W.E.B. GRIFFIN
ROGUE ASSET

Also by W.E.B Griffin

W.E.B. GRIFFIN
ROGUE ASSET

★

BRIAN ANDREWS &
JEFFREY WILSON

G. P. PUTNAM'S SONS
NEW YORK

PUTNAM
—EST. 1838—

G. P. Putnam's Sons
Publishers Since 1838
An imprint of Penguin Random House LLC
penguinrandomhouse.com

ISBN 9780399171215

Printed in Canada
1   3   5   7   9   10   8   6   4   2

FRI

Map illustration by Daniel Lagin

This is a work of fiction. Names, characters, places, and incidents
either are the product of the authors' imagination or are used fictitiously,
and any resemblance to actual persons, living or dead, businesses,
companies, events, or locales is entirely coincidental.

FOR THE LATE

WILLIAM E. COLBY
An OSS Jedburgh first lieutenant
who became director of the Central Intelligence Agency.

AARON BANK
An OSS Jedburgh first lieutenant
who became a colonel and the father of Special Forces.

WILLIAM R. CORSON
A legendary Marine intelligence officer
whom the KGB hated more than any other U.S. intelligence officer—
and not only because he wrote the definitive work on them.

RENÉ J. DÉFOURNEAUX
A U.S. Army OSS second lieutenant attached to the British SOE
who jumped into Occupied France alone and later became
a legendary U.S. Army counterintelligence officer.

FOR THE LIVING

BILLY WAUGH
A legendary Special Forces Command sergeant major who
retired and then went on to hunt down the infamous Carlos the Jackal.
Billy could have terminated Osama bin Laden in the early 1990s
but could not get permission to do so. After fifty years
in the business, Billy is still going after the bad guys.

JOHNNY REITZEL
An Army Special Operations officer who could have terminated
the head terrorist of the seized cruise ship *Achille Lauro*
but could not get permission to do so.

RALPH PETERS
An Army intelligence officer
who has written the best analysis of our war against terrorists
and of our enemy that I have ever seen.

AND FOR THE NEW BREED

MARC L
A senior intelligence officer, despite his youth,
who reminds me of Bill Colby more and more each day.

FRANK L
A legendary Defense Intelligence Agency officer
who retired and now follows in Billy Waugh's footsteps.

**OUR NATION OWES THESE PATRIOTS
A DEBT BEYOND REPAYMENT.**

—William E. Butterworth IV

AUTHORS' NOTE

We want to thank G. P. Putnam's Sons, and especially VP Editorial Director Tom Colgan and William E. Butterworth IV, for offering us the tremendous opportunity to carry on W.E.B. Griffin's Presidential Agent series. Being entrusted with a character as iconic and beloved as Charley Castillo is no small responsibility. It bears noting that it is neither our desire nor our objective to try to replace or supplant the creator of the series and his style, depth of knowledge, and flair. Far be it for us to try to replicate his prose. But while the style and cadence of this installment might feel different, we hope the ethos of the characters and the vision of the series shine bright. *Rogue Asset* is not a reboot or a revamping of the series. Rather, it's a continuation of the heroic journey of Charley Castillo—a character only the legendary W.E.B. Griffin could create—and his infallible dedication to safeguard the nation he loves. We hope you enjoy reading this new adventure as much as we enjoyed writing it. And thank you, as always, to our teammates and friends, still out there on the pointy tip of the spear, for your invaluable insight and commitment to our nation. You know who you are.

Brian Andrews & Jeffrey Wilson

THE MIDDLE EAST AND NORTHEAST AFRICA

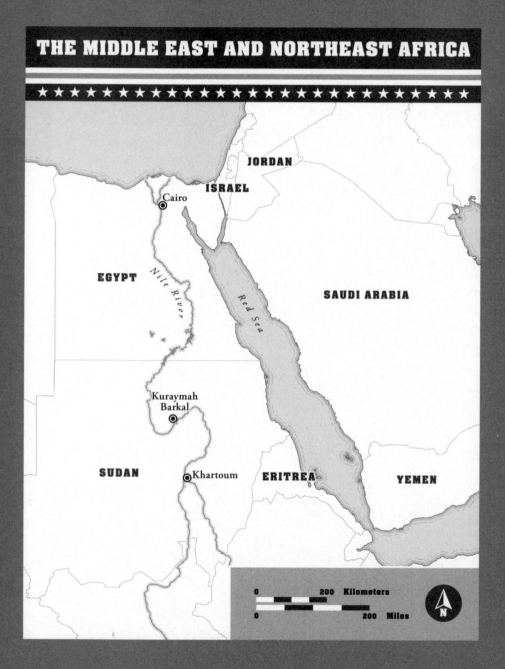

JORDAN

ISRAEL

Cairo ⊙

EGYPT

Nile River

Red Sea

SAUDI ARABIA

Kuraymah
Barkal ⊙

SUDAN

Khartoum ⊙

ERITREA

YEMEN

0   200 Kilometers

0   200 Miles

N

PART I

*"You shall know the truth, and the truth
shall make you mad."*

—ALDOUS HUXLEY

CHAPTER ONE

"You Americans and your conspiracy theories," the Egyptian ambassador to the United States said through a laugh. "I don't know how these crazy rumors get started, but I can assure you *extraterrestrials* were definitely not involved. Ingenuity and manpower—that's how the pyramids were built."

U.S. Secretary of State Frank Malone, who at six-foot-four and two hundred and forty-five pounds towered over the ambassador, smiled at the comment as he looked past the manicured courtyard and palm canopies at the four-thousand-year-old marvels in the distance. From the outdoor balcony of his Pyramid Suite at the Mena House, he could see both the Great Pyramid and the Pyramid of Khafre atop the Giza Plateau. He shifted his gaze from the pyramids to Ambassador Gamal. Malone had thrown out the "Did aliens really build the pyramids?" comment to see how the man would react.

The comment was clearly a joke, but it was also a test. The fifty-nine-year-old Malone, a self-made millionaire and the retired CEO of Malone Construction Ltd., had come to believe that everything in life was a test. Every task, every conversation, every interaction—no matter how insignificant or mundane—was an opportunity to rise or fall. Gain or cede. In this case, the Egyptian had proven himself to be affable, quick-witted, and someone who knew how to handle a curveball.

"As a former construction man, I can appreciate more than most why the Great Pyramid is the Seventh Wonder of the World," Malone said, contemplating how in the hell the ancient Egyptians had managed to stack more than two million limestone blocks, each weighing two-and-a-half tons, forty stories in the air without cranes and excavators. Blood, sweat, and bone built the pyramids, and he wondered how many slaves had died to fulfill the grand narcissistic desire of a man who believed himself a god.

Thousands? Tens of thousands? More?

"Minister Pasha is very much looking forward to meeting you this afternoon," Gamal said, referring to Malone's domestic equivalent—Egypt's newly appointed minister of foreign affairs. Pasha was Gamal's predecessor, serving as ambassador to the United States before being promoted. This was the typical diplomatic career progression in many countries, where the U.S. ambassadorship served as the ultimate litmus test and stepping-stone for promotion to the head of a nation's international affairs.

"I'm looking forward to meeting him, too," Malone said. "I understand he and my predecessor did not see eye to eye on most issues."

Gamal laughed politely. "It is true—there was great tension with the last administration, but now, with President Cohen's commitment to global diplomacy, Egypt is looking forward to renewed opportunities for dialogue and mutual prosperity."

Mutual prosperity? Malone thought, resisting the urge to roll his eyes. *Translation—the reestablishment of the United States' historically generous Egyptian foreign aid package that the previous administration unceremoniously gutted.*

"I'm glad to hear the minister feels that way. Egypt offering to host this summit to discuss the Middle East becoming a Nuclear-Weapon-Free Zone demonstrates—"

A hand forcefully grabbed him by the upper arm, stopping him mid-sentence.

"We've got a problem, Mr. Secretary," his security lead, Jack, said. "Time to go."

Movement in Malone's peripheral vision caught his eye—fast-moving, black-clad shapes flooding the courtyard outside his balcony.

"Jack, what's going on?" he asked as Jack pulled him away from the window.

The explosion knocked Malone off his feet and his enormous body hit the hotel room floor hard. He groaned, dazed, body alit with pain. The last time he'd felt like this was in the Rose Bowl, when Oklahoma University All-American defensive end Lamar Goodall had bulldozed him from the blind side and given him a concussion headache that lasted for a week.

Squinting, he coughed and scanned the room. Debris was strewn everywhere. Gray smoke and plaster dust swirled all around him, while tiny burning embers floated lazily toward the ground, reminding him of dust motes illuminated in a shaft of sunlight. Where a wall had once been, separating his suite from the one next door, now stood a charred and gaping maw. Had somebody been in that room? He tried to remember . . . wasn't that supposed to be Boaz Sharon's room, the Israeli minister of foreign affairs?

Automatic weapons fire reverberated outside and he heard shouting, but it all sounded funny—muffled, like his ears were filled with cotton. He rolled onto his stomach, then tried to press up to his hands and knees.

"Secretary Malone, are you injured?" a voice said, urgent and yet very far away.

"I don't think so," he tried to say, but what came out was a hoarse, pathetic croak.

"We've got to go, Mr. Secretary," the voice said, this time closer as strong hands gripped him under the armpit and pulled him up. "Right now."

Malone channeled his younger, college quarterback self, grunted, and got to his feet. As he did, a surge of adrenaline dumped into his veins—burning off the brain fog and making his lethargic body suddenly feel ten years younger. He looked right, where the Egyptian ambassador had been standing just seconds ago.

The Egyptian was now on all fours, crawling toward the bathroom.

"Gamal!" Malone shouted.

The ambassador froze and looked at Malone with wide, panicked eyes.

"You're coming with us," he said in a tone that left no room for debate.

Gamal nodded, scampered to his feet, and fell in behind Malone as Jack scanned over his weapon. They backpedaled away from the wide-open balcony doors toward the hotel room door leading to the inside hallway. A second explosion, this one farther away than the first, reverberated outside.

"Get low and hold here," his security lead said, gesturing quickly with his non-shooting hand to the space next to the door. "I augmented your detail with some shooters, former SOF and Ground Branch guys. They know how to handle themselves in combat and put together an emergency exfil plan for situations like this."

Malone nodded, crouching as instructed beside the doorframe.

While Jack conducted a rapid-fire tactical exchange over the radio—packed with acronyms and terms unfamiliar to Malone—a gun battle erupted outside. From his current vantage point, he could no longer see the courtyard, but the shooting sounded like it was just outside the balcony.

"We're going now," Jack said, opening the hotel room door.

Two vaguely familiar looking bearded Americans in plain clothes flanked the door. Both men were in tactical kneeling postures, wore headsets with boom mikes, and were sighting over assault rifles with optics packages. Seeing their steely, battle-hardened composure and slick tactical hardware, Malone suddenly felt a helluva lot better than he had just two seconds ago.

"One has the package," the younger of the two operators said, chopping a hand forward. "Maverick is moving toward the rally point."

They moved as a five-man, diamond-shaped unit—with one shooter front, Jack, Malone, and Gamal in the middle, and a shooter in back covering their six. The lead operator advanced in a tactical crouch, quickstepping so rapidly that Malone had to run to keep up. Viewed only from the waist up, the operator looked like he was riding on a conveyor belt, his torso gliding at uniform speed and elevation down the corridor.

"Just got a report the tangos are dressed as security personnel," the operator said over his shoulder.

"Shit," Jack said with a grimace.

"How you want to play this, boss?" the operator came back, the meaning of the query not lost on Malone.

"Kill house rules," Jack said, his voice a hard line.

"Roger that," the operator called back, and an understanding born from blood and brotherhood was reached . . . one that Malone decided could only mean *I trust you.*

Something exploded behind them, sending Malone instinctively into a squat-and-cover posture. He risked a backward glance and saw a hotel room door blown off its hinges and smoke pouring out into the hallway. The rear shooter sighted on the door, while the lead operator advanced toward a T junction ahead.

"Keep moving," Jack said, tapping Malone on the shoulder.

Malone nodded and scrambled to catch up to the lead shooter, who had reached the junction and was now pressed up against the right-hand wall just shy of the corner. Jack fell in behind him, against the wall, and Malone and Gamal followed Jack's lead. The lead shooter popped his head out for a half-second glance around the corner, then pulled back. Malone saw him take a deep breath, then repeat the maneuver, this time looking down the left-side hallway.

"Let's go," the operator said, over his shoulder.

A loud double crack behind Malone made him jump, as the rear shooter fired two rounds down the hallway behind them.

"We're being flanked—go, go, go!" the operator hollered, back-pedaling in a tactical crouch.

Muzzle flashes strobed at the far end of the corridor as lower-pitched machine gun fire erupted at them. Fresh adrenaline surged in Malone, and he ducked and ran around the corner, following the lead operator out of the line of fire.

"We gotta move, people!" the lead shooter barked, accelerating from his quickstep shuffle posture to a full-on run.

Malone's fifty-nine-year-old knees protested loudly as he lumbered down the hallway after the much younger and much more fit operator ahead. He could hear Gamal panting next to him and Jack's footfalls behind him as he'd somehow pulled ahead of his security lead. A security guard stepped into the corridor five meters away, sighting over an assault rifle. The lead American shooter dropped the man with a double-tap to the chest without even breaking stride. As he ran past the fallen guard, he put another round into the man's head and kept on going. Malone meant to avert his eyes, but his gaze went straight to the split-open skull and the bloody, clumpy gore spattered all over the tile floor.

"Don't look," Jack said, putting a hand on Malone's shoulder. "Keep moving."

They reached the next junction, a dogleg this time, and the lead operator cleared the corner blind—shrinking into a low tactical crouch and rounding the bend while sighting over his rifle.

"Clear!" he shouted.

Jack put pressure on Malone's back to get him moving around the corner. The five-man escape party moved down the hallway with speed and purpose, although Malone found himself getting winded. A mental image of his wife playfully scolding him the other day for eating too much red meat and not exercising popped into his head. *I know, I know, I'll try to do better,* he remembered promising, and now he wished he'd heeded her advice years ago.

"Coming up on the south stairwell," the lead operator announced. "We take the stairs down to the ground level, out the emergency side exit to where we have two vehicles ready to exfil in the circle. Secretary Malone, you're in the rear SUV. Do you understand?"

Malone nodded.

"Jack, help me clear this stairwell," the lead operator continued. "I'll take down, you clear up."

"Check," Jack said.

"On three, two, one, *go*," the operator said, barreling through the metal door and into the fire escape stairwell. Jack followed a split second behind and Malone heard the crack of gunfire followed by return fire a heartbeat later.

"Shit, I'm hit," he heard Jack say just before the door slammed shut with a resounding metallic *thud*.

"C'mon, c'mon, let's go!" the lead operator barked, pulling the door open and sticking his head out.

Malone ducked across the threshold, with Gamal and the rear operator in trail. As he entered the stairwell, he saw an Arab man sprawled prone and facing them on the landing above, his lifeless eyes peering off into space through the metal railing bars.

"Move!" the rear operator shouted, herding them down the stairs. "You guys are too fucking slow."

Malone shuffled his feet faster, catching up to Jack, who was hobbling and bleeding from his right side. "You okay, Jack?"

"Took one in the gut. Just outside my Kevlar," the Secret Service man said, his voice a little ragged now.

The lead operator stopped them at the emergency exit door, took a knee, and peered out the glass window at the circle drive a mere fifteen yards away. "Maverick is ready to load," he said into his boom mike.

Malone wasn't wearing a headset of his own, so he couldn't hear the reply, but through the rectangular pane of glass he saw two shooters with long guns step out of the passenger-side front doors of two idling black SUVs. The shooters opened the rear passenger-side doors on their respective vehicles and started scanning over their rifles.

"Secretary Malone, you're in the rear vehicle," the lead shooter reiterated. "Jack, you and the ambassador are in the lead truck. I'll ride with the secretary."

To Malone's surprise, his security lead didn't argue and instead simply nodded. Jack didn't look good. His face had gone completely gray and his forehead was dappled with perspiration.

"Keep your head low," the operator said, and shouted, "Go!"

Malone exhaled and went. Just like his college football days under center, he imagined he'd taken the snap and was running the option. Only this time, instead of a fullback running at his flank, he had a kitted-up operator with a machine gun alongside. And instead of running for the end zone, this time he was running for his life.

Twelve yards . . .

Staccato pops of gunfire erupted around him.

Nine yards . . .

He ducked his head, lowered his shoulder, and mustered more speed.

Six yards . . .

He heard bullets hitting the pavement behind him.

Four yards . . .

I'm almost there.

Two yards . . .

One . . .

Malone dove into the backseat like he was catapulting a goal line pile for a touchdown. He landed half-on, half-off the rear bench seat, his face buried into the lap of the terrified U.S. ambassador to Egypt, Jillian Hendricks. He scrambled quickly off her and into the middle seat as the lead operator jumped in beside him and slammed the door. A bullet plowed into the tailgate back window, leaving a starburst pattern but not punching through.

"Ballistic glass," the operator said, as the big SUV roared to life, tires laying rubber as the driver piloted them away from the Mena House with extreme haste and prejudice.

As they turned onto Al Haram Road, a building exploded a mere hundred yards in front of them, erupting in a giant fireball before imploding and sending a chimney column of black smoke and dust skyward.

"What the hell was that?" Malone said, gawking through the windshield.

"That was the El Ahram Police Station," the driver said.

"Shit," the lead operator barked. "Shift to exfil plan bravo."

The lead SUV whipped a U-turn and their SUV followed suit, leaving the burning police station and the Marriott Mena House in their rearview mirror as the two-vehicle caravan sped east on the four-lane Al Haram thoroughfare. Just as they cleared the first roundabout and accelerated to speed, a semitruck cut across the median and blocked the road, causing a pileup that forced them off the highway and onto a side street.

"What is this road?" the lead operator asked the driver, scanning nervously out the windows.

"Sidi Hamad El-Semman," the driver answered. "It runs along the Mena House Golf Course."

"What's wrong?" Malone asked, dread settling in his stomach like a ten-pound lead weight.

"These things aren't coincidence. They're herding us," the operator said, scanning this way and that out all the SUV windows.

"They have been from the beginning . . . Pete, you gotta get us off this road. I don't like it. I don't like it at all."

"Check," the driver said, just as two panel vans—parked and hidden in the tree line along the perimeter of the golf course—pulled out onto the road, blockading the convoy in front and back.

"Don't stop, dude!" the lead operator shouted, but it was too late. The lead SUV skidded to a halt and so did theirs. "Shit, shit, shit!"

Malone watched in horror and disbelief as the van's front-panel sliding door opened, revealing a man sitting behind a massive machine gun bolted to the cargo compartment floor. "What the hell is that?" he heard himself say, his voice ripe with fear.

"Fuck all," the operator beside him said as the machine gunner went to work obliterating the engine compartments of both Secret Service SUVs.

Everything that unfolded next seemed to happen in punctuated time—as if God himself pressed SKIP on a cosmic remote control. There was a great deal of shouting and confusion. A great deal more of shooting and people dying. And the next thing he knew, a man with a beard the color of onyx who was missing most of his left ear was yelling for him to climb inside an empty, dilapidated ice chest—like the meat freezer he'd once had in his own garage, but a slight bit larger—strapped to the bed of a pickup truck. Malone said no, and the man struck him in the side of his face with the butt of his rifle.

After that, he climbed inside, his one-time football player's frame only fitting by lying on his back and tucking his knees to his chest. The man with the missing ear slammed the lid closed and locked it. A few seconds later, Malone felt the truck begin to move. A small hole had been drilled in the bottom corner, letting in a shaft of light the diameter of his index finger.

Claustrophobia set in moments later.

I can't breathe . . . I can't fucking breathe . . . oh, shit, what are they going to do to me?

Soon his quads began to burn. Followed not long after by cramps in his hamstrings and calves. And he couldn't do anything about it because he couldn't straighten his legs.

He screamed in agony.

Then he screamed in frustration: "Stop! Let me out! Let me out, you fuckers!"

But they didn't stop.

And they didn't let him out.

Frank Malone, construction mogul, Wall Street darling, and secretary of state of the United States of America, screamed until he tasted blood in his mouth and pissed his pants.

CHAPTER TWO

President Natalie Cohen paced behind the *Resolute* desk in the most powerful office on the planet—*her* office—and tried to calm her anger with a short round of four-count tactical breathing. It was something she had learned years ago from someone she disliked but respected immensely. She had always taken great pride in her self-control, but the paucity of information on which she could act was fraying her nerves to the breaking point.

She met the eyes of Director of National Intelligence Marty Fleiss, a retired general, army intelligence officer, and one-time deputy director of the CIA. He stood straight and tall, his hands clasped behind his back in a weird blend of attention and parade rest.

"What the hell do you mean we have nothing, Marty? It's been over twenty-four hours since the attack. Ambassador Hendricks was murdered, and Secretary Malone is still missing. We had a legion of

agents from multiple agencies on the ground at the time of the attack. There are literally millions of bits of video evidence. The attack happened right in front of the international media. There must
be something—some thread or trail we can follow—by now."

"In fairness, Madam President," the DNI began calmly, "many of
the organic assets involved in the security of the summit—and thus
eyewitnesses to the attack—were killed or seriously injured. We have
several teams working the problem, but as you well know, trustwor-
thy assets in the region are hard to find. All the information coming
from the various agencies in the field in Cairo and throughout the
region are reporting the same thing—none of the usual chatter ahead
of the attack that might point a finger toward the players involved. It
would appear most of the bad actors in the region were as surprised
as the rest of us. Whoever pulled this off, they did it in a vacuum."

Cohen knew that Fleiss had been, and still was, the best pick to
head up the American intelligence community in her administration. Fleiss had the perfect blend of military and intelligence community experience to serve as DNI. He came from a long line of
soldiers he could trace back all the way to the Spanish–American
War, on both sides, and was a third-generation West Point graduate.
Unlike the infantry officers in his family tree, Fleiss recognized and
embraced the growing need for organic intelligence officers in military service. During his career, which spanned thirty years, army
intelligence had played a vital role in navigating the shift from the
Russian Cold War threat to Islamic terror and back again. He'd cut
his teeth supporting the mujahideen in the mid-'80s and come full
circle leading the intelligence efforts in Afghanistan in 2009 in his
last tour before retiring from the army and serving with the CIA,
eventually rising to deputy director.

The decision to bring him on had been easy, but she never would have guessed the IC would be taxed with an attack with nearly 9/11-level implications. Only two months after taking office on a platform of healing division in the U.S. and improving international cooperation, the U.S. secretary of state had been kidnapped, sending a clear message to the world: If America cannot even protect its own chief diplomat in the Middle East, then what business does it have dictating policy?

Cohen stopped pacing and leaned forward, hands on the desk from behind which she led the most powerful country in the world.

"It sounds to me, Marty, like our agencies might be slipping back into a rice-bowl mentality instead of working together. The previous administration undid a lot of great progress in joint operations over the last eight years, sowing seeds of distrust and fostering a self-preservation mentality. I fear we may be paying the price now."

"Perhaps so, Madam President," Fleiss agreed.

She smiled at his polite confirmation. Fleiss was perhaps one of the last remaining truly nonpartisan military leaders to survive the toxic environment of the last President, and she knew he was as frustrated as she was about the current state of affairs. He was still trying to get his house in order, and yet she knew he would always give it to her straight.

"Let's come back to Cairo and Malone in a moment, Marty. We have other things we need to think about, scenarios we need to game out."

"Like what, Madam President?"

"Like who will be emboldened after this attack and what does that mean for us. There's blood in the water now, and when sharks smell blood . . ." She paused, feeling her self-control slipping again, and collected herself before continuing. "My point is we need to anticipate the next blindside. We need to think about what shit could shake loose in the region as a result of the attack. I do not want to be standing here a week from now having a similar conversation with you."

"Understood, ma'am. We have CIA working with the Joint Terrorism Task Force on that as we speak. No major red flags just yet. I do, however, expect some pushback from certain foreign partners as a result of the attack, which may limit our tactical options in North Africa."

She looked hard at her DNI, but there was no condemnation or judgment in his eyes. He was providing her with information she needed, nothing more.

"Yes, well, the political implications will be horrific, but that will be my problem. This summit had to happen because this conversation has to be started. We simply cannot live in a world where weapons of mass destruction are proliferating in the Middle East."

"I agree, ma'am," the DNI said.

She gestured to the two opposing couches across from her desk and he took a seat, sitting straight and tall with his hands in his lap. She took the seat across from him and gestured for him to continue.

"The media is ganging up on us over this right now," he said. "The talking heads are saying the likelihood of a nuclear arms race accelerating in the Middle East is remote at best and so the risk of the summit was not justified."

"Do you agree with them?" she asked, crossing her legs and holding the gaze of the man to whom the entire American intelligence apparatus answered. Fleiss stared past her, his eyes in the middle distance, as he seemed to truly consider her question.

"Not entirely. Like you, I feel that the conversation must be started, but we may have rushed. I think it's impossible to say, in light of the attack, that agreeing to meet in Egypt proved more dangerous than was acceptable. Perhaps a summit in Europe would have been more appropriate."

"And pointless," she said back calmly. "Iran refused to participate, as did Pakistan, in a summit outside of the Middle East. For this to work, it's either everybody or nobody. There are five regional Nuclear-Weapon-Free Zone treaties currently in place. The Central Asian treaty is ten years old, and the entire southern hemisphere of our planet is now covered by a NWFZ treaty. Only the Middle East remains stubbornly volatile and uncooperative. Nuclear war between nation-states is not what keeps me up at night, Marty. What worries me is access to weapons of mass destruction—including our own weapons still in Turkey and the presence of weapons in Pakistan—to non-state players. All it will take is one fringe group like ISIS or Al-Qaeda or PKK getting a nuke and we'll have an event where deaths are measured in the millions somewhere on the planet. That's a scenario where superpower strategic dogma—like mutually assured destruction—doesn't apply. Terrorists aren't nation-states, they don't have land, infrastructure, a population they need to protect."

She rose and started pacing.

"I understand, Madam President, and I agree. But right now my job is to find out who is behind the attack, where they've taken the secretary, and prevent whatever the next action is in their endgame. That, not geopolitics, needs to be my singular focus at present."

"I know, Marty, and I trust you above anyone to get that done. My job is to provide you with the tools and resources you need to do your job. And to that end," she forced herself back into her seat on the sofa, crossing her legs, intent on projecting the control and confidence she had spent a lifetime developing for just such moments, "I would like to propose we add another tool to your toolbox."

"Of course, Madam President. What tool might that be?"

"I'd like to bring back the Presidential Agent program that was shut down by my predecessor. I believe we need a resource that can work within and across the alphabet soup of agencies we've created that have become a stumbling block to the flow of consistent and reliable information to this office. We need a small-footprint, black ops asset that is managed and responsible only to you and me."

She watched as Fleiss pursed his lips in consideration.

"Are we talking about the program or the man, if I may ask, ma'am?"

"Both."

The DNI let out a long breath through his nose. "May I speak freely, ma'am?"

She rolled her eyes and waved a hand. "The day you don't is the day your position in this administration ends. I trust you and your judgment, Marty, or else you wouldn't be here."

He nodded. "While I understand the appeal of the Presidential Agent program—and there is no arguing with the results achieved in the past—I'm not sure in the wake of this disaster, especially so early in your administration, is the right time to bring back someone as controversial as Carlos Guillermo Castillo . . . as tempting as it might be."

"I appreciate your candor, Marty. And I've considered the risk of bringing back a program that skirts oversight when I'm the candidate of transparency and cooperation. But I would argue that no event more desperately demands the program be brought back."

"It was also my understanding—and this is just rumor and legend, I suppose—that you didn't exactly get along with Charley when you were secretary of state."

"Between you and me, Marty," Cohen said, watching her DNI

closely, "you're half right. While I may not have cared for Charley personally, professionally his record speaks for itself. And I trust him completely. He is a patriot and dedicated beyond reproach to the security of our great nation."

"Of course," Fleiss said. "I simply meant it would be a bad time to have a rogue asset out there in the field, and Charley can be, well, difficult."

President Cohen laughed at this one.

"I don't disagree with that assessment. But I trust him, and anyway, I don't intend to have a rogue asset out there in the field."

"What do you mean?" Fleiss asked, clearly confused. "If he's not in the field, then what value . . ."

She held a hand up. "We need Castillo. He understands the program better than anyone because, well, he invented it. That said, Castillo is getting a little long in the tooth to be kicking in doors. What I want from him, what I need from him, is to resurrect the program. Under your supervision, Charley will recruit, mentor, and manage the next Presidential Agent—an asset who will answer to no one but Charley, and Charley will answer to no one but you and me. And we need that asset in the field twelve hours ago, so get Castillo to D.C. and in my office immediately."

"Yes, ma'am," Fleiss said, turning to leave. "But I'm not sure how much Charley is gonna like this idea."

"I'm sure that he will answer the call for his nation as he always has," Cohen said, but she wondered just how well this was going to go. "Perhaps, if you can find him quickly, you might want to bring General McNab with you when you go to see Charley."

"Bruce McNab?" Fleiss said with a smile. "Talk about long in the tooth . . ."

"The general still consults frequently with both JSOC and

NCTC," she said. "He stays pretty read in, but he's also someone Castillo might listen to."

"All right. I'll go to Texas to speak with Charley personally, and I'll ask Bruce to tag along."

"Good, but Marty, this needs to happen ASAP. I want Castillo read in and ready to roll by tomorrow morning."

"Understood."

"And I forwarded a file to your chief of staff on a candidate suggested by McNab to be our man in the field."

"Yes, ma'am, Madam President. Anyone handpicked by McNab is good enough for me. Is he local?"

"Unfortunately, no. He's a MARSOC Raider deployed to Tal Afar, Iraq," she said. "So get the wheels rolling to have him here in the next twenty-four hours."

He nodded. "Unless you have something else, I have a plane to catch to Texas."

She watched as Fleiss turned to leave, then hesitated and spoke over his shoulder as he reached for the door.

"One more thing?" Fleiss said, hesitating.

"What's that?"

"Can I be here when you tell Charley he's too old to operate in the field?" Fleiss asked, a smile on his face. "I'd really like to see that."

Cohen chuckled. "That's not exactly what I said. And you most certainly will be in the room, since I'm tasking you with managing Castillo."

Fleiss grimaced. "Awesome," he said under his breath, and then was gone, shutting the door behind him.

Cohen returned to her desk as the intercom buzzed. She dropped into the seat and pressed the red button. "Yes?"

"Chief of Staff Perkins asked me to let you know that Senator Gardner is requesting time with you this afternoon, Madam President."

She sighed.

Of course he is. The old dinosaur would use this tragedy to trash me and my administration and an audience with me legitimizes him.

"It won't be today. Please let Shannon Perkins know to coordinate a meeting with the senator tomorrow afternoon, but tell him I want Senator Rodriquez from the Senate intelligence committee present as well."

"Yes, ma'am."

"Let Shannon know I'd like a tentative agenda for that meeting by the time we do our daily debrief at 1800 today."

"Yes, Madam President. And you asked me to remind you that you want Director Powell present for your call with Chancellor Hecht at 1630."

"Yes, thank you, Sheila. And let the ODNI know to send a proxy for Director Fleiss. Perhaps Deputy Director Darner. The director is working on tasking that will take him briefly out of D.C. and he won't make it back in time for that. Keep my schedule open tomorrow morning for a follow-up meeting with Director Fleiss and his guest."

"His guest, ma'am?"

I hope to God he doesn't say no.

"Yes, and you'll need to coordinate for all the necessary clearances."

"Yes, Madam President."

The intercom went dead.

She would see if Castillo was up to a management role bright and early tomorrow. That was a pretty short fuse to put together a plan for a new agent he would mentor.

Unless he just tells me to kiss his ass and stays retired in Texas.

She shook her head and said a short, silent prayer that she wasn't making a mistake.

CHAPTER THREE

United States Marine Corps Captain P.K. McCoy Jr. scratched at his bushy auburn beard with his left hand as he brought the cup of thick tea to his lips with the other. The thirty-year-old Special Operator had come to like the sickly-sweet Iraqi chai, actually, but his ass ached from the three hours of sitting on the stone floor. The paper-thin pillow under his backside offered little comfort and his back was starting to protest now as well—a reminder of an injury he'd sustained during a HAHO insert with a bunch of Green Berets in Afghanistan five years earlier. The SCAR assault rifle in his lap and the full kit he wore made it impossible to find comfort by leaning over on an elbow beside the ground-level table as the clan leader of the Jabur tribe's modest population of people in northwestern Iraq did.

They sure as hell didn't teach us how to deal with this at the Naval Academy, he thought.

Everyone at the table laughed again, and Captain McCoy—"Pick" to his teammates—raised his cup and smiled at the joke Yasim al-Jebouri had made about the weight of a corpulent neighboring clan leader.

"In ancient societies, such massive weight was a sign of wealth," McCoy quipped in Arabic. "But here it may be that he is eating his children's meat."

Everyone erupted in laughter again, and Yasim pounded a leathery hand on the low table, toppling a small tower of sweet, honey-drizzled bread his family had spread out for their visitors. McCoy set his tea down, readjusted the rifle in his lap, and let his face turn serious.

"You have been an ally to us for many years, Hakim Yasim," he said, assigning the man the title of a wise leader. "And you have been a friend to me and my men for these several months. You have our respect. What I ask of you, I ask out of friendship and that respect."

Yasim took on a somber look as well. He waved his hand, shooing out the women and the younger men, leaving only himself and three elder tribal men in the small dirty room of the low, crumbling stucco building.

Sitting beside McCoy, Gunnery Sergeant Billy Dean caught his eye and shot him a "let's wrap this up" look.

Apparently, his ass is hurting too.

It was not unusual for the social aspects of these meeting to last nearly a day, and more than once he and his team had stayed well into the wee hours, leaving bloated on sweet bread and goat stew. But they had built a relationship over these months. It was time for the ask.

Three other MARSOC operators were in the room with them, leaning against the wall. McCoy turned to them and nodded, and each gave a slight bow before exiting to join three other Special Operations Marine Raiders outside. This would be a show of respect for McCoy—as their "clan leader"—that would carry weight with Yasim.

When they were gone, McCoy placed a hand on his own heart in a gesture of respect and friendship before speaking.

"Hakim Yasim, your assistance is more than just what you and your men can do to help us and our friends. You are a respected leader of your clan, and as you do, so will your neighbors."

Yasim stroked his long gray beard and smiled. McCoy knew the man well now, and knew that he was not likely to be swayed by flattery, but the words were true.

"You have been a friend to Jabur, Mak-Koy," Yasim said, pronouncing the name in two distinct barks of his gravelly voice. "But America is an unreliable partner. American soldiers come and go and come again. When the devils from ISIL return, who will then fight beside us? Will you be here, Mak-Koy? To help the Josh and the Peshmerga invites wrath on this region when you are gone. If you are not here, who will fight with us then?"

McCoy nodded at Yasim's use of the Josh slur when referring to regional Kurdish tribal leaders. Tribal rivalry was a problem he was growing accustomed to as his country's foreign policy shifted with each new political wind. It was true—the Peshmerga were not always a reliable partner, and he would not lie about that to Yasim to achieve his goal.

"We wish to work together with you and the Kurd fighters to achieve a peace, so that you may again rule your own land. You must surely see that."

Yasim laughed, a loud barking laugh, and shifted over to his other elbow, reclining beside the low table.

"Always foreigners come here with promises of peace. There is no peace here, Mak-Koy. That is a dream of the West. We are not the Iraqi peoples of the east and south. We are Jabur and beside us are Khazraj or Kindy or Malik or Laith. Always will we defend our land from those who would take it. We no longer seek peace, as it is not the will of Allah for our people. We seek strength to protect our people. From where will that come, Mak-Koy, next year, or the next, when you are gone and we are known for having helped the Peshmerga fight against the Islamic state here and in the West?"

This was a question he was prepared for and he leaned in.

"From one another, Hakim Yasim," he said, holding the dark eyes of the man across from him. "As it has always been, since long before my country even existed. By working with the Peshmerga now, you will not only bring other clans and tribes together in the defense of your region, but you will form a powerful alliance with fighters who have for thousands of years—since before even the Prophet walked the earth—fought to the death against oppression and assimilation. They will be your ally, and they are a powerful ally indeed."

Yasim waved his hand.

"The Kurds themselves say they have no friends but the mountains."

"I said *ally*, not *friend*," McCoy corrected. "You have long shared an enemy in the radical elements who would demand you lead your people this way or that, that you share with them your land and follow their rules. Together, you are stronger than apart. Together, you won't need American soldiers."

He had him. He could tell by his face. But he also knew Yasim well enough to know that he had likely already decided to respect the alliance the MARSOC Marines were forging with both clans and the Kurds in their work to clear the remnants of ISIL from both sides of the border in this region of Iraq—and to keep them from returning when America, inevitably, left *again*. Yasim's pleas were probably little more than a formality and the debate Yasim's show of power and control. The fact that America came and went was all the more reason to ally with one of the most ferocious fighting forces in the history of mankind. The Kurds were still around for a reason.

"I will agree to meet with them, and then we will see," Yasim said.

There was a knock at the door and a tense voice hollered through it.

"Captain McCoy . . ."

"One moment, Marine," he said in English. They needed to button this up.

"Apologies, sir, but we have a situation."

McCoy felt his pulse quicken and he instinctively moved his hand to the grip of his rifle.

"What is it, Mak-Koy?"

"With apologies and your permission, I need to speak to my soldier," he said, resisting the urge to rise.

"Of course," Yasim said, sitting up and crossing his legs.

"Come in, Santiago," Gunnery Sergeant Dean called out.

Santiago was in complete control—Marine Raiders were a select group of operators and his team was well blooded in Iraq, Syria, and Afghanistan—but the worry on his face spoke of a threat his demeanor downplayed.

"My apologies," Santiago said in Arabic, and bowed to Yasim with his right hand on his heart. He continued in English. "Sir, the head shed reports four trucks and about twenty fighters moving in from the west. They are well across the border and splitting into two elements of two trucks each, all four trucks with a technical, and appear headed to flank us north and south. Should I call for exfil, sir?"

McCoy looked at Yasim and for the hundredth time wondered just how much English the man actually knew.

Probably fluent, the sly bastard.

"Of course not, Corporal," he said in English. "We will gladly stay and fight beside our brothers of the Jabur against these devils. Tell Sergeant Lewis to prepare for the assault. We will be there in a moment."

"Yes, sir," Santiago said.

McCoy winked at him.

"But let's get some air support headed this way, Santiago," he added softly.

"Yes, sir." And then the Marine was gone.

McCoy shared the report with Yasim, but the man seemed already to know about the incoming threat.

"Together, we will slaughter these devils and show them that this is not where they wish to send their men to die," Yasim said, as he rose in one fluid motion that seemed impossible for a man his age. "Then, perhaps, we will not need to be friends with your Peshmerga." But he laughed at this.

"Before we begin this fight, may I have your word that we will meet soon with my allies from the Pesh brigade?"

"Yes, yes, Mak-Koy. I will meet your Josh friends and we will work together. Anyone who wishes to kill the devils who threaten my people can be my ally as well. Come, let us kill some devils and then we can have stew."

McCoy followed Gunny Dean out of the low, crumbling stucco

building and into the courtyard. The compound had ten similar buildings, all surrounded by a five-foot-tall wall. McCoy could see the dust trails made by the pickup trucks in the distance, one slightly north of the other as he looked west over the wall across a rocky desert toward Syria. His hands flew almost unconsciously over his kit, checking magazines, grenades, and the pistol holster on his chest. Around him, two dozen or more of Yasim al-Jebouri's men were slinging bandoliers of ammo over their shoulders and shoving long, banana-shaped magazines into the pockets of their pants beneath their long shirts.

McCoy checked his earpiece and keyed his radio, speaking into the boom mike by his mouth. "Raider Actual, Raider One," he said, querying his boss in the TOC.

"One, Actual—sitrep," came the gruff reply.

He could picture Colonel Bannon chomping on the unlit cigar, arms folded on his chest, in the TOC thirty miles east in the Special Operations FOB outside Tal Afar.

"Raider One—we are dug in with our partners and ready to defend the village. You know more than we do, sir." He was pulling a small computer tablet from his cargo pocket where he expected both real time intelligence and the opportunity to stream imagery from the drone somewhere overhead. "I understand four trucks with technicals split into two elements approaching quickly. We'd like air support standing by."

"One, we have two zulus from one-six-nine on approach from the east, on station in under five," his boss said, referring to AH-1Z Viper helicopters from HMLA-169.

It seemed like overkill for what they had approaching, but there was no such thing as too much backup. A "higher authority" was gonna finally support their mission with some serious-ass teeth. It would be nice to have them if needed, but he imagined that his team and Yasim's several dozen very experienced fighters could likely make short work of the insurgents heading toward them. As if to confirm this, he glanced over where tarps were being pulled off two Soviet-made DshK 12.7x108mm machine guns mounted to the roofs of two of the buildings in the compound. Yeah—they were gonna be just fine, and fighting alongside Yasim and his boys would seal the deal on his mission to unite forces against ISIL here in the far northwest.

"Copy that, Actual."

"Raider One, we have two Yankee Venoms in trail. Viper flight will engage the bad guys once on station, but I want you to exfil back to the FOB on the Hueys. How copy?"

McCoy pursed his lips. Why was Bannon pulling them out? As a Marine and an experienced Special Operator, he knew better than anyone how pivotal engaging ISIL together with Yasim could be in accomplishing their long-term mission before they had to redeploy home in a few months.

"Actual, Raider One—would prefer to stay embedded here, sir. Very close to achieving our objective with the locals."

Bannon will get it. He knows how this game is played.

"Negative, Raider One. Viper flight will do the shooting today. We have new priority tasking. I need you here—you personally. We have a visitor standing by to meet you with new orders."

New orders? What the hell is going on?

He could hear the thrum of the AH-1Z Vipers approaching, and a moment later they screamed overhead, splitting left and right toward the two dust trails in the distance.

"Copy that, Actual," McCoy said.

What else could he say?

"What's going on, sir?" Gunny Dean asked from beside him.

He looked over and saw Yasim al-Jebouri approaching. A pit formed in his stomach at the thought of having to give the bad news of their untimely departure, thereby undoing all the goodwill earned and progress made.

"I'm sorry, Hakim Yasim," he said, bowing slightly in deference. "I'm afraid we must depart. My men and I are urgently needed elsewhere. But my command is sending air support. I'm not going to leave you without firepower."

"I approve this plan, Mak-Koy," Yasim growled. "Your helicopters will destroy the ISIL dogs and I don't have to risk my men's lives."

Yasim raised his hands, holding his rifle in the air and giving a loud *WHOOP* as an explosion sounded in the distance. McCoy turned and saw a mushroom of fire and thick black smoke obscuring the northernmost dust trail as the attack helos launched their first salvo against the incoming jihadis.

McCoy nodded at Yasim. "There's your air support, as promised."

"Go in peace with Allah, Mak-Koy. You return in two days. We have stew together and meet with your Josh leaders. We will see if a deal can be made, yes?"

"Either me or another from my unit," McCoy said, reluctant to make a promise it appeared he wasn't going to be able to honor. Depending on what this new tasking was, there was a chance he'd not be having stew with Yasim before the deployment ended.

"What's going on, boss?" Gunny Dean asked.

"No idea, Gunny. New tasking," he said as two inbound UH-1 helos raised a cloud of moon dust on their approach. "Get the guys together. We're exfilling."

"You got it, sir," the Marine gunnery sergeant said, but his eyes had the same *what the fuck* look that McCoy felt.

Another explosion in the distance to the north and two more a mile or two south announced that the HMLA-169 Super Cobra pilots had dispatched the enemy to paradise to collect their virgins. McCoy saw them arc in opposite directions and then come together in a flight of two, tearing over the compound a minute later to the cheers of Yasim's men. Over the south wall he watched two Hueys flare into a massive dust cloud. He pulled his black-and-white keffiyeh scarf over his mouth and nose as he trotted over to where his men were exiting the compound through a narrow gate, held open by a smiling Jabur fighter apparently unaffected by the horrible dust. The fighter smiled and nodded at each American Marine, bidding them farewell in Arabic that couldn't be heard over the whine of the two helicopters.

Moments later the small compound was falling away beneath them, Yasim's men shouting and waving from the courtyard and rooftops as they departed.

Whatever this new tasking is, McCoy thought, *it better take less than two days. If we're not back here to meet Yasim with the Peshmerga representative, then the last three months of hard work will have been for nothing.*

He sighed as the helicopter banked and turned east toward home. *Fucking bureaucrats.*

CHAPTER FOUR

United States Secretary of State Frank Malone lay, cramped and still, in his black box tomb sweating and occasionally moaning.

He had no idea how long it had been since he'd been taken, and that sure as hell wasn't because he'd slept and lost track of time. He'd have paid in blood to sleep. In this protracted agony, time had mutated from a predictable metronome into an amorphous and abstract thing—losing its meaning. Hours had passed since his taking—that much he was certain of—but had it been days? Probably not. That was as precise as he could be.

He knew—from the motion, vibrations, and sounds around him—that he'd been driven by truck to an airfield where his box had been transferred to a plane. Despite his delirium, he knew it had been an airplane, as this was the only time that his box had been opened. They'd opened the lid and forcibly straightened his legs—an act that had made him scream in agony as his wrecked joints and spasming muscles were worked roughly about, perhaps to restore blood flow or perhaps just as a form of torture. Despite the abuse, he'd noted the turbulence and heard the whine of turboprop engines. He'd begged them for water, which they provided—jerking his head up by his hair and pouring it down his throat. He'd gulped it down eagerly, like an animal. But after, instead of letting him out, they'd folded his legs back in on top of him and slammed the lid shut as he screamed.

More time passed, long enough for him to piss himself again.

Not long after the plane landed, they loaded him onto another truck and drove him somewhere on much rougher roads—every pothole a fresh agony for his spine. He was deep in the third world now. Upon arrival, at what he assumed was his final destination, they'd roughly unloaded his box and set him on the ground.

For a long while, the box remained still and he was left alone.

Time passed.

He could no longer feel his arms or legs. His thirst became all-encompassing. He let out a shuddering breath and reminded himself of his mantra: Everything in life was a test. Every twist of fate was an opportunity to rise or fall, gain or cede—that was what he had always believed.

But he'd never fallen so far or so hard as this before.

"Is this my final test?" he muttered. "Where my willpower will decide if I live or die?"

The rattle of the lock and chains outside his box sent his heart rate surging. He realized, stifling an involuntary sob, that the only thing worse than being inside this damn freezer chest might be getting out of it. Images of videos he'd seen of captives brutally beheaded in front of Islamic terrorism flags flooded his mind's eye—like those streamed live on the internet to the cheers of believers and anguish of the rest of the planet. Tears ran down his cheeks.

This is not what I signed up for . . . why is this happening to me?

But Malone knew why.

He knew full and well that he represented a new generation of pseudo-politician who served as much for himself as for his country, but he saw no conflict in that. He'd spent a lifetime building his global construction business in nations ravaged by war and poverty. He'd always believed that this brought more prosperity to these regions, even if with that prosperity came a certain element of inequity. He was a capitalist—and capitalism worked, at all levels. Prosperity always trickled down, creating jobs, bringing infrastructure, and infusing capital to lift even the poorest peoples in the most impoverished countries to a higher standard of living. But as a CEO, this was not his mission. He answered to his shareholders, not his workers—and certainly not his foreign workers.

At Ohio State, where he'd led his team to back-to-back championship seasons as the starting quarterback, he'd learned that winning was what mattered. Winners inspired. Winners thrived. Winners moved the needle. He was a proven winner, and that's why Natalie Cohen had tapped him as her secretary of state. For a President committed to rebuilding wealth and jobs across the globe through American innovation, who better suited for the job than a man who'd spent his career building things. He'd built a dynasty at Ohio State football, and he'd built a dynasty at Malone Construction Ltd. And as secretary of state, he would rebuild America's reputation overseas. At the end of four years he fully expected to step down, pass the baton, and cash in on the fruit of those labors when he returned once again to take the helm at his company.

But this—this was never part of the deal.

The lid opened and bright light streamed in, painful to his dark-acclimated eyes. He heard talking—perhaps in Arabic, he wasn't sure—then three silhouettes broke the light from above, as men peered into the box at him. He couldn't make out their features, his vision blurred by his dry, light-blind eyes. He tried to speak, but his throat was impossibly raw, and his tongue was swollen and stuck to the roof of his mouth.

Another voice called out from behind the men. An image flashed of the angry man with the onyx beard and missing ear. He didn't want to see him again—the man with murder in his eyes.

"*Akhrajah min alealbati. Kun hadhrana. Wahdir la alma wa-nazafah,*" the voice said.

Malone was unsure what the first part meant, but he thought they were being told to give him water. Hands reached in and grabbed him roughly by the arms and his twisted legs, and he screamed in pain as they lifted him out of the ice chest.

"Ah . . . shit. Stop! You're hurting me!"

"*Qult hun hadhara!*" a man he could not see shouted, clearly in charge. It must have meant to be gentle because the three men lowered him carefully to the ground.

"*Jarhah wasayudhik baed dhik,*" the voice growled.

Malone was on a dirty blanket now, still twisted up, on the floor. The blanket stunk of mold and body odor, but felt like a feather bed after the hours spent in the freezer. Malone tried to move, but the effort brought pain and muscle cramps that took his breath away, so he instead tried something simple—just wiggling his fingers and trying to feel his toes. Pins and needles danced across almost the entirety of his body as circulation grudgingly returned to his limbs.

The commanding voice barked something else in what he now felt certain was Arabic, then he heard footsteps fading away. He wanted to peek, to see who it was, but the light hurt his eyes so bad he had no choice but to keep them shut. A moment later, a water bottle was held to his lips.

"Ashrb . . . ashrb bed alma," a softer—and much younger voice—said from beside him.

The water was not only clean, it was cold. He began to chug it down, feeling the cool water now running down his neck and onto his burning chest.

"Min fadlak bi bat," another voice said gently.

He thought they meant for him to drink slowly, but he simply couldn't slow himself down and in seconds the water bottle was empty.

"More," he managed to whisper, his voice sandpaper on wood. "Please."

"Akthar!"

And another bottle was held to his lips and a pillow—or perhaps just a bunched-up blanket or tarp—was pressed beneath his head so he could raise it to drink more easily.

Then they left.

Minutes passed and he was finally able to open his eyes, finding himself in a large, unfurnished room. Slowly, he stretched his legs out, each inch bringing screaming pain until, at last, his legs lay straight, or nearly so, as he lay on his side. He opened and closed his hands, and the tingling became a thousand bees stinging his fingers and forearms, but finally his angry, blood-deprived nerves stopped their grumbling and feeling slowly returned to his hands.

Time passed, perhaps fifteen or twenty minutes.

Three men returned, he thought them to be the same three as before, and now he could see clearly that they were young—maybe mid- to late teens at the most—and thin. Two of the boys were

African, the third an Arab, and only one carried a rifle, standing off
to the side with the weapon clutched nervously in front of him as
the others worked.

They first helped him, with some difficulty, to his feet. Then
they unceremoniously stripped him naked. He wanted to protest,
but had neither the energy nor the desire as they peeled the disgusting
clothes, covered in blood, urine, and feces, from his sweat-stained
body. They splashed cool water on him from a bucket and handed
him a large cloth, which he used to wipe himself down. Then he
was given a coarse towel with which he dried himself and finally
they handed him a pair of underwear and an orange jumpsuit.

Malone's throat tightened as he slipped into the fresh but stiff
coveralls, mental images of orange-jumpsuit-clad Christians kneeling on a beach in front of their executioners filling his head. But he
shrugged it on anyway, the glaring eyes of the young man with the
rifle suggesting to not do so would be a mistake.

A chair was brought to the center of the room by a fourth terrorist who gestured with his hand for Malone to take a seat. With great
effort, Malone took a seat in the metal folding chair. His back and
legs still ached, but the very act of sitting suddenly felt luxurious.
The three terrorist guards retreated behind their armed partner and
stood, all the while fixing him with their stares. The deep hatred in
their eyes was unmistakable.

And he hated them back even more deeply.

Together, simmering in their hate, they waited for something . . .
or someone.

The sound of a heavy door screeching open on rusty hinges
made Malone jump. Footsteps echoed on the cement floor—a man
walking with confidence, feet clad in western-style shoes. Malone
blinked as the new arrival came to a stop in front of him, the man's

hands clasped behind his back. The secretary of state swallowed hard and tried to stop his lower lip from trembling. He looked up, expecting to see the man with the missing ear, but this man was new to him. Despite his fear about what was coming next, Malone held the man's dark eyes.

The terrorist smiled at him, his well-trimmed beard splitting to show white teeth.

"It is an honor to meet you, Mr. Secretary," the man said in English, a thick accent lending an ominous weight to the words, which from the look of the man was perhaps meant to mock him.

He looked at Malone as if expecting an answer, but seemed equally unsurprised to not receive one. Malone thought of all the manly quips he could fire back, most of them movie lines he'd heard over the years, but decided such stupidity should be left for the movies.

The man looked over his shoulder and snapped his fingers.

"*Ahdir li kursii,*" he commanded, and one of the young fighters hustled off. Malone thought he remembered from his rushed consumption of the Pimsleur Arabic language tapes the last few weeks that *kursii* meant chair. Sure enough, the tall teenager returned with an oversized leather chair, his thin frame struggling under the weight.

"*Shukran,*" the man said to the young fighter, who beamed at the praise.

The boss terrorist sat, legs crossed and strong brown hands in his lap, across from Malone in his orange jumpsuit and simple folding chair. He gestured to the young man behind him.

The man stared at him hard a moment, eyes brimming with contempt, before saying, "Do not be fooled, Mr. Secretary, by my young fighters. Your American SEALs will never find us here, but if they did this compound is protected by an army of devout followers who will give their lives in service to the Prophet. The entire village surrounding this place is under my control. I have a legion of seasoned, blooded fighters ready to do my bidding."

Malone nodded. Decades at the negotiation table had taught him a thing or two about posturing and intimidation, but he knew better than to provoke a volatile personality from a position of weakness.

The terrorist leaned in, forearms on his thighs. "I tell you this because it would be a mistake to try to escape. I've ordered that you be shot on sight if you leave this room without an escort. And there is no one who will help you in the village. You are alone, Mr. Malone. Alone and helpless."

Again, Malone's mind searched for the best response, but finding none, he remained quiet, but did his best to hold the man's eyes. He was, after all, the secretary of state of the most powerful nation on the planet, which he reminded himself did give him leverage . . . even though right now it certainly didn't feel that way.

"At least nod if you understand, Mr. Secretary."

"I understand," he said simply. As the strength returned to his arms and legs, he felt some strength of will slowly returning as well. Even here, he must represent his country. Especially here, perhaps.

"Hu yatahadath!" the leader said over his shoulder to the young fighters behind him, and they laughed. "I was beginning to worry you had lost your ability to speak, that perhaps we did not provide enough air on your journey, giving you brain damage. I'm pleased that is not the case, because you are of little use to me brain dead . . . at least for now."

"Who are you, and what do you want?" Malone asked.

At the speed of lightning, the man smacked him with the back of his hand, snapping Malone's head to the right so hard it hurt his neck. The coppery taste of blood filled his mouth.

"You are not in power here, Mr. Malone. Allah has given me the power over you, so I shall be asking the questions." The man crossed his arms, but held Malone's eyes with malice. "In any case, your lies and other words are useless here. I have heard your blasphemy in your speeches to your fellow infidels. Worse, I have seen the damage of your lies here in my own country—lies for your profit and wealth—long before you became a spokesman for the devil."

He turned and said something in Arabic, and the young men nodded enthusiastically, the fighter with the rifle pumping it up into the air.

"I asked them: Who is more unjust than one who invents lies about Allah and denies His verses? This is from the Quran, and it applies perfectly to you. You have lied about Allah on behalf of your country, and denied His verses when you raped African countries for money, causing suffering for many, and allowing evil men to rise to power. But no more!"

The man stood abruptly, and Malone cowered backward, afraid to be struck again.

Malone felt his lip quiver and cursed himself for showing such weakness. Who was this man? What did he want? Before becoming secretary of state, his multinational company had done business in scores of countries throughout North Africa and the Middle East, but never in Egypt.

He chose his words carefully.

"I promise you I want nothing but peace and prosperity through-out the region, sir," he said, annoyed at the cracking of his voice. "As a businessman, I sought only to bring jobs, wealth, and develop in-frastructure in this part of the world, I assure you."

Again, the hand struck him so fast he could not prepare himself for the blow.

"These are more lies, and you should stop telling them so that I may keep control of my emotions," he said without smiling. "You brought jobs only to those who served you and stole the wealth of our resources back to your own bank accounts, standing squarely on the backs of our people, desperate to believe your lies." The man's voice began to rise, and Malone braced himself for another blow, but instead the man placed a bottled water on the floor beside Malone's chair. "Yet Allah, in His mercy, has seen fit to provide you now with the opportunity to make atonement for your many sins, and those of America. It is why He allowed you to be taken and delivered into my hands, so that with what is left of your life, you may serve His purpose."

Malone's mind raced. He had spent decades negotiating with people from all over the world, often taking from them things they believed they wished to give. He was a master at it—it was his true gift. Here and now, the stakes had never been higher. He had no doubt at all the joy this man would feel watching his young terrorists saw off his head as he filmed his execution.

"Respectfully," Malone said, bowing his head, "I feel you have misjudged me. If you knew me better, you would understand that everywhere I have gone in my life, always I have wished to leave things better than I found them. If you and your people have been unintentionally injured by my actions or those of my country, amends can be made. I can help you . . ."

"Oh, you will help me," the terrorist said. "Your ransom will repay the millions American corporations have pilfered from our people. I will return that wealth to the people who have suffered from your actions and your country's policies. And I will use this wealth to take power from the *kufaar* and infidels who wish to

make us a secular country, bowing at the feet of the Great Satan—
an unforgivable offense to Allah."

"I can help you, but only if you will let me. Ransoming me to
my government will not get you what you want. The United States
government does not negotiate with terrorists, sir, but perhaps together we can find another way."

Malone felt his hands begin to shake as a bead of sweat formed
on his forehead and sprinted down the side of his face.

"Very good," the man said, snapping his fingers and pointing at
him. "I was worried that, as so often happens in your American
politics, your assignment as secretary of state was payback for some
financial support you had given for this new President, or perhaps
an honor bestowed on you for being a winning quarterback from
Ohio State. Or maybe you are even fucking her, yes?" He laughed
and clapped his hands together at his joke. "But, despite your apparent lack of credentials for your job—other than decades of experience exploiting poor nations for profit—you show yourself able to
identify our problem—how do you say it?—right out of the gate."

Malone began to feel a new confidence—not just in himself, but
also in his situation. This man did not strike him as a typical jihadist. He was a true believer, to be sure, but far more pragmatic than
the brutal fanatics of ISIL. This man had done his homework; he
knew Malone's history all the way back to his Ohio State days.
Maybe that pragmatism offered Malone a shadow of hope. If this
terrorist's goal was money, rather than sacrificing another infidel
on the altar of jihad, then he had a chance. And even if Cohen refused to pay the ransom, Malone was certain he could personally
cover the tab. His liquidated stake of Malone Construction Ltd.
from the shares he'd been forced to divest before taking office was

more than fifty million. Still, best to keep this as his trump card and wait to see what the President did first. If he could get rescued without becoming a pauper in the process, all the better.

"You say America does not negotiate with terrorists, but we know that is not true. America is negotiating with the Taliban in Afghanistan as we speak. As secretary of state, you know that there is public negotiation and private negotiation. As a businessman, you have negotiated many contracts. Now you will put those skills to work, not for profit but to save your own life. You will help me find a way to convince your government that we are legitimate leaders of our people, working on behalf of our true nation to right some terrible injustices and restore prosperity to our country. We demand a voice in our government and country, a voice stifled by the corruption brought here by America."

So there it was . . . finally his adversary had tipped his hand. This was not just a ransom play—this was about legitimacy. About credibility. This man wanted what all men with a taste of power want: more power. Malone straightened up in the chair, ready now to begin the real negotiations. Now they were in his arena, but first, he had to establish himself as more than a cowering captive to be exploited.

"The problem, my friend, is that when you behave like a terrorist, the world will judge you like a terrorist," Malone said, raising his chin. He watched as the man gestured to one of the young men, who approached and leaned in. As the man whispered, Malone continued. "By kidnapping me and treating me as you have—by threatening my life and attempting to blackmail my country—you have put me in a situation where helping you under duress will not legitimize your standing. If you want my help to gain a voice in the

Egyptian government, then you must first treat me with respect. As secretary of state of the United States—"

With a nod from the leader, the young terrorist with the rifle smashed the butt into Malone's face with a force far out of proportion to his lithe body. Malone's head jerked back and blood exploded in his mouth. His head spun and he landed hard on the ground, his vision full of stars.

When his head cleared, he was looking up into the face of his captor, smiling at him while bent over at the waist to hold his eyes.

"It seems you have already forgotten. You are not in charge here. You will do what I say, when I say, or you will be punished. Maybe I was not clear enough on this point—I will kill you, unless you help me. And the manner of your death will depend on how you try. Serve me now, not the interests of the United States, and by doing so you may serve yourself. If, together, we cannot convince your government that I am to be taken seriously, then I will have no choice but to change tactics. I will give these young men what they want. And do you know what that is?"

"No . . ." Malone said, wincing and letting blood dribble from his mouth as he rolled onto his side.

"They wish to be people who are respected. They believe, from all they have seen in their lives, that such respect requires bloodshed. These men would consider it an honor to cut off your head for the world to see. Barbarism is counterproductive and, of course, a terrible mess, but if that is the path you choose, I will embrace your choice. The stakes for my people are too high to do nothing with you . . ."

He paced away, while Malone rolled over and struggled to get to his knees. The leader said something, and two of the young men scurried to Malone's side and hoisted him into the chair. Malone stared at the man, his back to him now, arms on his chest, through the one eye he could still open. So much for the negotiation. *Fuck it. This job isn't worth dying for. No amount of six-figure speaking engagements and seven-figure book deals in the world are worth this kind of abuse.*

"What do you want me to do?" Malone asked, realizing his voice sounded wet and mushy.

"I knew you could be reasonable. We will get you cleaned up, and perhaps even fed, and then we can discuss the terms of the negotiation with your government." He bent at the waist, leaning his hands on his thighs, and smiling that damn smile that now filled Malone with both terror and rage. "I knew I chose the right man."

Malone nodded deferentially, hating himself as he did, and watched the terrorist turn to leave.

"By the way, Mr. Secretary, you are not in Egypt anymore," the man said, pausing at the threshold. "We are in my country—a country with people whose suffering you have personally grown rich off over the years." The terrorist gave a little bow as if greeting a dignitary, then laughed, "Welcome . . . to Sudan."

CHAPTER FIVE

McCoy made safe his weapon and slipped out of his kit, leaving both against the wall on the inside of the door to the tactical operations center. He'd been told to report directly to the TOC on arrival, and orders like that from Colonel Nathan Bannon were not to be taken lightly. Bannon looked up from where he sat, talking to someone McCoy didn't recognize—yet another spook named Smith or Jones, he assumed. Bannon looked angry—not the disgruntled that seemed to be the man's baseline, but for real pissed off.

"McCoy, get your ass over here," Bannon said, seeing him now at the door.

McCoy headed over, starting to worry something was wrong and his mind scrolling through the last week of activities, trying to think if there was somewhere that he and his men had fucked up— something suggested by the boss's demeanor and the presence of a clear outsider. He stopped beside the colonel's wooden workstation and came to an approximation of attention. Beard and long hair be damned, he was still a Marine and his boss wore a full bird on his collar.

"Sir," he said simply.

"At ease, Captain," Bannon said, gesturing to a folding chair beside them.

He took the seat, sitting up stiffly. He could see around the TOC where MARSOC operators tended various workstations, including one where they were clearly working the streams from the helicopters that had decimated the ISIL convoy—trying to get body counts probably.

"How'd it go, McCoy?"

"Very well, sir," McCoy said, his eyes ticking to the clean-shaven civilian sitting beside Bannon, legs crossed in a relaxed recline. "We are a go to bring together a meeting with our Peshmerga leaders and Yasim al-Jebouri at Yasim's compound. I suggest we pull this together as soon as possible. He's requested a meeting the day after tomorrow."

"Colonel Bannon, I apologize, sir, but I really don't have time . . ." the civilian visitor said.

Bannon shot the man a chilling look.

"I don't have any idea what your shit is, son," he said. "But my shit is this mission and I'm gonna get a sitrep on my mission from Captain McCoy before you interrupt me again. Clear?"

"Crystal, sir," the man said, "but the commander in chief is waiting, sir . . ."

Bannon nodded to the man, but then rolled his eyes when he turned back to McCoy.

"Is Gunny Dean all read in, Pick?" Bannon asked.

"He is, sir," McCoy said, trying not to be distracted by their third wheel. "He's been at every meeting and is well read in. But you're not suggesting that I'm being pulled off—"

"I'm not only not suggesting it, Pick, I've fought tooth and nail against it for the last hour. But it's out of my hands. You've either wildly impressed or completely pissed off someone well above my pay grade because it appears you, specifically, have emergent tasking."

"What? Sir, all due respect . . ." he said, glaring at the civilian beside Bannon, who seemed utterly unfazed by the daggers McCoy was shooting the newcomer with his eyes. "I've worked my ass off to get this to finally come together. This meeting could determine the fate of any alliance we hope to build, and the security of this region moving forward. My relationship with Yasim—"

"You're preaching to the choir, son," Bannon said, cutting him off. "Give Lieutenant Chadwick a data dump while you pack your shit. You're headed out of here later today."

"Within the hour," their mystery guest corrected.

"Keep your mouth shut till I'm done talking to my Marine," Bannon snapped.

"Of course, sir," the man said, completely unruffled.

"Sir," McCoy began to protest, but Bannon stopped him with a look. "Can you at least tell me where I'm headed?"

"No fucking idea," Bannon said, rising, his face red and arms crossed as he chewed his unlit cigar. "Because our friend here didn't read me into whatever the hell this is." And with that, the colonel stormed off, leaving McCoy alone with the stranger.

"Captain McCoy, I'm really very sorry about this. I can see you're frustrated being pulled off mission. Believe me, I get it. But there is something much larger in play right now, and the country needs you elsewhere."

"Is that so?"

"Yes. POTUS has requested you by name."

"POTUS?" he asked, his eyes wide. Then, with a chuckle, he added, "Now I know you're full of shit. CINC doesn't make a by-name request of a nobody Marine captain. What in the hell is going on? Who the hell are you and where are we going?"

"We're going to the White House, Captain," the man said, grinning as he rose from his chair. "And frankly I have no idea what's going on. I'm just the guy they sent to fetch you."

"That's it?"

"That's it, I'm afraid. Pack your stuff. We're flying by helo to Qayyarah. I have a C-40 standing by to take us to Joint Base Andrews directly. Someone else will be waiting to pick you up and take you to the White House."

"This is ridiculous," McCoy said, his mind reeling. "I can't go from my FOB in western Iraq to the White House to meet the President of the United States. Why the hell would she want to talk to me? What kind of mission takes me outside of my chain of command completely?"

"These are all great questions, Captain," the man said, checking his watch, "but I've literally told you everything I know. Now, we really need to get going . . ."

"How much do I take with me?" McCoy asked, grabbing his weapon and kit and following the man out of the TOC. "How long will I be gone?"

"No idea. I recommend you take everything you can't live without until the rest of your stuff comes back to the States with your unit."

"That's not helpful. My unit is deployed. We're talking months."

"Mm-hmm," the man said with a disinterested smile. "I wouldn't worry too much about it. Whatever you don't bring that you need, we can get for you."

"'We'?" McCoy said, cocking an eyebrow.

"Yeah, we," the man said, pushing the door open to leave the TOC. The sun was already falling toward the horizon and turning the dusty desert air orange. "A UH-1 is waiting on us and I'd like to be in the air in thirty minutes."

"Can I at least clean up first?" McCoy asked. "I can't meet POTUS like this." He held his arms out, showing his dust-covered cammies and sweat-streaked arms and face.

The man sighed. "Look, Captain. The C-40 we're riding is a VIP jet with the 89th Airlift Wing out of Andrews. It's decked out. You'll have your own sleeping area with a full shower and we have civilian clothes on board for you to change into. You can clean up en route and get some sleep, since there will be nothing else for you to do, because, like I said, I don't have anything to brief you on."

"Where do we refuel?" McCoy asked, running through a mental inventory of what he needed to bring.

"Aerial refueling en route. Oh, and one last thing. All of this is top secret and compartmentalized, so tell no one where you're going. Your OC is reassignment to a counterterror task force."

"OC?"

"Official cover."

McCoy nodded, and felt himself falling into some strange, cosmic bunny hole from which he began to worry he may not have a return trip. "What's your name, by the way?" he asked.

"John," the man said, this time extending a hand, which McCoy shook firmly. The man's hands were callused in all the right places, meaning he was far more than just an errand boy, McCoy thought. "John Smith."

McCoy shook his head.

Of course it is.

"Look, seriously, McCoy," Smith said, "nobody can know where we're headed, including your boss Bannon, I'm afraid."

"Understood." Then, as the strange man hustled off to get a pickup truck, McCoy added, "Like anyone would fucking believe me anyway."

CHAPTER SIX

U.S. Army Colonel C.G. Castillo (retired) sat on the wide porch of the sprawling, red-roofed, Spanish-style "Big House," his boot-clad feet propped up on the railing in front of him, hands in his lap on his worn blue jeans feeling the cool wet of the longneck beer he held. This house, with the other buildings scattered around it— including the smaller ranch-style house just to his right, *his* house that he'd built when he'd finally, permanently, returned from the endless wars—formed the compound of the Castillo family. Three generations of Castillos lived here now, including his cousin and best friend Fernando and his family. Those generations, and the generations before them, had endured the sacrifice of service to country from long before terrorists had attacked America on her own soil, sending West Point graduate Carlos Guillermo Castillo down the bunny hole of deep, dark covert operations in his own war. He thought about it every day, missed it more days than not, but had resigned himself to the peace he now enjoyed.

Charley, as Castillo was known to his close friends, watched as the small black dot on the horizon grew, pulling behind it a small cloud of reddish brown dust as the Black Hawk helicopter approached from the east. He took a long pull on the beer and imagined that peace was about to come to an abrupt end.

Again.

He smiled as the familiar sound of the Sikorsky UH-60 Black Hawk's rotors beating the air into submission began to reach him. Had the call not come from General Bruce McNab, he might have told them to just piss off. But if McNab was willing to come personally . . . well, the shit had to have hit the proverbial fan for him to come all the way out here. Not to mention how urgent it must be for the new President, with whom he had, at best, a checkered history, to even entertain reaching out to him, of all people. Suffice it to say, President Natalie Cohen was not his biggest fan.

Castillo set his beer on the table beside his Adirondack chair and rose, shoving his weathered hands into the pockets of his jeans under his untucked plaid shirt.

This is gonna be interesting.

Truth be told, whatever they wanted, it would be hard to say no. Eight years at the ranch without any gunplay except what he enjoyed on his home range and the kill house he had constructed two miles away on the ranch was wearing on him. On the other hand, it had taken him most of those years to find contentment with his new life of peace. Did he really want to start that process over again? He was, after all, just a few years shy of sixty, and while he was still in better shape than most forty-five-year-olds, decades of combat had inevitably taken their toll. These days he felt the ache in his joints, not just after his daily five-mile run but often just as he slipped out of bed.

He heard the screech of the screen door and then the hand of his paternal grandmother and the Castillo matriarch, Doña Alicia Castillo—nearly eighty-five and full of more fire than most of her children—came to rest on his shoulder.

"These are the men you are expecting, Carlos Guillermo?" she asked. Her tone told him all he needed to know about what she thought of their arrival.

"Yes, Abuela," he said softly. Normally he would make a joke to lighten the mood, but he knew she was in no mood for jokes.

"And they believe you have not given enough—that our family has not given enough?" Her voice was flat—not angry, but clearly not happy. She had, after all, lost her son—his father—to war in Southeast Asia. She had nearly lost her grandson Carlos more than once, after taking him in at age twelve, when cancer took his mother. He inevitably followed in his father's footsteps and spent a lifetime in his own wars. It must just be in the genes—Doña Alicia had given enough.

"They only take what we are willing to give, Abuela," he said, reaching his hand up to squeeze hers. He turned his head and kissed the brown and wrinkled hand, sharply contrasted to his pale but weathered hand. "I serve our country, not these people. I will hear what they have to say."

"Then I should get together some tea, I suppose," Doña Alicia said. "I imagine you will entertain them out here, and I prefer that, quite frankly."

She reached for his beer as she turned to leave.

"You can leave that," he said.

She smiled, handed him his beer, and squeezed his arm.

"One day, it may be enough, Carlos Guillermo."

"One day," he agreed, raising his voice over the now deafening roar as the helicopter approached, flaring its nose up into a hover before settling to the ground.

Perhaps today, perhaps not.

He watched as the rotors slowed, the engine now at idle. The cloud of dust drifted to the east and settled to the ground around the green Black Hawk. Two men approached, one flashing an enormous smile when he saw Castillo.

In that moment, he knew he would likely do whatever it was they asked of him.

That man, retired general Bruce McNab, stepped up onto his porch, still with the grace and strength of a jungle predator, a smile on his weathered face beneath the aviator sunglasses, and extended his hand.

"It's good to see you, Charley," McNab said, his grip firm and confident—that of a young soldier, not a man now in his seventies.

"You, too, sir," Castillo said, unable to suppress his own smile. He had missed McNab and the world he represented. The weight of that hit him as McNab, in his black shirt and khaki cargo pants, hands on his hips, inspected Castillo.

"I'm retired, son," McNab said with a grin. "Maybe you can call me Bruce now."

Castillo laughed at that.

"Not sure it that's possible for me, sir, but I promise to give it a try."

He would have recognized the man beside McNab immediately even had he not known he was coming. It wasn't every day the Director of National Intelligence stood on the porch of a retired soldier in southwest Texas.

"Sir," he said, extending his hand. "It's an honor to meet you. Your time at CIA was something to be proud of."

"Thank you, Colonel Castillo," the DNI said, shaking his hand. "That means something coming from you. You have quite a reputation in the IC, one that extends beyond your retirement, as you can imagine."

Castillo shrugged.

"Call me Charley, sir," he said, gesturing to the small table on the porch, just beyond his Adirondack chair. "Care to sit?"

As if on cue, Doña Alicia came through the squeaky screen door, a tray with iced glasses in one hand and a pitcher of sweet tea in the other.

General McNab removed his sunglasses and introduced himself and the Director of National Intelligence, then added, "It is a pleasure seeing you again, Doña Alicia."

"Perhaps you gentlemen would care for a drink?" she asked, placing the glasses and pitcher on the table as they took their seats, "while you try to lure my grandson away from home?"

"Thank you very much, ma'am," DNI Fleiss said, with an almost bow as he took a seat, refusing to take the bait. "We won't stay long."

"I'm sure," Doña Alicia said, turning and heading back inside, letting the screen door slam behind her.

"So how are you, Charley?" McNab asked, taking a sip of his tea.

"I'm good, sir," Castillo replied, deciding that—especially under what he imagined to be the circumstances—he wasn't ready to call his old boss Bruce. He sipped his tea. "But I doubt you flew out here with the DNI to see how an old soldier is enjoying retirement. In fact . . ." he narrowed his eyes but let a grin spread on his face, "I'm betting you're only here with Director Fleiss because President

Cohen worried I wouldn't be receptive to whatever her request is, unless it came from you."

McNab laughed and smiled at Fleiss, who shook his head with his own grin.

"See?" McNab said. "You're never really far from the game, are you, Charley?"

"I suppose not, sir," Castillo said, placing his tea on the table and leaning in now on his elbows. "And I'm guessing this has everything to do with the kidnapping of the secretary of state?"

"It does, Colonel Castillo," Fleiss said, taking the lead. "We have a great deal of intelligence—most of it dead ends that tell us nothing, which in my experience can be telling in its own right—and various alphabet agencies spinning their wheels. We need someone who can move outside of the government bureaucracy and rice-bowl politics that have crept back into the intelligence community these last several years. Our feeling is that we—your country and your President—need you. And believe me when I tell you we know we're asking a lot and we don't ask lightly. We are running out of time to save a good man and prevent whatever the long game is of the assholes who took him."

"We don't have time to fuck around, Charley," McNab said, summing up. "We want to bring back the program."

Castillo nodded his head, marveling at the feeling of déjà vu. This felt so much like that day, a lifetime ago, when he'd heard the same pitch from another President and his proxies. Only that time it had been a missing Boeing 727 airliner instead of the secretary of state.

"The Presidential Agent program has been down a long time, sir," he said. "And it doesn't really seem in keeping with the transparent government President Cohen campaigned on, to be honest with you."

"Things change, Colonel," Fleiss said. "You of all people should appreciate that."

"Desperate times," McNab added, and sipped his tea again.

"We're aware you have had your differences with Natalie Cohen in the past, Colonel Castillo," Fleiss said. "But she's President Cohen now, and we need you."

Castillo smiled.

"I have no problem with this President, sir," he said. "Hell, I voted for her without reservation. She's quite capable. I'm just surprised you were able to talk her into this, is all."

"We didn't talk her into anything, Charley," Fleiss said, the switch to the familiar and collegial name not lost on Castillo. "She came to me with this. This is her idea completely."

"The program or the man?" Castillo asked.

Now Fleiss smiled broadly.

"Both, in fact," he said, leaning back and reaching for his tea.

Castillo felt the two men watching him, giving him time, as he sipped his tea again. Sure, he was fifty-seven, but he had no doubt he could still kick the ass of ninety-five percent of the young active-duty soldiers serving, the five percent left for only a portion of the SOF warriors—Army Special Forces, Marine Raiders, Navy SEALs—out on the tip of the spear. For those guys, it was his decades of experience that gave him the edge. He was fit, he was strong, and he had been there and done that more than almost anyone.

And his country—and right now, the secretary of state—needed him.

Castillo, of course, had decided on his answer the moment he saw Bruce McNab—fit for the fight and still in the mix himself, somehow—step onto his porch. That was the truth. What he needed now were assurances.

"So who's running the program then—assuming you're bringing it back permanently?"

"You are, Charley," Fleiss said. "Whether it's just for this or for a longer term, this will be your baby." The DNI folded his arms on his chest. "Again," he added with a smile, "you'll answer only to me and President Cohen."

"Is that your promise?" Castillo asked, already running an inventory in his mind of what he should throw in a duffel bag to head out.

"That's her promise, Charley," Fleiss corrected. "Something she'll tell you herself, if you're with us."

"When?"

"Tonight," Fleiss said. "We have a C-37B standing by at Lackland. If you're in, our orders are to have you in the White House for a meeting with her and then a full briefing this evening."

"I'm in," Castillo said. He felt a familiar fire grow in his chest. He drained his tea and rose. "Just give me a few minutes to throw some stuff in a bag and talk to my abuela."

"You want me to talk to her with you, Charley?" McNab said as he and Fleiss rose from their seats.

Castillo laughed.

"I wouldn't recommend it," he said. "She's meaner than she looks. Give me five minutes and I'll meet you at the helicopter."

Fleiss held out his hand, which Castillo shook firmly.

"Welcome back, Colonel," he said.

"Thank you, sir," Castillo said.

CHAPTER SEVEN

Castillo felt a strange combination of irritation and yearning as the limousine carrying him and General McNab rolled through the Secret Service gate. His retirement had come at the right time for him personally, but the way the Presidential Agent program had ended—abruptly and without warning or ceremony—had always chapped his ass. Scuttling one of the most effective counterterrorism tools in the American arsenal in the name of political expediency and optics was both foreign and disingenuous to a man like him. Even so, he had no regrets . . . other than the desire to be back in the know. That need, once habituated, never quite evaporated.

"Does it feel strange to be back?" McNab asked, from the seat next to him in the back of the limousine.

Castillo nodded. "A bit . . . but it also feels like coming home."

McNab flashed him a knowing smile.

Castillo admired how the retired general had kept a foot in the door, continuing to serve, while at the same time finding work and life balance for the first time in his lauded career. Castillo had certainly been offered more than his own fair share of "consulting" opportunities, but as tempting as it had been, his answer had always been no. He just didn't see himself as the old guy, clinging desperately to the past, by means of the odd contractor job here or there. He was an operator, not a consultant.

For Castillo, it was either all in or all out.

As the car pulled into the underground garage, he felt a gut-stirring sense of anticipation. Being the Presidential Agent again would feel good, like slipping on a favorite pair of shoes. Besides, his proverbial gas tank was still more than half full—he had plenty of miles left in him.

They parked by the security door. Director Fleiss, who'd traveled from the airport in a separate vehicle, greeted them by the security door. The DNI punched in his code and pressed his hand on the flat glass of the biometric reader. The door hissed open as the magnetic locks released, but that only gave them access to a short hallway that ended at another door with a kitted-up Marine standing guard.

The Marine studied the DNI's CAC card after scanning it with a handheld reader, then did the same with McNab's.

Finally, the Marine gave Castillo a hard look. "Identification, sir?"

Castillo looked at the DNI, who winked at him.

"I have his ID, staff sergeant," Fleiss said, pulling a thin case, clear on the front, from his coat pocket, then removing the CAC card from inside and handing it to the Marine. He gave the case with an attached black lanyard to Castillo.

"RFID blocker?" Castillo asked as the Marine scanned his CAC card, then got a green light and the expected chirp.

"Yeah," Fleiss said, "all the CACs for White House access are required to have them. Don't understand how exactly they work, but I know they're far more effective than the commercial ones you hear about on the radio. I'm told they're active instead of passive, whatever the hell that means."

"Means we're all getting thyroid cancer from whatever the hell they emit," McNab said with a wry grin.

The Marine punched in a code and the second door clicked heavily and hissed as it opened. Castillo glanced at his CAC card, which could not have been more than a few hours old, and smiled. Bureaucracy could be incredibly efficient . . . when properly motivated. His picture, which McNab had snapped on the plane ride here, was printed in the upper left-hand corner with the emblem of the Office of the Director of National Intelligence in the upper right. The ID listed his title as "Special Assistant to the Director of National Intelligence," a designation quite reminiscent to his OC role in Homeland Security a decade ago. That was in keeping with what Fleiss promised, that his chain of command was quite short—answering directly to the DNI and the President.

Perfect.

He slipped the lanyard over this head and followed Fleiss and McNab to the elevator.

Minutes later they were standing at the President's secretary's desk, waiting while the well-dressed, middle-aged man announced their arrival over the phone.

"Madam President? Director Fleiss and his party are here . . . Yes, ma'am. Right away." He looked up with a vacant smile and tired eyes, and Castillo imagined he'd been at this post for fourteen hours or more. "You gentlemen can go in. The President is waiting."

The Oval Office was just like Castillo remembered it, save for a few touches changed by the new occupant—a new Presidential seal rug and family pictures on a sideboard.

"Gentlemen, please come in," President Cohen said, rising from behind the *Resolute* desk.

Unlike her secretary, President Cohen looked fresh, confident, and in control. Her rise to the presidency made sense to Castillo. When he'd known her as Dr. Cohen, the national security adviser, she'd been the hardest working member of the staff, but, more important, seemed always to serve the people rather than herself—a rarity in the White House in his experience. He might not always have agreed with her, but he had never questioned her motives.

"Madam President," Castillo said, offering his hand. "It's an honor to see you again, ma'am."

Her grip was firm and self-assured.

"Let's cut the bullshit, shall we, Colonel?" she said, her eyes twinkling. "You and I were rarely on the same page when it came to politics and procedure."

"A true statement, ma'am," he agreed, releasing her hand. "But we were always in the same book. I have tremendous respect for you and was happy to see you win the election."

"Is that so?" she said with a curl of her lips. She gestured toward the opposing sofas for everyone to sit.

"Absolutely," Castillo said, taking a seat on the couch to the left, facing the President, who took her seat on the right side of the table between them. "Always happy when the best candidate wins, ma'am. And you were undeniably the best candidate."

She nodded as McNab sat beside Castillo. The DNI stood behind them, perhaps not wanting to crowd, but not willing to take a seat beside the President for this meeting.

Optics, Castillo thought.

"Will the chief of staff be joining us, Madam President?" Fleiss asked.

"No, Marty," Cohen said, crossing her legs. "I think it's best we keep this conversation just the four of us, don't you? A small circle is probably best."

"I agree, ma'am," Fleiss said.

"So, Colonel Castillo . . ."

"Ma'am, you are welcome to call me Charley," he said, crossing his legs and dropping his hands in his lap.

"Okay, Charley," she said, her eyes studying him carefully. "What has Director Fleiss told you so far?"

"Only the basics, Madam President," he said, preferring to let Fleiss speak for himself, always unsure what and how much the higher authority—in this case the President—wanted to share on their own. "That you're planning to bring back the Presidential Agent program—I'm speculating, in light of the short fuse, it's related to the disappearance of the secretary of state."

"Kidnapping," Cohen said, spitting the word out like a bad taste in her mouth. "Terrorists in Egypt have kidnapped the secretary of state and we're going to get him back."

"Yes, ma'am," Castillo said, watching her.

"Charley, I ran on a platform of transparency, and I will tell you it was a difficult decision to bring this program back. Not because the program was without value—your string of successes speak for themselves—but because it was always my hope that we could be effective doing things the right way. The intelligence community and counterterrorism entities that keep our country safe should be able to function within our constitutional checks and balances. I still believe that's possible, and yet here we are . . ."

"The world is a terribly complicated place, Madam President," McNab offered. "Americans want to be safe, and despite the bluster you hear from our divided population, at the end of the day, they don't really care about the nitty-gritty of how we provide that safety."

Cohen nodded, but seemed unpersuaded.

"Perhaps," she conceded. "Or at least there is some truth in that. But the bottom line is, we currently have an intelligence community that, over the previous administration, has returned to the pre-9/11 mindset and rice-bowl mentality that makes it inefficient and fractured. It is my hope that my administration can set us back on the right path of being a cohesive force working *together* for the American people and return us to the nonpartisan civil servants we should be. But, unfortunately, that will take time. And that's time that Secretary of State Malone simply does not have."

"Desperate times—desperate measures," Castillo offered.

Nothing like being called from the bench with seconds on the clock and the only hope being a Hail Mary play.

"Indeed," Cohen agreed.

It sure as hell didn't sound like job security, but then, at fifty-seven years old, how much career progression was he hoping for? This was a chance to do some good, and maybe this time end his service to the country he loved on his own terms.

"Madam President, I am honored to step back into the role of Presidential Agent, and I will do whatever it takes to bring the secretary home safely."

"I know, Charley," she said, this time giving him a genuine smile. "It's why I reached out to you. You're the last of a breed of truly apolitical patriots . . . I guess I just wanted you to understand my motives here, so as not to seem a hypocrite."

"Not at all, Madam President," he said, giving her the out. "The American people elected you to make the hard decisions no one else wants to make. This seems like the right one, and I'll be honored to do my part."

"I know you will," Cohen said. She uncrossed her legs and leaned forward, her forearms on her knees. She suddenly looked much more tired than when Castillo had entered the room. "Knowledge of this program must be kept within this circle," she said. "Charley, you will personally direct the operation and the small staff assigned to you. You will answer only to Director Fleiss and to me. General McNab will be available for counsel and to assist with personnel selection, but no one else is read into this program without direct consent. You can use whatever bullshit 'Special Task Force' NOC you choose, but this is highly compartmentalized to the people in this room and, of course, Captain McCoy."

Castillo looked at McNab, who shrugged, then at Fleiss before returning his gaze to the President.

"Who's Captain McCoy, ma'am?" he asked, with a heavy feeling in his stomach.

Cohen looked at Fleiss, who fielded the question.

"Charley, Captain McCoy is a MARSOC Marine Raider officer, currently serving with the 2nd Marine Raider battalion out of Lejeune. Academy graduate and a legacy Marine officer whom we have identified as the best candidate for the program."

"Candidate for what?" Castillo asked, still genuinely confused.

"For your successor as the Presidential Agent, Charley," Cohen said, watching him more carefully than ever. "You're the program manager and have full autonomy in running the operations, within the confines of ROE set out for you by Director Fleiss. McCoy will be trained, by you, to function as the next Presidential Agent."

"Wait, what?" he said, looking at McNab, then at Fleiss, both of whom looked down at their hands. To his credit, Fleiss then took a deep breath and met his stare.

"Charley," the DNI said, "we need the program to have a future, and that means we need to prepare the next generation. Captain McCoy has been identified as the best person for that job."

"Well, then why am I here, Marty? I'm a field agent, Madam President. Not a . . . a program manager . . . or whatever you called it." He felt his anger growing at the idea they thought he would come in to babysit a twenty-something Marine. For the program to function, and for this rescue mission to succeed, required a Presidential Agent with experience and blooded know-how.

"Because you are the best field agent there is, Charley," Cohen said. "And probably the only one who can properly prepare McCoy for this role."

"Look, with all due respect," Castillo began, feeling precious little respect for the reckless decision the President was proposing, "I'm not coming out of retirement to put on a headset and talk into the ear of some kid with no experience at all in this job. Not with the life of the secretary of state on the line."

"That's not what we're proposing, Charley," Fleiss said. "We need you there with him, but surely you don't envision yourself fast-roping onto a hot target at age sixty, which, last time I checked, is only a few years away. We need you to mentor this guy. Get him ready for the day he has to go it alone."

Castillo shook his head in frustration.

"Look, Charley, he's working for you, not the other way," the President said, her tone ending any debate. "This is still your program and you're still the Presidential Agent, but with that title comes the additional responsibility of mentoring him into the role. Somebody has to be the next guy. I would have thought you'd want to play the central role in nurturing your legacy."

Castillo took a deep breath, looking at the President, and then at McNab. He could read between the lines here. They needed him— Secretary of State Malone needed him—if they were going to get the job done, and everyone in the room knew it. So they wanted him to mentor some SOF Marine while he did the job? Fine. He owed a debt to plenty who had mentored him into what he'd become, including the retired general beside him on the couch. But there was no way they meant for him to hand the reins to the kid on *this* operation. You didn't call in the star quarterback with seconds left on the clock just to hold the ball for the kicker. They knew he would deliver and he sure as hell would.

"No problem, Madam President," Castillo said with a resignation and contentment he didn't feel. "When do I meet Captain McCoy?"

"In a few hours," President Cohen said, getting to her feet. He and McNab followed her lead and stood. "You'll have a few hours for Marty and his team to get you up to speed on the intelligence we have currently on the secretary's kidnapping and to review Mc-Coy's service record. Put your plan together for approval by Director Fleiss in the coming hours, so you can execute in the morning. We need you in Egypt ASAP."

"Yes, ma'am," Castillo said, shaking her hand again.

"Welcome back, Charley," Cohen said, turning and heading back to her desk.

"Thank you, Madam President," he said, feeling only slightly less enthusiastic than a few minutes ago. "And I promise we'll bring Secretary Malone home."

"I'm counting on it," she said, and returned to her seat behind the *Resolute* desk.

Castillo followed Fleiss and McNab out of the Oval Office, eager to get to work.

Hopefully this kid, this Marine captain, would be able to keep up.

CHAPTER EIGHT

Aboard 89th Airlift Wing C-40B
Over the Atlantic Ocean,
one hundred miles east of Joint Base Andrews
March 18, 3:50 a.m.

One of the most important tools McCoy had added to his toolbox in the five and half years he'd been deploying with Marine Special Operations was the ability to sleep anywhere and anytime. Sleep was a weapon to the SOF operator, one that could at times mean the difference between life and death. After a long, hot shower in a bathroom far nicer than the one in his town house back home in North Topsail Beach, North Carolina, and a delicious meal of perfectly cooked steak, lobster tail, and mixed vegetables served by a gorgeous woman made paradoxically more attractive by the green-bag flight suit she wore, he'd slept for nine straight hours.

Now after another shower, and a breakfast of chorizo, eggs, and orange juice, he was dressed in khaki pants, a light blue button-down shirt, and a dark blue blazer. He didn't bother asking how they knew his sizes. He sat in an incredibly comfortable oversized leather seat across a shared table from a matching seat and looked up as the man calling himself John Smith came out of the rest area.

"How are we doing?" Smith asked.

"Great."

"Get some rest?" the man asked, sliding into the seat across from him.

"Yup, and a great breakfast."

"More coffee?" The cabin attendant smiled at McCoy and held up a pot.

"Please."

"Sir?" the woman asked, holding the pot up for Smith.

"Yes, please," Smith said, and she set a cup in front of him as well.

"You take yours black as well?"

"Oh, God, no," Smith said, wrinkling his nose. "Do you have any flavored creamer?"

"I do, but I can make you a latte if you prefer. Vanilla? Caramel?"

"Now we're talking," Smith said, rubbing his hands together. "Caramel latte. Double shot of espresso, please."

"My pleasure. And I'll bring you some breakfast as well."

"Thank you." Smith grinned at McCoy. "These gigs ain't so bad, right?"

McCoy chuckled. "So, what's next, Mr. Smith?"

Smith leaned back in his chair.

"Well, next I hand you off to someone at the VIP hangar for transportation to the White House. Then, I head home to my wife and kids in Alexandria and enjoy a few days off."

McCoy nodded, not sure what to say to the strange man. For his part, Smith seemed to sense McCoy's hatred of meaningless small talk, so they ate breakfast together in silence. Not long after, the aircraft flared and rolled into a perfect landing at Joint Base Andrews.

As soon as they'd taxied off the long runway, Smith was up, pulling his bags from the back, no doubt eager to get his part of this strange play over. McCoy, for his part, had only his backpack and a small duffel, which he retrieved while the plane pulled up to the hangar.

"Just a moment," the flight attendant said, and he felt a gentle lurch as they began to again move forward. "We've been directed to pull inside the hangar for your transfer. You must be one of *those* passengers," she said with a wry smile that McCoy thought might mean she'd like to know more, but knew better than to ask.

"Must be," McCoy said, smiling back. "But it's news to me."

Halting inside a brightly lit hangar that out the window looked nicer than apartments he'd had, McCoy stood beside the spook waiting by the door, which the attendant was now unlatching and pulling inward. The cockpit door opened and a pilot—middle-aged but still fit with a touch of gray at the temples of his close-cropped hair—stretched his back and gave a nod.

"Hope it was a good flight for y'all," he said with a southern drawl. His nameplate on his flight suit said he was Lieutenant Colonel Chad Villanova.

"Great, sir, thanks," McCoy said.

"Love the rare chance to haul you guys around instead of some spoiled and entitled bureaucrat," the pilot said, not indicating who, exactly, he thought they were.

"We greatly appreciate the ride, Colonel," Smith said, shaking the pilot's hand.

McCoy shook his hand as well and followed Smith down the airstair.

"Have a great night—what's left of it," the attendant called after them.

The disorientation of stepping out of a combat zone and into this VIP hangar was suddenly overwhelming. He'd gone from sitting on the dirt floor with a tribal leader in Iraq to being whisked away to the White House. He decided it was time to wake up from the crazy dream.

"Hope that Town Car's for you, Smith," he said with a wry grin, eyeing the black Lincoln idling nearby. "More of a pickup truck guy myself."

Which was true, despite the vast family fortune available to him after his mother's inheritance of the American Personal Pharmaceutical Company. The McCoys had real wealth, but none of the entitled wealthy mindset, and he'd personally walked away from all of that to a life in a small-town home outside Lejeune, all paid for by his O-3 salary and housing allowance from the Marine Corps.

"Pffftt . . . Not hardly," Smith said. "My Chevy Tahoe's out back. That's all you, brother." The man offered him a hand as they stepped off the airstair onto the highly polished white floor of the hangar. "Good luck on your journey."

"Journey where?" McCoy asked, shaking his hand.

"Down the bunny hole," Smith said with a grin, turning and walking toward the back of the hangar and the exit door there. "Everything changes from here," he called over his shoulder.

McCoy walked to the idling Lincoln and, unable to see inside the vehicle through the blacked-out windows, rapped on the driver's-side window with his knuckles. The glass lowered with a soft hum.

McCoy looked at the driver, who then nodded to him.

"Hop in," the man said, his blue eyes studying him, or so it felt. The man looked a little old to be a limo driver, but had the solid fitness of a soldier. Perhaps he was as much bodyguard as driver, though McCoy hardly figured he needed one.

"Mind if I ride up front? I'm not much of a limo guy, and I hate the backseat."

"Suit yourself," the driver said with a shrug, but he grinned. The window slid back up.

McCoy tossed his coyote-tan backpack into the rear seat and walked around the back of the car, slipping into the front passenger seat.

"Thanks, my friend," he said. "Don't suppose you wanna tell me where I'm *really* headed?"

"The Situation Room," the man said as he put the vehicle in gear and pulled away.

McCoy glanced at his watch. "It's not even four-thirty in the morning."

"Must be important, then," the man said, his blue eyes twinkling under his blond hair—too long to be active-duty military.

"Well, I don't suppose *you* know what's up," McCoy grumbled.

"I might know something about it. But it's best I let the DNI read you in first, don't you think? Not good form to circumvent the President."

McCoy studied the man closely, certain now that he was a helluva lot more than just a driver. As they merged onto I-495, Capital Beltway South, McCoy let out a quiet sigh.

Eventually, I'm gonna meet a straight shooter who will tell me what is so important I had to be pulled away from my Raider Team in Iraq. And the answer better be damn good.

CHAPTER NINE

McCoy had never been to the White House, and it was a streak he had hoped to continue indefinitely as he was promoted through the Marine Corps ranks. The farther he could stay away from the halls of bureaucracy, the better. *Looks like that streak is about to be broken*, he thought as they cleared the E Street checkpoint and pulled up to the southwest gate of the White House complex. Two members of a Marine security detail manning the gate stepped up to meet them— one approaching the driver's door while the other walked the perimeter of the vehicle with an inspection mirror on a pole to survey the underside of the car.

"Good morning," the driver said, handing the stone-faced Marine a packet of what McCoy could only assume were both their credentials. McCoy had not given the driver his credentials, so he could not be certain.

"State your business at the White House this morning," the

Marine said, accepting the document packet but keeping his eyes on them.

Oh, this ought to be good, McCoy thought as he waited for the driver to answer the question. He was not disappointed.

"Colonel Castillo and Captain McCoy, here at the request of the President," his confederate chauffeur said.

"Just a moment, sir," the Marine said. "Please put your transmission in park while you wait."

"Colonel Castillo, huh?" McCoy said with a narrow-eyed stare at his *chauffeur.* "I'm assuming you didn't get your bird driving town cars around the beltway . . . sir."

"I've worn a lot of hats over the years, McCoy," was all Castillo said through a grin, both hands gripping the steering wheel at the two and ten o'clock positions.

"Mm-hmm . . ." McCoy said, studying the man in profile, trying to place the face and searching his memory for that name. After a long moment, he decided he couldn't place the name or the face and ruminated over which branch of service Castillo harkened from. He settled on army, but that was little more than a gut feeling. He estimated the colonel to be in his fifties—though with a level of fitness of a man much younger—and wondered about this whole "driver" charade. Clearly Castillo, whoever he was, enjoyed messing with people.

Yeah, definitely army . . .

The Marine sentry returned a moment later, and handed Castillo his envelope back, and said, "Sir, they're expecting you in the Situation Room. Park anywhere that's open, then walk to the south screening building on West Executive Avenue. Your escort will meet you there."

"Thank you, Corporal," Castillo said, easing them past the stout barricades after they'd fully retracted.

At this hour, parking was easy to find, and Castillo pulled nose-in to one of the angle slips on State Place NW. After killing the engine, he opened the envelope and passed McCoy his new credentials. McCoy looked at the badge, which had his full name, his photograph, and a title—SPECIAL ASSISTANT ODNI—printed in the upper-left corner. The badge was rimmed with a royal blue border and was fitted inside a thin transparent case.

"I think it's time somebody tells me what's going on," McCoy said, as Castillo pulled on his door handle to get out of the car.

"Yep," Castillo said. "That's what we're here for. C'mon, don't want to be late on your first day. Leave your backpack in the back."

With a grudging exhale through his nose, McCoy climbed out of the Town Car and followed Castillo to the south screening building where West Executive South met State. As promised, they were greeted by a White House staffer who introduced himself as Stephan Hart, ODNI liaison, and whisked them through screening before the two-hundred-foot march to the West Wing. When they reached the iconic white awning designating the west entrance, directly across the street from the Eisenhower Executive Office Building, McCoy paused.

"Ever been to the West Wing?" Hart asked him.

"Never," McCoy said, looking up at the monochrome gray Presidential seal affixed to the front of the awning.

"Then welcome to the People's House," Hart said, calling the White House by its nickname—a forgotten tradition that had been renewed and resurrected by the current administration.

A very American concept, McCoy thought.

Referring to the White House as the People's House, rather

than, say, the Presidential Palace, as a despot or dictator might, was a symbolic reminder that the current President—however important she may feel—served at the *pleasure of the people.*

"No guards?" McCoy asked, taken aback that the entrance was unattended.

"There's plenty of security here," Hart said. "Just not posted at every door. That's what the checkpoints are for."

McCoy nodded and quickstepped to catch up with Castillo, who'd already gone inside—none of this new to the colonel. Hart held the door for McCoy and they both stepped into the foyer. Castillo was talking to the night receptionist who was seated at a desk and he already had her laughing at something. When they stepped up, she smiled and greeted Hart by name. To McCoy's surprise, she didn't ask to see their badges.

"You know where you're going, Stephan, I believe," she said, more parting comment than question.

"Yep, thanks, Sandy. Have a good one."

"You, too. Nice to see you, Colonel Castillo."

Castillo took the lead, as McCoy was beginning to sense would be the norm, walking straight through a cased opening and into a lobby twice the size of the foyer. The ceiling was low and the décor was, while tasteful, far from regal—not nearly as grand and stately as he'd imagined the West Wing to be. As if reading his mind, Hart played extemporaneous tour guide.

"This is the ground level of the West Wing," the staffer began. "If you keep going straight, past that blue sofa and chair over there and head down the corridor, you'll pass the Secret Service office and find access up to the first floor. That's where you'll find the Oval, the Cabinet Room, the Roosevelt Room, et cetera—basically all the iconic spaces you're used to seeing in photographs and movies."

Ahead, Castillo disappeared around the corner.

"Most people think whizzer is underground," Hart continued, "but that's a common misconception. While, technically, you could call this level a basement, it's only halfway underground."

"What's whizzer?" McCoy asked, turning right and stepping through a set of open double doors.

"Oh sorry, not *whizzer* like it sounds. That's just how people say the acronym—WHSR stands for White House Situation Room," he said, leading McCoy down a half flight of stairs. "On the left is the Navy Mess. If you have time, I suggest grabbing breakfast there. Good eats." He turned right again into a dead-end hallway where Castillo was pressing the buzzer on a keypad beside a single door.

"Colonel Castillo, Captain McCoy, and Stephan Hart to see the DNI," Castillo said.

"Come on in," a male voice said, and the door buzzed open.

Castillo opened the door and led the trio into the cramped reception area at the entrance to the Situation Room.

"Welcome, gentlemen," the reception attendant said. "Please place your phones in one of the lead-lined cubbies and I'll give you a ticket. DNI Fleiss is waiting for you in the Briefing Room, straight ahead."

McCoy pulled his phone from his pocket and did as instructed, getting a little slip of numbered paper from the attendant that matched the numbered cubby he'd selected. He shoved the ticket in his pocket and followed Castillo across a transverse hall. As he did, he looked into a large room buzzing with activity. Two tiers of workstations staffed by a small army of analysts were working at computers or talking on phones in a setup reminiscent of many tactical operations centers he'd experienced.

He glanced at Hart beside him. "What's that?"

"It has lots of nicknames, but most people just call it the Watch Center—think of it as the nerve center of WHSR. Down here we have a staff of approximately thirty personnel organized into five watch teams—three duty officers, a comms supe, and two intel analysts. They prep the President's Morning Book and process thousands of cables and inquiries a day. It's pretty bad-ass how much data they crunch."

"Funny," McCoy said, "I always thought the Situation Room was an *actual* room."

"Once upon a time it was, but this space got completely renovated and updated in 2007. The name stuck, but the Situation Room is a moniker for this whole complex now."

"Quit gawking and gabbing," Castillo said, standing in the doorway ahead. "The DNI is a busy man and the clock is ticking."

McCoy turned away from the Watch Center, nodded, and followed Hart into the Briefing Room—a modest-sized conference room with a dozen black leather chairs arranged neatly around a large rectangular table. Seated at the head of the table was a man McCoy recognized instantly as Director of National Intelligence Marty Fleiss.

"Captain McCoy," Fleiss said, standing to greet him with an extended hand. "Welcome to the Situation Room."

"Thank you, sir," McCoy said, giving the DNI's hand a firm shake.

"Charley, I see you didn't get lost," the DNI said with a grin to Castillo.

"Not this time," the colonel said.

The DNI turned to Hart. "Thanks for playing escort, Stephan. If you could wait outside, please."

"Yes, sir," Hart said, and excused himself.

Fleiss gestured for McCoy and Castillo to sit as he took his seat back at the head of the table. "I imagine it's probably been a whirlwind twenty-four hours for you, Captain?" he said.

"Yesterday I was sitting on a dirt floor sipping tea with a tribal leader on the other side of the world, and now I'm in the West Wing talking with the DNI in the Situation Room—so yes, sir, this is all a bit surreal," McCoy answered.

The DNI nodded. "I assume Charley read you in on the basics of why you're here?"

"Uh, that's a negative, sir."

Fleiss shot Castillo a sideways look.

Castillo just smiled. "I thought it would be better to throw him in the deep end and see if he could swim."

McCoy resisted the urge to shake his head at this comment that perfectly encapsulated the difference between his father's generation of warfighter and his own. Today's leadership in the Corps didn't have time to make every assignment a test of character and mettle. In a Marine Corps at war for twenty years now, the job itself was the test of a Marine's character and mettle. As an officer, McCoy believed his number one responsibility as a leader was to effectively communicate information up and down the chain of command. Effective communication was the cornerstone of mission success. The world and the mission objectives were complicated enough; the last thing anyone needed was to waste time guessing and second-guessing the priorities, objectives, means and methods, and criteria for success. The days of "figure it out as you go along" were over as far as McCoy was concerned—and good riddance.

Apparently, Castillo hadn't gotten the memo.

"In that case," Fleiss said, "I think it's time we got down to business. As you are undoubtedly aware, Captain McCoy, the U.S.

secretary of state was abducted during a terrorist attack at the Middle East nuclear weapons nonproliferation summit in Cairo."

"Yes, sir, I'm aware," McCoy replied.

The DNI's expression turned grim. "So far, we've made precious little headway finding him. Whoever did this covered their tracks exceedingly well and they have made no attempt to communicate any demands . . ."

And what does any of this have to do with me?

"Now, I imagine you're sitting there wondering what all this has to do with you," Fleiss continued. "And that's a fair question, which is why I think this is the perfect time to turn this indoc over to Colonel Castillo."

"Captain McCoy," Castillo began, taking the proverbial baton from the DNI, "you've been identified and selected as the top candidate for the Presidential Agent program. As the Presidential Agent, your first assignment will be to locate the secretary of state and bring him home."

McCoy felt his mouth drop open. "Excuse me?"

Castillo flashed him a "no bullshit" smile. "Any questions?"

"Uh . . . yeah, a million," McCoy said, his head spinning. "First of which is, I've never even heard of the Presidential Agent program. What is it and who runs it?"

"The Presidential Agent program was created under a previous administration to fill a need that exists where the intelligence community, Department of Defense, and clandestine operations ecosystems intersect. Imagine, if you will, a giant Venn diagram where those three communities overlap—in the very center there's a tiny triangle where all the rings cross. Can you picture that in your mind?"

McCoy nodded.

"That hyper-connected space is where the Presidential Agent program was created to function. Our job is to execute emergent tasking, in denied areas, with zero footprint. We operate with the full knowledge and silent backing of the President of the United States, while offering her plausible deniability in the event we fuck up. In other words, the Presidential Agent gets the shit done that nobody else can—like rescuing the secretary of state from terrorists."

"Hold on," McCoy said, raising both his hands in disbelief. "Sounds like we're reinventing the wheel a little bit here. If you want to rescue Secretary Malone, send in the Tier One—this is the *exact* type of mission Delta or the JSOC SEALs were created for."

"Where do you want the President to send them?" Castillo asked, cocking an eyebrow. "I told you nobody knows where Malone is."

"Well, isn't that the CIA's job—to figure that out?"

"It is," the DNI answered, taking the baton back from Castillo. "And they haven't been able to find him."

"Okay, but what in the world makes you think *I* can?" McCoy said through an exasperated laugh. "Twenty-four hours ago, I was sitting in Iraq with the Raiders, leading an operation that has absolutely no connection with Egypt whatsoever. I'm sorry, gentlemen, but I have to be candid with you—I don't have the first clue how to go about executing the task you're suggesting. But even if I was arrogant enough to claim I did, I don't have the network or interagency connections to effect a successful mission."

Fleiss and Castillo looked at each other with matching knowing smiles.

"We know that," Castillo said. "But I do . . ."

"You see, Captain, you've been selected to be the *next* Presidential Agent, and Charley is going to teach you how."

In McCoy's head, the first puzzle piece clicked into place. "So, I assume that means Colonel Castillo is the former Presidential Agent?"

"Not former . . . *am*," Castillo said, beating the DNI to the punch. "I am the one and only Presidential Agent, and you'll be working for me."

In the corner of his eye, McCoy thought he glimpsed the DNI grimace at this. Maybe Castillo was having a little trouble accepting the idea of passing the torch . . . assuming that was what was going on here.

"In MARSOC vernacular," Fleiss said, "you're the operational element and he's command and control."

McCoy nodded, feeling a little better about this goat-rope he'd been sucked into . . . but only a little. "So, how exactly is this supposed to go? We work Malone's kidnapping in parallel to the rest of the IC and whoever finds him first wins?"

"In a manner of speaking, yes. Think of this as a counterterrorism fox hunt, and you're the lead hunter. The difference is, I'll make sure all pertinent intelligence uncovered is funneled to you in real time. In addition, you will have access to any and all intelligence collection means and methods at my disposal without having to jump through the hoops you'd normally be required to. As the Presidential Agent, President Cohen is basically handing you a giant pair of razor-sharp scissors and the authority to cut through any and all bureaucratic red tape that normally bogs down this giant machine we all work inside. I want you to understand that that takes an incredible amount of trust. The President is opening herself up to tremendous risk with this program, Captain."

So why in the hell did she choose me? POTUS doesn't know me from Adam . . .

"Understood, sir," McCoy said. When neither Castillo nor Fleiss followed up, he said, "So, about my orders. I never received the TAD paperwork."

"Sure, sure," Fleiss said, pressing back from the table and getting to his feet. "Charley, make sure you get McCoy a copy of his orders, please."

"Yeah, yeah," Castillo said. "Will do."

McCoy stood and the DNI clapped a hand on his shoulder and met his gaze. "The clock is ticking. Good luck, McCoy."

"Thank you, sir," he said, feeling as if at any moment Gunny Dean and the rest of his unit would burst in and yell *"Surprise!,"* putting an end to this charade.

And with that, the Director of National Intelligence walked out of the room—leaving him alone with a man who thirty minutes ago had pretended to be his Uber driver and now turned out to be his new boss.

"Well, don't just stand there with your mouth open, McCoy," Castillo said, turning toward the door. "We've got work to do."

"What's next on the agenda?" McCoy said, stepping after him.

"We hop on a plane to Egypt. Because if there's one thing I can guaran-fucking-tee, it's that the secretary of state ain't going to rescue himself."

CHAPTER TEN

McCoy stretched out in the wide, comfortable seat of the luxury Gulfstream 550 business jet, grateful for the few hours of sleep he'd been able to grab. His body had no sense of time whatsoever, but he was used to that, and the disorientation from traveling both ways across multiple times zone in just over twenty-four hours was unavoidable. The aircraft was far smaller than the large jet that had brought him to D.C., but was still extreme luxury for a combat SOF Marine used to living in the dirt overseas.

The lack of government or military markings on the plane—which they had boarded back at Joint Base Andrews, not far from the 89th Airlift Wing hangar where he'd arrived not quite six hours earlier—was in no way lost on McCoy. Equally noteworthy was the nondescript and unmarked hangar in which they'd boarded, and the pilots dressed in civilian clothes. The aviators weren't fooling McCoy, or anyone in the business, for that matter. Their military-style haircuts, swagger, and fraternity attitude said it all; McCoy had them pegged for naval aviators immediately.

"Need anything, sir?" a male voice asked.

McCoy looked up from where he'd been staring at the laptop in front of him, scrolling through page after page of TS/SCI-level intelligence on the attacks in Cairo, to see one of the pilots against the doorframe of the open cockpit door, arms folded, a smile on his face.

"I mean, I'm no stewardess," he said, smiling, "but I know how to work the espresso machine. Happy to make you a latte."

"Didn't have those on the Greyhounds," the other pilot hollered back with a chuckle from the cockpit, referring to the navy's C2A Greyhound Carrier Onboard Delivery aircraft, or COD, confirming McCoy's suspicion about the pilots' origins.

"Sure, thanks," he said, and the pilot gave a nod before turning left out of the cockpit, out of view in what McCoy remembered from boarding to be a spacious galley. He glanced toward the back of the aircraft at the door behind which Castillo had disappeared before departure and from which he'd still not emerged. For the tenth time in five hours, he found himself questioning his decision to be here at all—though as a Marine, he supposed it wasn't really a decision at all. The invitation felt more like an order, and if there was one thing Marines knew how to do—other than kill the enemy—it was follow orders. The Corps didn't pull an O-3 officer out of a current combat operation, fly him more than six thousand miles to meet personally with the Director of National Intelligence in the Situation Room, and expect him to say "no, thank you" and head back to his unit.

Like it or not, these were his new orders.

"Here ya go," said the pilot, who looked to be a mid-career officer, handing him an insulated paper coffee cup with the Starbucks logo. "Captain Starbucks at your service."

"Thanks," McCoy said with a chuckle.

"There's food in the galley as well. Sandwiches, snacks, and food you can heat in the microwave or oven—just prepared stuff, but still pretty damn good."

"Appreciate it," he said with a grin, getting the sense that the pilot's curiosity was getting the better of him. "How long till we land?"

"Nine hours," the pilot said.

McCoy glanced over his shoulder and saw the mysterious Colonel Castillo talking to someone from the doorway that divided the cabin roughly in half, though he couldn't see the person on the other side. He pursed his lips in annoyance—only he and Castillo had boarded the jet that he had noticed, so whoever was back there had boarded before them.

"Nine hours?" he asked, cocking an eyebrow.

"We make zero-point-eight-five mach and this thing has a helluva range, so no refueling needed."

"Wow. Plus, it's gonna go by quick in this five-star flying hotel," McCoy said with a grin, and raised his latte to the pilot in a mock toast.

The pilot laughed. "Yeah, well, a little less comfortable up front, but still way better than where I came from," he said, glancing over McCoy's shoulder to where Castillo was walking up to join them. "Anyway, enjoy the luxury now, cuz I'm guessing you'll have none of it in Egypt . . . or wherever the hell you guys are going."

"What makes you say that?"

"The weapons cases we loaded aboard," the pilot said, then nodded in greeting at Castillo, who'd arrived from the back. "Colonel . . ."

"Commander," Castillo returned, and with that the pilot headed back to the cockpit.

Castillo slipped into the wide seat across from him.

"All right, McCoy," he said, cracking his knuckles. "Let's get started."

"Yes, sir," McCoy said, straightening up and feeling a swell of excited anticipation. This may not be the style of service he'd planned for himself, but any mission serving the greater good of his country was worth being part of. Rescuing the secretary of state from terrorists in Egypt met all his requirements for a righteous mission—and then some. And he knew he'd learn stuff sure to serve him well when he returned to MARSOC.

"Call me Charley," Castillo said. "You need to stow the rank and title bullshit, but you also need to adapt to an environment where even seeming military or implying rank and title can be dangerous. You have some experience with this in the Raiders, I know, but you need to take it to the next level. Got it?"

"Yes, sir . . ." He caught himself. "Sorry. Old habits. Got it, Charley."

"Great. I've been chartered with the responsibility to mentor you, McCoy. But the priority of this mission is to retrieve the secretary of state before these animals do something that can't be undone. Watch and learn. Got it?"

McCoy nodded. That wasn't exactly his understanding of his role from the meeting with the Director of National Intelligence, but he decided now wasn't the time to point that out. He heard a door open behind him and turned to look, his eyes widening at the grinning man approaching from the aft of the aircraft.

"How're ya doin', Mr. McCoy?" the man said, slipping into the aisle side seat beside Castillo. "I'm Roy Jones," the man said, extending his hand. McCoy shook it.

"We met . . . um, I thought you said your name was John Smith?" McCoy said to the man who had escorted him home from Iraq.

The man reached down and grabbed the ID case hanging from the lanyard around his neck and turned it up awkwardly to look at it. Then he looked back up and smiled at McCoy, an unmistakable glint of humor in his eyes.

"Nope . . . This says I'm Roy Jones."

"Guess you didn't get to go home to your wife and kids for your days off," McCoy said, glancing at the book the man carried.

"No idea what you're talking about," the man said. "Never been married." He winked at him, before McCoy could object.

The man saw McCoy look again at his book.

"A covert ops thriller," the man said.

"*American Operator*? Any good?"

"I'm impressed—you read that without moving your lips. Unusual for a Marine. But, yeah. It's really good."

"All right," Castillo said, ending the confusing banter. "Mr. Jones here is with a joint interagency counterterrorism task force. He's here to help us coordinate working with various agencies operating in the area and to get us access to them, and any logistics or equipment we may need."

The man, now called Jones, gave him a double eyebrow raise and smiled.

"What agency are you with organically?" McCoy asked.

"A joint task force," Jones said vaguely, not answering the question.

"Right now he works for me," Castillo said, "and to a lesser extent for you. That's all that matters."

"Roger that," McCoy said.

"Dump the military-speak, Mr. McCoy," Castillo reminded him, annoyance in his voice.

"Okey-dokey, Charley," McCoy fired back, his own annoyance now rising. He knew the job, but nothing about the people he was working with. He was an SOF guy, and in his world, that was extremely dangerous. It was why they trained together, played together, deployed together, and fought together in his world. It was effective and familiar, and he wasn't liking this amorphous arrangement at all.

Jones chuckled and looked at his hands.

Castillo didn't react at all. "So," he said, ignoring McCoy's sarcasm, "Jones will be introducing us to some experts in the area when we arrive, some of whom, we hope, can get us a line on where to take the search."

"Or begin the search, from the sound of it," McCoy said. "Doesn't sound like the community on the ground has any idea what happened or where sec state is now, at least not from the intelligence I've read over." He gestured at the computer and the high side briefs on the attack and kidnapping he'd been scouring. "Lots of speculating, but nothing concrete and the theories that are put forward are all over the map."

Castillo nodded.

"Hopefully there will be some leads that shake loose," he said. "As was discussed earlier, the IC is badly fractured now—nothing like the more cohesive force that slowly evolved out of the ashes of 9/11. Which means there could be some useful intelligence not seen in those briefs."

McCoy shook his head. He understood. While the military joint operations abilities remained robust, he had seen, over his six years with MARSOC, a slow and steady degradation in the relationships with "other government agencies," which these days implied numerous communities other than the CIA. It made it frustrating, being on the pointy tip of a spear sometimes being thrust by nameless, faceless entities.

"That problem," Castillo continued, "is magnified by the fact that foreign governments and agencies can smell that kind of dysfunction from miles away. It makes them far less willing to share information, or at least to share in the broader sense of formally sharing it with the United States government."

"I agree with that," Jones said. "Assets in a country like Egypt have to be managed and run personally, in a relationship-based style, for them to be fruitful. An asset may not share with the American government, but they'll still share with the agent who got them out of a jam, or helped their child, or found their son a job. The first meeting I've set up for us is one I think most likely to bear some fruit. CIA is running a mature, very fruitful operation in Egypt, based out of Cairo. They run myriad assets, some embedded within a variety of radical groups and terrorist organizations in the country. If anyone has something of value, it'll be Ani Shaheen. She's worked a clandestine billet in Cairo for two and a half years now, and is the best field intelligence officer in theater."

"She's the officer in charge of operations in Cairo?" Castillo asked.

Jones laughed.

"Nah," he said. "She'd hang herself before running a desk. She's one of a half dozen CIA officers and agency contractors working Cairo in nonofficial covers."

"Her name sounds Egyptian," Castillo pointed out. "Was she recruited?"

"No, she's organic," Jones said. "We have a solid history. She's been working with my office for years."

"What office was that again?" McCoy quipped, now starting to like Jones even more.

"I'm with a joint . . ."

"Right, right," McCoy said, stopping him.

"What else?" Castillo asked, looking at Jones.

The man shrugged, and McCoy suddenly pictured the spook in tropical flower board shorts drinking beer on a beach beside a surfboard, instead of sitting in a covert operations jet over the Atlantic.

There's something almost comedic about this guy, he thought.

"I have other connections we can tap, but let's just start with Ani," Jones said, apparently not willing to show his cards just yet.

Castillo nodded.

McCoy waited for more, but Jones got up and headed forward to the galley.

"That's it?" McCoy asked Castillo when Jones was out of earshot.

"Whaddya mean?"

"That's the whole plan? We head to Cairo and meet some girl Jones knows. You gotta be kidding me."

"No, we're not kidding. These things are highly fluid, way beyond what you're used to. Jones is setting up assets in the area for us—as well as logistics—and he'll brief that a few hours out. We start with what we have, stay kinetic, and build it from there. The DNI has other agencies and assets exploiting every possible angle, and as that data gets sifted relevant information will flow to us quickly. If there was more to go on, they'd have JSOC making a hit already to recover the secretary. We're here to make sense of conflicting streams of data, cut through the bureaucratic BS, and find Malone by whatever means necessary."

"Then what? We just go and get him? You, me, and good ol' Spicoli up there?"

Castillo smiled now, leaning back in his seat. He crossed his thick, powerful arms across his chest, studying him a moment. "Look, McCoy," he said, his tone now softer for the first time since they'd met. "I know this is very new to you and you've gotten no time to get your bearings. I was SF myself, back in the day, and I remember climbing this steep learning curve to a whole new paradigm, just like you are now. I had a great man, General Bruce McNab, to help me get my bearings in this job, and I fully intend to do the same for you. What you need to do for me, right now, is put aside that Marine and see things in a different way. If we didn't think you were capable of doing that, you wouldn't be here."

McCoy sighed and resisted his compulsion to say, "Yes, sir," and instead nodded and said, "I'll try. But I have to say, if you didn't want an SOF Marine, I'm not sure why you picked me in the first place."

"I didn't," Castillo said, rising now himself. "Picking a Marine Raider wasn't my call. But together, we will get this job done. And you know why?"

"Why?" McCoy asked, not sure he wanted to hear whatever old-school, bullshit answer Castillo had for him.

Castillo smiled, his blue eyes sparkling in his weathered face.

"Because we have to," he said. "There's no one else."

"Okay," he said. That was a mindset he was familiar with, one he could relate to. "Always Forward, Charley," he added, using the second half of the Marine Raiders motto.

"Always Faithful, McCoy," Castillo said. "Refill your coffee? I'm gonna grab some, then you and I can go over some of the field intelligence reports together and see if anything jumps out at us."

"Sounds good," McCoy said, not quite able to ask the old man to make him a latte.

CHAPTER ELEVEN

Castillo glanced at McCoy in the backseat of the taxi, wondering for the umpteenth time why McNab had picked an uptight "I do everything by the book" Marine captain as his successor. On the flight, he'd stolen some alone time to peruse the kid's service record, read his fitness reports, and dig into his military lineage. There was no denying that McCoy had a helluva pedigree. His grandfather was an intelligence legend in the Korean War and his father had carried on the family military tradition as a Marine aviator, becoming an ace in Vietnam with five kills.

Why Captain P.K. McCoy Jr. went for special ops was unclear to Castillo, but he figured it probably had to do with stepping out of the very long shadows of his father and grandfather—a desire Castillo understood all too well, albeit for different reasons.

Whatever his motives, Castillo thought, *McCoy is well on his way to being his own Captain America.*

Quotes from McCoy's superiors in his evals rattled around in Castillo's head:

"Incorruptible integrity . . . puts the well-being of his men before self . . . embodiment of Marine Corps values: honor, courage, and commitment . . ."

Captain America must have felt Castillo's eyes on him, because he turned to meet Castillo's gaze.

"Have you worked with this agent before? Can you vouch for her?" McCoy asked, a very McCoy question, he decided.

Castillo shook his head. "Nah, this one is Jones's connection, but I have a couple of old contacts we can try next if she turns out to be a dead end."

McCoy looked like he was about to say something, but apparently thought better of it and returned his gaze out the window to scan the bustling early afternoon Cairo city streets.

I can't believe Cohen brought me back to train my own damn replacement, he thought with a scowl. *How visionary of her . . . And McNab knew and still played along. That shifty bastard is gonna owe me a crate of expensive scotch when this is over.*

He shifted his gaze to Jones, or Smith, or whatever the spook's name was in the front passenger seat as he chatted up the taxi driver. If he didn't know better, he'd have thought the two of them were long-lost brothers by the way they were carrying on, laughing and joking around. This was his first operation with the spook and the jury was still out on the guy. Jones was apparently Fleiss's boy, just like he was McNab's boy, and so even though Castillo had been given no explicit instruction to work with Jones, the implication was obvious. It was also obvious that Jones's nebulous role and credentials were driving McCoy nuts, but that didn't bother Castillo. Credentials didn't impress him, results did. If this bizarre spook got results, then Castillo would happily welcome him to the team. If not, he'd get the boot. That was the unspoken rule with his Merry Outlaws back in the day—they were as eclectic and diverse as the day was long, but together they got shit done.

And it sure would be nice to get the band back together . . .

He smiled at the thought, but it soon transformed into a grimace as he remembered the funerals for all the friends he'd lost in the near decade since their last operation.

Closing his eyes for a moment, he pushed the thoughts out of his head and centered himself. He took several long, deep breaths, and that's when he realized just how bad the taxi stank. He was already in a foul mood, and the smell just made it worse. Stale cigarette smoke and body odor—the hallmark mélange of the third world. The hot "fresh" air streaming in through his rolled-down window— a refined blend of petrol exhaust and *eau de sewer*—didn't offer any relief. *In fact, it might even be worse*, he decided, and contemplated rolling up his window, but the heat prevented that. Even in March, Cairo was blazing hot in the middle of the afternoon. The armpits of his shirt were already drenched with sweat in six-inch rings and the small of his back was damp against the seat.

They'd just gotten here and he was already thinking about his next meal, next shower, and next six down in a real bed inside a nice air-conditioned hotel room. He'd only gotten an hour of shut-eye on the transatlantic flight, and he felt a caffeine headache threatening in a band stretching from temple to temple across the middle of his forehead.

"Stop right here," Jones ordered the driver, latent urgency in his voice.

The driver slammed on his horn and cut across traffic, narrowly missing not one but two bike delivery boys, and came to a hard stop in front of their destination. The spook handed the cabbie a large note and thanked him for the ride.

"This is us," Jones said, hopping out of the taxi.

McCoy, who was seated on the passenger side, exited next while Charley checked their six through the back window. Seeing nothing of concern, he slid across the rear bench and climbed out to join his fellows on the dirty sidewalk.

". . . and if she asks if you want a coffee, say no," Jones was saying to McCoy.

"Why?" McCoy asked.

"Ani only drinks Lebanese coffee. I swear, three ounces of that shit is guaranteed to send you into A-fib. It should be illegal," the spook said with a chuckle.

"I'll keep that in mind," McCoy said.

Something about Jones's demeanor made Castillo suddenly wonder if their house call was unannounced.

"She's expecting us, right?" Castillo asked Jones.

"Sure," the easygoing spy said.

"*Sure?*" Castillo echoed. "That's not an answer."

"Right." Jones smiled, turned on a heel, and waved them to follow.

He led them into the five-story building with an electronics store on the ground level and, Castillo presumed, apartments on the levels above. Jones took the stairs, ascending in an annoyingly sprightly clip to the fourth floor. He turned and paused outside the second door. Lime green paint was flaking off the wooden door and someone had carved the words FUCK OFF in big block letters with a knife into the slab.

Jones turned to both of them and did his signature double eyebrow raise. "You're going to love her," he said, then knocked on the door.

A heartbeat later, Castillo heard a woman's voice call out in Arabic something to the effect of, "Go away."

"Nothing gold can stay," Jones said loudly, and it took Castillo a moment to place it.

The last line and title of the Robert Frost poem. Must be a challenge-authentication phrase.

He heard a rustle, the sound of multiple door locks being disengaged on the inside, and then the doorknob turned. Castillo resisted the urge to reach inside the flap of his travel shirt to touch the pistol grip of his compact Smith & Wesson M&P nine-millimeter he wore in a concealed shoulder holster.

The door opened.

"No, no, no—not you," a woman in her thirties said the moment she saw Jones.

She tried to slam the door, but the spook slid his right boot into the gap and the wooden door bounced off it with a resounding thud, vibrating on its hinges.

"Oh, c'mon, Ani," Jones said with feigned offense. "Don't be like that."

"If Bob had told me it was you they were sending, I would have said fuck off and changed apartments," she said, glaring at him through the six-inch gap between the door and the jamb. "Move your foot."

"No," Jones said.

"Move your damn foot," she repeated, this time with a growl.

"No."

Castillo looked at McCoy and shook his head—*spooks*.

The Marine to Castillo's surprise, whirled and started to walk away.

"Hey, where do you think you're going?" Castillo called after him.

"Back to the plane," McCoy said, already halfway down the hall. "This is a waste of time."

"Get your ass back here, McCoy," Castillo said, summoning his command voice.

On that cue, McCoy stopped and the female agent opened the door, more interested in this new development in the hall than the tiff she was having with Jones.

"I apologize," she said, looking at Castillo but projecting so McCoy could hear her. "If you can't tell, me and Jeremy Rogers here have something of a sordid past."

"'Rogers,' huh?" McCoy said, turning around and glaring at the spy with three different names. "Imagine that."

Enough of these reindeer games, time to take control of this situation, Castillo thought.

"Ma'am, my name is Charley Castillo and I apologize for showing up unannounced like we did to put a kink in your day. I also apologize on behalf of Agent Rogers, here, for whatever offense he might have caused you in the past and any and all future offenses I can virtually guarantee will follow." Castillo extended his hand to her.

She flashed him a courteous smile, the kind of smile a pro used that said *I appreciate the olive branch, but your Jedi mind tricks won't work on me.*

"All right, Mr. Castillo," she said. "You and your uptight friend there can come inside. Jeremy has to wait in the hall."

"Sounds good," Castillo said, giving their spook friend's shoulder a squeeze. Then he turned to McCoy. "You coming?"

With a sigh, McCoy walked back to rejoin the group. "Pick McCoy," the Marine said when he stepped up and extended his hand to the woman.

"Ani," she said, shaking it, and opened the door to let them inside.

Smith-Jones-Rogers ignored the tongue-in-cheek agreement Castillo had made with Ani and followed McCoy into the apartment anyway. Ani let the spook inside but rolled her eyes as he walked past her. She then shut and latched the door, engaging multiple locks at different heights on the slab. The back side of the door was covered top to bottom with what looked like woven black fabric used on bulletproof vests.

Ani saw Castillo studying it and answered the question. "Cordura antiballistic fabric . . . and yes, for all the reasons you're thinking," she said, nodding to the two windows across the room. "The drapes are made of the same."

"Nice touch," Castillo said as he surveyed the rest of the apartment, which was to his dismay an absolute dump.

Leftover food containers were stacked everywhere. What furniture she had was shabby, and the Oriental rug that served as her carpet was so threadbare in most places you could see the wooden floor below. Dishes overflowed the sink in the tiny kitchenette. Transparent plastic cups, each filled with varying degrees of liquid, dominated all the modest counter space. Laundry was strewn about everywhere, including bras and underwear, and the sheets on her futon looked weeks overdue in washing.

"Sorry about the mess," she said, utterly and completely unabashed. "As you might imagine, I rarely entertain."

Without permission or prompting, Smith-Jones-Rogers took the liberty of converting Ani's futon from bed to sofa and tidied it up, tossing a set of Ani's undergarments onto a nearby pile of laundry. For her part, Ani let him, seemingly unperturbed.

Castillo chuckled.

Yeah, these two were more than just work colleagues. They were lovers.

As for the woman herself, Ani presented the same as her apartment. Her espresso hair was tied up in a messy bun. The cream-colored V-neck T-shirt she wore was so worn and thin it was almost transparent, revealing her bra beneath. Loose-fitting khaki pants sat high on her hips, tied at the waist with a drawstring. She was barefoot, wore no makeup, and no jewelry save for a braided black leather band on her wrist.

And yet, despite all this, her slim figure, handsome features, and smile that could earn her a toothpaste model contract were impossible to ignore. Combine that with her no-apologies persona and "don't fuck with me" spunk, and it was obvious why the spook had fallen for her.

"Can I get you guys something to drink? Water, coffee . . . both?" she asked.

Castillo saw McCoy's eyes survey the dirty kitchen, so he answered first and introduced clarity to his order.

"Bottled water would be great," he said, trying to ignore his caffeine headache just a little longer.

"Same," McCoy said.

"Make that three," Smith-Jones-Rogers added.

She walked to a noisy refrigerator that was half the size people used in the States, retrieved four bottles of cold water, and passed them around.

"Thanks," Castillo said. "So, I presume you know why we're here?"

"I do," she said with a sigh. "But like I told my boss, I don't have any solid leads on who took the secretary of state."

"Solid leads or just leads?" Castillo pressed as he unscrewed the cap from the water bottle. He took a long swig, draining a third of the half-liter.

Ani looked at Smith-Jones-Rogers and an unspoken message passed between them.

"Look, Ani," the spook said, "We've got nothing. I'm serious, nothing. NSA, CIA, DIA . . . they're all scratching their heads on this one. Whoever did this managed to pull off an operation with a zero SIGINT footprint. Satellite imagery reconstruct has failed to produce a viable trail. Which means, to find the secretary, we need to leverage any and all HUMINT we can here in Cairo. So, please, can you help us?"

"Translation, you want to squeeze my network?"

Rogers-Jones-Smith nodded.

"Fuck," she said through a sigh. "Jeremy, you know I've spent nearly three years building trust with these people. Three years!"

"I know . . ." he said, his tone apologetic but insistent.

"If I bring you guys in and escalate the pressure, then I could lose them forever—not to mention I risk burning my NOC and drawing the ire and attention of some real assholes I've managed to avoid so far."

Castillo understood where Ani was coming from, and as the Presidential Agent, arguably better than anyone. He didn't know her personally, but he'd been in her shoes many times, asking trusted sources to put themselves at risk.

"At the risk of sticking my nose in where it doesn't belong," he began, meeting her steely-eyed gaze, "we don't know each other, but you'll just have to trust me when I say I understand the place you're coming from. But it's situations exactly like this why CIA put you here in the first place. It's why you've worked so hard for the past three years. If you burn your NOC and your assets in pursuit of intelligence that results in the location and recovery of the secretary of state, that's okay."

"That, Mr. Castillo, is not my concern. My concern is burning my NOC and my assets in pursuit of presumed intelligence that does not exist and therefore does *not* aid in the location and recovery of the secretary of state while simultaneously ruining the nine other operations I'm actively monitoring and trying to effect in the name of national security."

Castillo frowned.

Guess it's time to play my trump card.

He retrieved the signed letter from President Cohen giving him the authority to marshal and draw upon ODNI resources everywhere and anywhere as he saw fit.

He handed it to Ani.

"What's this?" she said, taking it.

"Just read it."

Office of the President
The White House
Washington, D.C.

To Whom It May Concern:

The bearer of this letter is operating on a mission of vital national importance with grave consequences to the safety and security of the United States of America. Full cooperation is expected from all to whom this correspondence is presented, and demanded of all who serve at the pleasure of the President.

The contents and knowledge of this letter are classified TS/SCI and divulgence of its contents or existence, even if only by implication, will be punished to the full extent of federal law as treason against the United States of America.

Natalie Cohen

NATALIE COHEN
PRESIDENT OF THE UNITED STATES OF AMERICA

She pursed her lips and stood in stoic silence for what felt like an eternity before finally answering. "Okay, Mr. Castillo, I think I finally understand what's going on here. What exactly do you want from me?"

CHAPTER TWELVE

McCoy looked in turn at each of his three new partners riding with him inside the cramped sedan and resisted the urge to judge.

But damn it was hard.

Really, really hard.

Forty-eight hours ago he'd been leading a platoon of the finest, most professional, locked-on Marines in the entire Corps and today he was riding bitch in the backseat with the Three Stooges.

No wonder Ian Fleming had written James Bond the way he had. In real life, spies were strange ducks.

The sedan hit a deep pothole and the suspension bottomed out, lifting McCoy out of his seat. His head hit on the ceiling and he cursed under his breath.

"You all right, bud?" the spook with three names asked him.

"Fine," he grumbled.

Thank God the assignment was TAD. As soon as this temporary tasking was finished, he was getting his Marine Raider ass on the first flight back to Iraq. And with that thought he realized that—despite having asked repeatedly—he'd never been given a hard copy or digital copy of his orders.

Oh, shit, I bet they don't exist. I'm out here, operating in the black with absolutely nothing to backstop me if this all goes to hell. Castillo, you sly dog—you were never gonna issue TAD orders in the first place, were you?

Dread washed over him as this entire operation he'd been goat-roped into took on new color.

"Tell us about this first guy we're going to see," Castillo said to Ani, who was sitting in the front passenger seat. "What's his story?"

Ani craned her neck around to address Castillo. "His name is Omar Fathy. He works in the import-export business. His father was Haim Fathy . . ."

"Haim Fathy of SSI fame?" Castillo asked.

"That's the one. Did you know him?" she asked.

"By reputation only. Did he survive the purge in 2011?"

Ani nodded, "He did, but died not long after . . . supposedly of natural causes."

"Mm-hmm," was all Castillo said.

McCoy had no idea who they were talking about but decided there was no point in bringing that to everyone's attention. Hopefully, Castillo would fill him in on all the relevant bits later.

McCoy glanced at the driver, who Ani said was OGA and had all the proper clearances. The man looked and acted like an operator, albeit one who'd been out of the game for a very long time. McCoy pegged his age at late fifties, but his lean frame and sinewy forearms were clues he maintained a high level of fitness. The driver had introduced himself as "Hatchet," but didn't clarify if that was a nickname, a surname, or NOC.

Hell, it wouldn't surprise me if it was something the dude had come up with on the spot. Spooks change names like normal people change underwear.

McCoy chuckled at the thought. Case in point, he wasn't even sure what name to call the dude sitting beside him.

"What's funny?" Smith asked him.

McCoy shook his head. "Nothing . . ."

"So, listen, guys," Ani said, her tone serious. "There's no way this is going to work if I show up with three white dudes who look like models out of a government contractor catalog. Omar is going to get scared and either bail on the meeting or clam up and tell me nothing. So, here's my rules. I'm going to talk to him with Charley and only Charley. Jeremy, if you brought the necessary tech, you and McCoy can listen in, but I want you at least thirty meters away. Okay?"

Castillo nodded. "I second that plan."

Of course you do, McCoy thought. *Once again, why am I here?*

"Sure," Smith said, completely unfazed as usual, and pulled out a small black zipper case from his back pocket. McCoy watched as the spy unzipped the case and folded it open like a book, displaying an array of slick micro-tech devices all neatly arranged in little molded plastic indentions. He gingerly removed and handed out five tiny earbuds, one to each team member, including the driver. Then he handed each person a tiny black box—half the size of an iPhone. "That's a signal relay booster/transceiver. It works in tandem with the earbuds, the same way an iPhone works with AirPods. It will manage all the traffic and relay encrypted comms to the other receivers using the cellular networks. The earbuds are fully charged and work pretty much flawlessly after they sync. It's plug, play, and forget—once it's in your ear, you don't have to do anything. The volume auto-adjusts based on ambient noise."

Ani smiled as she pocketed the transceiver and pressed the miniature earbud into her ear. "See, I knew you'd come prepared."

McCoy inserted his own earbud into his ear canal and felt the tiny device bottom out.

"How do I get this thing out?" he asked, realizing too late he'd probably pushed it in too far.

"Fingernails, but, if that doesn't work, I have a little tool. It's supposed to fit deep and disappear. Don't worry, you put it in correctly." After he and Castillo had inserted theirs, Smith said, "All right, I'm syncing them now . . . Check, one, two, three . . ."

McCoy heard a chime in his ear, followed by Smith's crystal-clear amplified voice with virtually no echo.

"Almost zero lag," Castillo said. "That's impressive."

"Yeah, these are super state of the art," the spy said. "Wait until you see how well the noise-cancellation works. You're gonna want to wear it all the time."

"Two minutes," the driver announced. "Where do you want everyone, Ani?"

"I want you to drive past the café and drop me and Charley on the northeast corner of the block. That will give a chance for a quick survey before we exit the vehicle in case something seems off. We'll backtrack to the café if everything looks good. After that, you loop around and park out of view on the southeast side of the block. Don't round the corner, just be ready if we need you. Jeremy and McCoy can get out there and find a good spotter location across the street."

The driver nodded, undoubtedly liking her plan that had no left turns nor the need to cross intersections.

"Straight numeric call signs, I assume?" McCoy prompted.

Castillo nodded. "I'm One."

"Two," Ani said.

"Three," Smith added.

"Four," McCoy said, continuing the count.

"And that makes me Five," Hatchet said.

"All right, everybody packing concealed heat?" Castillo asked and got nods all around.

"One block out," Hatchet said, eyes forward and scanning traffic.

"Check," McCoy said, reflexively taking the lead as he slipped into Raider mode.

From the middle position in the back seat, his vision was limited compared to his teammates'. Castillo on his left and Smith on his right were scanning out their respective side windows, while Ani looked through the windshield. This particular district of Cairo was hopping with activity—cars, trucks, scooters, and cyclists everywhere, along with hundreds of pedestrians moving in all directions. The entire block was a security nightmare. If there were bad guys waiting in ambush for them, it would be virtually impossible to spot the threat.

"Passing the target location on the left," Hatchet said.

"I see Omar," Ani said. "He's sitting at an outdoor table, alone, just like we discussed."

"Good," Castillo said. "The meet is on."

The driver cruised north to the next intersection and turned east as agreed. He pulled to the curb halfway down the block and let Ani and Castillo out, then took the next two right turns to loop around the block and drop McCoy and Smith on the southwest corner. McCoy exited after Smith on the passenger side and scanned the area. He'd never been to Cairo before, but it had a similar feel to other large Middle Eastern cities he'd visited—managed chaos was the simplest description that came to mind.

In his ear, he heard Ani greet her asset, Omar, followed immediately by his nervous response.

"Who is this?" Fathy said, his voice ripe with anxiety.

"I'm Peter Jackson," Castillo said, using the NOC on his travel documents. "No relation to the *Lord of the Rings* director."

This little icebreaker seemed to work, because McCoy thought he heard a chuckle from Omar.

"Okay, but I thought I told you to come alone, Ani," Omar said.

"Peter was either going to be in my ear asking questions or meet you and do it face-to-face. I thought you'd prefer I be sincere," Ani replied. An awkward pause followed, before she added, "We all need to smile, look happy to see each other, and take a seat."

He and Smith had rounded the corner now and were walking north on the opposite side of the street from the outdoor café where their teammates were talking with Omar. McCoy scanned the crowd. Over the years, the way he looked for threats had evolved. These days, instead of looking for shifty or menacing characters, he scanned for people who were eyeing him—especially people who were trying *not* to look like they were watching him.

"The enemy could be anyone," Smith said, a jovial expression on his face as he pointed to an outdoor café on their side of the street. "If you see someone take our picture or glancing repeatedly at us while texting or talking on their phone, let me know. It's typically the first indicator we're blown."

"Check," McCoy said, multitasking now—listening to the conversation happening in his left ear, Smith in his right, and surveying the crowd all at the same time.

He vectored toward an open, two-top bistro table positioned nearest to the exterior wall of a restaurant with an outdoor seating area. McCoy and Smith pulled their chairs around so that their backs were to the wall and they could watch across the street. Despite seeing no tangible threat, McCoy suddenly found himself longing for his kit, his helmet, and his tricked-out M4A1 with USSOCOM upper receiver and holographic optics package. In a real firefight, a pistol just didn't cut it.

He pushed back that unproductive thought and focused on maintaining his hyper-alert state. He shifted his gaze across the street and decided to listen and learn as Castillo went to work—because from the sound of it, things were just beginning to get interesting.

CHAPTER THIRTEEN

Bab Ash Shaareyah District
Cairo, Egypt
March 19, 2:45 p.m.

Castillo knew the Egyptian man was hiding something—he'd known it from the second they'd sat down with him. From Ani's demeanor, Castillo suspected she knew it, too. The question was whether she would wilt under the pressure and let her asset off the hook, or would she squeeze him until they got the intelligence they needed.

If she won't, I will . . .

"Look, Ani, I told you everything I know," the asset said. "I'm sorry, but there's nothing else I can do."

Ani held the Egyptian's gaze, taking a page from Castillo's playbook—trying to let her silence do the work. Omar quickly broke eye contact and wiped the sweat from his forehead with a napkin. It was blazing hot, and Castillo was sweating himself, but he suspected the other man's dappled forehead was more a product of nerves than the heat.

"Well, I should be going," Omar said, balking. He slid his chair back from the table. "I need to get back to work."

"Sit your ass down. We're not done here," Castillo said, taking control of the deteriorating situation.

Omar reflexively took his seat at the command, but he did not scoot back to the table.

"Now, I want you to listen very carefully to me, Omar," Castillo then said. "It's obvious from how nervous you are that there's something you're not telling us. It's also obvious you're concerned about your safety. I can appreciate that. I can also appreciate that none of us are in the charity business. So, let's stop playing games. Why don't you tell me what you want in exchange for the information you're not sharing. Do you want money? Protection? Information? A favor? I have the full power and backing of the United States government to negotiate with you here today. I can give you any of those things in exchange for information that leads to the safe return of Secretary of State Malone."

Omar shifted in his seat, but his eyes were now fixed on Castillo instead of darting about nervously like they had been.

"My family has been in this business a long time," the Egyptian said, "so I know how these things go. You pressure me. You make big promises. But after I tell you what you want to hear, I never see or hear from you again. Maybe Ani stays in Cairo, maybe she doesn't. When I contact her, she makes excuses and changes her phone number. After that, I'm on my own—abandoned and left to the wolves with nothing to show for my efforts."

"I've worked with you for almost three years, Omar, and during that time, I've always been true to my word," Ani said. "I would never abandon you. That's not who I am."

"I like you, Ani, and I believe you have a good heart, but this is not a nice game we are playing. Let's not deceive ourselves, okay? The information you're demanding puts both our lives at risk, but where you have the option to run home to the safety of America, I do not."

Castillo looked at Ani, and her expression said it all. She felt she'd been played the fool, trusting Omar implicitly, only now to discover he'd not been completely honest with her. And yet, Castillo knew that was only part of the story. Her subconscious had known her asset was holding back. That's why when Smith-Jones-Rogers had pressed her, she'd picked Omar first. Somewhere, in a quiet corner of her mind, Omar's lies of omission had been noted and catalogued. Harvesting intelligence was a lot like harvesting crops—one could spend an entire career picking only the low-hanging fruit. It was so much easier that way, but the sweetest and juiciest morsels withered and died just out of reach.

"Why didn't you tell me this before?" she said, aggravation plain in her voice.

Omar sighed. "I didn't tell you before because, quite frankly, Ani, you're not a big enough player."

"What is that supposed to mean?"

"It means it wasn't worth the risk. Better for me to pretend I know nothing and carry on with my life and business than to try to broker a deal with you. You're a mid-level CIA officer. You don't have the authority or the pull to give me anything other than mid-level table scraps."

She glanced at Castillo, the look in her eyes signaling she was in uncharted territory and unsure what to do next.

"Just tell me what you want, Omar," Castillo said, forging ahead. "Like I said, I know you're not in the charity business."

Omar took a sip of the Coca-Cola he'd been drinking when they arrived and said, "I want a million U.S. dollars for the information, wired into my bank account. On receipt of funds, I will tell you what I know."

Castillo kept his expression neutral, his gaze fixed on the Egyptian.

"Omar, I can't authorize that kind of money until I know the quality of the information you're selling. For a million, you'd need to provide the secretary's current geographic location, the identity of the group that took him, and proof of life. The look on your face tells me you can't deliver on even one of those."

"I can't give you proof of life. What I can provide is the name of the group rumored to have taken him and his probable location," Omar said.

"How specific can you be on the location? Can you provide us with target compound coordinates?"

Omar shook his head. "Country and probable city."

"No deal," Castillo said with a huff, and turned to Ani. "We're done here."

"Wait," Omar said. "I can give you something else."

"What?" Castillo growled, not even attempting to hide his irritation at this bullshit negotiation.

"Another contact," the Egyptian said, his voice eager. "Someone I trust who I believe can get you proof of life and potentially broker the secretary's release."

"If this man can negotiate the secretary's release, why has he not contacted the United States offering to do so?" Ani asked.

"For the same reason I did not volunteer my information. There is great risk in doing so. This is a high-stakes game we are playing. People get murdered for less in Africa every day."

Castillo pursed his lips and stared at Omar.

"What is this look?" the asset said, his tone defensive.

"Omar, what you're offering is not worth a million dollars. First of all, I'm going to have to pay your contact for the very information I was hoping to get from you. Second, if your contact doesn't agree to help us, then we're no better off than when we started. So here's what I'm willing to do. You tell me the rumors on the street and provide me with your contact's information and I'll have my people wire a quarter-million dollars into your bank account right now. Assuming your contact proves helpful, I'll wire another quarter-million after we recover the secretary. How does that sound?"

"One, this is Three—I've got the back office standing by to support a wire transfer if you close the deal," Smith-Jones-Rogers said in Castillo's ear.

Castillo didn't acknowledge the report, but he loved the fact that the spook had brought his A-game and wasn't just sitting somewhere sipping a beer and enjoying the show. Hopefully, McCoy was taking good mental notes, because there was a lot to be learned from this engagement.

Omar shook his head. "Half a million up front or no deal."

Castillo didn't get angry. Instead he smiled and nodded, and repeated his original offer in a smooth, even voice. Then he added, "Of course, there is a third option. As you've said, you have been in this business a long time, and know how these things go, so I'm sure you are aware of that option. Now that we know you have information of vital importance to the safety of the secretary and the security of the United States, we can always just take you now, disappear you into a black site, and find other, more compelling ways to have you share what you know."

Castillo crossed his hands on the table, holding the man's gaze and still smiling.

"Of course," he went on, "that is not our preference. Ani tells me you have been a reliable partner and, quite frankly, it would take more time than I prefer. We want to maintain a healthy relationship with you, but the choice, as they say, is yours."

The Egyptian man sat staring at him for a long moment.

"Fine," he said, pulling out his phone. He tapped on the screen for several seconds and handed the phone to Castillo. "This is the account at Crédit Lyonnais where I want you to wire the money."

Castillo took out his own phone and pretended to make a call. It was a charade, of course; Smith-Jones-Rogers was listening to his every word and that was the point.

"This is Peter Jackson, authorization code Whiskey Papa Bravo two, niner, four. That's correct . . . I need to execute a wire transfer in the amount of two hundred and fifty thousand U.S. dollars to the following account number at Crédit Lyonnais . . ."

As he play-acted, Castillo prayed that somewhere across the street, his spooky colleague was executing the wire transfer.

On cue, Smith-Jones-Rogers said in his ear, "Funds transfer in progress—I sure hope this guy doesn't screw us . . . wire complete."

Castillo refreshed the screen of the banking application and watched the account balance increase by more than four million Egyptian pounds, the current exchange rate equaling a quarter-million U.S. He handed the phone back to Omar.

"The wire transfer is complete. Tell us what you know."

The Egyptian checked his account balance, smiled, and forced his expression back to serious.

"The rumor is that Secretary Malone was kidnapped by the

Sudanese Islamic Front. Like their predecessor, the National Islamic Front, this reincarnated version rejects the concept of a secular state. They are hard-line Islamists with aspirations of wresting control of the transitional Sudanese government. For decades, Sudan has been governed by Sharia law, but pro-democracy activists are pushing for religious freedom protections and women's rights. The Islamic Front wants to see an authoritarian, conservative regime take control of the government and the military."

"But why would the Islamic Front kidnap the secretary of state?" Ani asked. "How does that possibly help their cause?"

"Obviously, I don't consult with them," Omar said, shaking his head. "But I would imagine the reason could be as simple as that Secretary Malone has expressed support for the post–al-Bashir transitional government after the coup d'état. And the Cohen administration appears to be backing Awadiya Khalil as the first female President of Sudan. Remember, the Islamic Front are ethnic Arabs, mostly Rasheeda. They're funded by Saudi Arabia. The last thing that the Saudi ruling family wants to see is an Arab Spring in Sudan. A woman rising to power in the next election would be a nightmare for the Saudis. Also, consider the fact that one of the provisional government's top priorities has been to convince the U.S. to remove Sudan from its list of state sponsors of terrorism."

"And we have made prosecution of the Islamic Front a condition for that to happen," Ani said, nodding.

"That's right," Omar said. "The provisional government in Sudan is now incentivized to root out the Islamic Front, so that is another possible reason for targeting Secretary Malone."

"Retaliation?" Castillo said.

"Exactly."

"So, you think he's being held in Sudan?"

Omar nodded. "Yes, somewhere outside Khartoum is my guess."

Castillo considered everything Omar had just told them, and it made sense—especially when viewed through the lens of an Islamic extremist.

"But something is still bothering me about all this," he said, looking at Ani, then Omar. "How could they have pulled this off without any chatter, without any intelligence finding its way back to the United States?"

"The answer is simple, my friend—operational security," Omar said with a strained smile. "Today's terrorists know they won't last a day without it. They have learned how to—what's the American expression—fly under the radar."

Castillo tugged at his chin. "Yeah, I guess . . ."

"Your Sudanese contact," Ani said, leaning in to put her elbows on the table. "The man you said could potentially broker a deal for the secretary's release. What is his name and how do we contact him?"

"His name is Irshad Khalil and he works in the Sudanese government. He is a native-born Sudanese and a very strong nationalist. He hated the Bashir government and he's working very hard to make sure that the country does not fall into civil war."

"Khalil? Isn't that the same surname you just mentioned of the woman running for President?" Castillo asked.

"Yes, Awadiya Khalil," Omar said with a smile. "Irshad is her brother."

"Why would he know how to get in touch with terrorists?" Ani pressed.

"Because Irshad is one of those people who knows everybody."

"Are you saying he's dirty?" she asked.

"Is anyone in the business of politics clean?"

"Can he be trusted?" Castillo asked, butting in.

"More than most," Omar said, and drained the rest of his Coca-Cola. "What number should I have him contact you at?"

"Uh-uh," Castillo said, shaking his head. "I want *his* number."

"I'm sorry, but if you're going to use my name, then I need to contact him first," Omar said. "The introduction will work better that way."

"That wasn't the deal," Castillo growled.

"If I recall correctly, we didn't specify on this point," the Egyptian said. "Besides, you know his name now. If you don't hear from him, your NSA can surely find him anytime they want."

Ani cocked an eyebrow at him as if to say, *He makes a good point.*

"One, Three—give Omar this number," Smith-Jones-Rogers said in Castillo's ear, and rattled off a ten-digit phone number.

"All right," Castillo said, answering Omar and the guy in his ear simultaneously, and repeated the number while Omar entered it into his phone.

"Is this your mobile number?"

"Yes," Castillo lied.

"Very good," Omar said, looking from Castillo to Ani. "Please, no more surprises, Ani. We had trust; I didn't like how you changed the rules today without warning me."

"Well, you came away a half-million dollars richer, Omar," she said, pushing back from the table without apology. "So I don't feel too bad about it."

"A quarter of a million richer," the Egyptian corrected. "You still owe me a quarter-million."

"Assuming your contact in Sudan comes through for us, then I'm sure you have nothing to worry about."

Omar stood and shook hands with Ani, then Castillo. Then he dropped several Egyptian pounds on the table to cover the bill for his Coke and bid them goodbye. Once Omar was out of earshot halfway down the block, Ani turned to Castillo.

"What do you think?" she asked. "Is that what you were hoping for?"

Castillo smiled at her. "I wouldn't call it a home run, but that was definitely an RBI double—"

The sound of squealing tires, car horns, and a woman's scream interrupted him. He whirled and dropped low, jerking Ani down with him by her arm.

"Stay low," he barked, and scanned the sidewalk and street.

"Hey, guys, the asset's down. I repeat, the asset is down," Smith reported. "He just got hit by a truck while trying to cross the street."

"Holy shit!" Ani said, all the color draining from her face.

"Hit and run?" Castillo asked.

"Nope," the spook said. "The truck is stopped, and the driver got out. He's kneeling by the body."

"Is the asset alive?"

"Stand by, moving in for a closer look . . . uh-oh, he's not moving. Looks bad. I'm gonna try to snap a pic of the driver and the truck."

Castillo scanned the crowd for possible gunmen or suicide bombers in case the accident was the first of a two-part hit. Seeing no imminent concerns, he tugged on Ani's arm and got to his feet. "We're leaving. Keep your eyes open for threats."

"Shouldn't we try to help him?" she asked, falling in beside him as he strode south, away from the accident and toward their waiting sedan.

"No. We can't help him now, and we don't know what this was," he said, picking up the pace. Then to their two partners he issued the order, "Three and Four—time to exfil. Double-time it."

CHAPTER FOURTEEN

McCoy brought up the rear of the Presidential Agent entourage as they returned to Ani's messy apartment, thinking again that he was probably not the right person for this assignment. While he appreciated at times the hard work the spooks did to bring actionable intelligence to the table, this day had proven that he seemed much better suited as an instrument—a weapon—for acting on the intelligence once it had been harvested and vetted. He appreciated the opportunity to see how the sausage was made and imagined a new appreciation for intelligence reports he would read once he returned to his real job, but the freewheeling style of this team was just not his thing.

He followed the team into the shitty apartment. Ani locked the door behind him, leaned her back against the slab, and let out a long, weary sigh. Her rich caramel-colored complexion had taken on a gray pallor and she looked emotionally exhausted.

"I can't believe Omar is dead," she said, her voice ripe with self-blame.

"Don't blame yourself," Castillo said. "It's not your fault, Ani."

"We don't know that," she said.

"I, for one, don't like it," McCoy said, leaning against the tiny counter that separated her kitchenette from the rest of the studio-style apartment. "I don't believe in coincidences and this doesn't feel right. Are we now blown?"

He needed a target to prosecute. This sniffing around and waiting to see who might be hunting *them* was not the life he'd joined the Marine Raiders to find.

Castillo nodded. "The timing is certainly suspect, but we made it back here without incident. Nobody came after us and the driver of the truck that hit Omar didn't try to flee the scene."

"That's not a guarantee," Ani said. "Not all assassins hide in the shadows. It could have been planned this way, since we were there. Call it good tradecraft."

McCoy turned to Smith. "Any facial rec hits on that pic you took of the driver?"

"Still waiting on the back office," the spy answered.

"The back office?" McCoy echoed, his irritation at the spooky ambiguity that had been simmering since he'd first met the man finally about to boil over. "Dude, don't you think it's about time you knock off the games and just read us in on what group you work for? We're all on the same team here."

"You know who I work for," Smith replied. "ODNI."

"Right, just like we know your name? Agent Smith, I mean Jones, I mean Rogers . . ."

"Hold on, that whole time we were together you were NOC'ing me?" Ani said, anger returning a little color to her cheeks.

"Yeah, but you knew that . . . right?" the spook said with surprise.

"Uh, no," she said, still seeming to struggle with this revelation. "So your name's not Jeremy?"

The spook shook his head. "Nope."

"Even after I told you my name . . ."

"Yeah, well, you chose to use your given name with your NOC. That was your prerogative." He turned to McCoy and said, "I wouldn't recommend it, by the way, but each to their own."

"You're such a dick," she said, the words tinged with venom.

"What do you want us to call you for the rest of this engagement?" Castillo said, chiming in on the matter. "Ani met you as Rogers, I met you as Jones, and McCoy met you as Smith. You know our names and our stories, but we don't know jack shit about you."

The spook blew air through his teeth. "Look, don't take this the wrong way, but you guys are making *way* too big of a deal outta this. In my particular line of work, I interface with a lot of people. Also, the nature of my work tends to make a lot of those people very unhappy with me. Charley, I imagine you—of all people—can relate."

Castillo shrugged. "Not really. I always have considered myself a pretty straight shooter."

"Yeah," McCoy chimed, "he's a real people person."

Castillo shot him a disapproving look.

"Okay, fine," the spook said, unfazed. "My point is, this is how I roll. Chances are, after this engagement, the four of us will never see each other again. Charley will go back to his ranch, McCoy here will go back to the sandbox to play with his Raiders, and Ani will continue to live in this gem of an apartment with her takeout boxes, dirty laundry, and encrypted laptop . . ." Ani gave him the middle finger as he continued. "And I will be off to some other city, to help some other operatives clean up some other mess. I'm just sayin' . . . that's reality."

"I hear you, and you're probably right," Castillo said, "but we still need something to call you besides Smith-Jones-Rogers. Don't you have a nickname or something?"

"How about Tiny?" Ani said, a vulpine smile curling her lips as she held up her fingers to pinch a one-inch length in the air. "I can vouch for both relevance and accuracy."

Now it was the spook's turn to give her the middle finger. "Oh, really? I never once remember hearing you complain."

"How about Kevin?" McCoy said, "You look like a Kevin."

"No Kevin," Smith said, shaking his head. "Kevin happens to be my dad's name."

"Okay, then in that case, we'll call you Junior," Castillo said, grinning.

The spy rolled his eyes. "Really? My choices are Tiny, Kevin, and Junior?"

McCoy nodded along with his cohorts.

"I think Big Richard has a much nicer ring to it, and anatomically speaking it's a much better fit," the spook said, laughing despite himself, which got them all laughing. "How about we just stick with Smith for now?"

McCoy looked from Smith to Ani, who was still leaning with her back against the apartment door. He understood why the spook had fallen for her.

When she smiled, she was quite beauti—

Gunfire erupted in the hallway outside.

Time slowed and McCoy watched Ani's expression morph from jovial laughter to agony as she jerked forward and collapsed to the floor. McCoy dropped low and rushed to her, quickly pulling her clear and behind the futon that Smith had upended, the only viable cover in the spartan apartment.

"You hit?" he asked while running a hand across her back. His palm came away dry and blood-free.

"I don't think so," she managed, wincing as she pressed up onto all fours. "Feels like I got hit in the back with a hammer. Thank God I hung that Cordura over the door."

"Stay low," McCoy told her and pulled his Sig Sauer P365 XL from the waistband holster under his shirt.

In his peripheral vision, he saw that both Castillo and Smith had pulled their weapons and were firing through the wall, hoping to hit the kill squad in the hallway. His gaze ticked to the apartment door, where the antiballistic fabric was doing its job—mushrooming inward in multiple places, catching bullets but not losing integrity. Stopped slugs tumbled out the gap at the bottom in a nice, benign little pile on the wood floor. Unfortunately, the same could not be said for the rounds being fired through the walls at them, which were zipping across the room with increasing intensity.

"Shit!" Smith yelled as he jerked down behind the sofa as massive and prolonged strafing from outside sent plaster dust and chunks of wood flying. "How many shooters are there out there?"

"Three," McCoy said, his MARSOC mind having automatically already worked that problem. "One with an AK-47 and two with something smaller—nine-millimeter machine pistols, I think."

"Ani, you got anything heavy in this apartment? A long gun or a shotgun?" McCoy asked, hopefully.

"No, just my primary and my compact," she said. "Sorry."

"They're going to breach after this barrage," McCoy said, turning to Castillo.

"How do you know?"

"Just call it Raider intuition," he said, shifting his stance. "I'm going to the kitchen—gonna try to plink 'em from the blind side as they come in."

"Good idea. I'll reposition to the bathroom doorway and we can shred them in a cross fire," Castillo said.

"What about us?" Smith asked.

"This futon is gonna get shredded," McCoy said. "You two should get small behind those ballistic curtains."

"Check," the spook said.

"Get ready . . ." McCoy said, feeling the breach was imminent and nodding to Castillo. Abruptly, the maelstrom outside stopped. "Go!"

Legs churning, McCoy crossed the twelve feet from behind the tipped-over futon to the kitchenette in a flash, aware in his peripheral vision of Castillo moving swiftly to the other doorway across from him, his movement powerful and fluid—the movements of an operator and a predator. No sooner had they slid in unison into their new positions than he heard a loud crack, and the front door to Ani's apartment burst inward. He sighted around the corner and squeezed the trigger just as the lead insurgent barreled into the apartment, AK-47 blazing. His round hit the shooter center mass, but the assassin seemed unfazed—hosing down the futon just as McCoy had predicted. Puffs of feathers and splinters of wood filled the air as the upturned futon was annihilated with 7.62-millimeter fire.

McCoy shifted his aim upward and squeezed off two rounds—putting the first in the assassin's right ear and the second a little higher. At the same time, successive muzzle flashes in McCoy's peripheral vision confirmed that Castillo was in the fight, firing from the darkened doorway of Ani's bathroom at the other end of the apartment. The old man's rounds flew true and Castillo dropped the second breacher almost simultaneously with McCoy dropping the lead guy. A third insurgent stood in the doorway, machine pistol up but frozen with indecision, seeing his comrades dropped dead directly in front of him. His gaze swept center to right and he locked eyes with McCoy. In that split second, each man made his decision.

McCoy squeezed the trigger, aware of a nearly simultaneous crack from where Castillo positioned himself in the bathroom doorway.

The shooter bolted.

McCoy was pretty sure one of their rounds clipped the fleeing terrorist in the flank, who spun momentarily as the dude disappeared out of view beyond the doorframe.

"Everyone okay?" McCoy called, his pistol still leveled at the open gap.

"Check," Smith said.

"I think so," Ani called out.

Castillo didn't say anything, just stepped out of the shadows from the bathroom, standing tall and angry—his defiant stance his answer. McCoy suddenly saw the former Special Forces and more recent super spy in the older man. Perhaps he had misjudged him . . .

"I'm going after the dude that got away," McCoy said, the compulsion to pursue the lone remaining assassin overwhelming now that he'd confirmed his teammates were intact.

"Alone?" Castillo growled. "Like hell you are. We saw one guy but there could be more."

"Then I hope you've been doing your PT, Charley," McCoy said, already moving toward the apartment door, weapon at the ready, "Cuz I ain't jogging just so you can keep up."

CHAPTER FIFTEEN

McCoy aimed over his Sig Sauer pistol as his booted feet pounded the stairs to the first landing. There he stopped, pressed into the corner wall, and scanned over the pistol both up and down the stairwell, searching for threats and targets. His eye caught the bloody handprint on the wall to his left and he saw a few bright red drops of blood on the cement stairs as well, confirming that one of them—likely Castillo, he admitted to himself—had wounded the fleeing shooter.

As he descended to the next landing, he realized that safe, single-operator clearing procedures right now would do little, other than ensure that their attackers were gone by the time he reached ground level. Taking a long, slow breath, he sighted over his pistol and changed tack, sprinting down the steps two at a time, clearing as best as he could.

"McCoy!" Castillo hollered from above, his voice echoing in the stairwell. "McCoy, wait!"

"No time!" he shouted upward, making the turn at the second-floor level landing. A door beside him burst open and an old woman emerged carrying two canvas bags and wearing a scowl of disgust, not fear, on her face.

"Arjie lildakhil! 'anah khtatar!" he shouted, warning her of danger and ordering her back inside.

"Baaahh," the old woman said, shaking her head, the sound clearly conveying the same dismissive annoyance in any language. But she went back into her apartment, slamming the door shut behind her.

Seconds later he reached ground level and was moving through the narrow hallway toward the dirty glass entrance door, passing, on his right, a red wooden door marked in Arabic, which he imagined must be an interior entrance into the electronics store beneath the apartments. He felt the door with his hand as he passed, not sure what he was feeling for, but seeing no blood on the handle or masked in the red paint, he advanced quickly toward the entrance ahead of him, where he now saw two bright drops of blood beside the glass door.

As he passed, he heard the red door behind him swing open, and he spun rapidly, dropping to his knee as he did, just as the deafening explosion of the rifle filled the small space and a 7.62 round from the shooter's AK-47 whistled over his head. He fired as he raised his pistol, the first round hitting the man in the hip, giving him enough pause that McCoy aimed his second shot and fired center mass. The man—whom he could now see was a man in his early twenties with a thin beard—pitched backward, his head striking the doorframe, and he came to rest half in and half out of the

door, his foot shaking in a death throe and a whistling sound ema-
nating from the hole in his chest. McCoy kicked the AK-47 out of
reach and into the apartment hallway. For a moment, he considered
transiting through the store—perhaps there were more fighters
there and he could create an opportunity to take one alive.

That's not what I would have done, the operator inside his head
whispered. *This kid was the disposable distraction to cover the leader's
exfil. Clearing through the store will take time.*

He turned on a heel and sprinted for the main door, aware of the
sound of Castillo, and perhaps Smith as well, descending the stairwell behind him. He broke out onto the north side of the street and
glanced toward the merging large roads at Ramses Square, but saw
nothing as he pressed his back against the wall to make himself a
smaller target. He swiveled left, searching over his pistol for a target, and spotted two men scrambling toward a dented dark blue
Renault on his side of the street a half block away, a man standing
beside the open driver's door, screaming at the men in Arabic and
gesturing for them to hurry. The man locked eyes with McCoy and
froze for a heartbeat, before raising a compact machine pistol McCoy
now saw hanging beneath the right armpit on a sling.

McCoy exhaled as he sighted and squeezed the trigger of his Sig.
The man's head jerked back and he fell backward into the open
door, his weapon discharging a stream of bullets that licked up the
side of the five-story building, tearing away chunks of stucco
and concrete. McCoy thought of the old woman on the second
floor, praying no stray rounds struck her or other residents, as he
shifted to open a better lane of fire and dropped again to his knee.
He tried to sight on the two fleeing shooters who now rounded
the Renault to take cover, delighted to see one dragging his leg
awkwardly behind him. Having no line on either fleeing shooter,

he instead shifted his aim, letting loose a barrage of nine-millimeter rounds, blowing out the rear window and destroying both rear tires of the vehicle. He spun back to the right, pressing against the side of a gray car parked along the curb. He ejected his spent magazine and replaced it with a fresh twelve rounds.

The passenger-side door opened into the street and at first he thought the shooters were trying to crawl into the disabled vehicle— a fatal mistake—but instead a third man exited, spinning around and firing a burst of automatic fire from his machine pistol. The rounds tore up the sidewalk beside him—way off target—and McCoy was back on his feet, firing at the man who quickly ducked behind the vehicle. As he did, McCoy watched as the two men he'd been chasing disappeared onto a side street headed north.

McCoy kicked off a sprint just as the shooter behind the Renault popped back up, aiming where McCoy had just been. McCoy sighted on the move, squeezing his trigger twice, at least one round appearing to catch the man in the side of the neck. The shooter stumbled backward just in time to be struck full-on by a delivery truck that had come rumbling up the road at high speed toward McCoy. The man's body rode the front panel awkwardly for a split second, then disappeared under the right front tire with a nauseating crunch as the truck locked up its brakes. McCoy looked away and cleared the Renault as he passed, seeing only the dead driver. Five strides later, he rounded the corner and sprinted north after the fleeing terrorists.

This street was much narrower and densely packed with parked cars, leaving a modest passage in the middle for southbound cars to navigate. He scanned over his pistol in all directions, but between the doorways and parked cars there were simply far too many places for the shooters to hide. He could see straight up the street for two blocks to where the road intersected a much larger and busier street, but he didn't see any running figures causing a commotion on the crowded sidewalks.

McCoy held his pistol tightly against his thigh, making it less obvious, and crossed the street to the east side where fewer pedestrians were scrambling for cover. His eyes scanned every shadow, every potential hide, as he forced himself to move leisurely up the sidewalk north. As he approached a recessed doorway into a three-story building, he slowed, glancing around. Just as he was about to step even with the recess, a woman approaching him in the other direction did a double-take into the recessed doorway.

"Madha tafeal hunak?" she exclaimed, angling away from the doorway.

Instead of retreating backward, McCoy sprinted around the corner into the doorway of the building, just as a man in a long gray tunic moved forward. He saw McCoy and his eyes widened with both fear and rage as he growled at him, trying to raise his weapon.

The man screamed a death curse at him in Arabic, but McCoy locked his left hand on to the man's right forearm, pinning it and the machine pistol against the man's side. The gun burped a burst of rounds harmlessly into the pavement beside them as McCoy shoved the man backward and into the glass door. He saw the blood soaking the man's tunic and trousers on the left side. As he forced the man backward and off balance, he spun and twisted the terrorist's shooting hand out and around, feeling the crunch of bones breaking as he did, and the man released his grip on the weapon, which dropped but still hung from a sling between them. Keeping the broken arm tightly in his grip, McCoy then headbutted the fighter, breaking the man's nose and stunning him. He released his grip and shoved the terrorist backward, where he fell to the ground against the door as McCoy pulled his pistol up, aiming it at the man's face.

"Drop your weapon and stop resisting. You're coming with me," he said in Arabic.

But the man had no intention of coming quietly and screamed a battle cry. Then, in rage and pain, the insurgent tried to lift the machine pistol despite his broken arm. McCoy had no choice and ended the man with a bullet to the head. The machine pistol burped as the terrorist fell, missing McCoy but spraying the side of a black sedan on the street instead.

People screamed.

McCoy spun around the corner of the doorway onto the street, pistol up and searching for the next shooter. The once busy but peaceful scene on the street had now, in the wake of gunfire, deteriorated into chaos, people running in both directions. An old man a few yards to his north fell to the ground in the panic. McCoy's eyes locked on the one man who seemed out of place, a smile on his face as he jogged toward where he must have assumed his injured partner had gotten the drop on the American. He froze and his dark eyes widened at the sight of McCoy stepping out onto the street. McCoy raised his pistol, but the crowd of fleeing civilians swirling around the man prevented a shot, and just as they cleared, the man ducked to McCoy's right and disappeared into another doorway.

"Son of a bitch," McCoy grumbled, remembering how he had hated the chaos of the urban tactical combat course. He preferred a straight-up gunfight of good guys and bad guys—and one where he was leading a team, not dashing through a foreign city on his own.

The sidewalk cleared as he jogged to the edge of the next recessed doorway, ready to try his luck again with the same tactic.

But this time he spun around into an empty nook around a slowly closing door that led into what looked like a coffee shop filling the space beneath yet more apartments. Keeping low, he jerked the door open, twisting left as he entered the shop, weapon up, scanning the frozen, terrified faces that greeted him. At the sight of the weapon, half of the fifteen or twenty patrons of the coffee shop, thick with cigarette smoke, dropped to the ground and the other half rose and rushed for the door beside him or the hallway across from the coffee counter, which he assumed led to a rear entrance. One man, at the head of the crowd, looked over his shoulder and at McCoy, the face easily recognizable as his prey.

McCoy pushed through the crowd rushing for the door beside him, shouting in English for everyone to get down, a command completely ignored by the crowd, even when he repeated it in Arabic. He then fought down the narrow hallway, beside two doors he guessed to be restrooms, and his eyes were suddenly assaulted by bright light, someone pushing through the door at the end of the hall. McCoy surged forward, no longer gentle as he parted the crowd, elbows up and pistol muzzle pointed skyward. He charged out the door into a tiny courtyard, which was closed off by a building on his left but had a narrow exit alley crammed between the buildings to his right. There he spotted his squirter, and kicked off in a sprint after him, just as the man disappeared around the corner.

McCoy made the corner in a half-dozen long strides, but as he did, he worried about falling into an ambush. Castillo and Smith, and probably Ani, were no doubt in the hunt, but he'd lost them in this convoluted warren of alleys, dogleg turns, and intersections. If he didn't catch this asshole in the next few minutes, the chase might well end with them having nothing to show for this very shitty day.

At the corner, he crossed fast and low instead of hugging the wall, hoping to spoil any potshot from the fleeing terrorist.

Just as he predicted, a gunshot rang out. He momentarily locked eyes with his quarry, who was standing at the next corner aiming at the exact spot where the courtyard alley intersected the street. The bullet missed him but managed to find another target instead. A woman screamed, and McCoy glanced over his shoulder to see a young woman looking down at an older woman lying at her feet on the dusty pavement.

"Dammit," he grumbled, as the shooter disappeared around the next corner.

He knelt beside the old woman, relieved to find her wide awake, but her wrinkled face distorted in pain. McCoy ran hands over her while she grimaced and moaned. When he reached her right shoulder, he found a gaping, scythe-like wound in the fleshy part of her shoulder. A squeeze confirmed no broken bones but earned him a slap on the hand. He turned to the uninjured woman, who had both hands clasped over her mouth in apparent horror and disbelief at it all. He tried to give her the best smile he could muster and explained that the wound was just a graze. He got to his feet and squeezed the younger woman's arms gently. *"Almusaeadat qadimat . . ."*

Help is coming . . .

"*Shukran* . . ." the woman said, right hand over her heart. "*Shukran jazilan lak.*"

"You're welcome," he said, spinning on a heel, sprinting back up the alley at top speed, trying to make up for the lost time.

He turned left without pausing, clearing at the corner before continuing his sprint north toward the larger, crowded street of Habib Shalaby. He cleared corners and doorways as he ran, weaving around the pedestrians. At the sight of McCoy pounding up the sidewalk, gun in hand, this new crop of pedestrians panicked, many going to the ground, arms over their heads in fear.

At Habib Shalaby, he paused only a moment, glancing back toward El Zaher, but his gut screamed that the man had gone right. He saw him in neither direction, but turned right and ran full speed east, scanning in all directions for the fleeing terrorist. When he reached the traffic circle at Berket Al Ratl, McCoy spotted his target hunched over low, trying to mingle in a small crowd of people waiting to cross the street.

McCoy vectored that direction and the target panicked, ditching the crowd and taking off running across the traffic circle toward the city campus of the small college, one with a long name he could not remember on the map of the area he'd studied earlier in the day.

If he's headed there, this could get messy.

McCoy pushed through the crowd and sprinted out into traffic where he was greeted by the blaring of horns and the sound of locking brakes. He pressed his hand onto the hood of a long, black sedan—one free of chips and dents for once—and slid across the hood on his hip, taking a single step before leaping over the front end of a motorbike that appeared next, like a hurdler in track and field. One more step and he was at the curb and crossing the small park in the center of the traffic circle, weaving past a couple holding hands and nearly crashing into a well-dressed, middle-aged man staring down at his phone.

He glanced right, picking up his target, who was crossing the street forming the south spoke of the circle. The man had his weapon concealed beneath his shirt and was glancing in the wrong direction, apparently having lost his visual on McCoy. Using this to his advantage, McCoy dropped onto a park bench and hunched over his phone, glancing up to confirm the target was still headed toward the campus.

"Four—where the fuck are you?" Castillo huffed in McCoy's ear. "Or should I just keep following the trail of dead bodies you're leaving behind?"

"I'm pursuing the last guy, who I'm *trying* to take alive," he said. "He's heading north on Berket Al Ratl getting ready to enter the campus of that college there. I don't remember the name."

"Collège De La Salle," Castillo replied, surprising him with his knowledge of the area. "I assume the dead guy in the doorway on Heret Attaby is your work as well?"

"Well, if they'd stop trying to murder me, I wouldn't have to shoot them."

"I'm serious. We need this last guy alive, do you copy?"

"Copy," McCoy said curtly. "Hurry up and get here."

He disappeared his pistol underneath his untucked shirttail and back into the holster inside the waistband of his cargo pants, aware he was drawing a lot of wary stares. After losing the target for a few seconds, McCoy picked him up crossing the small courtyard between two of the academic buildings, the space swarming with young people, perhaps in the middle of changing classes. With some effort, he maintained his distance, but also kept sight of his prey, keeping a reasonable crowd of people between them. The target was glancing over his shoulder frequently, but he wasn't looking in the proper quadrant to spot McCoy.

They moved in tandem—hunter and hunted—along a wide path, crowded with students and older people with shoulder bags who he imagined to be professors, into the heart of the city campus. The target angled right, and for a moment disappeared around the corner of the building. McCoy followed, passing between two buildings and emerging into a large courtyard ringed by buildings designed in a Mediterranean style, with cream stucco and tall arched windows. A gaggle of students, mostly young men in khakis and blue polo shirts, were waiting in front of the three-story building to the north—waiting to go in for classes, he assumed. He scanned the courtyard and found his target sitting on a cement bench seat at one of a dozen umbrella-covered tables in front of the building to his right. The other tables were mostly crowded with young people eating, sipping coffee or tea, and chatting enthusiastically. The terrorist, however, was alone—still breathing heavy and trying to recover from his harrowing escape—sweat dribbling from his brow.

McCoy drifted east to stay out of the man's line of sight and come up behind him. He moved slowly but deliberately, eyes focused on his quarry as he approached. A few students glanced at him curiously, but then ignored him, returning to their conversations as he passed by their tables.

Thirty feet to go . . .

Twenty . . .

McCoy reached under his shirt, grasping his pistol, intent on waiting until the last minute to bring it to bear, lessening the chance that the panic that would ensue would provide cover for yet another escape.

You're mine, you bastard . . .

Ten feet . . .

The target was hunched over on his elbows now, still unaware of the predator bearing down on him, his breathing now normal, sweat stains down the back and sides of his dark gray shirt. McCoy tensed, preparing to grab the target by the neck when a hand gripped McCoy's shoulder and he felt the unmistakable cold muzzle of a gun press into the base of his skull.

"La tataharak," a voice growled from behind him, commanding him to remain still. "Or I will be killing you here now."

The terrorist at the table turned slowly, a malevolent grin plastered across his face—unable to conceal his joy that the foolish American had fallen into this little trap he'd set in the courtyard.

Where the hell are you, Castillo?

The flutter in his chest was all the proof McCoy needed to decide this was no time to wait for the cavalry. Knowing that offense was always the best defense in a fight, McCoy dropped and whirled hard to the left, playing the odds that the shooter behind him was right-handed. As he spun, the pistol that had been pointed at his skull discharged overhead, the bullet screaming off toward the building across the courtyard. The gunshot rang painful and loud in his ears, but he was no stranger to the roar of combat and did not lose his focus. Still rotating, he brought his elbow up, connecting perfectly in the man's temple—snapping the shooter's head violently to the side. The terrorist shrieked in pain and dropped his pistol, the gun clattering to the ground at their feet. McCoy looped a foot behind the killer's ankle—capitalizing on the shooter's off-balance lurch—and shoved him hard. The man pitched backward, his head smashing onto a cement bench with a crunch. As McCoy finished his spin, he drew his pistol and drove it up under the chin of the other terrorist, who had been slow to react.

The man's eyes widened in shock and fear, and McCoy lifted him up onto his toes using the gun under his chin.

"Stay very still," he growled in Arabic.

Screams now filled the courtyard, and chaos followed as students and faculty ran in all directions.

McCoy saw hate and intention in the man's eyes.

"Don't do it," he hissed.

But the man was already turning, raising his hand, trying to re-create the move McCoy had just used. But when the terrorist's hand impacted McCoy's wrist, the gun stayed lodged in the flesh under his chin, blocked in place by the V of his jawbone. His eyes filled with terror just as he realized his mistake and the Sig Sauer discharged, blowing off the top of the man's head, its contents raining down on the terrified crowd like wet, gory confetti.

The dead man dropped in a heap to the ground.

McCoy spun in a circle, searching for other targets, but let out a whistle of relief when he saw Castillo and Smith in lockstep sprinting toward him through the crowd.

CHAPTER SIXTEEN

Lungs on fire, Castillo sprinted across the wide brick courtyard, elbowing his way through the crowd of panicked students and staff, a rock in the riverlike flood of people fleeing the violence behind them. As the crowd thinned, he saw McCoy, consummate Marine Raider, scanning over his pistol, looking for targets.

"There he is," he growled at Smith, who had apparently spotted him as well and already angled in that direction. Castillo slowed to a jog until he reached McCoy and stopped, looking back and forth between the two dead men at McCoy's feet.

"Damn, son," Castillo said, in between breathless huffs. "You a little unsure of what the word 'covert' means ahead of the word 'operative'? My God, you left a trail of bodies from here to Ani's apartment."

McCoy didn't answer, just holstered his weapon and glared at him with what Castillo took for aggravation at not having anyone left alive to question. In the near distance, police sirens began to wail. In his peripheral vision, he could see a crowd of students and university faculty beginning to coalesce in the courtyard. Castillo holstered his weapon, pulled his phone from his front pants pocket, and quickly popped photographs of the lifeless faces.

"Okay, done. Time to go, Killer, before Egyptian Homeland Security scoops us up and tries to interrogate our asses."

Castillo saw him bristle at the nickname, once the call sign of his Marine aviator father.

"The enemy brought the battlefield to the city, not the other way around," McCoy said, scanning for the best escape route. "The only thing I'm guilty of is risking my neck to save innocent civilians and trying to stop a jihadi hit squad that just tried to murder us before they could disappear into the wind."

"Simmer down, kid," he said. "I'm just busting your chops."

"One, Five," said their OGA driver's voice in Castillo's ear. "I'm parked at the northwest corner, just off campus. Look for me in El-Malah Alley off Berket Al Ratl."

Castillo got his bearings and scanned northwest. There was no break in the courtyard at that corner, and he glanced back over his shoulder to the south and the only outdoor exit. He was about tell McCoy to follow him, but the MARSOC officer took off at a slow jog, joining in with the moving crowd exiting the courtyard with a cursory "This way" over his shoulder. Castillo shook his head and followed the Marine, glancing at the spook, who shrugged and smiled.

They exited campus via the wide sidewalk between the buildings at the southwest corner and crossed a large open lot full of parked buses, then reached Berket Al Ratl. Together they crossed the road, Castillo spotting their beat-up sedan at the corner a half block up.

"You injured?" Castillo asked McCoy, who'd said barely a word since it all went down.

"No," McCoy came back, the answer hard and clipped.

Looking at his protégé, Castillo decided that he might have misjudged the man. While McCoy's failure to follow his directive in the stairwell was frustrating, it also showed that he'd gotten more than he'd bargained for with McCoy. He'd issued the stop order because his brain had made a cost-benefit calculus in that moment— a gun battle spilling over into the city streets of Cairo would likely result in heavy civilian casualties and not further their mission objective. McCoy's brain had conducted the same calculus and reached a different conclusion. With a typical Marine, that wouldn't have mattered. A typical Marine follows orders, but McCoy wasn't a typical Marine, was he? McCoy was a Raider—the Marine Corps version of a Green Beret or a Navy SEAL. McCoy had demonstrated "tactical disobedience," adapting fluidly in a combat situation. Sure, Castillo's calculus had proven more accurate than McCoy's, but the kid was already showing himself to be more than just a rule-following Marine. And truth be told, McCoy did exactly what Castillo himself would have done fifteen years ago, back when he was more fleet of foot and brazenly overconfident.

Castillo smiled.

Despite having no terrorist captives to interrogate in the aftermath, the kid had executed under pressure. He was fast, had good reflexes, and was a good shot . . . a one man-killing machine.

There might just be a Presidential Agent lurking under that clean Marine yet.

The sedan sat idling at the corner, the passenger door wide open, and Castillo scanned the crowded street for threats as Smith and

McCoy jumped inside. Ducking his head, Castillo crowded in last and slammed the door shut behind him. The vehicle took off before his ass cheeks had made contact with the seat. The whole team now accounted for, with Ani in the front passenger seat, the spook sitting behind the driver, and McCoy riding bitch in the middle as usual, Hatchet turned and accelerated south on Berket Al Ratl Street.

Looking past McCoy at Smith-Jones-Rogers, Castillo said, "I assume we have you to thank for the exfil?"

"Yeah," the spook said. "No point in twiddling our thumbs back in Ani's apartment. We're blown, so best to get the hell out of Dodge while we still can."

A trio of police cruisers—lights blazing and sirens wailing—zipped past them going the opposite direction toward the scene of the gun battle, or at least the most recent gun battle. Castillo reflexively looked away as the cops passed. He tensed, fully expecting to hear the sound of squealing brakes and horns blaring as the cruisers executed U-turns.

Don't turn around, please don't turn around. Otherwise this is going to get real ugly real fast.

In his peripheral vision, he saw Smith glance over his shoulder out the back window.

"Are they whipping a U-turn?" McCoy asked, holding his gaze front and center.

"Nope," the spook said.

Castillo exhaled with relief and only then did he notice that Ani was animatedly murmuring to herself in the front seat.

". . . they told me Cairo was the most important post in Africa. Everyone said, *You gotta take the job, Ani. You'll do great, Ani. It will be a launch pad for your career, Ani.* So, I say yes and take the job, and now it's all ruined—my NOC's blown, I'll never be able to work in Cairo again, and I can forget about that promotion . . ."

The spook—who Castillo decided then and there he would henceforth call Junior—reached up and squeezed her shoulder. "It's okay, Ani. These things happen all the time. It's the nature of our work."

"It's *not* okay," she said, whirling in her seat to glare at him. "I blame you, Jeremy, or whatever the hell your name really is."

Junior flashed her that easy, unflappable smile he always wore.

The man could be on fire, Castillo thought, *and he'd still be smiling.*

"Ani," Castillo said, hesitant to stick his nose into this one but feeling he had no choice, "I know you've dedicated the past two years of your life to this—"

"Three years," she snapped. "I've dedicated the last three years of my life to this assignment."

"Right, three years," he said. "But like we discussed before, harvesting critical intelligence like this—even when it goes bad—is the reason why the agency invested in you and your NOC in the first place. Nobody in Langley is going to condemn you for what happened today. This is not a failure—professionally or personally on your part. The hit on your apartment is confirmation we're on the right track. You're stressing out about this being a black mark on your record. Trust me when I tell you the opposite is true."

"How can you know that? Hmm? Do you know the director of the CIA, Charley?"

"No, but I'm in pretty tight with his boss and his boss's boss," he said, suppressing a smile. "I will personally convey to both the DNI and President Cohen your contribution and sacrifice. You'll come out on top of this, I promise, Ani."

She nodded, seemingly placated. "So . . . what now?"

"When we get to the airport, we part company. You fly back to CONUS on the next available flight and we head to Sudan."

"Back to CONUS?" she said, indignant. "Fuck that—I'm coming with you guys."

Castillo shook his head, baiting her. "Sorry, not gonna happen."

"Sorry, my ass. You came to me and asked for my help to locate Secretary Malone and effect his safe return. I burned down my house for you—my NOC, my network, my entire operation are all gone, thanks to you. No way in hell I'm walking away now. We're going to see this through to the end . . . *together*."

This was exactly the response Castillo hoped to hear. When it came to recruiting, he was only interested in candidates who knew what they wanted and could not be easily dissuaded from their goals. He wanted a team rounded out by more than just him and McCoy. He had Junior, of course, but having a woman as bright as Ani who was also fluent in Arabic and blended in with the local population could prove invaluable.

"Are you sure?" he said, opening the door just a crack for her.

"One hundred and ten percent sure. Besides, how far do you think three American white dudes are going to get in Sudan without drawing the terrorists' attention? I speak Arabic, Egyptian, and a little bit of Sudanese. I can easily pass for a local, where none of you can. Also, I do have a couple of contacts in Sudan we can call on for help if things take a turn."

Castillo looked at McCoy, smiled at him, and turned back to Ani. "Okay, you're in." Castillo extended his hand to her. "Consider everything up to now an unofficial job interview for an unofficial position in our little unofficial program."

"Whoa, whoa, whoa," McCoy said, turning to look at him. "What are you doing?"

"Building our team," Castillo said, looking at the Marine but leaving his hand still extended to Ani. He felt her fingers close around his own and squeeze, cementing the deal.

Seeing this, McCoy sighed in defeat and stuck out his own hand to Ani. She shook it.

"Did you talk with the pilot?" Castillo asked, looking past McCoy to Junior. "I'm hoping he knows we're coming and is in preflight."

"Relax, you're working with pros, Charley," Junior said. "The pilots never left the plane. I told them to assume we'd need to leave in a hurry. I texted them, like, twenty seconds ago, and they'll be preflighting and lighting up those engines as we speak."

Castillo felt a stab of regret as he thought about the "good old days" when flying to an exotic locale like Cairo meant staying at a fancy hotel, having drinks and dinner out, and sleuthing around for a couple of days before moving on. He missed that era . . . when going on a boondoggle meant *going on a boondoggle.* This felt a lot more like work.

"Charley, shouldn't we be talking next steps?" McCoy said, snapping Castillo back to the present.

"Yep, when we're in the air," Castillo said. "Let's just get to the plane first, then we can deal with next steps." He knew the reply wasn't the answer the Marine Corps officer wanted to hear, but the simple fact was they weren't out of the proverbial woods just yet. "For now, let's just all stay sharp and focused on getting the hell out of Cairo."

PART II

*"It is absolutely necessary, for the peace and
    safety of mankind,
that some of earth's dark, dead corners and
    unplumbed depths be let alone . . ."*
    —H. P. LOVECRAFT

CHAPTER SEVENTEEN

Kuraymah Barkal

Sudan

March 19, 6:00 p.m.

Malone stared at the ceiling.

The small, windowless cinder-block room they had moved him to—replete with a brick of water bottles, a cot with an actual blanket, and a bucket for relieving himself—was more humane an accommodation than he'd expected. He wasn't chained to a wall, eating food off the floor, or being subjected to frequent beatings . . . Thank God.

Nonetheless, his fear of what was coming next grew with each passing hour. Each time the key rattled in the lock, he expected the well-dressed terrorist—whom he'd nicknamed Fifth Avenue in his head—to walk through the door. But as the hours passed without a second meeting, he imagined that maybe things were not proceeding as well as the terrorist had planned and that the next time he saw Fifth Avenue it would be to drag Malone out for his beheading.

He decided to do some calisthenics to get his blood moving and break the fear cycle, but the attempt was cut short by his hip and knee joints, apparently torn up worse than he'd thought by the time he spent folded like a pretzel in the freezer box. He rolled over and heaved himself up into a sitting position with a grunt, wondering when his next meal of roasted bread and rice paste would arrive. Without a window, his sense of time was further muddied, and he couldn't distinguish day from night. He tried counting to keep the time, but that was too tedious and monotonous. The best evidence he had that more than twenty-four hours had passed since moving him to this room was that a scab had formed over the cut created by the blow he'd taken to his cheekbone. Also, the number of meals, he realized. His next plate would be number seven.

So, I've been here about two days.

And in that time, no one had explained to him what they wanted from him. In fact, no one had spoken to him at all—they simply slid food on a metal plate into the room or silently replaced his full toilet bucket with an empty one.

Had they contacted the State Department yet? Had they already made a ransom demand? The hope he'd be tapped to participate in the negotiations for his ransom and release faded with each passing minute. Cohen would never negotiate a cash settlement for his release—not after criticizing prior administrations for paying cash to other groups, money that had later been used against America in the never-ending war on terrorism.

Unless some miracle leads a team of Navy SEALs to my location, I'm totally screwed. Even then, I'd likely die in the cross fire or be executed before they find me in this cell.

It seemed his only hope of survival was to endear himself to Fifth Avenue—a man who'd slapped him twice and ordered a teenager to smash a rifle butt into his face. If Cohen wouldn't pay, should he try to negotiate his own ransom? Certainly Fifth Avenue had thought of that . . . and if money was his primary objective, why not lead with that?

Maybe because he wants me hopeless. If he can convince me that my government has abandoned me and refused to pay, then he figures he can get more from me.

Or maybe the political leverage is truly what he craves. He did seem to hold me personally responsible for the poverty and suffering in Sudan—

A key rattled in the lock, sending his pulse through the roof. His bucket had been replaced not long ago, and it seemed too soon for a meal. This was it. They were coming to do the deed. His mind conjured imagery of his bloody, headless body being crammed back into the freezer box for shipment home to his wife.

A wave of nausea washed over him.

Oh, Linda . . . I'm so sorry.

The door swung open and Fifth Avenue strode in, rifle slung on his chest and his hand on the grip. Unsure what to do, Malone rose to his feet, his knees and hips screaming in protest, and lowered his head, hands clasped in front of him.

Dear God, please don't let this be it. Please don't let this be how it ends.

His throat tightened and he stared at a spot on the floor halfway between him and the terrorist, noticing again the man's clean, well-polished shoes. This man had money from somewhere.

"Please, sit, Mr. Secretary," the terrorist said, his English well practiced but his accent thick, making his words seem so much more ominous.

Malone sat, folding his hands in his lap, still not quite able to look up into the man's face, afraid of what he would see there. The silent pause drew out, the man perhaps waiting for Malone to speak first. But he wasn't about to make that mistake again, and so he sat in silence.

"It would seem that your government is quite upset about your disappearance, and have many, many people scouring North Africa to find you," Fifth Avenue said, sounding bemused.

At that, Malone was unable to resist looking up, feeling hope rising in his chest.

The look in the man's eyes dashed any such promise.

"But I'm afraid they're looking in the wrong places—the wrong country, in fact. No Special Forces team will arrive to get you anytime soon. We are quite safe here. I also have been busy setting in motion what must happen once your *sharira* President Cohen gives us what is right and due—both financial restitution and the public acknowledgment of our legitimacy."

Not sure what else to do, Malone nodded. But his mind was spinning around something just out of reach—something very important, not about what the man was saying, but perhaps how he was saying it?

"Because our plan must lead, inevitably, to a rise in political power, there are many things that must be put in place, people who I assume must be prepared, ahead of our deliberations with your *sharira* President. You understand?"

"Yes," Malone said, looking up now at the man. "Except, and I apologize, but I do not know this word 'sharira.'"

The man chuckled and nodded. "It means 'dishonorable.' *Aimra'at ghyr sharira* is a dishonorable woman—an apt description of your President, who shames herself and Allah by her actions. Our intention is to prevent a similar heresy from happening here in Sudan."

"Of course," Malone said softly, trying to sound respectful.

"You see, Mr. Secretary, we wish only to govern ourselves, free of interference by imperialist infidels who treat us as children, so we may live in freedom and prosperity the way Allah intended."

"May I speak freely?" Malone asked, with the distinct feeling he was on the verge of making a connection—an epiphany just out of reach.

"Speak," the terrorist said, irritated.

Malone chose his words carefully. "As I listen to you now, I hear a man who desires what is best for his country and his faith. A man who wants prosperity for his children and a future. A man who wants peace."

"Is that not what all good men want?" The man raised an eyebrow as if daring him to disagree. Malone had already felt the sting of that path and avoided it.

"Yes, exactly," he said. "And as I listen to you now, I fear I may have misjudged you. It would appear that you want respect and stability for this troubled nation—and as secretary of state, that is of course something I want for Sudan as well. Despite my comments before, a stable Sudan is in the best interest of the United States. The provisional government that replaced Bashir had lent temporary stability, but we all know it is not the long-term solution. For real peace to exist, the government must represent the true will of the majority of the people. I assure you, if that is what you seek, we seek the same thing for Sudan."

The terrorist paced back and forth, his face a mask. When Malone finished, he turned to face him. "Understand, I would as soon slit your throat and bleed you to death rather than cooperate with you as an emissary of the United States. And while it may yet come to that, it has been determined that keeping you alive, for the time being, is the best way forward if we are to achieve our goals."

"I will help you however I can, so long as your true goals are peace and prosperity for your people, and not war against the United States."

Fifth Avenue laughed. "You Americans are so full of shit. Always you think that your needs, your wants, your goals, your safety are all that matter. I have no interest in helping the United States and would prefer to rise up our people without the help of infidels who pat themselves on the back as we eat scraps from their table. But for now, it is felt that your cooperation will bring us more quickly to our goals and so we will allow it."

"I understand," Malone said subserviently while the dull ember of epiphany suddenly burst aflame in his mind.

You're not in charge, Fifth Avenue, are you? You desperately want to be, but you're just a lieutenant in someone else's army.

In his tenure as CEO, Malone had regularly negotiated with Japanese companies. He was reminded of this now, because typically in those meetings, the Japanese negotiator who purported to have authority, was in reality either a mid-level proxy or a figurehead standing in for the true decision maker. Only when the shadow boss was happy with the progress of the negotiation would they reveal themselves.

And only then did the real work get done.

Malone resisted the urge to smile.

"I will return in one hour," the terrorist said. "In that time, I have instructed my men to allow you a hot shower and clean change of clothes. They will also provide you with a desk. When I return, we shall have a conversation about how, exactly, you might properly represent our demands to your government. Together, we shall write a speech for you to share on video. There you will help promote the legitimacy of our requests and your personal desire to help us achieve

our goals. This video will also serve as our proof of life as we prepare to reach out to your President."

"We" again . . .

He knitted his fingers together and stared back at him.

"Will you do this?"

Malone rose cautiously, not wanting to insult the man and get a
rifle butt to the other cheek.

"Yes," he said.

The look on the terrorist's face seemed a combination of smug
satisfaction of the power he held over the American secretary of
state and also a bit of regret that he would not, for now, be permitted to execute violence on a man he despised.

Without another word, the terrorist turned and left.

Malone sat back on his cot, hands in his lap as the door closed,
heartened by the opportunity to bathe. He reeked, his stench an
omnipresent reminder of how far he'd fallen.

In the meantime, he silently congratulated himself for the de-
duction he'd made. He'd managed to check his fear and keep his
wits about him enough to make a key observation.

Knowledge was power.

And he definitely had new knowledge about his terrorist captor.

CHAPTER EIGHTEEN

McCoy shifted in his seat and looked out the porthole window as the plane taxied to the corporate hangar. He spied two white Toyota Land Cruisers with dark tinted windows parked on the skirt—vehicles that he assumed were waiting for them.

"Hey, Junior," he said, using Castillo's new nickname for the spook. "Looks like we might have a problem. I see two blacked-out government SUVs waiting for us. It appears somebody in the Ministry knew we were coming."

"Oh, I wouldn't worry about them," the spy said, and winked.

McCoy shook his head, trying to remember the last time in his professional career somebody had winked at him. As a Marine . . . never.

"Lady and gentlemen, this is your pilot speaking," came the voice over the cabin PA system. "We have arrived in beautiful Khartoum and we're taxiing to the hangar. The weather outside today is sunny and scorching—presently ninety-nine degrees after a day-time high of one hundred and fucking ten—so please wear sun-screen during your visit. Be sure to check the seatback pockets and overhead compartments for any firearms, incendiary devices, and electronic warfare equipment you may have brought with you. On behalf of EXFIL Airlines, I want to thank you for flying with us today. We know you don't have any damn choice in your air travel, but please come back and see us the next time you need to flee mis-hap, murder, and mayhem in extreme haste."

McCoy chuckled.

Dude must have been a pilot for JSOC in a former life, before joining Air America or Evergreen Aviation or whoever the hell these guys are.

Sarcasm in this business seemed to be the one thing he could always count on to brighten his day.

A moment later, the plane jerked to a halt and he heard the en-gines immediately winding down. McCoy pressed up from his seat, the last of his team to do so, and grabbed his duffel from the over-head bin. He followed Castillo out of the plane, pausing at the open cockpit door just long enough to give a two-finger salute to the pi-lots before stepping out onto the airstair and the still blazing early evening sun.

Instantly light-blind, he squinted hard and donned his Gatorz shades before descending the staircase to the tarmac. Thirty feet away, a Sudanese man of African descent stepped out of the driver's seat of the lead Toyota SUV and walked up to greet them. Junior, who walked ahead, met the man halfway between their jet and the two-vehicle welcome wagon. To McCoy's surprise, the spook and the stranger greeted each other with a bear hug.

"It's good to see you, my friend," McCoy heard the spy say as they stepped back from their brotherly embrace. "You look good. I see Ruba is feeding you well."

"Yes, but I'm eating only kids' food these days. It's like a feeding frenzy, I tell you. These kids eat twice as much as me and twice as often," the man said.

"How old are the boys now? Ibrahim must be ten or eleven . . ."

"Yes, Ibrahim is eleven and Kariem is eight, but looking at the boys you would think that they are the same age. Kariem is just as big as his older brother."

"I told you I thought he was going to be a big boy," Junior said with a laugh. "Turns out I was right."

"You were indeed, my friend. And how are you? Please tell me you have someone special in your life at last and you're not just working all the time."

In the corner of his eye, McCoy noticed Ani fold her arms across her chest at this comment.

"Ahh, you know me too well," the spook said, turning to face McCoy and the others. "Speaking of working all the time, I should probably make introductions. Team, this is my good friend Abdul-Baatin Wardi. He will be managing our transportation and security while we're in country. We've known each other for . . . gosh, Wardi, how long has it been?"

"Twelve years," the African said, nodding cordially at the rest of the group. "Welcome to Khartoum. Most people call me Wardi, but you can call me Baatin if you like. Either is fine. While you're here, you have nothing to worry about. I will handle all the logistics of your stay. If you need anything, anything at all, you let me know, okay?"

Castillo stuck out his hand to the man. "Charley," he said, in greeting.

Wardi shook it and traded handshakes with Ani next and McCoy last. McCoy was impressed with the man's strong grip and concluded from the way he held his left arm that Wardi was right-handed and had a concealed carry in a shoulder holster.

"I brought two vehicles as requested," Wardi said, turning his attention back to Junior. "But since there are only four of you, it looks like we only need one."

"I want two," the spy said, shaking his head. "We had a little trouble in Cairo earlier today and I want redundancy."

"No problem. Both Land Cruisers are yours as long as you need them." Then, scanning their gear, Wardi asked, "Do you have more luggage or is this all of it?"

"We've got luggage in the cargo hold, if you catch my meaning," Junior said, referring to a couple of over-sized hard cases—one with their long guns and ammo and the other with electronics.

"Understood," Wardi said with a nod.

They split into pairs, Ani and Junior going with Wardi, McCoy and Castillo riding in the other SUV. While Wardi and Junior loaded the hard cases into the back of the first Land Cruiser, McCoy and Castillo made small talk with their Sudanese driver, who'd introduced himself as Shaker.

"Nice vehicles," McCoy said.

"Nothing but the best for Mr. Smith," Shaker said, seemingly reading his mind. "This vehicle has bulletproof glass and doors. It was a special order."

"Up-armored? Really?"

"Full antiballistic package," Shaker said, professional pride in his tone, "courtesy of the USA."

"Of course," McCoy said, exchanging a knowing glance with Castillo.

Five minutes later, they were underway and exiting the airport grounds.

"Shaker," Castillo said, "do you know the place where we're staying? Is it a hotel?"

"No, not a hotel," the driver said. "You're in a very nice house in a very nice district called Al Amarat. It is one of the most prestigious neighborhoods in Khartoum. Very safe and very close to the airport. This house is the place where Mr. Smith always wants to stay. It has a wall and a nice garden. Also, a water filter system. A German family used to live in this house, but I think your government is owning it now."

McCoy, for his part, looked out the window as they drove. He'd not been to Sudan's capital city before, but the pink-brown dirt, square stucco buildings, and chaotic traffic reminded him of so many African and Middle Eastern cities he'd visited during his tours in the Corps.

"Have either of you been to Khartoum?" Shaker asked as he trailed Wardi's Toyota using what McCoy noticed was a proper tactical standoff.

"No," McCoy said.

"Neither have I," Castillo said.

"Then let me tell you a little about my city," the man said. "Khartoum is one of the biggest cities in Africa, with over five million people. It is a desert city, with little rain, but it was built at al-Mogran, giving us a valuable supply of fresh water all year round."

"What is al-Mogran?" McCoy asked.

"The confluence of the Nile," Castillo answered, surprising McCoy. "Where the two main tributaries—the Blue Nile and the White Nile—meet."

"That's right," Shaker said, apparently excited by Castillo's trivia knowledge. "Very good."

Out the window, McCoy watched an Arab boy, no older than eight or nine, dragging a heavy cart, his cargo covered with a tarp.

"Here you will see many children working," Shaker continued. "That's because almost everyone is poor. This neighborhood is rich, but the country itself is one of the poorest in the world. That is why there was a coup d'état in 2019 to get rid of the dictator Omar al-Bashir. The people were starving and prices were going to the sky, so we had no choice."

"And how are things now?" McCoy asked, already knowing the miserable answer but wanting to hear what the man had to say about it anyway.

"Now there is hope, but it is a fragile hope. The provisional government is an uneasy alliance between civilians and the military regime. The country is trying to transition from dictatorship to a democracy, but the old generals do not want to give up their grip on power. Many of the promised reforms of the transitional government have not come to pass. We were supposed to have a parliament in place by this time, but the Islamic hard-liners and the *Kizan* do not want this to happen."

"What is the Kizan?" McCoy asked, shifting his gaze to catch the driver's eyes in the rearview mirror.

"The Kizan is what you Americans would call the Deep State. These are Bashir loyalists and those in powerful positions who survived the coup and don't want to be accountable to a parliament or the people. They want to go back to the way it was before."

McCoy gave a grim nod.

Different place, different people—same old story.

"So, what about this woman politician I've been reading about?" Castillo asked. "What's her story?"

"Are you talking about Awadiya Khalil?" the driver asked.

"Yes."

"She is a reformer and very popular with the people. Many people want her to be the country's next President."

"Is she a member of the transitional government?"

"No," Shaker said. "No one in the transitional government can run for President in the election. It was one of the conditions to help ensure a legitimate election and transition to the new democratic people. As you know, most coups simply result in toppling one dictator only to birth another in his place. We cannot let that happen in Sudan."

"Has Awadiya Khalil announced her candidacy and launched her campaign?" Castillo asked.

"Yes, and at every protest and march you will find her leading the crowd and speaking out against the Sovereignty Council and the Council's chairman, General Shandi, who is increasingly at odds with the acting prime minister."

"Is she trying to create a movement for another coup?"

"No, no, no," Shaker said with a chuckle. "This is not the point. She wants to hold the Sovereignty Council accountable. There was an assassination attempt on the acting prime minister after he repealed Bashir-era laws restricting women's freedom to work, study, travel, and dress as they choose. After this attack, the Sovereignty Council said nothing. They did nothing. It would be convenient for General Shandi if the prime minister were out of the picture, because the reforms he is passing threaten the status quo."

"Interesting," Castillo said.

McCoy looked at Castillo and saw from his expression that he'd reached some silent conclusion.

"We have arrived," the driver said, slowing and following the lead SUV into the driveway of a large, well-appointed brown stucco estate. The two-story home had a boxy, modern design, very few front-facing windows, and looked to McCoy to be somewhere in the neighborhood of four to five thousand square feet. An eight-foot-tall privacy wall, also constructed of stucco, enclosed three of the four sides of the property, but did not prevent access to the driveway or front entrance. Two stately palm trees stood sentry in the front "yard"—a patch of grass that couldn't have measured more than fifteen square meters. McCoy couldn't help but wonder the annual cost for water to keep that little statement piece of turf alive.

As soon as their Land Cruiser stopped, Castillo hopped out. McCoy did the same, slinging his duffel over his shoulder as he scanned a one-hundred-and-eighty-degree arc for threats. Seeing nothing and no one of concern, he walked over to the open tailgate of Wardi's SUV and he and Shaker unloaded and jointly carried inside the second of two hard cases with their gear. To his relief, the house was air conditioned and a blast of cold air greeted him as he stepped through the front door into the property's modest foyer. He kicked the front door shut behind him with a thud and set the hard case down on the glazed ceramic tile floor.

"The house has four bedrooms, one for each of us," Junior said, smiling. "Three upstairs and one downstairs. I'll let the three of you fight over rooms and I'll take the leftover. There's a kitchen, of course, on the main level, and a nice common room with a large-screen television. Also, there's a safe room in the basement in case of emergency. I'll take you down and review the lock codes. I believe Wardi stocked the fridge with beer, bottled water, and snacks, so feel free to help yourself."

"Nice work, Junior," Castillo said. "This sure beats the hell out of staying at a hotel."

With Castillo's comment, it suddenly clicked for McCoy what their spooky friend's job on this team actually was.

The dude is a one-man logistical wizard, he realized.

While McCoy had dozed on the flight, after running through the streets of Cairo like a crazed vigilante shooting terrorists, Junior must have tapped his network and set them up with secure and reliable transportation, lodging, and local help. Wardi and Shaker were personally vetted by Smith and so was this property. You couldn't put a price tag on peace of mind like that in this line of work.

McCoy realized that now, as part of this Presidential Agent program, he had forfeited all the logistical luxuries he'd come to depend on as a Raider. As a MARSOC officer, he was backstopped by the infrastructure and supply chain that was the U.S. Marine Corps. At the end of an op, he returned to a base—a facility with reliable medical care, sleeping quarters, rations, and security. For his entire career, he'd been unwittingly coddled under the DoD umbrella known as force protection. In his current assignment, he had none of that. In a city like Khartoum, he wouldn't even know who to turn to for help. That's where guys like Junior came in, and he hadn't even realized how comfortable and secure he'd felt until this moment.

"How about we each take twenty minutes to get settled and use the facilities and then we regroup in the common room to map out next steps," Junior suggested.

After getting nods all around, the spook walked over to McCoy.

"Thanks for doing this," McCoy said.

"My pleasure," the spy said. "Why don't you take the room on this level. It's the nicest."

"You sure?"

"Absolutely, you earned it." Then, wrinkling his nose, added, "And you might wanna hit the shower while you're at it, because, um, dude, you reek."

CHAPTER NINETEEN

Safe House

Al Amarat District

Khartoum, Sudan

March 19, 8:15 p.m.

McCoy hit the shower and damn did it feel good.

Now, if I could only get a six down, he thought, glancing at the queen-sized bed in his bedroom suite, *I'd be ready to take on the world.*

It took all his willpower not to recline on the bed, knit his fingers behind his head, and close his eyes. The rest of the team probably was already waiting for him in the common room, so instead of risking falling asleep, he brushed his teeth and got dressed. Why Junior and Castillo had forfeited the master suite to him was beyond McCoy, but he was never one to look a gift horse in the mouth. *Take the win* had always been his motto.

He reached for his Sig in its holster lying on top of the bed but stopped short before his fingers touched the pistol butt.

No, he told himself. *We're safe here.*

Leaving the weapon took willpower. He felt naked without it, just like he felt naked without his kit, which he'd not donned since Junior had picked him up in Iraq. After a decade of operating with MARSOC, *kitting up* had become synonymous with *survival*. That was simply what operators did. It was not what spies did, however, and for the foreseeable future that meant walking around in short-sleeve, button-up shirts and cargo pants with no body armor, no helmet, no night vision goggles, and no rifle.

Awesome.

With a heavy, mind-cleansing exhale, he walked out of his bedroom without his pistol, down the short hallway, and into the common room. He glanced to the corner where the Pelican cases held their long guns, glad to have them within reach. He saw Ani curled up asleep on the sofa and Castillo in one of the room's two club chairs with his feet up on an ottoman and a notebook computer in his lap.

"Whatcha reading?" McCoy asked.

"Working some back-channel commos," Castillo said, not looking up. "Looking for anything on Awadiya Khalil, trying to connect dots."

McCoy nodded and made his way to the kitchen, where he found Junior dropping fresh-cut limes into the bottom of four rocks glasses. Next he spooned a couple of sugar cubes into each glass and muddled each in turn. McCoy watched him top the sugar–lime blend with a handful of ice cubes and pour a clear spirit over the top.

"What are we drinking?" he asked when the spook finally caught his eye.

"Caipirinhas," Junior said, as he gave each cocktail a stir with a long-handled teaspoon. "You ever had one?"

said, glancing at the bottle. "Is that rum?"

"......... That's cachaça—a Brazilian spirit distilled from sugarcane. Rum is made from sugarcane by-products like molasses. Cachaça has more of a bite, and it's not as sweet . . . hence the sugar cubes."

Junior extended McCoy one of the finished cocktails.

"No, thanks, I don't drink on the job."

"It's not like we're sitting down with Irshad Khalil tonight. Government offices are closed now," Junior said. "So, technically, we're not on the job until tomorrow. I figured we can relax, have a nice dinner, a cocktail or two, and everybody can get some needed sleep. Then we'll hit it hard tomorrow."

McCoy's mind went immediately to a mental image of the secretary of state curled up in the fetal position and lying in the bottom of a dark pit—battered, bloody, and dehydrated. That image suddenly contrasted with another—the four of them having a dinner party—and simply didn't sit well with his sense of duty and honor.

"We're not going to get Malone out tonight, if that's what you're thinking," Junior continued, thrusting the cocktail at him. "So, you might as well put that idea out of your head completely. We have no idea where to look or what we're up against. It's not dereliction of duty to rest and regroup."

McCoy held the spook's eyes for a long moment and finally accepted the cocktail. "You're right, but it just feels wrong."

"I know, but you gotta trust me when I tell you it's not," the spy said.

McCoy nodded and took a sip. "It's good. Sorta like a mojito without the mint."

"And not quite as sweet," Junior added.

"Yeah, good call," he said, accepting a second cocktail to carry for Castillo.

"Shall we?" Junior said, gesturing toward the common room.

Castillo looked up as they entered. Seeing the cocktail in McCoy's hands, he said, "Thank you," eagerly accepting the rocks glass and taking a long pull. "Caipirinha . . . mmm, so good."

Junior sat down beside Ani, who was taking up two of the three sofa cushions, while McCoy dropped into the lone remaining club chair catty-corner from Castillo. Ani stirred and opened her eyes and looked at him with drowsy lids. He smiled at her and she smiled back, before stretching out her legs and slowly sitting up.

"Man, I needed that nap," she said, receiving her drink from Junior.

Junior smiled at her, then extended his glass to the middle of the room.

"To finding the secretary," he said.

"To finding the secretary," McCoy repeated in unison with Ani and Castillo, and consummated the toast with a sip. It had been months since he'd had a drink, and a few sips later, he already felt a slight buzz coming on.

"So," Castillo said, his gaze settling on Junior. "I think it goes without saying this is not your first rodeo in Khartoum."

"I know my way around the neighborhood, if that's what you're asking," Junior replied.

"When was the last time you were here?"

"Twenty nineteen, during the weeks leading up to and through the coup d'état."

"Of course," Castillo said with a knowing grin. "I suppose you had nothing at all to do with that . . ."

The spook grinned back. "You know, Charley, it's bad form to kiss and tell."

Castillo chuckled. "Sure, sure—that would never happen with this crew," he said, his gaze flicking from Junior to Ani and back again.

"And for just a minute, I thought we were all getting along so well," Junior said, with a hint of irritation in his voice.

McCoy wasn't sure why Castillo was trying to push the spook's buttons—he didn't see the point—so he jumped into the fray and redirected. "In your past travels here, did you ever have any dealings with this guy Khalil?"

Junior shook his head. "No, he wasn't on my radar. His sister was, of course, but I think the brother has only recently become somebody of import."

Ani got up from the sofa and walked over to her shoulder bag, which she'd yet to unpack, and retrieved her notebook computer. She returned to the sofa and opened it on her lap. Fingers working the keyboard, she said, "Let's see what we can find on him, shall we?"

"Omar said that Irshad Khalil was a very strong nationalist who hated the Bashir government," McCoy said, remembering the conversation he'd listened in on between Castillo, Ani, and the Egyptian asset. "That tells me he probably got his position after the coup."

"That appears to be the case," Ani said, looking down at her screen as she spoke. "According to the provisional government website, he's the acting minister of interior, appointed nine months ago. In Sudan, the interior minister is responsible for internal security, supervision of local governments, policing, immigration, emergency management, and the conduct of public elections—it's a pretty powerful position with tendrils in lots of different sub-agencies."

"If Khalil is the acting minister, who's the minister?" McCoy asked.

"Akram Mandi was," she said. "But apparently, he was killed in an auto accident a few months ago. It appears that, for now, Khalil is the acting minister of interior. I'm guessing that's unlikely to change until the entire provisional government does."

"Well, after what happened to Omar in Cairo, it's a chilling coincidence that the guy he replaced died in a car accident," McCoy said.

"Well, yes and no," Junior said. "Auto accidents are one of the leading causes of death in Sudan, and that's in a country with poverty and pretty shitty health care. The accident rate in Sudan is like forty times higher than other countries in the region, and the fatality rate is more than ten times higher per vehicle than the rest of the world. If someone told me a relatively young man died in Khartoum, my first guess would be that it was in a car crash."

"Yeah, well, I still hate coincidences," McCoy grumbled, but began to wonder just what the hell Junior didn't know about Sudan.

"So, Khalil is the minister of interior, huh," Castillo said, and took a long swallow from his cocktail. "I definitely want to talk to him now."

"Sure, but no one else sees the inconsistency here?" McCoy asked. "I mean, a nationalist in the provisional government whose sister is expected to run for President—a woman President in a majority Muslim country with a terrible record on women's and religious rights? This guy seems like the exact opposite of what we're looking for, don't you think? Hell, he's probably pretty brave to be serving in this government and not in hiding for his life somewhere.

In what world is he tied to terrorists kidnapping the American secretary of state?"

"The world of North Africa, bro," Junior said. "Look, I'm not saying he's involved—we have no reason to think that yet—but this is Sudan. Loyalties are complex and political power is the only real path to prosperity here. I'm just saying anything is possible."

"And Omar didn't say he was involved, just connected enough to get us information," Ani added.

"Okay, fair enough. So then what's the plan? We just show up at his government office and question him?" McCoy asked, overwhelmed by a sense of operational déjà vu.

"Khalil is the only lead we have," Castillo said and polished off what was left of his cocktail. "Do you have a better idea?"

"Yeah, maybe we surveil the guy first instead."

"Why not do both?" Junior chimed in. "We meet with Khalil, push his buttons, then watch and see what he does. I'll get us set up in an OC related to the diplomatic corps and get State to press for the meeting."

"By morning?" McCoy said, getting a little tired of being constantly amazed by this new world. Whoever Junior really was, and whatever spooky acronym he worked for, he got shit done.

"Bro, I could have it set up during the drive over," Junior said with his frat boy smile and wink.

McCoy shook his head. The bunny hole he'd fallen through had taken him to a very strange world indeed.

"Sounds like a plan," Castillo said, and with an old man grunt got to his feet. "I could use another one of these. Junior, you got enough limes for more?"

"Got plenty," the spook said, moving to get up. "I'm happy to make you another."

"No, no, relax. I got this."

On that cue the doorbell chimed. Junior looked at his phone and said, "Looks like Wardi is back with our dinner."

McCoy pressed to his feet and made his way to the kitchen, but his eyes ticked to the Pelican hard cases. He felt his muscles automatically tense, a predator primed to spring into action, until he heard Junior at the door say, "Wardi, my man!"

Relaxed now, McCoy rounded the corner and found Castillo already preparing another round of drinks.

Castillo looked up. "Ready for a refill?"

"No, thanks," McCoy said, and suffered a look like he'd expect to get at a college party, peer pressure to drink with the boys.

Castillo set McCoy's glass aside.

Very strange world indeed . . .

Wardi walked into the kitchen carrying a paper sack in each hand and grinning large. The aroma of grilled meat and spices hit McCoy's nostrils a second later and his stomach growled with anticipation.

"What did you get for takeout?" McCoy asked.

"Not takeout," Wardi said, shaking his head as he set the bags on the kitchen table and began unloading a hodgepodge of plastic containers. "This is home cooking. Beef with roasted spices and vegetables, salad, flatbread, and peanut stew with okra and eggplant—which is my wife's specialty."

"Smells delicious," McCoy said, inhaling deeply. "I'm starving, so thank you."

"Will you join us for dinner, Wardi?" Junior asked.

"How could I say no," the man said with an expression that said it would take a semitruck to drag him away. "It is my favorite meal of all."

The dinner exceeded McCoy's expectations on all fronts—socially, professionally, and gastronomically. Castillo's rough edges fell away and whatever ghosts were haunting the man, tonight seemed to give him a respite. With alcohol playing Cupid, Ani and Junior were quickly rewarming to each other. And Wardi turned out to be a helluva storyteller, and just as clever as a comedian, as he regaled them with funny stories about Junior from the "old days."

McCoy, for his part, just sort of let himself bask in the sunshine of it all and enjoy the moment for what it was. Turning "it" off had always been one of McCoy's weaknesses, and being an officer in the Marine Corps had only reinforced his naturally guarded persona. But with these people, despite having only just met them, he slipped into an easy but surprising camaraderie he'd only ever really found in his Special Operations team.

Strange . . .

"You sure I can't get you another drink?" Castillo asked, giving McCoy's shoulder a squeeze as he pushed back from the dinner table. "I'm gonna need one before calling the boss, that's for sure."

"You're calling the DNI?" McCoy asked, a little surprised.

"Comms are secure here, don't worry."

"Oh, I'm not," McCoy offered. "Just impressed we can just hop on the phone with the director of national intelligence whenever we want."

Castillo laughed as he headed to the kitchen.

"Then you'll be really impressed to find I'm not calling Director Fleiss," he chuckled. "I'm calling Cohen herself. She wants frequent updates, and I think she may be pissed we waited this long."

"And that we don't have more to report," McCoy grumbled.

"Nature of the beast." Castillo peered around the corner from the kitchen and raised both eyebrows, imitating Junior. "How about that drink?"

"Nah, man, I'm good. In fact, if I don't get some rack soon, I'm gonna pass out on this table. Wardi, please tell your wife that dinner was delicious and give her my sincere thanks. I'll see everyone bright and early in the morning."

And with that, McCoy bid them good night, wandered to his bedroom, and fell hard asleep within sixty seconds of his head hitting the pillow.

CHAPTER TWENTY

"Secretary Malone is running out of time, Charley. Which means we're running out of time. I need you to find him by any means necessary," President Cohen said, doing her damnedest to keep her tone collected and Presidential.

"Yes, Madam President," Castillo said, his voice as clear as if he placed the call to her from the next room.

"And you need to do a better job of keeping me in the loop."

"Yes, Madam President. As the situation and operational security allows."

She could hear the smile in his voice, which really pissed her off. She ended the call by loudly returning the phone into the cradle on the *Resolute* desk—with more vitriol than she intended. She could feel Marty Fleiss's gaze on her, but she wasn't ready to meet his eyes.

"Tell me this wasn't a mistake, Marty," she said through a sigh, rubbing her temples in a futile attempt to stave off the stress headache coming on. "Tell me this wasn't a mistake resurrecting the Presidential Agent program and putting Charley Castillo in charge of it."

"It wasn't a mistake, ma'am. It was your best worst option," Fleiss said, his comment either patronizing or brutally honest—she couldn't tell which.

"Don't be an asshole, Marty," she chastised, her gaze snapping to him.

"I'm not trying to be, Madam President, I promise," Fleiss said.

His face softened with sympathy as he stood before her, hands folded in front of him. No matter how casual he appeared—and today he was wearing khaki chinos and a dress shirt—his body language was that of a man in uniform. Perhaps that many years of service made permanent changes to a person's spine.

"I believe that Charley and his new band of Merry Outlaws may well be our best shot at recovering Secretary Malone," Fleiss said.

"Did you know that they left Cairo and are in Sudan now?"

"I didn't have confirmation, but suspected they were heading there. We had some"—he seemed to choose his words carefully—"'activity' is the best word, I suppose, in Cairo that I suspected to be Castillo and his group, and there was continued utilization of the air asset they took to Egypt."

"By 'activity,' are you implying some international incident we'll be cleaning up in the coming weeks?"

She did not like where this was going. She'd chosen to resurrect the Presidential Agent program under Charley Castillo's management to *avoid* international incidents, not create them.

"I don't think so, ma'am. Honestly, there was some gunplay and a few enemy casualties, but there is nothing concrete tying it to our guys. Even the intelligence community in the region has chalked it up to rival radical groups having a go at one another. The exception being a CIA case officer, whose agent has now apparently joined the team."

"What's his name?" she grumbled, wondering how many names she would be either denying or defending in the coming days.

"*Her* name, ma'am. Ani Shaheen. She's a stellar Clandestine Services officer from CIA."

"Great. So now CIA knows we have someone not just playing in their sandbox, but pilfering their agents." Her words to the intelligence community after taking office about teamwork, cooperation, and joint operations echoed painfully in her mind.

"Not at all," Fleiss reassured her. "I've smoothed it over in anticipation of a problem. CIA believes we've embedded her with a joint counterterror task force to bring them to the table rather than circumventing them."

"Nice work, Marty," she said, feeling the throbbing in her head ebb a little. "Thanks for getting ahead of this thing."

"That's what you pay me for, Madam President."

She nodded, aware that the American government wasn't paying him nearly enough for his service.

"But no contact from Charley until now," she pressed.

"No, ma'am," he agreed with a shrug, appearing far less annoyed by the fact than she.

"Didn't we tell him to keep us apprised of his progress?"

"Yes, ma'am, but remember his team is working quickly and with very little in the way of backup or resources. We should expect that his ability to update us is limited, and encourage him to make that call based on his operational security, and our *need* to know rather than our *desire* to know."

"That's fair. But still, this whole rogue asset mentality Castillo loves to embrace . . . it just needles me. Even now, after all these years, he still needs to be managed. This is precisely what made me nervous about going this route in the first place."

"I understand, ma'am," Fleiss said. "But if I may, you put your personal feelings and self-interest aside and did what was best, despite the personal risk. Madam President, I think that's exactly the type of leadership that drove most of us to vote for you in the first place."

"Thank you, Marty," she said, smiling for real this time. "But I want your unfiltered opinion, do you think the team is on the right track?"

"Hard to imagine Charley Castillo on the wrong track, ma'am. I've always believed the best predictor of future success is past success, and ol' Charley has pulled some amazing successes out of his ass over the years, if you'll pardon the expression."

"Indeed," she agreed. It was why she had thought of Castillo to begin with.

"We know Sudan is a powder keg, Madam President," Fleiss continued. "The provisional government is holding a tenuous grip on order, much less power, and the shift from Sharia law to a secular government is not sitting well with any number of conservative groups and extremist organizations in the country, who are stirring up all kinds of trouble. I may not be able to predict exactly who or what their endgame might be, but it certainly isn't out of left field. It also goes a long way to explain why none of the tree shaking inside of the radical groups in Egypt knocked anything loose. Time will tell, but it's sure as hell a lead they should follow. Especially after what happened in Cairo."

"So, you want to tell me what happened in Cairo?" she snapped, sharper than she meant to.

He shot her that same gentle half smile she found herself growing to both love and hate.

"No, ma'am," he said simply. "Unless you insist. Plausible deniability is the primary benefit of the program. I know it's difficult, but you have to resist the urge to self-sabotage."

She sighed, knowing he was right.

"Very well," she said, her way of dismissing him. "But do keep me posted on their progress."

"Of course, Madam President," he said, spinning on a heel as if released from parade rest and heading for the door.

"Hopefully Castillo and his new protégé can resist the urge to upset members of the provisional government in Khartoum while they're in Sudan. Our relationship with the provisional government is strained enough."

"Hopefully, ma'am," he said, turning to her.

"Why don't you convey that message, please."

"Yes, ma'am," he said as he exited and closed the door softly behind him.

But the DNI's tone didn't fill her with much hope that it would matter.

She went back to rubbing her temples.

Fucking Charley Castillo . . .

CHAPTER TWENTY-ONE

"Please try not to piss off any transitional government members while you're there," Ani said in McCoy's earpiece as he, Castillo, and Junior walked toward the modern, six-story government building. "The United States has a strained relationship with Sudan as it is. We don't need you throwing gasoline on the fire."

"Oh, Ani," Castillo said, his voice feigning injury. "You hurt me with such comments. It's like you don't know me at all."

"I *don't* know you at all," she fired back, but there was humor in her voice. She sat in their safe house, running the operation from their low-level TOC, with little or no signals intelligence. Junior had promised them some satellite coverage on loan from NSA in the coming hours, but for now Ani had little to contribute other than running commentary. "Since I met you *yesterday*, you obliterated my NOC, burned the intelligence operation I'd built in Cairo to the ground, got my best asset killed, and left a trail of bodies in your wake. That's the kind of thing that pisses a girl off . . . not to mention governments, Charley."

Junior looked over at McCoy and gave his signature double eyebrow raise. McCoy shook his head, but couldn't help but smile at the banter. He realized that dinner and socializing with this band of misfits had brought them together and done more for his attitude and confidence in this mission than anything else since getting yanked out of Iraq.

"Since we're apparently keeping score, I would like to point out that all of those bodies in Cairo bear wounds from Captain America here, not me," Castillo said, elbowing McCoy.

"That's fair," Ani said with a chuckle. "So, I'm adding him to the list of people I don't like along with you and Tiny."

"I agreed to Junior, I believe," Junior said with an eye roll. "Not Tiny."

"Okay, people," Castillo said as he approached the obstacle course of barriers leading to the building, flanked by tan-uniform-clad soldiers, a security checkpoint visible inside the lobby through the glass door. "Here we go. Let's get our cover on."

McCoy had been impressed already by the beauty and relatively modern, urban feel of Khartoum, which was not the dreary, run-down city he had expected. He knew well about the many slum neighborhoods from the city central, but in the Al Amarat district, at least, the city was well kept, clean, and attractive with well-paved and well-marked roads and modern buildings mixed with older, but still beautiful, architecture. The district contained myriad international embassies, including the United States Embassy just south of where they were now, and the Saudi Arabian Embassy a few more blocks north.

The building they approached was a boring, tan, narrow-windowed government building just like one might find in America, though this one had barriers in place with armed Sudanese soldiers, including several troop carriers with heavy weapons mounted on top and a maze of cement barriers meant to keep vehicle-borne IEDs at bay. He nodded to a soldier beside the entrance door, a machine gun on his chest, who looked them up and down and opened the door for them with a curt nod.

The lobby of the government complex was gray tile and, after a few feet, they arrived at a security checkpoint where they showed the diplomatic corps identification that Junior had given them on the drive over.

"Which offices will you be visiting?" the guard asked after scanning their identification, his English flawless but clipped and tinged with a heavy accent.

"We have an appointment with Minister Khalil in the Ministry of Interior," Castillo said.

The guard scanned through several printed pages on a clipboard, rather than on a tablet one might see in the West, but found their names.

"Very well," he said, opening a red velvet rope between two stanchions, as if they were to be seated at an exclusive restaurant. "Please empty all of your pocket contents into the bins and pass through the scanner when directed. Have a pleasant day."

McCoy dropped what he had in his pockets—just the ID carrier and wallet with a fake international driver's license and some American cash—into a bowl, then passed through the metal detector behind Castillo when waved through by another soldier. The detector beeped and he stepped forward, raised his arms as directed, and was scanned with a wand, his belt buckle the only culprit, and retrieved his wallet and ID lanyard.

A few minutes later they left the slow elevator on the fourth floor and followed the signs down the hall to the impressive, ornate wood door, much different from the ordinary wood doors flanking them along the hallway, behind which presumably less important and impressive work was being done. Above the door, in Arabic and then English beneath, gold letters announced they had arrived at the offices of the Ministry of Interior.

On the other side of the door, a well-dressed man in coat and tie sat at a reception desk.

The attendant greeted them in Arabic with a sincere smile. McCoy imagined American diplomats were afforded the same deferential courtesy as the Saudi Arabian representatives, in light of Sudan's desperate need of financial support from both sources.

"Do you speak English, please?" Castillo asked, though all three of them spoke reasonable Arabic.

"Of course," the man replied, still smiling. "How may I help you?"

Castillo passed over his identification.

"I'm Charles Whittaker and these are my colleagues, Mr. Mason and Mr. Thomas. We are a few minutes early for our appointment with Minister Khalil."

"Certainly," the man said, reaching for his phone. "I'm sure the minister will see you right away." He then spoke into the phone briefly in Arabic, telling his boss the Americans had arrived. He replaced the receiver and rose. "He'll see you directly," he said, moving around the desk to open the door for them. "May I bring you coffee or tea?"

"Nothing for me, thanks," McCoy said.

"I'll have a black coffee, thanks very much," Junior said.

"Sounds great. I'll have one also," Castillo said.

McCoy followed Castillo through the door, Junior behind him, to find a man circling his desk, buttoning his suit coat closed with one hand as he did, the other already extended in greeting and a broad, white-toothed smile on his face.

"Good morning, gentlemen," he said in practiced English with a Sudanese accent, shaking Castillo's hand first and moving down the line. "I'm Acting Minister of Interior Irshad Khalil. I'm most honored to meet with you. I would ask you to please make yourselves comfortable." He gestured to the three heavy, leather-cushioned chairs in front of the desk, a small round end table beside each with a pen and pad of paper. "Did Asim offer you something to drink, I hope?"

"He did indeed," Castillo said as they all took their seats and Khalil returned to his on the other side of the modest desk. "It is certainly our pleasure to finally meet you as well. It is long overdue, though I know the ambassador has met with you more than once. We were saddened by the tragic loss of Minister Mandi."

"Yes," Khalil said, making a steeple with his fingers. His face changed to what seemed most sincere grief at the mention of his predecessor's death. "He was a great man and a greater friend. He taught me so much. I'm not sure I could ever hope to fill his shoes, but I work hard to honor his memory by continuing his work for our country."

"Well, from all we've heard, you're doing amazing work."

"You are too kind," Khalil said with a humble nod.

McCoy's first take of the man was he seemed rather benign, though quite well spoken and well dressed. And, with years of reading people in far more stressful situations, he felt the man to be sincere, not at all what he'd expected.

"Your sister is quite inspiring as well, if I may say," Junior added with a nod. Then he smiled. "I have to tell you, I'm quite a fan of hers."

Khalil beamed with pride. "You can't imagine how proud I am of her. You may not know, but she is my younger sister—by two years—and yet she is my inspiration. I follow her example and work hard for our people. She is a fearless woman and one of great vision. We are all trying only to secure a prosperous future for the people of Sudan, and the friendship of your ambassador and your country is both appreciated and desperately needed. Perhaps you have come with good news regarding removal of our government's status on the list of state sponsors of terrorism? That would be good news indeed, as it would allow us to pursue corporate partnerships to begin the rebuilding of our country after the corruption and degradation of the Bashir years. While I know President Cohen has her own politics to manage, this next step is needed for us to succeed."

"That is something we all desire, including President Cohen, I assure you, but there is something you can do that will accelerate that process."

"My assistance with American interests in Sudan is always available, and free of strings, as you say, I assure you. How can my office be of assistance?"

His assistant and receptionist, Asim, returned, balancing a silver tray, with three china cups and saucers and several bottled waters. He placed a cup beside Junior and Castillo, then a cup on the minister's desk, before distributing a bottle of water to each of their guests as well.

Asim said to McCoy with a smile, "You are certain you don't wish to have a coffee or tea?"

"Yes, quite certain, but thank you," McCoy said.

Castillo watched over his shoulder as Asim left, closing the door behind him, and turned back to the minister, raising his coffee and taking a tentative sip. "Delicious," he said with a smile, then set the cup down and his face turned serious. "I'm afraid the matter we wish to discuss is a bit sensitive, and to be frank, top secret, as dramatic as that sounds."

"I'm intrigued," Khalil said, and his expression suggested as much, and perhaps genuine concern.

"As you know," Castillo continued, "the American secretary of state was kidnapped in a terror attack in Egypt."

"I'm quite aware and offer you and your country my deep condolences," Khalil said, and for a moment actually looked a bit choked up. "These are quite difficult times we live in, I'm afraid. I am so sorry that this has happened to a man who appears quite committed to helping bring peace to North Africa on behalf of his President. Your President's Nuclear-Weapon-Free Zone summit was a courageous and brilliant piece of diplomacy that should be bringing nations together, and yet—again—ideologically driven religious zealots have stolen the narrative and brought more violence to our region. It is infuriating, and one reason why Sudan has, as a people, rejected Sharia law and religious government in favor of a secular government representing all of our people. It is the only hope for a prosperous future for Sudan, but also for the region and the world."

"Minister Khalil," Castillo said, lifting his cup again. "Your passion is inspiring to me, I must say."

Again came the humble nod.

"I thank you. And I would be honored if you would call me Irshad. It is my hope we shall form a lasting friendship."

McCoy felt his boredom rising at this inane love fest Castillo had them in. As a MARSOC Marine Raider, he got the schtick—had executed it many times. He knew the value of partnerships based on real relationships, hell, he'd been exploiting the technique in Iraq just a few days ago before they jerked him out for this goat rope. But they didn't really have the time for this now, did they? He thought the plan was to squeeze this guy whom Omar had fingered, not offer the guy a back rub.

"It is because of my admiration for you that sharing this top secret information is so painful for me," Castillo said, the old spy so sincere that, had he just met the man, McCoy would have bought the act hook, line, and sinker.

"Go on," Khalil said, his face now troubled.

"We have reason to believe that Secretary Malone may be in Sudan . . ."

"What?" Khalil's shock at this, if contrived, was in McCoy's mind worthy of an Oscar. "Why on earth would you suspect this . . ." Castillo began to speak, but Khalil held up his hand. "No, no . . . of course you cannot reveal the source of your information."

"I would if I could," Castillo answered. "Military and intelligence communities have far too much power over diplomats in my opinion. That is something not unique to North Africa. But our spies and generals rarely share anything of value with diplomats such as myself."

"It is true here, as well," Khalil said, putting his coffee cup on the saucer beside him on the desk.

Junior did the same—but missed the small round table and his cup dropped to the floor and smashed into dozens of pieces.

"Grandma's ghost, look what I've done," Junior said, slipping from his chair to his hands and knees to pick up the broken shards.

"Please, it is no bother. Asim will clean it up," Khalil said with a dismissive wave.

"I'm so embarrassed. My apologies, Minister Khalil," Junior said sheepishly, reaching under his chair to pick up a piece.

"Accidents happen," Khalil said with a tight smile. "Please, you do not have to clean it."

Junior returned to his seat with an apologetic shrug to Castillo, who shook his head and closed his eyes.

Khalil summoned Asim, then returned his gaze to them. "What you have told me is disturbing. Even as we struggle and often risk our lives to save our country, there are radical elements within Sudan who still pursue their agendas using violence. If they are helping these terrorists, within our borders especially, they will be punished most harshly when we find them—and we will find them."

McCoy found himself believing the minister. He knew that torture and execution by crucifixion were both still legal under Sudanese law.

"I'm afraid it's worse than that, Minister," Castillo said. "Our intelligence people strongly believe that this may have been committed by Sudanese nationals—terrorists from your country linked to the Sudanese Islamic Front, though this is an organization I must confess I was not familiar with until the ambassador briefed us."

Khalil nodded, his eyes far away. Asim entered and began cleaning up the spilled coffee.

"A new name for an old problem," Khalil said. "SIF is the rebirth of the National Islamic Front, once swept away but now returned under new and younger leadership. Evil has many lives, unlike its victims, I'm afraid."

"Of course," Castillo said, while Junior dabbed at his slacks with a ball of paper towels Asim had given him.

Asim turned to Junior. "Another cup of coffee, sir?"

"No," Castillo answered for Junior, glaring at the spook and shaking his head.

"No, thank you," Junior agreed.

Asim nodded and left and Castillo's face became more solemn still.

"I'm afraid it has been suggested that there may even be links to some within the provisional government."

"I am sorry to hear that, but I'm not shocked, I'm afraid. Change takes time and courage and weeding out bad elements is an imperfect process."

"Can you help us?"

"I am willing to, but how?"

"Perhaps, through your position in this office, you can shake some trees in your own intelligence community and see if there is any information at all you can find that will help us locate our secretary of state."

"I will quietly see what I can learn, of course, but understand we are still a fractured government and there may yet be pockets of resistance and corruption within our walls. To not alert the terrorists holding Secretary of State Malone, I must keep the knowledge within very trusted circles."

"That would be most appreciated," Castillo said. He rose and extended his hand to Khalil, who rose and shook it. "I would like to offer that, if we can locate the secretary, we conduct a joint operation for his rescue, which will afford us the opportunity to give credit for the rescue to your government and, I am sure, removal of your watch list status would follow soon after."

"That would be appreciated," Khalil said with a slight bow, "but understand I will do this because it is right and because we simply must extinguish these radical terrorists from our country if we are to survive."

"It has been a true honor to meet you," Castillo said, bowing slightly himself. "And please let your sister know, at least unofficially, that we are rooting for her and know she could lead your country to a better future."

"I will tell her, and she will be flattered and honored."

"Now, that's from me personally, and not an official statement from the United States, you understand," Castillo added, his face that of a nervous government diplomat who had clearly overstepped and feared consequences. "It's important that you know that—I could get in big trouble."

"Of course," Khalil said with a smile.

Junior handed a card to Khalil.

"You can reach me at this number twenty-four hours a day and I can have Mr. Whittaker on the phone in minutes."

"Charles," Castillo corrected with another bow of his head.

"Thank you, Charles. I will call you the moment I have any pertinent information on the secretary."

McCoy wisely held his tongue, waiting to share his feeling on just how useless he thought this evolution had been until they were back in the lead Land Cruiser. He followed Castillo out of the office, giving a nod to the man at the reception desk, and down the hall to the world's slowest elevator. Minutes later, all three men slid into the SUV with Wardi at the wheel, Castillo and McCoy in the back, and Junior up front, beside his friend.

"Grandma's ghost?" Castillo said, cocking an eyebrow at the spook.

Junior laughed. "I was in character. Whatcha gonna do?"

"You guys played that differently than I expected," McCoy grumbled, in no mood for ass-grabbing banter. "I thought we were squeezing this guy for information, not kissing his ass every which way to Sunday. What the hell good did any of that do?"

"More than you might think," Junior said, turning in his seat, still wearing a self-congratulatory grin. "In my experience, it's more important to hear what an official like Khalil says after the American diplomats leave his office than what he says to their faces."

"Great," McCoy said. "And how the hell are we going to do that?"

"With the four listening devices I planted—one in the reception area, one on Khalil's desk, one under my chair, and one under the side table." Junior put a finger to his ear where the tiny transceiver rested. "We up, Ani?"

"Yeah, gonna stream to you directly. Give me a second."

"When did you . . . ?" He then pictured the spy on his knee beside the desk cleaning up broken china. He had not seen him do anything that looked like planting a bug—much less four.

"This ain't my first rodeo, dude," Junior said.

"I know on the surface that encounter felt benign and friendly," Castillo said, "but believe me, right now Khalil is feeling pressure. Sometimes waltzing like we just did is more effective than squeezing his balls as federal agents."

"When did this little plan come together?" McCoy asked, irritated as hell now.

"After the kids went to bed, the grown-ups stayed up and brainstormed," Ani said in his ear with a chuckle.

"So, boss," McCoy said, turning to Castillo and containing his anger as best he could. "How about next time you keep me read in to what we're doing, huh? I can be way more help that way."

"That's fair," Castillo said with a conciliatory smile. "But you're here to learn as well."

"As a part of the team," McCoy said, his voice a tight string.

"You're right," Castillo said, his blue eyes nonetheless amused. "I'm sorry," he added, but his voice didn't sound very apologetic. "Won't happen again."

McCoy shook his head. There was plenty of sophomoric bullshit and screwing around in his MARSOC team, but not when on mission, for Pete's sake.

"Hey, guys," Ani said, "I'm gonna monitor and record all four devices, but only live stream the best transmitter to you. Since we have multiple bugs, I can patch any gaps in the recording from low gain situations or signal interruption using timestamps."

"Check," Castillo said. He looked at Junior. "You and Wardi plant yourselves somewhere up here in front and we'll take the other SUV around back." He opened his door. "Gonna grab us some coffee on the way, though. Want anything?"

Junior shook his head. "Hate having to pee," he said, suggesting to McCoy they intended this to be a long evolution.

CHAPTER TWENTY-TWO

McCoy stifled a yawn, making his ears pop, and listened to yet another of the most boring conversations in the world—at least to those outside the adrenaline-neutralizing world of government bureaucracy. That all the conversations were being conducted in Sudanese Arabic made it a thousand times more painful. The Marine Raider in him wanted to bail something terrible, but instead he shifted in his seat and stretched his back. They'd been spying on Khalil all day since their morning meeting and so far nothing damning or insightful had come to light.

"Isn't this great?" Junior said in his ear from the other SUV. "It's like we're still sitting in Khalil's office. Some for real James Bond Q-level tech, right?"

McCoy couldn't help but laugh. The strange spook had irritated the hell out of him the first twenty-four hours, but now Junior's

Excellent Adventure demeanor was having a calming effect on McCoy, instead of just pissing him off. He rolled his head slowly, working out some kinks in his neck. At least they'd changed into jeans and open-collared short-sleeve shirts, so he was more comfortable than he'd been in the suit he'd worn posing as a member of the diplomatic corps during their meeting.

McCoy turned to Castillo in the back of the Land Cruiser.

"You think we're on the wrong trail?" he asked.

"Don't know yet," Castillo said, no apparent concern for the timer that McCoy felt counting down to zero on the secretary of state. "Sometimes these things take a while."

"The sec state doesn't have a while," McCoy grumbled, and now Castillo gave him his full attention. "I assumed, after our meeting, this guy would have been making a furious series of calls if he was involved, but even if he wasn't, the carrot you dangled should have had him contacting resources to gather information for us. But he's not doing any of that. It sounds to me like Khalil is just going about his ordinary day. Omar was full of shit. Khalil is just what he seems—an honest, hardworking, reformist bureaucrat."

"Hard to find an honest politician in any country," Junior said. "Even more improbable in Sudan."

"I'm just sayin' we offered quite a political reward to this guy if he could get us some real intel, or, if he was dirty, an incentive to bolt or at least notify his accomplices that we're on to him. He's done nothing of the sort over the last six hours. He's either a legit bureaucrat or one cool, calm sonuvabitch under pressure, and a hell of an actor."

"That it? That's all you got?" Castillo said, with that irritating smile.

"I guess," McCoy relented. He gazed out the window at the cars packed on Gama'a Avenue and a thought occurred to him. "Unless he knows we bugged his office? Maybe he found the devices?"

"Nah," Junior said. "The bugs I planted are state of the art micro-micro tech. Tiny as hell and made of biological material undetectable on a sweep. These would hold up in our own CIA headquarters, so this guy ain't finding 'em. And they're auto-degradable, so in thirty-six hours they'll be gone without a trace."

McCoy sighed. He had no idea what biological material in a listening device implied, or how the hell they would be "auto-degradable," but he grudgingly admitted to himself that he trusted Junior.

It's not that Khalil had done nothing—he had made a call to a general in Sudanese military intelligence, asking for help finding information for the Americans. He'd also asked for a report on anything available on recent activities or communications from the Sudanese Islamic Front that might indicate they could be involved. The conversation had suggested the two men were good friends and that Khalil had absolute trust in the general. But that had been well over five hours ago. In the time since, Khalil had worked tirelessly at his desk on conference calls and meetings related to typical Ministry of Interior government issues. One of the bugs, installed on a chair, had been moved to what they assumed was a conference room. This device transmitted an hour-long conversation during a budget meeting, which Khalil had not attended, and had otherwise been silent.

If Khalil was their only lead in Sudan, then Malone was as good as dead.

"He's taking a call," Ani said in his ear, her voice suggesting she was perhaps as bored as he, but at least a bit more focused. "Streaming his side to you, but he's not on speaker so you won't hear the other half. That reminds me, we should really get something so we can listen on the phone lines. Bet CIA station here could hook us up."

"Yeah, maybe. If this goes anywhere," Castillo answered. "They're probably listening to most of these guys already."

McCoy thought that maybe the old man was starting to see this wasn't working out as well as hoped. Or maybe he finally needed to pee after three cups of coffee. The dude was a friggin' camel.

"Laysat hunak hajat lilqalaq," Khalil said in the audio Ani streamed into his ear. Other than an almost undetectable echo, Khalil could have been sitting in the car with them.

Junior's spy tech was incredible.

A pause in the transmission lingered as the caller spoke, responding to Khalil's assurance there was nothing to worry about.

"Limadha la naltaqi."

Why don't we meet?

"Sa'arek fi almakan almuetad baed eshr daqayiq."

"Well," Junior said in his ear, "I don't know where the usual place is, but he's saying they're meeting there in ten minutes, so it can't be far."

"Game on," Castillo said, tapping the driver, Shaker, on the shoulder and pointing north. "Khalil is going to meet someone. Why don't you head up the west access road. We'll see if we pick him up there. Watch the east side, Junior. He'll more likely come out there if he's going to his car, but he might have a driver pick him up out front."

Shaker perked up at this and nodded enthusiastically. After hours of controlled silence and breaks only to fetch Castillo more coffee, he was finally getting to do something. Moments later they turned onto Gama'a Avenue heading west and skirted across both lanes to make the right turn onto the one-way access road to the government complex that housed the Ministry of Interior, the parallel access road to their left the exit after a loop just beside the Nile River. Just as they rolled past the main entrance they'd entered that morning, Junior called out contact with Khalil.

"I got him, boss," Junior said. "Coming out the east entrance alone. No briefcase or backpack or anything. Doesn't look distressed and he's not in a hurry."

"Okay, we'll loop around and hold at Gama'a Avenue until you see which way he goes."

"Cool," Junior said.

"Sitrep on the eyes in the sky, Junior?" Castillo prompted.

"Nothing yet, I'm afraid. I'll have satellite access beginning in another hour or so, but the request required some serious retasking. We'll have it soon. Sorry."

"No problem," Castillo said.

"Okay, so our boy is not headed to a car in the rear lot," Junior said. "Crossing the lot and now cutting across the road and headed between my building here and the one north. There's, like, a big courtyard between the two buildings. He could be meeting there. You want me to pick him up on foot?"

"Yes . . . go," Castillo said. "We'll circle back to the corner of Gama'a and Al Qasr Avenue in case he continues east, but let us know if we should reposition east of you if he stops."

"Gotcha," Junior said, instead of the "Roger" or "Check" McCoy was accustomed to.

"Maintain a decent setback, since he would definitely recognize you," Castillo cautioned.

"Yeah . . . duh," Junior said, and McCoy shook his head and suppressed a grin. What a band of misfits.

As they turned onto Gama'a and headed east, McCoy felt the familiar tingle as his mind and body sharpened for action. They passed the Sudan Post building on their left, and he saw the other Land Cruiser just up from the corner. He felt with his forearm for the comforting bulge of the Sig Sauer pistol in his waistband.

"Okay," Junior called out softly, "so he's crossing the courtyard and not looking like he's stopping. You guys might pick him up coming out the east side between the buildings, but I'm still on him."

Castillo tapped the driver on the shoulder.

"Turn left here and find a place to stop."

Off to his right, McCoy saw a sprawling green park just outside the grounds of the Republican Palace, which he could see in all its splendor farther east, the nearly as beautiful support building closer to them, both nestled along the Nile.

Shaker brought the Toyota to a stop, then pulled a pair of binoculars from the glove box and passed them back to Castillo.

"Great, thanks," Castillo said, pressing them to his eyes. "Yeah, that's Khalil. Hold at the corner. I got him crossing the street now."

"Okie dokie," Junior said.

McCoy shook his head at the goofy spook and looked across the road at a large gazebo with a blue glass roof partially blocking his view of the palace. Beyond, he saw a fountain statue that marked the entrance to the grounds, with a small but attractive park surrounding the entrance along the road on both sides. As he watched, Khalil bent south on his course, headed toward the gazebo.

"He's gonna meet whoever this is either by that gazebo-looking structure or maybe in the park across from the entrance."

"Looks right to me," Junior agreed. "Coming up on his ten minutes, so that makes the most sense, unless he hops in a car with the guy nearby."

McCoy looked at Castillo and raised both eyebrows.

Castillo nodded. "Go. But don't get seen, McCoy, or the whole thing is blown."

McCoy nodded and exited the Land Cruiser, putting on a gray ball cap and slightly hunching his shoulders. The heat hit him immediately, and he felt sweat bead up on his neck and face. He crossed the street, angling south toward the corner of Gama'a Avenue beyond the modern building with the impressive blue glass roof. He walked casually, playing the part of the tourist, looking up and admiring the architecture of the building beside the palace grounds, hands in his pockets.

He figured odds were very low that Khalil would recognize him. McCoy looked quite different than the suited diplomat who had said almost nothing in the meeting six hours ago. He slipped on a pair of Oakley sunglasses just to be sure.

"I've got a parabolic in the Toyota to listen with," Junior said. "Want me to go back and get it?"

"I'm not sure we'll have angles to listen from here, either," Castillo said. "Oh, shit. He turned and is headed right toward you. They're not meeting in the building."

"No problem," McCoy said, confident that he could go unnoticed in the crowd on the street. Nonetheless, he angled east up onto the patio of the building, pulling out his phone as if to take a picture.

"Just passed behind you."

He said nothing but glanced over his shoulder, holding the phone up as if taking a selfie, and watched Khalil continue to the corner. The man had lost the tie, but still wore his suit coat despite the heat, the temperature creeping into the high nineties. He watched the man, who walked casually and without apparent suspicion, to the corner, crossing the street and heading into the half-circle-shaped park, bisected by Al Qasr Avenue, which dead-ended at the entrance to the Republican Palace into two quarter-circle parks. Once he watched Khalil shuffle onto the path leading into the park, he hustled to the corner, looking for a break in traffic to cross.

He circled the outside of the park along the road, jammed with parked cars, until he reached a gap in the trees along the periphery. He watched as Khalil took a seat, hands in his lap and back straight, on a bench by himself. He certainly seemed to be waiting for someone, but again his posture and face were not that of a man prepping for a covert meeting, scanning about for threats or to see who might be watching.

"Eyes on," McCoy whispered. "But I can't get close enough to hear anything without being seen."

"Let's just hold and see what happens," Castillo cautioned.

"He could be meeting his mistress for all we know," Ani chimed in.

McCoy resisted the urge to pace back and forth along the break in the trees, aware that movement caught the eye far more readily than a static figure. He strained to see beyond the bench, where another line of trees ran behind Khalil. It seemed like the distance between the back of the bench within those trees along Al Qasr Avenue would be far less than watching from where he was. Perhaps he would be able to hear something from that location.

"I'm gonna reposition," he said.

He took the silence as consent, and began a leisurely stroll around the half circle until he hit Al Qasr, then he turned left, heading north and behind the bench where Khalil sat. Ahead, he saw the impressive entrance to the Palace grounds across Gama'a

Avenue. He couldn't see Khalil through the trees, but estimated where the bench would be, checked around himself casually, and stepped off the sidewalk and into the grove of trees.

After only a dozen steps, he could make out the figure sitting on the bench—no, two figures. Whoever Khalil was meeting with had arrived. He took a knee for a moment, straining to hear the men talking. Khalil sat upright, but the other man, dressed in casual but expensive trousers and a short-sleeve oxford shirt, leaned in toward him, speaking now in a hushed tone. As he watched, Khalil reacted to something the man said, snapping his head left to face him, his expression no longer the easygoing, relaxed bureaucrat. Whatever the guy had said both surprised Khalil and pissed him off.

"Unacceptable," Khalil barked in Arabic. "Take care of this immediately!" He then grumbled something else, too quiet for McCoy to hear.

McCoy rose from his knee, slowly and quietly, and took a few shorter, careful steps, bringing himself closer to the men on the bench. The second man was asking something else, his head again close to Khalil, and still he couldn't hear him.

". . . everyone he talks to . . ." Khalil said, just loud enough for him to hear, although it was difficult to parse because of the man's Sudanese dialect and accent.

He took one more long, tentative step, and to his horror, a twig snapped underneath his boot, his eyes on the two men instead of the ground. Instantly, he kicked his legs out behind him, burpee style, catching himself silently in a push-up plank and lowering himself to the ground as the two men turned to look in his direction. He watched them bob back and forth, probing in his direction, but apparently didn't see him. Then Khalil stood, pulled a thick envelope from his inside coat pocket, and handed it to the man, who rose beside him.

They exchanged words, which McCoy could not make out, and the other man took the envelope and disappeared it into the front pocket of his pants.

Without a farewell, Khalil headed north, back the way he came, while the other man headed to the path off to McCoy's right, leading back to Al Qasr. McCoy waited, moving south now with less stealth, to open some distance before calling in.

"Guys, it looks like Khalil just paid cash to a rough-looking dude to take care of something for him. No idea what it was, but he looked pretty pissed off, I can tell you. I couldn't hear much more, but whatever the issue was, it had him in a tizzy."

"Where are they now?" Castillo asked.

"Khalil is headed back toward . . ."

"Wait, I got him," Castillo said. "Heading toward me. Can you stay on the other guy? Khalil looks like he might be heading back the way he came."

"On it," McCoy said, turning back to the east and hustling through the trees on a diagonal to keep some distance between him and the other man.

He should emerge onto Al Qasr Avenue right . . .

McCoy sidestepped onto the road between the parked cars, pulling out his phone as if looking at a map or something.

. . . now.

"Got him," he mumbled.

"Khalil just passed us on our side of the street, headed for you, Junior," Castillo said.

"I'm ready," Junior came back.

McCoy watched his target cross Al Qasr Avenue and pull keys from his pocket. He pressed the fob and the taillights of a black sedan blinked twice.

"Tango One is heading to a car," McCoy said, feeling new urgency. "Come get me or we'll lose him."

"Coming now," Castillo said.

He watched the man slip into the driver's seat of the sedan, his foot still on the pavement as he pulled the envelope from his pocket. The man leaned in, a leg out the door, perhaps putting the envelope into the glove box. Then he closed the door and the brake lights lit as he fired up the ignition.

"Hurry," McCoy said tightly.

"Coming to you now . . ."

The sedan pulled out of the spot and McCoy heard the Land Cruiser approaching behind him. He turned and hustled to the SUV, double-parked now just yards away in the turn, and out of view of the sedan. He hopped into the backseat as Shaker pulled the truck forward, slowly.

"There," McCoy said, pointing at the sedan at the corner, the left blinker on. "That's him."

"Khalil is cutting back through the courtyard again, headed back to the Ministry of Interior, I'm guessing," Junior reported.

"Check," Castillo said. "Tail him wherever he goes. We're going to stay on Tango One."

"Will do, boss," the spook replied.

"Nice work, kid. What did you hear, if anything?" Castillo asked.

"I didn't get much beside what I reported—that Khalil is pissed off about something and gave the dude what looked like an envelope of cash and with what I understood to be orders to take care of the situation quickly." McCoy rubbed his bearded chin. "Maybe we shook the right tree after all."

"Maybe," Castillo said, but he was smiling. "Or he could be paying that guy to pick up his dry cleaning for all we know. But I doubt it. I'm not a believer in coincidences."

Shaker merged the truck onto Gama'a Avenue now, a few cars behind the sedan.

Castillo was right. The conversation he caught could mean absolutely anything, but his instincts told him this guy was a target worth following. Anything was better than sitting for hours parked outside Khalil's office listening to bureaucratic dribble.

More important, he didn't believe in coincidences, either.

CHAPTER TWENTY-THREE

Toyota Land Cruiser
Westbound on Morada Road
Khartoum, Sudan
March 20, 5:20 p.m.

From where he sat in the Toyota Land Cruiser's rear captain's seat, McCoy leaned in so he could see out the windshield. He kept his gaze fixed on the taillights of the black sedan three cars ahead as they crossed the White Nile on Victory Bridge heading west.

Shaker continued to impress McCoy with his considerable aptitude for tailing the target vehicle. Not only did he maintain a proper standoff distance, he didn't panic if he lost sight of the target for brief periods when interfering vehicles changed lanes or maneuvered in disadvantageous ways. Tailing a vehicle without aerial backup—satellite or drone support overhead—was a stressful and difficult operation. Most people, even pros, eventually got flustered and screwed up. With Shaker, so far so good.

"We're leaving Khartoum and heading into Umm Durmān," Shaker said, changing lanes and accelerating slightly to close the range to the sedan, which he'd let open up on the bridge. "Umm Durmān is a very large city, over two and half million people, that is growing very fast. Khartoum expansion is limited to the east by the Blue Nile and the west by the White Nile, so all of the growth is either west in Umm Durmān into the desert or north of the confluence in North Khartoum."

"Any guesses where this guy might be going?" Castillo asked.

"No. Umm Durmān is a huge, sprawling place. The farther west you travel the lower the economic status. Much of the city is what we call third-class residential—very poor areas and slums. This place has become a mecca for refugees, especially from South Sudan and Darfur, but at its heart Umm Durmān is an Arab city, which sometimes leads to conflict."

McCoy resisted the urge to look out the side windows as they continued west into the heart of the city on the main east–west thoroughfare—a four-lane paved highway that seemed to be increasingly populated by buses on this side of the Nile.

"When do we get eyes, Junior?" McCoy asked.

"Soon, bro," Junior promised in his ear. "I just checked back and we'll have Ani up on the satellite feed in thirty or forty-five minutes."

McCoy clenched his jaw. *Just exactly too late.*

"He just cut in front of that bus," Castillo said, urgency in his voice.

"Yes, yes, I know," Shaker said. "Don't worry."

"Watch that van. He's gonna cut us off and we'll lose the target."

Shaker accelerated and blasted his horn just as a dilapidated van attempted to cut them off and pass a bus in front of them. The van jerked violently right, back into its lane a split second before what would have been a collision with their Land Cruiser.

McCoy scanned the traffic ahead, looking for the taillights they'd been following.

"Got him," he said, locking his gaze on the target vehicle just before it maneuvered again. "He just moved back into the passing lane—the third car ahead of us."

Back at the safe house in Khartoum, Ani was still working as their coordinator. Without eyes in the sky, there wasn't much she could do. Nonetheless, she was tracking them via GPS, providing helpful details as she could.

"Hey, guys," Ani said in McCoy's earbud. "Looks like the highway you're on is about to dogleg right in a couple hundred yards. Get ready."

"Check," he replied, keeping his eyes on the target sedan. "Ani says a dogleg turn coming up in about two hundred meters, Shaker."

Shaker, who was not wearing an earbud, showed his expertise once again by closing range to the target and maneuvering ahead of one of the interfering vehicles prior to the turn.

"Got him," McCoy said as they came out of the turn. "He's still in the left lane."

"I see him," Shaker said, his gaze fixed dead ahead.

"You've got a roundabout coming up in three hundred meters," Ani reported. "If you've been made and your tango wants to ditch, that would be the place for him to do it."

"Looks like we've got a roundabout ahead," Castillo said.

"Yes, yes," Shaker said. "I'm going to close range."

"Good."

"If he circles completely, do you want me to follow him around or take one of the spurs?" Shaker asked.

"How many intersecting spurs?" Castillo asked.

"Three," Shaker said. "The first one continues north. If we pass it, the next one exits west, and if we skip that one, we are returning back to this road."

"Just follow him, whatever he does."

"Even if he loops around to check for a tail?" Shaker asked, surprise in his voice. "I would normally pull off and try to reengage."

"We can't afford to play games since we don't have backup," Castillo said, turning in his seat to look at McCoy. "Do you agree, McCoy?"

McCoy stared at Castillo for a beat, shocked that the old man had asked his opinion on the matter.

Now that's a first.

"Agreed."

"Okay, you're the boss," Shaker said as the black sedan entered the roundabout in the left lane. He followed suit, also entering the traffic scheme in the left lane, two cars back.

"He's exiting west," McCoy said.

"Okay, he's taking the Libya Street exit," Shaker said, steering around the circle in trail. "I thought he might . . ."

"What's down this road?" McCoy asked.

"Tens of thousands of shanty houses," Shaker said. "And the desert."

They trailed the target for four miles until the paved section of Libya Street ended and the sedan continued west on a dirt road.

"Kill our daytime running lights," Castillo said.

Shaker did as instructed, just as the only remaining car between them and the target vehicle braked and exited north into one of the neighborhoods.

"It's going to get tricky to follow him now," Shaker said. "This area is very crowded and confusing. There is no formal organization. Many small streets and they do not have names. If I don't stay close, I will lose him, but if I do, he will know we are following him. An impossible situation, I think."

"He's right," Ani said over the comms channel. "You should see what this area looks like on Google Maps. It's a warren of nearly identical housing blocks that just goes on and on and on. It's going to be really easy to get lost in there."

Castillo didn't respond for an uncomfortably long pause. "We need eyes in the sky," he murmured, then louder, with formality, he said, "Three, One—we need eyes ASAP. This is ridiculous."

Junior, who was tailing Khalil in the other Land Cruiser, answered promptly. "The request is in and people are working on it, Charley, but there is nothing available right now. It's coming, like I told Pick. You'll be the first to know when it happens, promise."

"I've been in situations like this before," McCoy said. "We use the shitty, dusty dirt road to our advantage. Don't keep eyes on him, just on his dust cloud from a proper standoff. I've seen almost no other vehicles. Follow the cloud, which will keep us masked in his rearview as well. We tail him until his *second* turn, then I'll get out and spot, following him on foot, while you guys loop around the perimeter."

"Okay, we try this," Shaker said, maintaining his standoff as the black sedan headed west, throwing up a billowing cloud of fine dust behind it.

Several minutes later, the target sedan—or at least its towering plume of dust—turned south and disappeared around a corner.

"Here we go," Shaker said, accelerating toward the street where the target had turned. "First turn."

McCoy reached into the back and grabbed a hard case, which he hoisted onto his lap. He undid the plastic clasps, flipped the lid open, and pulled a Sig MCX Virtus from the foam cradle inside. He set the assault rifle down on the floor between the captain chairs, chucked the hardcase behind his seat, and nodded at Castillo.

"Just in case," he said, patting the butt stock.

Shaker slowed and turned left at the street where McCoy had seen the sedan turn moments earlier. As soon as they rounded the corner, McCoy scanned the narrow street, but didn't see the target sedan's glowing red taillights anywhere through the dust.

"Shit," Shaker said. "He turned somewhere."

"It's okay," McCoy said. "We advance until the dust cloud fades."

"I'll look right, you look left," Castillo said.

"Check," McCoy said, and started scanning each intersecting cross street on the driver's side as Castillo did the same on the passenger side. "Got him," he said six blocks later. "He's a hundred yards down on the left . . . appears to have parked."

Instead of braking, Shaker coasted past the turn and only braked once he'd cleared the line of sight. He turned left at the next intersection and headed east on a parallel street, one block south of the target street.

"Let me out at the next block," McCoy said. "You guys loop around to the east side. I'll converge from the west."

Shaker stopped at the next intersection and McCoy hopped out, dusty gravel crunching underfoot. A pungent and cloying mélange of odors flooded his nose with his first inhale—urine-soaked earth, charcoal smoke, rust, decomposing garbage—the universal smell of extreme poverty. He pushed the thought from his mind.

"Hey, kid," Castillo said before he shut the door.

"Yeah?"

"Observation only. No Rambo shit, got it?"

"Got it," McCoy said with a wry grin, holstered his weapon, and shut the door.

Ani's description of this neighborhood as an endless warren was spot-on. He'd been in similar places in Iraq, but nothing of this scale. The shantytown was laid out in a grid pattern of rectangular housing blocks. He estimated each block at approximately four hundred feet long by one hundred feet wide, with residences back to back on the north and south sides and lined up in parallel rows east to west. Most homes were constructed of mud and bricks, but some were made with cinder blocks and concrete. They had corrugated metal roofs and open-air cutouts in place of windows. Every lot was enclosed by a six-foot-tall mud-brick wall that abutted and connected to the neighbor's wall, effectively creating a continuous perimeter wall that enclosed the entire block of shanty homes.

The setting sun made the dust-filled air take on an alien planet–like orange hue. The streets were deserted. But the sounds of communal living—a baby crying, music playing, a couple arguing—belied what his eyes could not see. Wandering the slums of Umm Durmān, he was definitely not alone. Hidden eyes watched him, and he knew to operate accordingly.

Leaving his weapon holstered, he ran north along one of the walls, ducking his head just enough so as not to be seen from the other side. When he reached the corner, he stopped and peered around the edge, spying the rear of the target sedan parked and idling in front of one of the houses only forty feet away.

"One, Two—I hold the target idling in front of a house," he reported. "Too dark to confirm number of passengers and I can't see into the house because of the perimeter wall. I'm going to observe from the corner."

"Roger that, Two," came Castillo's reply in his ear. "You should see us crossing, south to north, one block east of the target."

"Check," McCoy said, seeing the white Land Cruiser drift across the intersection.

"We're going to loop around to the west to pick you up and continue pursuit when the target leaves."

"Copy."

It killed him not being able to see or hear what was going on inside, but this was as close as he dared to go. He glanced over his shoulder, checking his six. Seeing nothing of concern, he returned his focus to the target car.

A few seconds later, two men emerged from the shanty, stepping out of an opening in the mud-brick wall. The taller of the two men—the target—handed something to the other man, a smaller envelope than the one he'd received from Khalil.

A stack of bills, McCoy guessed, because the recipient stuffed the rectangular wad into his pocket.

The taller man clasped the younger man on the shoulder, said something, then climbed into the sedan.

"The target appears to have just made a cash payment to whoever lives in the house . . . target just got into the driver's seat," McCoy reported. "Tango Two is heading back inside."

"Copy," Castillo said. "Stay put. We're going to loop around and pick you up."

"Hold," McCoy said, with a surge of adrenaline supercharging his senses. "Tango Two just stepped out of the house with a rifle. Shit, we might be made. He's heading my way."

"We're at the northwest corner," Castillo came back. "One block north of your position. We're going to shoot the gap and pick you up."

"Negative. You'll have to cross an open line of fire to get to me.

Let's just see what he does," McCoy said, glancing past the approaching shooter, watching as the target sedan drove away.

"Target is exfiling east. Advise you follow. I got this guy."

"Negative," Castillo came back, the rest of the message implicit: *We're not leaving you behind.*

McCoy whirled, looking for cover. On the opposite side of the street, he saw an opening on the east face of the perimeter wall encircling the cluster of homes that formed the next block. He sprinted across the street, ducked through the doorway-sized gap, and spun so his back was pressed against the inside of the wall. The shanty house inside the wall—which couldn't be any larger than five hundred square feet—was dark and McCoy didn't hear any voices inside. For numerous reasons, he resisted the compulsion to pull his weapon.

"Tango Two just crossed the intersection, walking west," Castillo reported in McCoy's ear. "He didn't even glance in our direction when he crossed. Dude looks like a man on a mission. You're clear to tail him now."

McCoy pivoted around the corner, clearing north and then south before stepping out to pursue the would-be shooter. He jogged north a half a block to the intersection, stopping at the corner. Straight ahead, he spied their Land Cruiser idling in the shadows with its headlights and running lights off as the shadows lengthened in the darkening streets. He exhaled, glanced around the corner, and jerked his head back. His brain quickly reconstructed the details of the split second's worth of data his eyes had taken in.

The shooter was now a hundred feet away, his back to McCoy, and walking west. He held what McCoy guessed was an AK-47 in a combat carry and looked like a modern-day outlaw walking the dusty deserted streets of some dilapidated cowboy town.

McCoy glanced east next, checking to see if the target sedan was still in play, but the familiar red taillights were now gone and the dust had settled slowly back into the street.

Satisfied with the tactical picture, he stepped around the corner and into trail. He hugged the mud-brick wall on the south side of the street—keeping track of every gate and hollow opening he could dive through for cover, should the shooter suddenly whirl and decide to strafe his six. McCoy slipped his hand under his untucked shirt and let it rest on the grip of his pistol as he took long, swift strides, slowly closing the gap between himself and his quarry.

"What's he doing?" Castillo asked in McCoy's ear.

"Still heading west," he said, glancing over his shoulder to check his six.

Clear, the Marine Raider in his head reported automatically.

At the next intersection, the mark turned south.

"Tango Two just turned south," he reported, accelerating to a jog that he held until he reached the cross street. He stopped at the corner and glanced left, just in time to catch a glimpse of the man disappearing around the corner of the next block's perimeter wall.

"Tango Two just doglegged west," he said. "I've closed to within half a block."

McCoy checked his six again, then cleared the street north and south for possible threats before rounding the corner in pursuit. Quickstepping now, he crossed the street on a diagonal vector to the next corner. But before he could glance around the wall, the staccato crack of gunfire echoed in the night and sent an adrenaline dump of liquid lightning into his veins. Muscles primed and senses on high alert, he pulled his Sig out and dropped into a tactical crouch. He rounded the corner, weapon out and held at a forty-five-degree down angle.

Eighty feet ahead, the gunman ran out of a house on the north side of the block, pausing to look right and left on the street. He locked eyes with McCoy and, despite the low ambient light, McCoy could make out surprise on the man's face. Years of operational experience took over, and McCoy sighted on the shooter, his iron sights hovering center mass. Instead of bringing his rifle up to fire at McCoy, the young man turned and fled west, running away into the long shadows.

"Stop!" McCoy hollered in Arabic, but the shooter just kept running.

"Sitrep?" Castillo said in his ear.

"I think Tango Two just capped someone. That cash money he took from Tango One must have been payment for a hit," he said, sprinting toward the house where the shooter had just exited. "I'm gonna check it out."

Twenty seconds later, he reached the place along the perimeter wall where he thought the shooter had exited. At the same time, the gunman reached the next intersection and rounded the bend, disappearing out of sight.

"Shooter is headed north, one block up," McCoy said, then hesitated for a split second, deciding if he should continue the chase or investigate the scene, before opting for the latter. Weapon raised, he ducked through the opening in the perimeter wall and stepped into the enclosed dirt courtyard. A single-story, mud-and-brick hut with a metal roof took up half of the lot. Inside the hut's doorway, an amber light flickered. Leading with his Sig, McCoy stepped through the doorway into the shanty where he found two bodies sprawled on the dirt floor. A young African male lay facedown and motionless, with half the back of his skull missing. A young woman, possibly the dead man's wife, was in her death throes. She had multiple gunshot wounds to the chest and McCoy knew immediately that she was bleeding out.

"*Saeidni,*" she said in a hiss, bloody bubbles forming at her lips as she pleaded for help.

McCoy took a knee beside her and collected her hand in his. Meeting her terrified gaze, he spoke to her in calm, soothing Arabic. "Do not be afraid. You are a daughter of Allah. Love and good fortune await you in the next life."

She took a shuddering breath, but the fear left her eyes.

"I see him," she said, her lips curling into a bloody smile. "It's beautiful . . ."

She squeezed his hand tight for a moment and her fingers went limp inside his grip.

"Tango Two capped two people—a male and a female, both young, under twenty, is my guess," McCoy reported, getting to his feet.

He pulled his phone and snapped pictures of their faces. He scanned the inside of the little hut for anything of interest: a pair of folding chairs, a plastic crate with dishes and a couple of pots, a dirty mattress on the floor, a kerosene lamp, and an AK-47 leaning against the back wall.

"You need to get out of there," Castillo said in his ear.

"Roger that."

McCoy slipped the Sig into his waistband holster and walked out of the house, across the little yard, and out a doorway in the perimeter wall onto the street. Where moments ago the street had been deserted, now a small crowd of locals had gathered. He counted eight—five males, three females—and they did not look happy. In his peripheral vision, he saw more figures stepping out of doorways onto the street.

"What you do here?" the largest of the men said to him in broken English.

"It wasn't me," McCoy replied, meeting the African's reproachful gaze. "Another man entered this house with a rifle and killed two people inside. I was following him. I can show you where the killer lives."

The crowd was twelve now and the men were drifting into a circular formation around him.

Shit, this is not good . . .

McCoy repeated what he'd just said in English in Arabic to the crowd.

The ringleader, looking unconvinced, motioned for one of the other men to go inside the house and take a look.

"I'm telling you, it wasn't me," McCoy said in Arabic, raising both hands in a placating gesture.

"They're murdered," the house-checker yelled, running back out onto the street.

The news lit a fire in the crowd. Their expressions morphed into outrage and everyone started shouting at him, their voices a discordant, angry chorus.

"Listen to me," McCoy said, turning in a slow circle. "I did not do this."

"Liar!" the ringleader said.

"Murderer!" someone else yelled.

Something smacked McCoy in the back of his head so hard he saw stars.

A rock, he realized as it landed beside his foot.

They rushed him as he belatedly reached for his Sig. He managed to get it out of the holster, but that was all. The body blows came hard and fast and the next thing he knew he was on the ground, curled on his side in the dirt, protecting his head with his arms as they kicked and beat him.

As the blows rained down, a single thought reverberated in his head.

I'm going to die . . .

CHAPTER TWENTY-FOUR

"There!" Castillo hollered at Shaker, pointing through the windshield at the mob of twenty or more people. He couldn't see McCoy, but had no doubt the kid was the object of the kicks and blows being delivered to the middle of the tight crowd, dust rising from the center. The Land Cruiser slid to a stop, and Castillo snatched the Sig Sauer assault rifle, opened the door, and stepped out onto the running board. Castillo saw a tall black man standing in the middle of the circle raise a long-handled axe over his head.

Oh, shit!

"Stop!" he screamed in Arabic and fired a burst of 5.56 into the air. "Stop or I'll shoot."

The tall man with the axe stopped mid-swing and turned to look at him in surprise.

Castillo placed the red dot of his holographic sight directly in the center of the man's face.

The man, apparently no stranger to having a gun pointed at him, did not panic. Slowly, grudgingly, he raised his arms in surrender—axe still in his hand—and fixed Castillo with a *fuck you* stare.

The crowd, transfixed by the standoff and battle of wills, didn't move.

"Go back to your homes," Castillo ordered, using his command voice.

When no one moved, he shifted aim and fired two rounds into a mud wall beside the crowd. Jaw clenched and murder in his eyes, he swept his targeting laser across their chests and gave the command again. This time, they listened—fleeing in all directions except, gratefully, toward the Land Cruiser.

Castillo leaped off the running board, dropped into a tactical crouch and moved forward quickly toward McCoy, who still lay balled up tightly on the ground. The man with the axe stood over the Marine, defiance on his face and still in a position to deliver a death strike. Castillo stopped a few yards away and hovered his red targeting dot just above the bridge of the angry man's nose.

"Back away!" he commanded in Arabic.

The man smiled, slowly lowered the axe to his side, then sauntered off to the corner twenty yards away where he stopped and watched.

Castillo repositioned so he could keep an eye on the threat and knelt beside McCoy.

"McCoy?" he said, shaking the Marine by the shoulder.

To his relief, the kid groaned and rolled onto his back.

"Where ya been, boss?" he said, blinking, staring up at Castillo in the fading light, a bloody grin stretched across his battered face.

"We gotta go, brother," Castillo said, one hand pulling him up by his arm, the other still leveling the rifle at the axe man at the corner. "They'll be back any second and this time they'll be armed."

McCoy surged to his feet, groaning again in pain and grabbing his side where Castillo imagined he was nursing one or more broken ribs. The Marine spit blood into the dirt, and Castillo pulled the kid's arm around his neck, still keeping his rifle at the ready and scanning back and forth as they shuffled to the truck.

Just past the man holding the axe, two younger men emerged from a mud shanty, jogging with AK-47s in their hands. Castillo shoved McCoy roughly into the rear of the truck, stepped up on the running board again, and sighted on the wall just beside the armed men, firing a three-round burst that drove them back toward the shanty.

"Go!" he shouted to Shaker, ducking into his seat and slamming the door.

The Land Cruiser accelerated as Shaker turned back to the southeast, a rooster tail of dust spraying toward the man with the axe. Castillo heard gunshots as they tore away and a loud *TING* sounded as a bullet found the tailgate but didn't punch through.

"Where we go?" Shaker asked.

"Anywhere, just get us the hell out of here."

"No problem, boss," Shaker said, shooting him a relieved grin. "What about the shooter who ran away?"

Castillo cleared around the truck through the windows, then glanced back over the seat. McCoy was awake, but collapsed against the door, half on the floor and half on the left captain's seat, clutching his chest, streams of blood running down his bruised and battered face from wounds somewhere up in his hairline.

"Forget about him," he said, crawling over the center console and dropping into the seat beside McCoy. He set the Rattler onto the floor beside the seat and leaned over his comrade. "We need to get Pick back to the safe house."

Castillo leaned over his teammate, placing a hand on the Marine's shoulder.

"What's your sitrep, McCoy?" he asked. "You still in the fight?"

Castillo watched McCoy run his hands over his upper body and neck, then gently palpate his face. His right eye was almost swollen shut, but Castillo saw the pupil dilating normally in the fading light.

"Broken ribs, probably," McCoy answered, his voice strained with pain. "Otherwise good. No broken bones in my face, I don't think. Never lost consciousness, so I doubt a major head injury."

"That's good," Castillo said. "Because from what I hear, Marines don't have much in the way of spare brain cells in reserve."

This made McCoy laugh, then cough.

"Damn it! Don't make me laugh," he wheezed, wincing at the pain as he struggled into the seat.

Castillo leaned over to help him, lifting him gently into the other seat. He searched for a towel, found one behind him in the back, and cracked open a water bottle, soaking half the towel and handing it to McCoy. "Here ya go."

The Marine took the wet towel and began to dab gently at the blood and dirt on his face. McCoy managed a crooked smile, and Castillo felt an enormous weight lift off him. His teammate would be fine. "Good plan hanging back instead of following the sedan," McCoy said, the gratitude in his eyes unmistakable.

"Yeah," Castillo agreed with a tired sigh. "I get it right sometimes."

"Well, thanks for saving my ass."

"No one left behind, brother," was all Castillo could think to say. Castillo checked in with Ani and Junior, sharing what they'd learned from their misadventure in Umm Durmān. For now, he decided to leave out the part about McCoy almost being murdered by a mob.

The Land Cruiser weaved through the confusing sea of poverty that was the shantytown—or shanty *city*, Castillo supposed—of central Umm Durmān, Ani occasionally calling a turn into his ear, which he relayed to Shaker. Shaker was a skilled tactical driver, and he quietly thanked Junior in his head for putting him on the team.

As the sun dipped below the horizon behind them and the dirt road again transitioned to pavement, Castillo finally began to relax. It wouldn't be long until they were on the bridge crossing the White Nile River back to Khartoum. He glanced at McCoy, who was pressing the towel tightly against the back of his head to stem the bleeding wounds. The Marine's eyes had regained their fire and alertness. Unless the kid had some internal injury they didn't know about, they were probably out of the proverbial woods.

McCoy said, "Well, we learned one thing."

"What's that?"

"We're definitely pushing people's buttons. First the hit on Ani's apartment after we get the tip from Omar in Cairo, and now this kid and his wife get whacked right after we shook Khalil's tree."

"No coincidences," Castillo said, finishing the thought.

"No coincidences," McCoy agreed. "Maybe Khalil ordered both hits?"

Castillo shrugged. "We have to be careful not to mistake correlation for causality. We don't know what role Khalil might have in all of this. He could be a true believer working for the Saudis or the Islamic Front inside the Sudanese government. He could be a geopolitical mastermind, pulling levers and planning the next coup.

Or, most likely, he's just your everyday corrupt politician who's been taking bribes from bad guys, trying to cover his tracks, and suddenly realizes he's in over his head."

McCoy rubbed his face with his hands. "I don't know, the way Khalil behaved in Al Qasr park gave me the impression he's more than just your stereotypical bureaucrat trying to line his pockets."

"What do you mean?"

"It's just a gut feeling," McCoy said, hedging. "It's hard to explain, especially with the language barrier, but the Khalil at the park wasn't the smiling diplomat we chatted with at the Ministry of Interior. He was the boss, issuing orders. It was the way he carried himself and more so the way the guy from the sedan responded to him. I've spent a lot of hours with tribal leaders and warlords in Iraq and Afghanistan, more time than I ever thought imaginable. And what I've learned is that men in power—or, more important, men who stay in power—learn how to manage their audience. When we met with Khalil this morning, he was exactly the man he was supposed to be. He managed us during that meeting, just like we tried to manage him, and he did a bang-up job at it. Hell, after six hours of listening to him on the phone, he even had me convinced he was just a bureaucrat. But in the park, I saw a different man. The collegial bureaucrat was gone and the warlord took center stage. Now I don't know what all of that is worth . . ."

"In our business," Castillo said, interrupting him, "it's invaluable. Sure, signals intelligence is great, but what you just described is the human factor. You took a measure of the man in the park, and you saw a different side of him. That's something you can't get from a drone feed or a satellite image."

McCoy nodded, then turned and looked out the window, deep in thought.

Castillo studied the kid—no, the man—and was impressed. This was the type of thinking and gut instinct that mattered in the spy business, and especially in the Presidential Agent program, where so often you were out completely on your own. And, in his experience, it wasn't something you could teach—you either had it or you didn't.

Maybe the Marine Raider did have what it took to be the Presidential Agent . . .

Someday.

They skirted through downtown Khartoum, sneaking south on Ghaba Street to circle around a protest near the government complex, before cutting back to the east on Ahmed Khair Street into the luxury neighborhood at the fringe of the embassy district. Turning onto the street that led to their safe house, Castillo spotted the black sedan parked just ten yards from the gate to the driveway. Anger flared in his chest. The government plates on the sedan confirmed what he suspected—that the Sudanese government, and therefore Khalil, knew about their presence all along, probably even before today.

"Pull behind that sedan, Shaker," he ordered.

"Safe distance?" Shaker asked, slowing.

"No," he growled. "Right fucking behind him. Tap him if you want."

Shaker didn't tap the sedan, but did stop mere inches away. Castillo was out of the Toyota before it rocked to a stop. He walked up to the driver's door, finding only a single person in the vehicle, a Sudanese Arab in a dark suit. He rapped on the window, his face masking the fury inside.

The driver stared at him a second, then went to roll down the window. Castillo capitalized on the moment and jerked the door handle. The door went flying open, sending the driver off balance; he almost fell out.

Castillo seized the man by his ear, twisting and pulling as the man shrieked, and yanked him out of the car. As the man fumbled to his feet, he said, "I am an agent with the—"

"Shut up," Castillo barked, reached into the man's coat, and relieved him of the Glock 19 pistol on his hip. He handed the pistol to McCoy, who walked up to join him and—still twisting the man's ear—dragged the government agent toward the safe house.

"Ani, open the gate, please," Castillo said, and the gate began to swing on its hinges. "Shaker, pull the truck up, then pull his car into the drive."

"You got it, boss," Shaker called from behind the wheel of the Land Cruiser.

McCoy walked beside him with a slight limp.

"Ummm . . . what are we doing, boss?" he asked, real concern in his voice.

Castillo wanted McCoy's caution to be contagious, but it wasn't. He was furious, and he was going to find out more about their situation the old-fashioned way.

"We're gonna have a chat with our new friend here. It's high time we figure out what the hell is going on."

CHAPTER TWENTY-FIVE

Safe House

Al Amarat District

Khartoum, Sudan

March 20, 8:25 p.m.

"Tie him up," Castillo snapped at Junior after forcing the fit, dark-skinned man into one of the wooden dining chairs in the kitchen.

Junior started to protest but Castillo cut him off with a look. "All right, all right," the spook said, disappearing into the basement.

Ani, who had been working at the kitchen table, was on her feet and looked terribly confused. "What's going on?" she said, her gaze going from Castillo to their guest, then to McCoy. "Oh, my God, what happened to you?"

"I got my ass kicked," McCoy said, shifting his tender jaw side to side.

"By this guy?" she asked, gesturing to the man in the chair.

"No," the Marine said with a chuckle, and winced in pain. "Angry mob."

"So that's what I was hearing when your transmitter went dead," she said, shaking her head. "Why didn't you guys tell me?"

"We'll talk about that later," Castillo said. "Right now, the guy in the chair is our primary concern."

Junior returned carrying a spool of black paracord. He unwound and cut off a length of the woven nylon material and quickly and deftly tied their guest's ankles to the chair legs and bound the man's wrists behind the chair back.

"Do you speak English?" Castillo asked the man.

"Yes," the man answered.

Thank God, Castillo thought, *because this trip has reminded me how much my Arabic sucks.*

"Who do you work for?" Castillo asked.

The man didn't answer.

"Look, we can do this the hard way or the easy way. It's up to you. The hard way means you end up looking like my colleague here," Castillo said, jerking a thumb at McCoy. "The easy way means you walk out of here under your own power with all your teeth and appendages intact and unbroken. The choice is yours."

The man exhaled loudly, making his decision.

"As I tried to tell you outside, I work for the Sudanese government. I was assigned to watch you after your sudden and unexpected arrival. Your customs paperwork flagged you as persons of concern."

"Go on," Castillo said, pleased with where this interrogation was heading straight out of the gate.

"There is little to tell. My assignment is to watch you and report back to my chain of command."

"Do you work for Irshad Khalil?" Castillo asked.

"No. I work for a group within the Internal Affairs Defense Force. It is like your Homeland Security. It is important you understand that I was not sent to harass or harm you. You understand that you are foreign agents in *my* country, correct? My orders are to watch you and report your activities and whereabouts—that is all. Would it be any different were I to be on assignment in New York or Washington, D.C.?"

Castillo looked at McCoy. "You believe him?"

McCoy responded with a noncommittal shrug. "Let's run his picture through facial rec. See if it pops."

Castillo nodded. "What's your name?"

The man hesitated a beat. "My name is Mohammed Tawer, but I am no terrorist. You will not find me in your American CIA database."

"Who said we work for the CIA?"

The man snorted and rolled his eyes.

"It is obvious, is it not?"

Castillo frowned at Junior and the spook took the cue.

"I work for the State Department. My friend here is the head of my security detail," Junior said, jerking a thumb at Castillo. "His job is to assess and prosecute all threats to my safety, which is the reason why you are in that chair."

The man stifled a laugh and looked at Junior. "I am to believe that *you* are a diplomat?"

"That's correct," Junior said, his expression serious.

"Oh, I didn't realize tying people up was in a diplomat's job description."

"You'd be surprised what diplomats are required to learn these days," Junior said with a little half-smile. "Especially when the assignment is in Khartoum."

Ani took the man's picture with her phone and walked back to the workstation she'd set up at the kitchen table to, Castillo assumed, run Mohammed Tawer's image through the database.

"Tell me everything you know about Irshad Khalil," Junior continued.

"I don't know much about him."

"Try harder," Castillo growled.

Tawer sighed. He showed no real signs of fear at the threat of being tortured, but did appear resigned to the fact that he would not be leaving without at least cracking open Pandora's box. Castillo guessed the guy was a pretty good agent—maybe a good asset to recruit in a different situation, one with a slower tick on the clock. In any case, Castillo had made his play and this was it. No turning back now.

"Khalil is the acting minister of interior," the Arab said. "I don't know him personally, but I understand he is doing a good job."

"Understand from who?"

"People talk. Khalil is doing more to support the police and the Internal Affairs Defense Force than the previous minister."

Castillo nodded, making a mental note of this comment. "What about his sister, Awadiya Khalil? What do you think about her?"

Tawer hesitated, just a heartbeat, but long enough that Castillo registered the subtle shift in the man's demeanor. "I know she is a political activist and reformer."

"Go on."

"Some people say she's the people's choice for our next President."

"Have you ever been tasked to observe her?"

"No."

"But Internal Affairs Defense Force is watching her?" Castillo pressed.

"It is not my assignment, so I cannot speak to this," the man said, making a point of meeting Castillo's eyes.

Castillo held eye contact until Tawer looked away, then he turned to McCoy. "You have any questions for him?"

The Marine nodded. "Are there others like you assigned to observe us?"

Tawer didn't respond.

"Answer the question," Castillo ordered.

"I don't know. Probably," Tawer said.

"Is the Ministry of Interior investigating the kidnapping of U.S. Secretary of State Malone?" McCoy asked.

"I don't know."

"Is Internal Affairs Defense Force investigating the kidnapping of U.S. Secretary of State Malone?" McCoy asked.

"I don't know. It would be routine for there to be some activity to investigate possible connections to groups operating in our borders. We do not generally involve ourselves in international matters involving Egypt and their relationship with the United States. We have our own problems, as you know."

"But you do know that U.S. Secretary of State Malone was kidnapped during a terror attack in Cairo five days ago?"

Tawer nodded. "Of course."

"Do you have any reason to believe the secretary is being held in Sudan?"

"What? No . . . I have heard nothing to support such a claim."

"Tell us everything you know about the Sudanese Islamic Front," McCoy continued.

Tawer laughed. "You know more about these terrorists than I do, I'm sure. This is your job at CIA, is it not?"

"We don't work for the CIA," McCoy said, his voice a hard line. "My colleague already made that clear. Now answer the question."

"Where do you want me to start? It is a terrorist group. The Islamic extremists who represent a fringe and minority position. They want to destabilize the provisional government. They do not support democracy or religious freedom. They are hard-line supporters of Sharia law and do not tolerate any ideology except for their own. They most certainly do not support the rise of women to positions of power. You know this story well."

"Do you think the Sudanese Islamic Front could have been behind the attack in Cairo?" McCoy went on. "Do you think they could have kidnapped Secretary Malone?"

"No," Tawer said without hesitation. "This is a small group. They have neither the power nor the resources to do these things. Even if they had the manpower to pull off such a feat, they lack the money required, to say nothing of the training and foreign connections that would be required. Nor do their interests intersect well enough with allies they would require within Egypt to do the job."

"Where do they operate out of?"

"They are here in Khartoum, of course, hiding in the shadows. There was an attack in Port Sudan six months ago, so maybe they have people there, too. Probably they have a camp in the desert somewhere, but I don't know. Again, this is not my job. I am internal security, not part of the counterterrorism unit."

"Okay, so what happens next?" Castillo said, jumping back in. "We let you go, and then what?"

"I could lie and promise you I will say nothing," Tawer said, "but we know that is not going to happen. I will leave here, tell my boss everything that happened, tell him I think you are CIA and trying to find Secretary Malone and that you think the Sudanese Islamic Front is involved in the kidnapping. He will remove me from the observation detail, because you know what I look like. And because I got caught, he will give me some terrible assignment now. No one wins from this situation."

"Cut him loose," Castillo ordered McCoy this time instead of Junior.

The Marine did as he was told. After the paracord was cut, Tawer shook out his hands, but stayed sitting in the chair. "Are we done with questions?"

Castillo nodded.

"I can leave?"

He nodded again. "Tell your boss to back off. We're not here to cause any trouble."

"Somehow I don't think he's going to believe you," the man said, flashing them a mouthful of white teeth.

"Just make sure you give him the message, or I might not be so nice next time."

Tawer stood and his expression hardened. "You would do well to remember which country you are in when you make your threats. You are in Sudan, not America. The terrorists you are hunting are enemies of my country, too. Did it not occur to you to solicit our help? You Americans always assume you are in charge in every room you enter. Be careful, my friend—I think you are the one who needs to back off."

Castillo didn't respond, just pointed at the front door, the message implicit: *Go now, before I change my mind.*

"Can I have my phone back, please?" Tawer said.

"No," Castillo said, tapping his front pants pocket where he'd stuffed the man's phone after confiscating it. "I think I'll hold on to this for a while. But don't worry, I'll be sure to turn it over to officials at the airport with return instructions when we leave Sudan."

Jaw clenched and eyes burning, the Sudanese agent walked out the front door without a backward glance. Junior locked the door and reactivated the security system and looked through the security peephole for fifteen seconds.

"He just drove away," the spook announced, returning to the kitchen. He walked straight to the fridge and grabbed himself and no one else a beer. He opened it angrily, using the counter edge and a hard, downward blow of his palm on the cap. "Well, thanks for that, Charley. Now we're all completely blown and you've just antagonized the secret police. Nice one."

"We were already blown," Castillo said, glaring back at the spook. "That's the entire point."

"Yeah, but what you just did torpedoed any chance of decorum and cooperation with the Sudanese we had right out of the water. That guy wasn't wrong. If we had selectively solicited help . . ."

"Listen to me very carefully," Castillo said, trying hard to keep his temper in check. "We can't trust the Sudanese government. We can't depend on their cooperation. Irshad Khalil is the fucking minister of interior and he's responsible for the murder of two people in Umm Durmān. We don't know who they are and we don't know why, but we know with near absolute certainty he ordered the hit. And he only ordered the hit after we showed up at his office and started asking questions. I yanked Tawer from his car because we're running out of time and running out of leads. I *wanted* to antagonize the bastard. Sometimes the only way to get the hornets out of the hive is to shake the damn thing. We need to accelerate this process before Secretary Malone hits his expiration date."

"I agree," McCoy said. "Khalil is not just some bureaucrat. He's moving chess pieces on the board and we need to figure out which ones and why."

Junior took a long pull from his beer, then said, "Yeah, but if we're not careful, one or more of us might take a bullet in the back."

"Agreed, so what's our next move?" McCoy said.

"I think we talk to the sister," Ani said, leaning back in her chair and knitting her fingers behind her head. "I would really like to hear what she has to say about all of this. And if anybody is going to know where Khalil hides his dirty laundry, it's her."

"I like it," Castillo said. "In fact, I think you should be the one to talk to her, Ani. Are you good with that?"

"Hell, yes," Ani said, smiling for the first time since they got back. "I'm tired of being cooped up in this house."

"All right, then, it's settled. Junior, do you think you can facilitate that meeting?" Castillo asked, walking to the freezer to fill a plastic bag with some ice.

"I'll make it happ'n, cap'n . . . that's why I'm here," the spook said with a crooked grin.

Castillo nodded and turned to McCoy. "You know, kid, you really should put some ice on that face of yours. You're swelling up like the Stay Puft Marshmallow Man."

"Thanks," McCoy said accepting the bag of ice and pressing it against the side of his face. "But, uh, what's the Stay Puft Marshmallow Man?"

"Really?" Castillo said, rolling his eyes. "You know, *Ghostbusters?*"

McCoy shook his head.

"Sorry, I'm not much of a classic movie guy," the Marine said, with a hint of a smile.

"It's not that old of a movie," Castillo said, glancing from McCoy to Ani to Junior for backup. "Right, guys?"

"It came out almost forty years ago," Ani said, after a flurry of keystrokes on her computer. "I mean none of us were born then . . . but sure, Charley, it's not *that* old."

"Right," Junior said, jumping onto the dog pile. "It's not like *Casablanca* old. I mean, *Ghostbusters* was shot in color."

"And most of the actors are still alive," McCoy added, with a painful grin.

"Screw you guys," Castillo said, feigning offense. Then, earning himself a raucous round of laughter, added, "On a different note, anybody seen my Metamucil? I could've sworn I left it right here on the counter last night . . ."

CHAPTER TWENTY-SIX

"Every time I think you've pulled your last rabbit from that magic bag of tricks of yours, you go and surprise me yet again," Castillo said, shaking his head at Junior, who was decked out like an ENG cameraman, complete with a cable news vest, press ID badge, and Sony HD professional ENG camera.

"Press corps is my favorite NOC for places like this," Junior said.

"Where did you get all this shit?"

"That second hard case we unloaded from the plane had all this stuff inside, along with other electronic goodies."

"Other goodies . . . like what?"

"NVGs, a thermal imaging scope, a laser microphone, surveillance and countersurveillance detection gear, and so on."

"Good, we may well need all of that before this is over."

Castillo turned his attention to Ani, who was coming down the stairs. Like Junior, she was also in character—dressed like an international correspondent, wearing khaki trousers, a cream-colored button-down blouse, and a gray-blue headscarf wrapped loosely around her head and neck. It was the first time he'd seen her with eye makeup and lipstick. She looked like an entirely different person from the grungy spy he'd been hanging out with for the past two days, the transformation so profound he probably wouldn't have recognized her on the street.

"I'm going to stop you right there," she said, her gaze meeting his. "I don't want to hear it."

He pretended to zip his lips shut. Grinning, he turned to McCoy and said, "Sorry, Killer. I'd let you tag along with us, but your face would draw too much attention . . . Jesus, kid, you look like you went ten rounds with Jack Dempsey."

An irritable McCoy murmured something Castillo couldn't quite make out.

"What's that?"

"I said I'll stay in the truck," McCoy replied. "I've never been one for hanging out in the TOC when the action is in the field."

"Yeah, I know," Castillo said, "But for today's op, the TOC is where I need you."

"Fine," McCoy said, letting out a long sigh of defeat as he walked over to the kitchen table and the two notebook computers that comprised their tactical operations center.

"All right, let's roll," Castillo said, giving McCoy a two-finger salute before heading to the front door.

Outside, Shaker waited in his Land Cruiser parked in the driveway, engine running and windows rolled up. Castillo climbed in the front passenger seat while Ani and Junior got in back. Shaker had the A/C cranked up and the temperature difference between

the cabin and outside air had to be at least thirty degrees. Castillo
didn't mind, but he knew Ani probably would.

"Hey, Shaker," she said a heartbeat later. "Can you turn the A/C
down a bit? It's freezing in here."

"Sure thing, Ms. Ani," the driver said. He turned the control
from 20°C to 24°C and the cabin air flow immediately dropped
from gale force wind to a gentle breeze.

"At some point, I imagine we're going to want to break cover,"
Castillo said, looking over his shoulder as Shaker piloted them onto
the street. "I'm going to leave that call with you, Ani."

"I don't understand," she said.

"This is not Awadiya Khalil's first interview. We should assume
she's experienced, savvy, and not prone to naïve or fanciful thinking. Anyone running for President is going to be on the lookout for
wolves in sheeps' clothing, if you catch my drift. I imagine as soon
as you pivot from policy and reform questions to interrogating her
about Irshad, her antennae are going to perk up. We can't afford for
her to clam up or kick us out because she decides the interview is
disingenuous."

"Hmm, good point," Ani said. "Maybe we break cover as soon
as we sit down with her?"

"Hold on, that's not how this is supposed to work," Junior said.
"And you know it, Charley. We never break cover voluntarily. That's
Tradecraft 101."

Castillo smiled. "You're right, that is Tradecraft 101, but we're
not freshmen in the introductory class anymore. We've graduated
and moved on to the real world. The rules are designed to keep the
rookies and their bosses out of trouble, and we're way past that
point. In fact, the authority and freedom to make calls like this one
is the reason for this operation in the first place: no armchair

quarterbacking from Langley, no layers of bureaucracy to penetrate to get answers, and most important, no middle management intermediary with an 'I need to cover my ass so I don't get blamed' attitude interfering with our ability to make decisions in the field. We have the authority to make the hard calls as we deem appropriate and only one person who we need to satisfy, and that person is sitting behind the *Resolute* desk."

"Wow," Ani said, staring at him.

"Wow, what?"

"That was a pretty bad-ass speech. Gave me goose bumps," she said, showing him her forearms as proof.

"That's what it takes to give you goose bumps, a diatribe about breaking the rules?" Junior said, turning to her.

"Yes, apparently," she said, with a coy grin. "I hope you're taking notes."

Something smacked against Castillo's window, giving him a start. "What the hell was that?" he said, whirling in his seat to look out.

"I think it was a shoe," Shaker said. Traffic slowed to a crawl as they moved into a section of town where a crowd of thousands had gathered.

"What is this? What's going on?" Castillo asked.

"A protest against the Sovereignty Council and the provisional government. The people are not happy," Shaker said.

Outside the Land Cruiser, marching protesters carried signs on poles and were chanting in Arabic. None of them were brandishing firearms or Molotov cocktails, so that was at least a plus, but Castillo still didn't like being trapped in the middle of it. His and McCoy's little misadventure in Umm Durmān last night seemed proof enough of how quickly a seemingly innocuous crowd could turn into a murderous mob.

"We need to turn around and take another route," he said to Shaker. "This is no good."

"I am sorry, I did not know this was happening here," Shaker said, braking to a complete stop. "But I think we are stuck now."

Castillo knew that, as a melting pot for the Middle East and Africa, Sudan was widely considered the most ethnically rich and diverse population on the African continent. Looking out the window now, Castillo saw that sentiment to be true. Arabs, Africans, and Nubians of every size, shape, and shade were assembled under a common banner—to end state corruption and promote democratic reform.

The crowd, which had been maintaining a two-meter standoff from the line of traffic, suddenly converged on the Land Cruiser en masse, with people shouting and slapping their open palms against the windows, hood, and roof. Castillo pressed the door and window lock buttons.

"Why are they angry with us?" Shaker asked, his face strained with worry. "I have no government markings on this vehicle."

"I don't think they're angry with us," Junior said, cradling his camera rig on his lap. "Quite the opposite, in fact. They want our attention."

"Should we take off our press badges," Ani said, smiling and nodding at the wall of faces outside her window.

"Too late. Just don't engage, or we'll never get out of here," Castillo said, turning around in his seat to face her.

"Sorry," she said, meeting his gaze. "I thought it was better than ignoring them."

"No, it just encourages them," he said, as a young man standing next to Ani's door started pulling the handle, trying to open her door.

"I see what you mean," she said, shifting her gaze to out the windshield.

"Shaker, we need to start moving," Castillo said. "We can't stay here."

"But I don't want to run over them."

"You won't, just start moving at idle speed," he said. "They'll move out of the way. I promise. Just ease your foot off the brake."

Shaker, whose brow was now dappled with sweat, nodded. The Land Cruiser began to inch forward. The movement incited the crowd, causing the shouting and the pounding to intensify.

"It's okay," Castillo said. "You're doing great. A little less brake, we need to get up to idle speed, faster than they can walk. The traffic ahead is moving now . . ."

Somebody slammed a bottle against Junior's window, breaking the bottle but failing to crack the bulletproof glass of the up-armored vehicle.

"Damn it," Junior said, leaning away from the window.

In front of the Land Cruiser, people were starting to get the message and hurrying clear of the bumper. Alongside the SUV, the incited protesters were now walking and shouting.

"Now start accelerating," Castillo said, encouraging Shaker. "Give it some gas."

Shaker, clutching the wheel tightly with both hands, accelerated past human-running speed and ten seconds later they'd left the throng behind.

"That was a close one," Ani said. "Shaker, let's be sure to take a different route on our way back to the safe house."

"Don't worry, I will," Shaker said, his composure coming back.

The remainder of the forty-minute drive to Awadiya Khalil's office across the river in North Khartoum unfolded without incident.

On arrival, Castillo, who was posing as the news crew's security man, hopped out of the Land Cruiser first and surveyed the area. Finding nothing of concern, he opened Ani's door for her while Junior climbed out the other side with his camera.

"Keep the engine running," Castillo said to Shaker through the gap.

"Will do, boss."

Castillo shut the door and turned to Ani. "You ready?"

"Yeah," she said, instantly stepping into character. "Come on, Larry," she said to Junior, her camera operator. "We're late."

"I'm coming," he said, hoisting the 4K HD Sony camcorder up onto his shoulder.

"I hope you brought the extra battery this time," she said, with maternal annoyance in her voice. "Let's not have another Cairo ever again."

"Got it right here," he said, tapping a pocket on his vest, just as a young African woman stepped out the front door of the modest ground-level storefront Awadiya Khalil was using as her campaign office.

"*Marhaban,*" the woman said, "My name is Nadima."

"*Marhaban bikum,*" Ani answered, with a warm smile. "I'm Rayan Reshma of BNC. We are here to interview Awadiya Khalil."

"Yes, I know. We are grateful for your coming."

"Do you speak English?"

"Yes, pretty good," the young woman said. "Follow me inside, please. Miss Khalil is expecting you."

Bringing up the rear, Castillo followed the rest of the party inside. The tiny campaign office was cooled by a lone, overtaxed window air conditioner. A few curious staffers looked up at them from their desks as Nadima led them to the office in the back, where they could see their host waiting for them.

"Welcome. I'm Awadiya Khalil," she said, greeting them with an open-armed gesture. "Thank you for this opportunity to share my story."

"Thank you for agreeing to the interview. I'm Rayan Reshma from British News Corporation," Ani said, then, gesturing to Junior and Castillo, added, "This is my ENG camera operator, Larry. And my security escort, Frank."

"Very nice to meet you," Awadiya said, then surveyed her tiny office, which was barely large enough to hold all of them. "Maybe we do the interview outside, where there is more room and good lighting."

"I think that's a great idea," Ani said, "But first maybe we should have a discussion off-camera in your office. I find it is usually helpful to discuss the questions in advance, so we are both prepared."

"Wonderful," Awadiya said, her shoulders visibly relaxing at this. "I wish all reporters did this."

"Frank, maybe you could wait outside," Ani said, turning to look at Castillo.

The request caught him off guard, but instead of bristling he just rolled with it. They were all wearing micro-earbud transceivers; he'd still get to hear everything said in the room. This was Ani's show and he needed to trust her instincts.

He nodded at her and stepped out of Awadiya's office. Like a sentinel, he stood with his back to the door, arms folded across his chest. And with the gaze of a half dozen strangers lingering on him, he forced himself to wait patiently for what was coming next.

CHAPTER TWENTY-SEVEN

Irshad Khalil sat in the rear of the Mercedes-Benz E-Class sedan, legs crossed, sipping a strong coffee the driver had poured him earlier from the thermos up front. The man beside him, Hafez—his enforcer and trusted second who he'd given the critical tasking to handle the loose-lipped youth in Umm Durmān yesterday—was talking on the phone.

". . . make sure the minister stays inside for a minimum of thirty minutes . . . yes . . . yes . . . call me when you're departing for the next precinct," Hafez said, ended the call, and turned to Khalil. "Your body double is at the polling precinct manager's office in Ad-Damir now."

"He knows to leave the vehicle inside the garage?" Khalil asked.

"Yes," Hafez replied, as their driver pulled up to a gate next to a construction trailer at the end of a dirt road. "He reports no unusual activity and no apparent tail but understands that the Americans may well be watching from the air or from a satellite in space."

"It is imperative that my double adheres to my published schedule until our business here is finished and I can take over this afternoon."

"Don't worry, he knows."

"He'd better not fuck this up."

This was the first time Khalil had used a double, so there was reason to be nervous. Most people were incompetent. Unfortunately, given the scrutiny he was under, he had no choice. He could not dare risk visiting this compound without a cover story. Today, he was making stops to inspect the security of election polling sites throughout the north precincts. The upcoming election would be Sudan's first *real* democratic election and it was critical that the vote be legitimate. The tour had been on his schedule for weeks and would not arouse suspicion with anyone in the government or the Americans. But he needed to see Secretary Malone with his own two eyes. He didn't trust the SIF leader, Yasir Aldama, and so this had been his solution.

The trailer door opened and a heavily armed guard stepped out into the morning sun. He approached them with menace in his eyes, but when he spotted Khalil through the window, he straightened up, jogged to the gate, and opened it. He gave Khalil's car an awkward stiff salute as they passed, then hustled the gate closed behind them.

The driver parked beneath a tin awning beside the warehouse in the center of the complex. The former manufacturing compound included several smaller, cinder-block buildings with corrugated tin roofs along the river, and a small cement and stucco office off to their left. As the driver opened the rear passenger door, Khalil's phone rang.

He looked at the screen and said, "Give us a moment," to the driver, who dutifully closed the door and stood patiently beside the car. Khalil showed the screen to Hafez, who frowned, then he pressed the button to answer the call on speaker.

"Yes?"

"It's the Americans," said Sadiq, a trusted lieutenant who functioned as their eyes and ears in the city.

"What of them?"

"They are at your sister's campaign headquarters," Sadiq replied, the worry thick in his voice. "They are meeting with her right now, pretending to be an international news team. Three of them are there. We trailed them from their safe house at a safe distance but lost them in the city. Our surveillance team picked them up at her campaign headquarters. They are there now!"

Khalil thought for a moment in silence. In truth, there should be nothing that Awadiya could tell the Americans that would arouse suspicion—a few missteps in his youth, comments about his ambition, but that was a family trait, was it not? In her mind, he was a committed civil servant, dedicated to bringing prosperity to Sudan. There was nothing in the world she knew of to suggest he would have any ties to Islamic terrorists—in fact, one might assume him to be a target, just as she was, for promoting secular government over Sharia law and a democratic Sudan.

But the fact that they are meeting her at all . . .

He glanced at Hafez, who held his gaze, eyes full of worry.

"One moment, Sadiq," he said, muting the line. "What are your thoughts, Hafez?"

Hafez tensed his jaw and stared past him out the window.

"That they would choose to speak with her suggests our plan is in danger," Hafez said, mirroring Khalil's own thoughts. "If they are digging into your past, then everything will be under intense scrutiny. We must accelerate the timeline. The assassination will cause mayhem and buy us time."

"We should hit them first, I think. Before they put the pieces together."

Hafez smiled and cut his eyes toward the warehouse. "Perhaps we should task that to our partners . . . let them do what they do best."

Khalil smiled and nodded. He had the same thought. It was not without risk, but then what in his plan was without risk? And as long as nothing linked him to the SIF . . .

"I agree," he said, then unmuted the phone and said, "Continue careful surveillance, Sadiq, but be prepared to pull your men at a moment's notice."

"You mean stop watching them?" Sadiq sounded surprised. "I assure you I have my best men on this and there is little risk of detection . . ."

"There is always risk, Sadiq. We are dealing with trained professionals. Maintain your distance and take pictures. Send any images you have to Hafez right now."

"Understood," Sadiq replied, and ended the call.

Khalil rolled down the window, and the driver leaned in. "I wish to meet with Yasir Aldama in the car before we go in."

"I will see to it."

Hafez climbed out and moved to the front passenger seat to make room for the leader of the Sudanese Islamic Front. Moments later, the warehouse door beside the car opened again and their driver held open the passenger-side rear door.

Yasir Aldama slipped into the seat beside him, a tight smile on his rough, hard face. Seemingly annoyed to be summoned to the car, he smoothed his suit pants, folding his hands into his lap. Gone were the dirty street clothes and sandals from their last meeting—Yasir was now dressing like Hafez. With both his bank account and ego on the rise, the terrorist was apparently already fashioning himself as something he was not.

"I apologize for this unexpected visit, Yasir," Khalil said, his right hand over his heart, giving the terrorist leader a slight nod of deference. "I am afraid there have been some changes I wished to discuss with you privately. You have met Hafez, I believe."

"I have," was all Aldama said, without looking forward at Hafez. "What kind of changes?"

"I assume you have heard of the incident in Umm Durmān last night . . ."

Rage suddenly flashed across the man's face. "I have, but I am quite surprised to hear that you had heard of it. If you were involved—"

Khalil raised a hand, cutting the man off before his threat could be floated.

"We are well past such things, Yasir," he said. "We are partners now, and each of us acts only in the best interest of the other. Your young fighter was bragging of his involvement in the kidnapping of Secretary of State Malone. Hafez went to talk with him about the dangers of such talk," he shook his head, the sadness on his face an exclamation point to the lie, "but when Hafez arrived, American agents were already there, preparing to take him. A shoot-out with the Americans ensued, and regrettably your man and his wife were killed. You have my deepest sympathy for the loss of your man."

"Is that so?" Aldama said, his eyes narrowing and gaze shifting to Hafez. "But it would have been better for me and our *partnership* had you discussed this with me and allowed me to police my own people. I could have handled it privately. Thanks to the public violence, there will be an inquiry now."

"There will be no inquiry," Khalil said. "I control such things."

"But you do not control the Americans," Yasir snapped. "Like a bloodhound, they now have a scent to follow . . . and that scent will eventually lead them here!"

"I believe I have a plan that will both satisfy your desire to avenge your martyr, and also buy us more time."

"I am listening."

"We believe that the Americans involved are a small and elite team acting undercover. We have the location of their safe house, which is not well guarded. They appear to be a four-person team with two Sudanese contract drivers. Presently, one American and one driver are at the house and the others are in North Khartoum."

"You have them under surveillance as we speak?"

"Yes."

Yasir rubbed his bearded chin. "If you give the locations, I could strike them now—before they close in on our operation."

Khalil resisted the urge to smile. "This would seem to be risky with all we have going on. Are you sure you have the manpower to execute this?"

"I have weapons and men in Khartoum ready at a moment's notice," the terrorist snapped. "I expected the Americans to come. I do my part, you do yours, remember? That was our deal. After I eliminate the threat, you play the grieving diplomat and servant to the West, condemning the attacks."

Khalil nodded. "Yes, very good. And maybe we consider accelerating the timeline for the assassination. With the opposition party eliminated, it would solidify financial backing from our supporters in Saudi Arabia and all but assure my rise to power."

"*Our* rise to power," Yasir corrected, leaning in and holding his eyes.

"Of course, my brother," Khalil said, choosing his words carefully, as Yasir was a true believer and a ticking time bomb. "But we have discussed this. You are advocating a path that has not worked in any country in Africa or the Middle East. It is time to show our Muslim brothers the proper way to flourish, gain power, and eventually vanquish our enemies. Is Taqiya not permitted, even demanded by the Quran, so that we may defeat the infidels? Are we not told 'let us smile to the face of some people while our hearts curse them'? The Prophet himself tells us war is deceit."

"Yes, yes," Yasir said with a wave of his hand, clearly annoyed to be lectured by Khalil on Islam and the Prophet. "These are for those silver-tongued, such as yourself, who excel at Taqiya and less for those of us who prefer to strike at our enemies directly."

"But have we not agreed which strategy is a winning one? And is it not the perfect marriage of our individual talents that assures our success?"

"Of course," Yasir said, but his eyes suggested he still did not entirely trust Khalil.

No matter, they were well past that. Through the connections Khalil had built in Saudi Arabia and now his power in the transitional government, he held more power over SIF than Yasir, and they both knew it. Not only did he hold the purse strings, but he could— with a phone call—wipe the organization from the face of the earth by reporting the location of this compound to the Americans.

This was something Khalil knew Yasir must think and worry about constantly.

"Do not fear—by next year, you and I will lead our people to a new era, I promise you, and we will do it together. I will need your spiritual and tactical counsel, more than you know."

"When do you want the assassination to take place?" Yasir said, shifting from the political, which Khalil knew he loathed, to something tactical.

"Soon, on the heels of what we have planned for the secretary of state, rather than in the final week before the election."

"Very well. Give me the American team's location. We need to move on this quickly."

"I just sent you an encrypted message with their locations," Hafez said from the front, bowing in deference. "I would be honored to work with your men and coordinate the attacks using my spotters as your eyes."

Yasir nodded, retrieved his phone, and pressed a name on his contact list. Then he barked instructions into the phone and hung up without waiting for a reply.

"You know where to go in the control building?"

"I do, teacher," Hafez said, placing his hand on his heart and bowing again.

Khalil watched his right-hand man get out of the sedan and walk to the small building beside the warehouse. *With a performance like that, you are destined for great things, my friend,* he thought. He turned back to Yasir.

"I am ready to meet with the American secretary of state now."

"You received the recording we made of him begging that we be recognized as legitimate leaders of the people of Sudan? It was just as you scripted."

"I have and it was perfect. We will use it with the American government shortly after I return to Khartoum. You and your men are to be congratulated."

"Let me introduce you to our captive, then," Yasir said, grinning. "I look forward to observing your acting skills as well."

"I want only your most trusted fighters in place where I might be seen," Khalil said, his thoughts on the young fool whom he'd ordered killed in Umm Durmān.

No more mistakes just to feed the ego of this man who seeks adoration from young men.

"It has been done already as you asked," the terrorist said.

"And," Khalil continued, "with your permission, I believe it best if, beginning now, everyone currently on the compound must remain here until the end of the operation. I feel there should be no exceptions to this, now that we have accelerated our time line."

"I agree," Aldama said, clearly pleased to have been asked instead of told. "Now, please, let me introduce you to Secretary of State Malone."

CHAPTER TWENTY-EIGHT

Malone didn't know whether the fact that they had cleaned him up, allowed him a shower, and changed his orange jumpsuit should make him feel optimistic or terrified that he was about to make his gory YouTube debut. Twenty-four hours ago, he recorded a video where he pleaded—without sounding like he was pleading, he hoped—that his government acknowledge SIF as legitimate and engage in conversation.

He'd expected something, *anything*, to change in his situation for doing so, but nothing had. He'd sat here, isolated, in his small room waiting for his fate to be determined by a group of people who hated him with a zealot's passion.

The anxiety he felt made his stomach cramp, and for a moment he thought he might best return to the bucket in the corner for yet another painful bout of diarrhea. But the cramp passed, and he rose nervously from his tiny cot and began to pace the room. If he was forced to betray his country on video, Cohen would certainly see it for what it was—a desperate play on his part to delay his execution and secure his rescue. And he had done nothing to betray his oath so far, right? So why had a day passed with nothing? Had she sacrificed him in pursuit of a tough stance on terrorism?

When the key rattled in the door lock, he actually cried out, a pitiful sob he was glad no one was inside to hear.

Get your shit together, Frank. You're still the fucking secretary of state for the United States of America. Face this like a man . . .

Another wave of cramps rippled painfully across his insides, and despite his terrified nervous energy, he dropped back onto his cot as the door swung open, fearful he might vomit or shit himself at any moment.

The well-dressed man who entered, however, looked nearly as terrified and nervous as he felt, and for a moment he thought the man to be another hostage with whom he would now share the tiny room until one or both of them lost their heads. But the guard beside him nodded to the man with almost deference. Then he stepped aside, and another man—again, a rougher, more seasoned-looking terrorist than the teens he'd seen so far—brought in an oversized cushioned leather chair and positioned it in the center of the room, facing Malone.

Despite the bead of sweat trickling down from the well-dressed man's temple, he turned to the armed men and addressed them politely.

"*Shukran,*" he said, thanking them.

Then the door was closed behind him, and Malone heard the lock turn.

The man gave him a genuine smile as he took his seat, smoothing his suit coat, and crossed his legs. He let out a rattling sigh, shaking his head in disbelief.

"I can't believe it's really you," the man said, his English crisp and practiced. "I thought they made the whole thing up—that they lied, because how could they possibly have done this thing . . ."

"Who are you?" Malone demanded, evenly, the man's presence his first glimmer of hope since he'd arrived, balled up like dirty laundry in a box.

"Secretary of State Malone, on behalf of my people and the government of Sudan, I apologize for what has happened," the man said. He looked nervously behind him at the closed door and around the cell. "They are listening," he whispered, and straightened up and took a long, cleansing breath. "It is my sincere hope—"

Malone stood, placing his hands on his hips and feeling for the first time since his arrival like he might have a tiny bit of control over a conversation.

"I really need to know who you are," he demanded, cutting the other man off. "And if you are a representative of the Sudanese government you have a hell of a lot of explaining to do."

"My name is Irshad Khalil. I'm the acting minister of interior for the transitional government of Sudan. I assure you that the Sudanese government had absolutely nothing to do with your kidnapping. Until the ransom demand came, we had no idea you were in Sudan. Until just hours ago, the whole world thought you were in Egypt."

"Wait a minute," Malone said, holding up a hand. His mind went to his conversation with Fifth Avenue only yesterday—or three meals ago, at least. "You're telling me that no one knew I was here until today?"

The man nodded. "I'm afraid we all assumed the worst. Then

the video of you was sent to us and to your State Department. We have been working tirelessly ever since to help locate you. I have been tasked with the responsibility to negotiate your release."

"On behalf of whom?"

He felt a new, real hope surge inside. If this acting minister was working on behalf of D.C.—if this was the beginning of some back-channel negotiations—then maybe this really might be over soon.

"Well," the well-dressed man said, looking around as if nervous about choosing his words carefully, "officially I am working on behalf of the government of Sudan, but you should know we are working very, very closely with the *diplomats* from your country on behalf of your President."

The man stared into Malone's eyes with an intensity that suggested he was conveying some important message—but what? Was it simply that the United States was fully engaged? Was "diplomats" code for embedded CIA assets in country? Was it that a heroic rescue from SEAL Team Six or Delta Force was imminent? Whatever it was, Malone decided he was better off than he'd been only minutes ago.

"I understand," he said.

"I need to ask you some questions, please," the man said, opening a small leather notebook he pulled from his inside coat pocket. Malone saw the man's hands were shaking.

"Anything." Malone let out a slow, rattling breath.

"Can you confirm the car you drove in high school?"

"What? Why?" But then he realized—this was to confirm that this man Khalil had really met with him. "Sorry, yes, of course. I drove a white Dodge Dart until I left for college."

"What was the name of your childhood dog?"

"Ranger," he answered, smiling a moment at the memory of the black lab he'd gotten as a puppy when he was in first grade. Ranger had died the year before he graduated from UAB.

"In a moment they will come back and they will take a picture of us together. Is this okay for you?"

"Yes, of course."

If the terrorists were allowing this man—the minister of interior—to come and take a picture as proof of life, then some deal must be in the making. He didn't know Irshad Khalil from Adam, but he probably should if he was a minister in the transitional government. But the name Khalil sounded very familiar for some reason other than this man, he thought.

"What else can I do?" he asked, hoping he sounded brave and in control.

"If they ask you to make another video, I would ask that you comply. And to the extent your position allows, I would ask that you please comply with all of their demands as it will help us complete our negotiations quickly. Do you understand?"

"Yes," he said, embarrassed that this time his voice cracked.

Khalil gave him a compassionate smile. "It is okay. I am very frightened as well, but I think we are both going to be okay."

Malone nodded and tried to smile back.

"They have treated you well? You are healthy?" Khalil asked.

He thought of the pain still in his hips and back from his hours and hours in the ice chest. He thought of the aching pain that still remained from the blow to his face with the rifle butt. Then he thought of the possible consequences should he share that now, while his captors listened to every word.

"They have treated me very well," he said, staring into the minister's eyes, hoping he could see his own message reflected there . . . as if the fist-sized hematoma on Malone's face wasn't answer enough.

"They have kept me comfortable and well fed. I have no complaints, other than my strong desire to go home."

The minister nodded, signaling he understood the unspoken message. He appeared about to speak again, when the key rattled and the door opened again. Malone was not shocked to see one of the more seasoned guards coming through the door. The large, barrel-chested man dressed in a long, gray, traditional-looking tunic barked at him in Arabic, signaling with his hands for Malone to rise, which he did. The man roughly turned his chin, using a large hand that smelled of dirt and gun oil, apparently trying to hide his facial wound in the shadows. He then shoved Khalil backward roughly, pulled out a phone, and took two pictures of them together.

"*Yakfi alhadith. Tueal maei,*" the guard said.

Malone was unsure of the first phrase, but the second he was pretty sure meant *come with me*. Khalil stepped toward the door, but then stopped and turned, extending his hand. Malone shook it.

"I will negotiate your safe return, Mr. Secretary," he said. "I promise."

"Thank you, Minister Khalil. Thank you so much."

Despite his best effort, he felt tears well in his eyes as a second guard wrestled the large chair out of the room, leaving him alone. Suddenly weary, Malone collapsed onto his cot, pressed his hands painfully against his battered face, and began to sob. He didn't care if they could hear him or even see him. President Cohen had not abandoned him, after all. Backdoor diplomacy was under way. Chess pieces were moving.

Whatever they wanted him to say in the next video, he would say it.

Help was coming.

CHAPTER TWENTY-NINE

Go ahead and stare, see if I care, Castillo thought as he dragged his laser beam gaze across the room of staffers. The only thing that intimidated him at this point in his career was a gun pointed at his chest. And even then, it had to be a big damn gun.

On the other side of the door behind him, Ani was getting down to the distasteful business of doing what spooks are supposed to do best—recruiting and manipulating assets. Technically speaking, Awadiya Khalil was not being recruited, but the playbook was the same. Ani's job was to get inside Awadiya's head, identify and appeal to whatever motivated the woman, and win her trust and cooperation. Whether Ani succeeded depended on her ability to wear two hats simultaneously—psychologist and salesman—a feat that was much more difficult than the average person might imagine.

"Let me just start by saying how impressed I am with the work you've done here in Sudan and the reform effort your campaign has been leading," Ani began. "Thanks in large part to your efforts, for the first time in Sudan's history, the country has an opportunity to become a legitimate democracy and unwind decades of government corruption and the suppression of personal and religious freedom."

"Thank you," Awadiya said, "but I am not alone leading this effort. Thousands of Sudanese women and men are speaking out and risking their personal safety and livelihoods in the name of change. It takes the courage of the citizenry to stand up and face down a corrupt government and military that does not hesitate to shoot first and ask questions later."

Castillo listened as the dialogue between the two women unfolded in an easy, magnanimous manner over the next ten minutes. But the moment Ani broached the subject of Awadiya's brother, Irshad, everything changed. At first, Awadiya fielded and deflected Ani's questions with the seasoned polish he'd expect from an American politician, but as Ani continued to push, the conversation quickly soured.

"If you are so interested in my brother's opinions and policies, I suggest you interview him instead," Awadiya said, her tone so frosty Castillo practically felt a chill seeping through the door, all the way to where he waited outside.

"Do it now as we planned," Castillo said, prompting Ani to break cover, "before you lose her."

"Can you give us the room?" he heard Ani say to Junior. "I'd like to speak with Ms. Khalil in private for a few minutes."

"Certainly," Junior said. A moment later the spook was standing beside Castillo, both men ejected from the room.

"I'm not a reporter," Ani began, letting the words hang in the air for effect. "I work for the U.S. State Department. I'm part of an investigative team searching for Secretary of State Frank Malone who, as I'm sure you're aware, was kidnapped in Cairo six days ago. We have reason to suspect he's being held here, in Sudan."

"Thank you for being honest with me about your motives and your identity," Awadiya said. "I'm disappointed, however, you did not tell me the truth from the beginning."

"Would you have agreed to meet with me if I had?"

"Probably not . . ."

"Which is why I approached you as a journalist. I needed a vehicle to get an audience with you so we could have this conversation."

"I am not naïve," Awadiya said, a little melancholy creeping into her voice. "I understand how the world works. I probably would have done the same thing, if I was in your position."

"Despite misleading you about being a reporter, I was not lying when I said I admire your courage and the movement you're leading. As a Muslim woman, who has spent much of her adult life living and working in the Middle East and North Africa, I have witnessed the power of institutionalized suppression and discrimination firsthand. Thanks to your efforts, Sudan has a real chance of becoming a legitimate democracy. It is time for Sudan to move off the global terrorist watch list and become fully embraced by America and the rest of the world. But if we discover that a terrorist group is harboring the secretary in Sudan, that will never happen."

On this masterstroke, Castillo glanced at Junior, who nodded his approval.

Keep it up, Ani, you got this.

"But what does my brother have to do with Secretary Malone's disappearance?" Awadiya asked.

"We have intelligence that suggests that he might have been involved," Ani said, which was a stretch but also just an inflammatory

enough statement to potentially rattle candidate Awadiya into saying more than she might otherwise have been predisposed to share.

"In what capacity do you think he was involved?"

"I don't know—you tell me," Ani said. "Do you know if Irshad
embraces the tenets of radical Islam? Does he support or sympa-
thize with jihadists?"

Awadiya laughed and Castillo could picture her waving a hand
to dismiss the notion.

"My brother, a terrorist? Impossible . . ." she said. "Sure, in his
youth he had a few troubling incidents, but what young man doesn't
test boundaries and social norms?"

"What type of incidents?" Ani asked, the piqued curiosity in her
voice matching Castillo's own.

"He fell in with an undesirable crowd. There were a few incidents of theft and vandalism and . . ." Her voice trailed off.

"And *what*?"

"And . . . nothing, really. One incident with a woman, but that
was years ago. Look at him now. He has put all those things far
behind him, embraced the mission of reform, and risen to the position of acting minister of interior. He has been very supportive of
my campaign and even offered me a government security detail for
protection."

"You have security here, now?"

"No. I refused it because it would send the wrong message to the
people. I'm not . . . *we* are not from a family of means. We grew up
poor, like ninety-nine percent of Sudanese. My campaign is one of
truth and integrity. I am the same as the people I hope to represent
as President."

"So, where does Irshad figure into your campaign and aspirations? Is this a shared vision the two of you have had from the beginning? Would he have a role in your administration if you win?"

Awadiya didn't answer for a moment, and Castillo could sense that this question had hit her like a bucket of cold water in the face.

"Like all serving members of the transitional government," Awadiya then said, "my brother understands that after the election those in provisional government posts will be filled with new appointments. No one on the Sovereignty Council, nor the prime minister himself, is permitted to run for office. This is by design to prevent corruption and power grabs during the transition. The last thing Sudan needs is to oust one dictator from power only to replace him with an opportunist with similar aspirations."

"So, you've discussed this with Irshad?"

"He supports my vision, which is why election security has been one of the most important things he's focused on during his time at the Ministry. He travels the country, setting up voting facilities to ensure all Sudanese will have a place to vote without fear or intimidation."

"That's wonderful, but you didn't answer my question. Are you certain he understands there will be no place in your government for him should you win the election? Are you certain he is willing to give up his newfound power and influence so easily? I mean, surely, your ascension to President must figure into his plans somehow?"

That's it, Ani, Castillo thought. *Nicely done.*

Awadiya sighed and said, "I don't know . . ."

"What don't you know?"

"I have always given Irshad the benefit of the doubt—that's what siblings are supposed to do . . . but I have seen another side of him. Even as a child, he was very good at manipulating people. He has this uncanny ability to look inside a person and see who they want him to be and become that person."

"I don't understand. What do you mean by that?"

"I mean, sometimes, I feel like Irshad is a mirror—reflecting back at me the traits and values I cherish and admire most. The funny thing is, I remember him using this trick with our mother and thinking how blind she was to his adolescent lies, but now, maybe I am the one who is blind. Maybe I am the target of some grand scheme he's orchestrating," Awadiya said, frustration creeping into her voice. "But what could it possibly be? All his actions for the past two years have focused on helping me with my mission and reform. How can he be a terrorist when he is working tirelessly on the very reforms hated by the terror groups wishing to keep Sudan from pursuing a free society and secular government? He works with government officials and political activists dedicated to these principles and reforms every day."

Ani started to answer, but a brick smashed through the office's front plate-glass window, usurping Castillo's attention. A woman screamed as the window imploded, spraying shards of glass in all directions. He unholstered his weapon as a second incoming object sailed through the gap where the window had once been.

"Molotov cocktail!" he shouted, as the flaming bottle tumbled end over end in an arc and smashed into a desk.

A potent petrol–bleach mixture exploded, sending tongues of fire licking out in all directions along with a cloud of noxious smoke. The front office workers shrieked and fell over one another as they attempted to scramble to safety.

"Everybody fall in on me!" Castillo shouted, waving the panicked staffers toward him.

Behind him, the door to Awadiya's office flew open.

"What's going on?" the candidate asked, her eyes wide.

"We just got firebombed!" Castillo shouted.

He scanned over his weapon, looking past the flames to the sidewalk outside for a target readying the next fiery salvo.

"We have a rear exit," Awadiya said. "Let's go out the back!"

"Wait!" he barked, his mind's eye imagining a team of gunmen staged in an alley to cut them all down as they exited. "This could be a trap—they might be trying to force us out the back. Do you have security cameras in front and back?"

"No," she said.

Awadiya's staff was now huddled around Castillo, while Junior used a fire extinguisher to put out burning clothing on two screaming staffers who'd been closest to the impact zone.

"Stay here," Castillo ordered the group, and sprinted down a short hallway to the rear entrance.

He stopped at the door and took a knee. With his free hand, Castillo unlocked the door's dead bolt and grabbed the handle.

God, I fucking hate this part . . .

With a fatalistic exhale, he raised his pistol, turned the handle, and opened the door to the alley.

CHAPTER THIRTY

Castillo scanned the alley over the iron sights of his pistol looking for threats, certain that any second, a barrage of automatic weapon fire would cut him to ribbons.

The bullets never came.

"Clear!" he shouted, after sweeping the alley and scanning the rooftops. "Junior, get everybody back here!"

"Check," the spook said, and Castillo heard him immediately begin directing traffic.

"I'm coming around the back to pick you up," Shaker said, talking on the radio Junior had given him earlier that tied into their comms channel.

"Roger that," Castillo said, stepping out into the alley, still not entirely convinced of their safety.

Moments later, they were all gathered in a cluster in the alley behind Awadiya's campaign office.

"Is this the first attack on you or your office?" Castillo asked Awadiya.

"No," she said with a cynical laugh. "But it is the first Molotov cocktail."

"I'm calling the police," one of Awadiya's female employees said, pulling a phone from her handbag.

Awadiya looked to Castillo, as if checking for his consent, and he nodded.

"I know it's not my business," he said, "but I think it's time you got yourself a security detail."

"Maybe you're right," she said through a sigh, and repeated the line as if trying to convince herself. "Maybe you're right."

"It's not just about your safety, Ms. Khalil," Ani said, squeezing the woman's arm. "Democracy is at stake."

Nice, Ani. Keep it going.

"Yes, you are right, of course."

"What do you see?" Castillo asked Junior, who was looking through the back door into the office.

"They haven't thrown any more Molotovs," Junior said, "and it looks like the fire is burning itself out."

"Good," he replied as the squeal of rubber on asphalt grabbed his attention. He turned and saw their Toyota Land Cruiser tearing around the corner and into the alley. "Don't worry, he's with us," Castillo said to the group, some of whom looked panicked by the fast-approaching SUV.

"Do you want to evacuate with us?" Ani asked Awadiya. "We can take you somewhere safe."

"Thank you for the offer, but I'm safe here," the candidate said.

"Your campaign office just got firebombed," Ani said, her brow furrowed. "I wouldn't call that safe."

"They are just trying to scare me. Millions support me, but many still see me and my message of reform as a threat. I'm advocating a secular government built on constitutionalism and human rights—that's a threat to the status quo. More important, it's a threat to Islamism and Sharia. But trying to stop change is like trying to stop the flowing of the Nile. Block it in one place, and it will gather in pressure and flow around the impediment. If they silence me, another will rise to take my place."

Ani looked at Castillo as if to lobby him to change the woman's mind, but he knew too many strong-willed women like Awadiya to even bother trying. So instead of arguing, he simply handed the people's candidate a business card with a phone number written on it.

"If you think of anything else you want to share about your brother, or, more important, if you need our help, call this number and ask for Charley," he said.

"Thank you," Awadiya said, and with a wry smile added, "but I thought your name was Frank . . ."

"To my friends, it's Charley," he said with a wry smile of his own, and turned to the Land Cruiser.

"Are you okay?" Shaker asked after Castillo climbed into the front passenger seat and shut the door.

"Yeah," he said. "Did you see what happened?"

"Unfortunately, I was circling the block when it happened," Shaker said. "I wanted to get a good tactical picture of the surrounding streets since I have not been to this area before. I am very sorry, Mr. Charley."

"It's probably a good thing. If you'd been parked in front, they might have firebombed the Land Cruiser, too."

"I think this was a drive-by assault. I was looping around the block when it happened. It could not have been more than three minutes before I got back, and I saw nobody in front of the office and nobody running away."

Castillo gave Shaker's shoulder a squeeze. "You did great, but we should probably get going before the police show up. I don't want to get roped into the investigation."

With Junior and Ani settled into their seats, and a wave goodbye to Awadiya, Shaker piloted the Land Cruiser out of the alley. They made their way to Al-Ma Una Street and headed south, toward the bridge that would take them south across the Blue Nile and back to Khartoum proper.

"Sounds like you had a little excitement," McCoy said in Castillo's ear from where he'd been listening from their kitchen TOC inside the safe house. The Marine had essentially maintained radio silence for the past hour and, truth be told, Castillo had forgotten the kid was on the line with them.

Some mentor I am . . .

"Yeah, it got a little rowdy there for a few minutes, but turned out to be an intimidation job rather than a hit."

"You think it had anything to do with you being there?"

"I don't think so. If they were coming after us, they would have brought more firepower."

"You're probably right," McCoy said. "What are our next steps?"

"We're gonna head back to the house and regroup," Castillo said. "Have you got eyes on us?"

"Yeah, good eyes," McCoy said. "Not a cloud in the sky and the satellite feed is good."

"Now that we finally got eyes, nobody's gonna take them from us—isn't that right, Junior?" Castillo said with a backward glance.

"We'll have dedicated satellite coverage for the rest of the operation," the spook said. "The DNI personally assured me as much."

"Okay, in that case, Killer, why don't you stop watching us and track Irshad Khalil. Follow him everywhere he goes. Are those bugs we planted still transmitting?"

"Check, but they're quiet. He's not in his office today."

"Where did he go?" Castillo pressed.

"I don't know. He never came in and I didn't get the bird until 0900."

"Then start monitoring everyone he talks to. It's probably time to get our friends at the Fort involved."

"Roger that," McCoy said. "I'll see you guys in a few."

Castillo turned back once more to look at Junior, this time just staring at the spook.

"What?" Junior said, shifting uncomfortably in his seat under Castillo's gaze.

Castillo narrowed his eyes at the spy. "There's something you're not telling me."

Junior laughed. "I don't know what the hell you're talking about, Charley."

"You've got something up your sleeve, and you're just waiting on the right time to read me—" Castillo stopped mid-sentence as a vehicle traveling behind them caught his eye. "How long has that van been behind us?" he said, directing the question to Shaker.

"The white one?"

"Yeah."

"Not long," Shaker said. "A few minutes, why? Are you concerned?"

Junior turned and stared out the rear window for a look. "Two serious-looking dudes in the front . . . and they're looking at us."

Castillo swiveled back around to face front and scanned the

vehicles driving on the road ahead of them. "Change lanes," he said, his voice a tight cord. "Use your blinker."

Shaker did as instructed, moving from the driving lane into the passing lane of the four-lane highway they were traveling.

"Did the van change lanes?"

"No."

"Accelerate past that bus. As soon as we've cleared his front bumper, I want you to move back to the right lane, but this time don't signal. Keep it close, so they lose their visual on us."

"Okay," Shaker said, doing as instructed.

As soon as the maneuver was executed, Shaker glanced in his side-view mirror. "The van changed lanes and is speeding up to pass the bus."

"I think we have a tail."

"One exit remains before we reach the bridge. Do you want me to take it?"

Castillo grimaced, wracked with indecision.

"I need an answer, the exit is coming up . . ."

"No, I want to get to the other side of the river, but instead of driving back to the safe house, let's divert to the airport. We'll see if the van follows us there," he said.

"Okay, boss," Shaker said.

"Where are they now?" Castillo asked.

Shaker glanced in his side-view mirror. "Holding position in the passing lane beside the bus. Do you want me to accelerate?"

Castillo scanned the traffic ahead and noted brake lights and that the traffic on the bridge was coming to a stop. "Damn it . . . Shaker, try to put some space between us and that van. I don't want to be stopped with them directly behind or beside us."

"I'll try," Shaker said, accelerating despite the brake lights ahead. "Hang on, everybody."

Castillo grabbed the oh-shit handle on the Land Cruiser's A-pillar as Shaker swerved left and threaded the gap between two slightly offset vehicles occupying the left and right lanes. The maneuver earned them a chorus of angry horn blasts but Castillo didn't care. Shaker had accomplished his task and that was all that mattered as the southbound traffic came to an abrupt standstill.

Castillo whipped around in his seat to look out the rear window at the white van, which was stopped in the passing lane one vehicle back. A third head appeared in the gap between the front seats to talk to the driver, then quickly disappeared into the darkened cargo compartment. Both the driver and passenger were staring at the Land Cruiser.

"I don't like it," he murmured, turning back front to scan the road ahead and see what the hell was going on.

About a dozen cars ahead of them, an orange dump truck appeared to be stalled in the right lane. It had its hazard lights flashing and a burly African man was standing at the back left corner of the truck, directing traffic. He wore a fluorescent yellow mesh vest with reflector panels and was ushering cars in alternating trios from the passing and driving lanes around the dump truck.

"Junior, please tell me you packed more heat than just a camcorder and boom mike for today's outing," he said, glancing back at the spook, who feigned offense and smiled.

"Is that a trick question?" Junior said, swiveling in his seat to grab a hard case from the cargo hold. He dragged the case through the gap between his and Ani's captain's chairs and turned it so it was resting on both their laps. The two spies simultaneously undid their respective side hold-down clasps and opened the clamshell-style lid. Inside the hard case, Castillo spied two Sig 716I Tread rifles, a half-dozen extra magazines, and a row of percussion grenades neatly arranged in foam cradle cutouts. "I've got vests in the back and another little somethin' somethin' back there, too, in case things get really out of control."

"Now we're talking," Castillo said. "You two kit up and ready those rifles just in case."

"Roger that," Junior said, pulling the first rifle out of the case.

Castillo turned back to face front and scanned the vehicles stopped ahead of them. The stalled construction vehicle would make the perfect tactical ruse—allowing a hit squad to stop and control the flow of traffic. Executed properly, they would be locked into the perfect kill box—blocked in front and back, with no escape routes and dozens of civilians trapped in the mix to create confusion, chaos, and collateral damage.

Damn, I'm getting paranoid in my old age, he thought, suddenly feeling like a new parent seeing danger lurking in every innocuous situation.

Unable to help himself, he glanced out the back window where the white van was still creeping along in the stop-and-go traffic behind them with single-vehicle separation.

Fuck it—it's my paranoia that's kept me alive all these years.

"Shaker, put on your blinker and nose over into the left lane," Castillo said, facing front.

"You want me to merge early?"

"Yes."

Shaker nodded and started angling left.

Castillo looked at the man in the yellow vest directing traffic, and saw that the worker's gaze was fixed squarely on their Land Cruiser even though they were still fifty meters back from the choke point. They stared at each other for a long moment, when movement in Castillo's peripheral vision caught his attention. His gaze flicked to the bed of the orange 8x4 Mercedes Arocs dump truck. For a split second, he spied a head peeking over the top of the tipper's double-action tailgate.

"Shit . . ."

"What?" Junior said, his voice hardening now.

"I just saw a head pop up in the bed of the orange dumper. There's somebody in there and I think he was ranging us," Castillo said, pulling his pistol. "This is a setup. We're being funneled into a trap."

"What do you want me to do?" Shaker said, gripping the steering wheel tight with both hands. "We're on a bridge, blocked front and back."

"I know," Castillo grumbled.

"There's nowhere to go. I can't even turn around."

"I know! Let me think . . ."

"One, this is Homeplate," McCoy said from the the TOC in his ear. "Sitrep?"

"I think we're about to get our dicks slapped," Castillo said. "No offense, Ani."

"None taken," she said from the back, her voice tight with pre-combat anxiety. She reached into the rear cargo hold and tossed a Kevlar vest to Castillo. "Last one."

"Thanks," he said, then turned to their driver. "Shaker, you should probably take it."

"No way in hell I'm getting out of this SUV," the man said with a fatalistic laugh. "And besides, I'm not a soldier. It is better if you wear it."

Castillo nodded, then slipped the vest on over his shirt.

"All right, guys, I just zoomed in on your position and I'm looking at that dump truck," McCoy said over the comms circuit. "Charley was right, it's a trap. I count five shooters crouching in the bed. Looks like they've got rifles, but nothing heavy. I don't see a fifty or a technical . . . so you got that going for you."

"Wonderful," he murmured. "What about the van? How many thermals?"

"Wait one. Okay . . . looks like six tangos—two up front and four sitting in back."

"Sure would be nice to have that Sentinel *now*, Junior," McCoy said, looking over his shoulder at the spook. "We're outnumbered four shooters to one, and the bed of that dumper is made from reinforced plate steel. Nothing we're packing can touch it."

"That's not exactly true," Junior said, pulling a second bulky case from the back, with MBDA stenciled on the outside. "Remember that little somethin' somethin' I mentioned before?"

"Yeah . . ."

"Well, this is it," the spook said, opening the case to reveal a rectangular sleeve a little less than a meter long, painted green with an integrated optics package and double pistol grips and the word ENFORCER printed on the side in yellow block lettering.

"What the hell is that?"

"A present from a friend of mine at MBDA," Junior said with a crooked grin.

"Is it an RPG?"

"No, this is what every RPG dreams of becoming. This bad boy is a fire-and-forget shoulder-launched, guided aerial munition."

"You brought a fucking missile launcher with you?" Castillo said, shaking his head with a smile.

"Well, I just thought—"

A round ricocheting off the windshield abruptly ended the conversation. Castillo whirled to see a tiny starburst pattern directly in front of Shaker's face. A second round slammed into the windshield on the passenger side at head level, followed a heartbeat later by a coordinated barrage from both their front and rear.

"Son of a bitch," Castillo growled as bullets plinked off the up-armored SUV like hail in a thunderstorm. "I hate it when I'm right."

"Why are they engaging now?" Ani said from the back. "It's too soon, we haven't reached the choke point."

"Because they realized we made them," Junior said.

"Oh, God, what do we do?" Shaker said, ducking down in his seat.

"We have to fight back," Castillo answered.

"Can't we just hide inside? The glass is holding."

"I wish we could, but if we don't fight back now, they're going to shoot out the tires, swarm the vehicle, and detonate an incendiary device under the chassis—either killing us immediately or forcing us out with heat and we'll be slaughtered by firing squad."

"You've got five shooters up in the dump truck, and two—no make that three—shooters out of the van behind you moving to covered firing positions behind civilian vehicles," McCoy reported over the comms circuit.

"Shit, there's no way we get out of this without collateral damage," Junior said. "There's people everywhere."

"We have to try our damnedest," Castillo said, swiveling to look out the rear window, where he saw a tall, skinny fighter with an AK-47 moving around the rear bumper of the car behind them. He shifted his gaze to the van and a counteroffensive plan began to formulate in his mind. "Junior, what type of projectile does that Enforcer fire? Is it an antitank missile like a Javelin?"

The spook shook his head. "Light armor only, but it packs a punch."

Castillo pursed his lips, really wishing he had McCoy with them. The Marine was a one-man annihilation machine. Now, as the only person in the SUV with a Special Operations pedigree, the burden of making kills would fall disproportionately on his shoulders.

I'm just gonna have to find a way to make it work.

"Junior, have you fired that weapon before?"

The spook nodded. "Yeah, at a boondoggle in Germany. MBDA put on a clinic, hoping I'd convince OGA to place a big order."

"All right, in that case, I want you to blow up the van with it. I'll cover you while you take the shot out the rear tailgate."

"But what about the dump truck?"

"We've only got one shot, so we need to make it count. We can't risk the missile not punching a hole through that plate steel. And anyway, I have an idea how to handle the dumper, but first, we need to get out of this cross fire," he said, shifting his gaze to Ani. "How good are you with a long gun?"

"I'm not," she said, meeting his gaze. "I'd be lying if I said otherwise. You should take it, Charley. I'm proficient with pistols, but even then, only an average shot."

"That's okay," he said, unbuckling his seat belt. "Trade places with me."

As bullets pounded the Land Cruiser from both directions, they made the awkward switch, taking turns climbing over the center console between the two front seats. Outside, pandemonium ensued as bystander vehicles jockeyed for position, trying desperately to get clear of the firefight.

"Shaker, listen to me," Castillo said. "On my mark, I want you to turn the Land Cruiser back in the other direction to face the dump truck."

"What!"

"You heard me, we're at the wrong angle. I need an offset so I can get out without being cut to ribbons and also, when you open the tailgate, we don't want a straight firing lane so the guys behind us can hose you down inside."

"Okay, I understand," Shaker said, his hands trembling on the wheel.

He turned to Junior to tell him to prep the Enforcer, but the spook was already on it with the missile launcher out of the case and being powered up. He opened the rifle case laying on the floor across the footwells and pulled two frag grenades from their foam cradles. After pocketing the grenades, he unlocked the right rear door and grabbed the door handle.

"How much longer, Junior?"

"I'm ready," the spook said, his voice all business.

"One, Homeplate—you've got three tangos behind you. Suggested kill order is Tango One, who's in cover at the right rear corner of the white sedan directly behind you. Followed by Tango Two, who's crouching behind the silver pickup truck beside the white sedan, also right side. Tango Three is sweeping southeast, around the other side of the pickup," McCoy reported, his timing perfect.

"Check. How many thermals in the van?"

"Two. The driver is still behind the wheel, but the dude who was seated in the front passenger seat has moved aft into the cargo compartment. I can't tell what he's doing back there."

"Copy all." Castillo looped his rifle sling over his head and said, "It's now or never. Shaker, execute the turn."

The Land Cruiser's engine roared to life and the SUV lurched forward and angled hard to the right. Castillo flung the passenger door open and jumped out. His boots hit the pavement with a thud and both his knees screamed in protest, still sore and stiff from the action in Cairo. *Get moving, old man,* he told himself and brought his 716 up to the ready and sighted through the Sig ROMEO8H holographic optic. He advanced in three strides to the rear bumper, took a knee, and hovered his target reticle at chest level at the northeast corner of the white sedan where McCoy had reported Tango One in cover.

"One, Homeplate—I got your back," McCoy said in his ear. "You have a good line on Tango One."

While McCoy talked, a torso popped out around the rear corner of the white sedan and into the ballistic circle of Castillo's holographic sight. Without even needing to adjust angle or elevation, Castillo squeezed the trigger and sent a 7.62-millimeter round into the insurgent's forehead. The body fell away from view and he swiveled left, shifting his aim toward the silver pickup to look for Tango Two.

A bullet careened off the D-pillar just above Castillo's head as he found Tango Two standing beside the silver pickup unloading a volley directly at him. Castillo pulled back just in time as the shooter dialed in his elevation and unloaded a prolonged strafe where Castillo had just been.

He exhaled and readied himself to return fire.

"Now," McCoy said in his ear, as the distinctive *crack-crack-crack* of the shooter's AK-47 fell silent.

Castillo popped out and engaged. His civilian variant 716I Tread was limited to semiautomatic action, but the weapon more than made up for it with precision and balance.

Trigger squeeze.

Trigger squeeze.

Trigger squeeze . . .

The second and third rounds found their marks, hitting the shooter in the left arm and center mass respectively. The body crumpled and Castillo pulled back into cover.

"Nice shooting, One," McCoy said. "Tango Three is—hold on, we've got a problem. Tango Four just stepped out of the van and he has an RPG!"

"Open the tailgate. Fire the missile now!" Castillo shouted. "I'll distract both of them."

Fresh adrenaline surging through his veins, Castillo sighted around the Land Cruiser's D-pillar and hosed down the cargo van, forcing the RPG-wielding shooter to drop low below the roofline of the white sedan between them for cover. In his peripheral vision, Castillo could see the Land Cruiser's tailgate coming up. He rotated left and fired three rounds over the hood of the silver pickup where he sensed Tango Three had repositioned and was about to pop up. His instincts were correct. The crown of the enemy shooter's head broke the plane momentarily, but then quickly disappeared as Castillo's bullets gave him an unexpected haircut.

To Castillo's surprise, Junior jumped out the back of the Land Cruiser, ran four strides, and fired the missile. The jet of fire out the back of the launcher answered his unspoken question, and he thanked God the spook had been smarter than he was. Had Junior fired from inside the SUV, the back blast from the launch would have fried Shaker and Ani. Propelled by a rooster tail of orange-yellow flame, the Enforcer missile—with its multi-effects warhead—screamed toward the enemy van. A heartbeat later, the van exploded in a massive fireball, sending burning hunks of metal and plastic in all directions.

"Tangos Four and Five are down," McCoy called.

But Castillo's elation at the direct hit instantly turned to dread as the melee around them was evolving at lightspeed.

"Junior, on your left!" McCoy shouted over the comms circuit.

The sequence of events that transpired next, Castillo would not fully piece together until it was too late. Tango Three had repositioned again in cover to the north side of the silver pickup truck. Only Ani had noticed, with Castillo's attention—along with Junior's and McCoy's—fixed on the RPG threat. Ani, recognizing the impending blindside, stepped out of the Land Cruiser to engage Tango Three with her pistol. On McCoy's warning, Junior got small, while Castillo swiveled in time to see Tango Three turn on Ani.

Ani fired two shots and smartly dropped prone as Tango Three unloaded a prolonged burst. Unfortunately, she'd left the front passenger door wide open. The barrage of bullets missed her but flew true and through the gap. Castillo watched in horror as blood spattered the inside of the driver's-side window. Then the Land Cruiser's engine roared and it abruptly accelerated, driving right toward the dump truck, leaving Ani, Junior, and Castillo stranded in no-man's-land with no cover as the shooters in the dump truck lined up along the top of the dumper tailgate for a turkey shoot.

"Oh, shit, they're going to die," Castillo heard McCoy say over the comms circuit, followed by a burst of static and a click.

But he didn't have time to worry about McCoy and comms at the moment, because everything had just gone to hell, with enemy bullets ricocheting off the pavement all around them.

Castillo took a knee and prioritized his targets.

Tango Three first.

Time slowed.

He brought his rifle up, his holographic sight in line with Tango Three's chest, only to find himself staring straight into the barrel of the terrorist's AK-47.

Castillo squeezed his trigger.

So did the enemy.

CHAPTER THIRTY-ONE

"Junior, on your left!" McCoy barked over the comms, furious with himself.

He'd been so focused on the van and the terrorist with the RPG that he'd taken his eyes off Tango Three. And while he'd been snoozing, that fucker had snuck around to the other side of a pickup and was about to cap Junior.

McCoy zoomed out on the live feed and watched as Ani jumped out of the front passenger seat to engage the terrorist before he could shoot Junior. Meanwhile, farther south, inside the dump truck, fighters were lining up like a firing squad to cut his teammates down.

Oh, my God . . .

McCoy felt his chest tighten as he watched Ani hit the deck as Tango Three swiveled and strafed her direction. From his bird's-eye view, he couldn't tell if Ani had been hit or dropped prone just in time to miss the AK-47 barrage. Then, in high-definition horror, he saw blood splatter on the Land Cruiser windshield and watched it suddenly accelerate toward the dump truck.

"Oh, shit, they're going to die."

Ripping off his headset, he turned to Wardi.

"We gotta go get them."

"By the time we get there, it will be over," Wardi said, his accent thicker than usual under the strain.

McCoy pushed away from the table, tucked the laptop under his arm, and grabbed the Sig Sauer 716G2 rifle leaning against the chair beside him. "Maybe, but we have to try. We can't help them from here and we can't leave them stranded."

"Okay," Wardi said, and McCoy looked up to find the man already slinging his own rifle and pack over his shoulder. "Let's go. I'll drive," the Sudanese man said, his eyes showing the same fire McCoy felt.

"One, I'm coming to you," he announced.

He got no response from Castillo, but even if Castillo had tried to shoot down the plan, McCoy was coming anyway. The team was badly outnumbered and outgunned, and if Shaker's Land Cruiser was disabled, they'd be stranded on the bridge with no way to exfil on foot. Rifle and backpack in hand, McCoy turned to leave just as the foyer exploded. The blast tossed him backward like a rag doll. He slammed into the coat closet door hard enough to splinter the wood before he slid down onto the tile floor. Despite the stars in his vision, he rolled right, spinning onto one knee and bringing his rifle up as he blinked his eyes to clear his vision.

Fire and move, the Marine in his head reminded him.

He shifted the shot-mode selector switch with his thumb to

three-round burst and squeezed the trigger twice, firing blindly into the smoke-filled hole where the front door had been moments ago. He heard a scream of pain, his ears confirming what his eyes couldn't yet see.

The assaulters were coming.

McCoy shifted left and squeezed off another three-round burst into the smoky void just as a barrage of heavy gunfire shredded the closet door he'd been leaning against just seconds ago. He backpedaled out of the foyer, ran through the dining room and into the kitchen. With some separation and a better angle, he whirled around and took a knee. He watched three figures emerge from the smoke, each clearing like pros in different directions as they entered the house. As he positioned his holographic red dot onto the lead shooter's forehead, McCoy clicked the selector switch back to single shot. He squeezed the trigger, dropping the leader—which instantly diverted the other two fighters away from the line of fire in search of cover.

Not wanting to be flanked, McCoy repositioned.

He quickstepped in pursuit of the closer assaulter and dropped him with a shot in the middle upper back. He took a knee and scanned for the third assaulter, but the man had disappeared around the corner.

He's probably looping around through the great room, to try to catch me from the other side.

As he swiveled left to prepare for that, his thoughts went to Wardi, who he'd not seen anywhere. He wanted to call out for Wardi but didn't dare for fear of giving up his position. But the driver, operator—and now friend—must be alive, because had the blast at the front door killed him, his body would have been in the foyer.

C'mon, you bastard, he silently cursed, hovering his red dot three inches off the corner of the wall where he expected the shooter to emerge. *Come and get me.*

He heard a metallic rattle.

Grenade!

Operating on pure reflex, he dodged toward the heavy dining table they'd been using as their workstation and flipped it on its side. The grenade exploded a millisecond later, driving the table into him and sending him sliding across the floor. He came to rest with the table pinning him against the back wall, but damn if the thick wooden top didn't hold. Ears ringing, he pushed the table clear a few feet and scrambled into a crouch. He took a deep breath and sighted over the table edge to see four more men entering the foyer. He dropped the leader first, his 7.62 millimeter round taking off the top of the man's head and spraying gray matter on the far wall. He shifted his sight to the next shooter and fired twice. The first bullet tore through the man's throat and the second hit him in the temple as he fell.

The other two infiltrators repositioned, but so did McCoy.

Fire and move . . .

Fully automatic rifle rounds tore through the table McCoy had been hiding behind, but he was already gone and flanking. He found his target in a combat crouch moving toward the table and shot the assaulter twice in the chest and once in the head. Heart pounding, he continued his sweep, quickstepping out of the foyer and into the great room. There, he finally found Wardi, sitting hunched in a pool of blood on the white carpet between the modern sofa and glass coffee table. Suddenly, Wardi's hands shot up over his head and his eyes went wide—staring at something behind McCoy.

McCoy hit the deck as a volley of bullets screamed past overhead. He landed hard on his side but ignored the pain. He rolled, brought his rifle up, and fired—sighting on a tall and powerfully built black man kitted up with a plate carrier vest and a half-dozen extra magazines in pouches on his chest. McCoy's bullet struck a glancing blow to the side of the man's kit, spoiling the assaulter's shot, which went wide. Before McCoy could get off another shot, the man skirted around the corner to cover. His Marine Raider mind had the count at two enemy shooters still alive in the house, but how many more were waiting outside? He was almost out of bullets in this magazine and with Wardi wounded, there was no way he could fend off this attack indefinitely. Scanning over his rifle, McCoy duck-walked back to Wardi.

"Where are you hit?"

"My . . . right . . . chest . . ." Wardi said as he strained to get up, a slight whistling sound framing each word.

McCoy could try to drag him to the master bedroom suite and make a stand there, but that would buy them little time. Their odds of surviving were much better if they could make it to the panic room in the basement. Also, there would be a full medical kit and possibly working comms inside. The decision was a no-brainer. The hit squad would reorganize and attack any second and put them in a cross fire from two sides.

"Grab your rifle, brother," he grunted. "We're moving."

He rolled the powerful Sudanese man onto his shoulder in a combat carry. Securing Wardi's wrist and leg to his chest with his left hand, he rose and surged forward. He stayed low and sprinted clear, while someone shouted and fired behind him. He took his pursuers by surprise again, ducking through the narrow doorway to the basement, knocking Wardi's head accidently into the doorframe as he did. Halfway down the staircase, he felt and heard Wardi fire two three-round bursts behind them up the stairs with his rifle.

Hell yeah, brother, he thought as the man he was carrying covered their six.

At the bottom of the stairs, he looped right, just as gunfire tore down the staircase and pinged off the washer and dryer that sat along the basement wall. He vectored toward the safe room, the bank vault–style door their only salvation. He pressed the green button and it hissed open just as the sound of boots on stair treads reached him. He charged into the void, dumped Wardi unceremoniously off his shoulders, and pulled the heavy door closed just as he heard two grenades *tink*ing off the cement floor. He smashed his elbow into the red button beside the door, listening as the magnetic lock engaged and the four titanium bars slid into place. The grenades exploded sequentially—a deadly one-two punch—but inside the panic room, the detonations registered as only a dull *whump whump.* They were safe—for now. Junior had briefed the team that not even an RPG or breacher charges could penetrate the door and walls to the panic room.

McCoy pressed his forehead against the steel door and let out a long sigh.

A wheezing gurgle from Wardi on the floor snapped his attention to the next crisis he had to deal with. He scanned the room for a med kit and spotting it hanging from hooks on the wall beside a communication panel. He grabbed the bag and took a knee beside the wounded man while bullets ricocheted harmlessly off the safe-room door outside. Wardi's lips had gone blue and his rapid breaths were coming in short, panicked gasps. McCoy noted the man's neck muscles straining as he tried to pull air into his lungs.

"I gotcha, bro," McCoy said, trying to sound calm. "You have a pneumothorax—a collapsed lung—but I can fix it and you'll breathe much better."

Wardi nodded, but his eyes were already glazing over.

McCoy now noticed that Wardi's windpipe seemed crooked, displaced to the left side by the mounting pressure in his right chest. Racing against time, he tore open the pneumothorax kit that he pulled from the bag, spreading the tools and instruments out on a blue paper drape he laid on the floor. He grabbed the large-bore, twelve-gauge needle and the small silver package of betadine. He pulled open Wardi's shirt, the buttons popping off and plinking on the polished cement floor, and tore the betadine open with his teeth. The brown liquid spattered onto Wardi's upper chest and dribbled into a little pool at the base of his neck and McCoy tossed the package to the ground. He removed the large needle from its package and yanked off the cap.

With two fingers, McCoy probed the man's right chest, feeling the collarbone and ribs below. He found the second space between the ribs, pressed the point of the needle into the skin just above the rib to avoid the blood vessels nestled beneath each, and jammed the needle deep into the space, hard, and pulled the inner needle out of the catheter.

Immediately he was rewarded with a long, loud hiss, like someone had just punctured a car tire, and he held the catheter in place against the pressure. The rush of air continued for several seconds before slowly tapering off and becoming a wet gurgle, and blood dribbled out of the hub of the catheter.

With the pressure relieved that had been compressing his lung, Wardi gasped for air in one long breath. He blinked, in cadence with his respirations, his eyes clearing seconds later.

"I can breathe, thank you," Wardi said with a tenuous smile. "I did not know you were a doctor."

"Not hardly," he said. "In Special Operations we get some advanced medical training for stuff like this."

He tore off two pieces of tape from the kit, tearing each down the middle halfway, and used them to secure the catheter in place. Then he attached a small flutter valve to the hub of the catheter, allowing any air that built up again in the driver's chest to escape, while preventing air from being drawn in.

There was another barrage of distant-sounding rifle shots and the accompanying sound of bullets bouncing off the heavy steel door. They had air enough inside for two days and the terrorists could literally blow the house up around them and they'd be fine. The problem was, they didn't have two days, and for sure Charley, Junior, Ani, and Shaker didn't. And there was no Ranger battalion a quick flight away to serve as QRF and rescue them or Charley's team. Even if there was a covert team in Khartoum, he had no idea how to identify and contact them, not without Junior.

Shit.

He felt for Wardi's pulse, which no longer pounded out of control but instead was a bounding, regular one hundred beats per minute. Whatever damage had been done to his lung, Wardi wasn't bleeding to death—at least not yet.

McCoy scanned the room, which included two cots, a second medical bag, a gun cage with four assault rifles and several pistols as well as stacks of magazines for both, a narrow door he assumed to be for a water closet, and a desk with two computers and chairs. There were four bricks of water bottles and a box of military MRE bags beside the desk. McCoy had no idea how to reach anyone on the computers, or who, but they couldn't just sit here.

"One, this is Homeplate. One—do you copy?"

He heard nothing in his earpiece. He had no idea if a signal could reach him in this bunker of a room, but he doubted it.

"You okay?" he asked Wardi.

The man nodded, and McCoy gently helped him to one of the two cots and reclined him as gently as possible. The man needed a surgeon pretty soon but seemed stable for now.

"I'm gonna see if I can get someone on the computer," he said. "We're safe for now, but we need to get you to a hospital and warn the rest of the team."

CHAPTER THIRTY-TWO

Castillo felt the terrorist's bullet nick the top of his shoulder strap as it screamed past. Had it been three inches to the left, it would have plowed through his neck and he'd be a gurgling, suffocating pile of useless flesh, bleeding out on the pavement. Castillo was the better shot. Only one of the 7.62-millimeter rounds fired simultaneously hit its mark, and that round had been his. Through his ROMEO optics, he watched Tango Three's head whiplash backward and the terrorist's body drop like felled timber.

With no time to savor his win in the duel of long guns, Castillo whirled counterclockwise and unleashed a barrage of covering fire at the dump truck—firing five rounds in rapid succession at the row of shooters in the bed. Only one of his rounds scored a hit, but the salvo accomplished its primary objective of forcing the enemy shooters down.

Shoot and move, the Delta operator inside reminded him, and Castillo got his legs churning.

Trigger squeeze.

Trigger squeeze.

He pinged two more rounds off the dumper's tailgate as he charged toward their Land Cruiser, which had crashed into a silver sedan, plowing it into the back corner of the dump truck. The Land Cruiser's wheels spun in place—burning rubber and squealing terribly—confirming in Castillo's mind that Shaker was dead, the weight of his lifeless right foot still depressing the accelerator. In his peripheral vision, he saw both Junior and Ani up and moving in hunched crouches toward cover.

Trigger squeeze.

Trigger squeeze.

"That's right, keep your heads down, assholes," he growled, firing more suppression rounds as he closed on the Land Cruiser. Five strides later, he was crouched at the rear bumper under the Land Cruiser's still open tailgate, which he now used as a very handy bulletproof awning. In the lull, the four remaining terrorist shooters reengaged, taking pot shots at the Land Cruiser and the silver pickup truck, behind which Junior and Ani now sheltered.

"Two, One—sitrep?" he called to Junior.

"We're both intact, you?" came the spook's reply.

"Intact and pissed off."

"You got a plan?"

"Yeah, I'm going to frag these motherfuckers. I need covering fire," he said, pulling out one of the two grenades he'd pocketed.

"Check. On your mark," Junior said.

Castillo took a deep breath and listened to the cadence of the enemy fire. When the pattern lost its rhythm, he gave the order.

"Now!"

The crack of Junior's Sig to his right interrupted the enemy fire.

Castillo exhaled, pulled the pin, and stepped out of cover. It had been ages since he'd thrown a grenade and it showed. His toss sailed over the top of the high-walled bed of the dump truck, off the side of the bridge, and detonated in midair as it plummeted to the river below.

"Shit, too much," he murmured, ducking back under the raised tailgate.

"You put too much on it," Junior echoed. "Wanna go again?"

"Yeah, but this time instead of trying to sink a three-pointer, I'm going in for a layup."

"What?"

"Just cover me . . . on my mark. Three . . . two . . . one . . . covering fire," he said, and a split second later he heard Junior go to work.

"God, I hate basketball," he mumbled, ducking around the other side of the Land Cruiser and taking off in a sprint.

Instead of trying to make a lob, he ran straight at the dump truck. As he passed the Land Cruiser's driver's-side door, he pulled the pin. With a leaping stride, he catapulted himself up onto the hood of the silver sedan. His booted foot put a crater in the sheet metal as he did his best Michael Jordan impersonation and delivered the frag to the hoop—the hoop in this case being the bed of the dump truck. He traded wide-eyed stares with one of the terrorists who'd popped up in the exact moment he delivered the goods, *too late* recognition flashing in the man's eyes at what had just happened.

Castillo came down awkwardly, one foot landing on the hood but the other missing, and he tumbled into the narrow gap between the side of the sedan and the dump truck. He bounced off the side of one of the Arocs' massive rubber tires as he fell and hit the pavement hard. Above him, the grenade detonated inside the bed of the dump truck with a terrible, resonating clang—the explosive force magnified in the five-sided heavy steel box that forced the blast in only one direction—up. Debris, weapons, body parts, and blood rained down on him like some hellish, gory squall from above.

"Oh, hell, yeah!" Junior shouted in Castillo's ear. "That was incredible, dude."

"Did I get all of them?" Castillo groaned, his right shoulder and left ankle both barking mad with pain. He was rolling onto his side to reengage with his rifle if anyone had escaped the blast.

"You got 'em, all right," the spook came back. "Now let's get the hell out of here while we still can."

Castillo got to a knee and brought his 716 up to scan overhead, just in case one or more of the enemy shooters survived. But, when no heads or rifles appeared over the sidewall of the dumper bed, he lowered his weapon and limped his way back to the Land Cruiser. Junior and Ani showed up a moment later, both sighting the bed and cab of the dump truck with an abundance of caution.

"Help me with this," Castillo said to Junior and opened the driver's-side door to the horror show inside. Shaker's slumped body fell as the door swung open, but Junior caught the dead man before he could tumble out. Blood and chunks of gore decorated the cabin—splatter on the driver's-side window, door panel, instrument cluster, and windshield.

"Oh, my God," Ani said behind them.

"Don't look," Junior said. "Just keep covering the dump truck."

The roar of the Land Cruiser's engine went quiet and the wheels stopped spinning as Shaker's right foot came off the accelerator. Junior grunted as he pulled the Sudanese man out of the vehicle and onto the road. Castillo grabbed Shaker's legs and together they carried the corpse to the cargo compartment and closed the tailgate.

"I'll drive," Castillo said, slipping into the driver's seat while Ani and Junior both climbed into the back.

Ignoring the blood and other bits, Castillo put the Land Cruiser's transmission into reverse and backed clear of the silver sedan whose occupants were either hiding or had run away. Over the course of the firefight, most of the civilian vehicles had fled—leaving only those that were damaged or boxed in. To Castillo's relief, the path in the left lane around the dump truck was now clear. He floored the accelerator and the Land Cruiser took off south, leaving smoldering carnage straight out of *Mad Max* on the bridge in the rearview mirror.

"Homeplate, One—come in," Castillo said, querying McCoy. "Homeplate, One—do you copy?"

When no reply came, he met Junior's gaze in the mirror.

"I think he lost comms," the spook said. "I thought I heard him drop out during the firefight."

"Call his mobile."

"Roger that," Junior said, pulling his own mobile from his pocket.

"I got a bad feeling about this," Castillo said through gritted teeth. "I think they hit the safe house, too."

"Oh, my God," Ani breathed behind him. Castillo looked at her in the rearview mirror and what he saw concerned him. The CIA officer was shaking with emotion. She was an experienced undercover operative for Clandestine Services—which meant she probably hadn't discharged her weapon in a real gun battle. And she had certainly never experienced the heat of battle the likes of which they'd just survived—a Task Force Green level firefight for certain.

"You good, kid?" he asked.

She met his eyes in the mirror, her own haunted with images he knew, from experience, would likely be with her the rest of her life.

"I . . ." She looked back down into her lap.

"You did great, Ani," he said. "You saved our lives today."

"Not . . . not everyone," she said, her voice cracking, tossing a glance over her shoulder toward the rear cargo area where Shaker's body lay.

Castillo understood, but also knew he needed her sharp. This wasn't over by a long shot.

"War is like this, Ani. Things happen and they're not our fault. You performed where ninety-nine percent of people would freeze or run. I mean it when I say we are alive because of you. But we have more work to do. We have two more teammates in trouble and I need you sharp. These assholes don't get to kill any more of us today."

"Okay," she said, her jaw twitching as she clutched her weapon in her lap.

Junior leaned over, pulling her toward him, forehead to forehead as she clung to the spook's forearm and closed her eyes. He whispered something to her, too quiet for Castillo to hear. She sobbed and he whispered something else and she nodded. Then she looked up again, a new confidence and fire in her eyes.

"She's good, Charley," Junior said, giving him a curt nod and knowing look in the mirror.

Castillo scanned the road in both directions as he exited the bridge still heading south. Sirens screamed toward them from the west, heading for what would now be assumed to be a terrorist attack on the Al Mak Nimir Bridge. The investigators weren't going to find much evidence to piece together.

Two blocks in, the traffic was already heavy. Castillo turned east on Al Jamhuriya Avenue, accelerating east to pick up the faster-moving four-lane road a few blocks away.

"Can you access the satellite feed, Junior?" he asked, looking

again in the mirror and this time seeing Junior already tapping
away on his tablet.

"Working on it," the spook said.

Castillo turned right, cutting off a delivery truck who answered
with a blast of his horn and a shaking fist out his window. The four
lanes, with extra lanes for major turns, allowed him to accelerate
rapidly, weaving in and out of the much lighter traffic. They would
be at the safe house in minutes now.

"Got it," Junior said, triumphantly. "Had to clear my head and
recall the access code and double password that they . . ." the spook
stopped.

Castillo glanced in the rearview where the man raised his eyes
from his tablet, mouth open. "Oh, shit, dude."

Ani leaned in and looked at the tablet.

"What is it?" Castillo barked, eyes on the road and pressing
down on the accelerator.

"You're right—they fucking hit the safe house. Our other Land
Cruiser is still there. I got heavy smoke rolling out of the front door.
I show only two shooters outside, holding a perimeter on the driveway near the house. No other motion, but there could be shooters
inside. They came in two SUVs, so could be up to a dozen guys
we're up against."

Castillo tightened his jaw and let out a long breath. Then he
thought of the bodies left behind by McCoy in Cairo.

"Not if McCoy was still in the house when they came," he predicted. "Our guy is a one-man killing machine."

"True that," Junior said with a grin and a nod. "And if they
killed or captured our guys already, they'd be gone. McCoy must
still be in the fight."

"Then God help them all," Castillo said, now grinning for real.

They would be there in just a few more minutes. He had weaved his way back to Street 60 southbound.

One more turn . . .

"Junior," Castillo called out, his mind assembling an order of battle already. "Come up here."

Junior squeezed between the seats, landing awkwardly in the passenger seat and turning to look at him, the tablet in his lap.

"What're ya thinkin', boss?"

He approached the turn, headed east, then pulled abruptly to a stop along the curb.

"Take the wheel," he said, grabbing the tablet and squirming between the front seats to drop into the passenger-side middle captain's chair beside Ani. "When we get there, don't even slow down," he said. "Looks like the gate is already open so plow right up to the house, bending left as you do. After I drop those two assholes out front, follow me into the house."

"I'll be on your right," Ani confirmed, no hesitation in her voice at all. "Junior, stay left."

"You guys know standard room-clearing procedures?" Castillo asked, picking up his Sig 716 and replacing the magazine with a fresh one.

"I kind of remember from the Farm . . ." Ani's response confirmed what he would be working with. But both spooks had drive and smarts. And they were highly motivated.

"Okay," Castillo said. "Pay attention. I enter first, and I'll turn left, clearing my left rear corner and the dining room to the left. You follow right on me, clearing right. Junior will surge straight in between us, and we clear and fall in on him, repeating it in the great room to the rear. Got it?"

"Yeah, I got it," Ani said, and he believed she did.

"Kill anything that isn't McCoy or Wardi. You good with that?"

"Oh, I'm all good with that," Ani said.

Good. Harness that rage, girl.

They were a block away now.

Castillo rolled his head and took a long, slow breath. A moment later, the SUV was in the turn, bouncing over the dip at the end of the driveway, moving fast toward the house. He opened the door, positioned his rifle on the roof, and pressed his cheek against the stock, sighting on one of two enemy shooters flanking the front door. As predicted, both men began firing, but at the windshield on the driver's side, their barrage of bullets plinking off the hood and frame and starring the ballistic glass. His first round dropped the shooter in his tracks. His second caught the right-side fighter in the chest, spinning him around. The man stumbled to his knees, and Castillo lined up his second shot carefully, putting a 7.62 round through the back of the man's head.

Both men were dead when the Land Cruiser braked to a stop.

Castillo was already on the brick pavers, rounding the hood of the truck and sprinting to the door.

"Tight on me," he commanded over his shoulder.

Thin smoke billowed from the wrecked doorway, the door itself part of the debris on the front stoop and in the hazy foyer, he assumed. His breathing controlled and steady, Castillo entered the foyer sighting over his rifle. He crossed the threshold and swept left, clearing the corner and then the dining room. Without seeing her, he felt Ani enter behind him.

Dead bodies littered the floor—two on the left, one in the dining room, and another in the short hallway leading to the great room. He surged forward while chopping a hand right for Junior to circle around and flank whoever might be waiting for them in the kitchen. Castillo's pulse pounded in his temples, not from the adrenaline of combat—years of killing had numbed him to that— but from a visceral fear for the lives of McCoy and Wardi. He cleared quickly left, saw a body on the floor, then pressed forward. At the same time, a man stepped out of the doorway leading to the basement, his eyes going wide and mouth open in surprise as he came face to face with Castillo. The shooter's weapon made it up barely thirty degrees before Castillo's round tore off the side of his head. Junior's rifle roared from behind him dropping a second assaulter coming up behind the first.

He nodded to Junior, then felt Ani tap him on the shoulder as he stepped over the bodies, leading the descent down the stairs into the basement.

Please, God, if you ever listen to operators like me, let McCoy have made it into the panic room . . .

Three quick turns confirmed the basement was clear and he was beside the bank vault–style door, the black glass plate red, the door magnetically locked.

Castillo smiled at Junior.

"They made it," he sighed. "They're inside."

"Oh, thank God," Ani breathed from behind him.

Junior pressed his hand onto the glass and punched in his code. The door clicked and hissed as the compressed air inside escaped.

"Don't shoot, Killer," Castillo hollered, not wanting to get shot by his boy. "It's us. We're coming in."

The heavy door swung open.

McCoy sat cross-legged on the floor beside Wardi, who opened his eyes briefly, then smiled and let out a long, pained laugh. "I knew you would come, my friend."

"We're here, Wardi," Junior said, taking a knee beside his man, inspecting the needle assembly that Castillo recognized as a catheter decompression set up for a pneumothorax.

"What the hell took you so long?" McCoy asked, taking a sip of water from the bottle cradled in his lap.

"Stopped for drinks," Castillo said with a grin.

"Well," McCoy said, as he grunted and got to his feet, "I hope you brought me one."

Castillo stared at the Marine, remembering the dead bodies scattered around the upstairs of the house. The kid really was living up to his inherited nickname.

"I'm just glad you guys are okay," McCoy said, sticking out a hand.

"Back atcha," Castillo said. "Let's get the hell out of here and get Wardi to some decent care."

"CIA safe house is not far away. They're expecting us," Junior said. "I already got it coordinated."

"Of course you did," McCoy said, pulling the spook in for a bro hug.

CHAPTER THIRTY-THREE

McCoy slipped into the molded plastic chair beside Ani and let out a long exhale. The compound they'd relocated to was reminiscent of most of the CIA complexes he'd seen in Iraq and Afghanistan. The location—the Faki Jad Allah District, south of downtown Khartoum along the White Nile River—was a low-rent, industrial area with more of the Middle East vibe he was accustomed to. Naturally, they'd set up camp in the GRS breakroom. Replete with kitchenette and gun racks, the space normally served the five contract operators who worked as security specialists safeguarding the CIA compound. An arrangement that had not worked well in Benghazi a few years ago, he reminded himself.

But this time was different, he thought with an ironic frown. *The bad guys already hit our compound and we walked away . . . at least most of us.*

A heavily bearded GRS man—a former military shooter in all likelihood—gave McCoy a nod from where he poured a tall coffee into a metal tumbler, a Sig pistol in a drop holster on his thigh.

"Coffee?" the contract operator asked.

To McCoy, that sounded better than a week at the Ritz Plaza right now.

"That'd be awesome," he said.

The man turned to Ani. "How about you?"

"No, thanks," she said.

McCoy turned to her and caught her eye. She tried to smile, but only managed a grimace. He felt it, too. He'd known Shaker only a short time but had liked him—the loss was hard.

"How's Wardi?" she asked, needing some good news to offset the loss of Shaker. He thought he detected something in her voice and that worried him. In fluid combat operations, there was no room for second-guessing and guilt. That was for back home in the clear light of day . . . or the dark prison of one's dreams.

"He's gonna be okay," McCoy said, accepting the coffee from the black-T-shirt-clad operator who took a seat at the table beside him. McCoy had helped another GRS operator—an 18-Delta Special Operations combat medic who went by the handle "Flash"—insert a chest tube into Wardi and start an IV for antibiotics on arrival at the safe house.

"The medic says he doesn't think he's bleeding internally anymore, so the bullet missed all the important veins and arteries with Latin names, I guess. The lung has stayed reinflated and he's awake and resting."

"We'll get him to our surgical support team once you guys are gone," the bearded man said. "I'll take care of it personally and make sure we circumvent any political and bureaucratic bullshit for you."

"Thanks, bro," McCoy said, giving the man a grateful nod.

"For the brotherhood," the man said simply. CIA was packed with bureaucrats at the head shed level, but the GRS guys in the field were mostly former operators who got it.

The brotherhood, indeed.

"What're the chances you could have been spotted heading here on your exfil?" the man asked. "What's your footprint?"

"Anything is possible," Ani answered. "For what it's worth, all the assaulters who hit us are KIA and Junior scraped for ticks multiple times en route during our drive here. Still, we need to be vigilant. I think it's safe to say our presence here in Khartoum has not gone unnoticed."

"Junior is the guy that Flash knows?" the operator asked.

McCoy gave a tight chuckle. "Junior appears to be the guy that everyone knows, just never by the same name."

The GRS man leaned back in his chair and looked back and forth between them, undoubtedly wondering about the pair of outlaws sitting in his breakroom but knowing better than to ask questions.

"But Ani's right," McCoy continued, "we should prepare for the worst and plan accordingly."

The operator nodded. "Already done, bro. We're on alert and tagging assets in the neighborhood to be on watch. We also have a second QRF from Ground Branch on short-fuse standby just a forty-minute hop away. And of course, there's a JSOC element in Djibouti. We're locked in. No more Benghazis."

"Good," McCoy said. "Hope we didn't cause a problem for you

guys coming in here unannounced. If we coulda given you a heads-up, we would have."

"Nah," the man said, waving a hand. "This is the kinda shit we exist for."

"Well, I just want you to know we appreciate the hospitality," Castillo's voice boomed from behind him and McCoy turned to see his boss with Junior in trail. Castillo's cargo pants were still stained with Shaker's blood, which had seeped up onto the dirty T-shirt he wore as well. "But we won't be here long."

The GRS operator stood and gave up his seat to Junior as Castillo slipped into the empty chair on the other side of Ani. "Stay as long as you need."

"I hate to ask," Castillo said, sounding like he might actually mean it, "but could we have the room for a minute?"

"Yeah, of course," the man replied with a *don't mention it* wave of his hand. "Gotta check in with my guys anyway." He left, closing the door behind him.

Castillo scanned the team's faces, his gaze settling on McCoy.

"Sorry I couldn't get to you guys on the bridge," McCoy said.

Castillo shook his head, almost as if he found the sentiment annoying.

"You wouldn't have gotten to us in time in any scenario, Killer, so it didn't change the outcome. You made the right call, secured in place, and saved Wardi's life. So, what the hell are you apologizing for exactly?"

Not sure what to say, McCoy shrugged.

"I'm sorry, too," Ani said, looking down.

"Enough of this mea culpa bullshit," Castillo said. "Combat is fluid. You make the best decision in the split second you have, and it works out or it doesn't. You can find time to kick your own ass when the mission is over if you want, but I don't recommend it. In the present, it is combat ineffective. Understood?"

"Understood," Ani said, looking back up.

McCoy just nodded. He looked over at Junior, who stared at the water bottle in his hands, his solemn face looking nothing like the easygoing spook he'd come to know.

"Sorry about Shaker, bro," McCoy said, squeezing the spook's forearm.

Junior nodded without a word. He glanced at Ani, and wondered just what she thought her role in the death of the man—who was clearly much more to Junior than just an asset—had been.

Junior looked up at him, a fire in his eyes that McCoy had not seen before.

"Yeah, well, that's the job, right?" Junior said, turning to Castillo. "What's our next move, boss?" he asked, his voice more pointed and professional than McCoy had heard from the laid-back spook since they'd met.

"Okay," Castillo began, looking from face to face, "so, Junior and I have just spent the last hour and a half poring over imagery provided by his office and the boys at the Fort in Virginia. The geeks were able to piece together archived data from the last several hours, back to early this morning. We know that Khalil was in one of two vehicles that headed out of Khartoum and went north before sunrise."

"Khalil had this series of visits scheduled well ahead of what's going on," Junior said, taking over for the boss. "These were scheduled inspections of voting sites throughout the region, something he's been doing about once a week. We can't confirm which vehicle he was in, because they only exited under cover—suspicious in and of itself, in my opinion—but we know they were in two regions."

Castillo had pulled a tablet from a pocket of his cargo pants and opened up a map application, handing it to Junior, who set it in the middle of the table.

"One vehicle headed northwest on Khartoum-Shendi Road, stopping here . . ." Junior said, tapping a town on the map about sixty miles northwest of Khartoum, ". . . in Shendi, where they made two stops, then continued on to Ad-Damir, a big town about one hundred and twenty miles northwest of us. They then went on to the smaller town of Atbara just beyond. That vehicle is headed back toward Khartoum now. The other vehicle"—Junior used a finger to scroll the map west, revealing another highway heading north out of Khartoum after passing through Umm Durmān, where McCoy had gotten his ass kicked—"drove north and then west along this road here. They stopped at government complexes along the route, including here in Kurti and Kanasah, before continuing on to the larger city of Kuraymah Barkal here, about a hundred and seventy miles north of us."

"Okay," Ani said, a little skepticism in her voice. "So, first off, if this was a series of voting site visits scheduled before all of this, I don't see what it tells us. And second, even if we believed that the secretary was being held in one of these sites, how the hell do we tell which one? This is a lot of towns over a very large area."

"I agree," Castillo said, and McCoy felt the same disappointment he saw in Castillo's eyes. So far, the information seemed pretty underwhelming.

"But," Castillo continued, "one interesting thing did pop up. While we can't confirm that it was Khalil's vehicle that went north into the Kuraymah Barkal area, we can confirm that Khalil made five trips up into that region in the last three months, three of them in the thirty days leading up to the kidnapping of Secretary of State Malone."

"How does that compare to other travel and visits to other regions?" Ani asked, now sounding more intrigued. "As acting minister of interior, he must travel a lot."

"The department as a whole does travel a lot," Junior confirmed. "But much of it is assigned to his deputies. Khalil does visit regions throughout Sudan, but none with this frequency—not even close."

"Okay," McCoy said, picking up the thread now. "And his frequent visits to the region only began three months ago?"

"Well, obviously we have rather incomplete records," Castillo admitted. "But our sources at CIA and NSA as well as the Activity guys working the region don't show that he made any visits to the Kuraymah Barkal region at all in the twelve months before they began three months ago."

"It would make sense that he began making more frequent visits recently as they gear up their voting program for a fair election," McCoy said, stroking the beard on his chin now and playing devil's advocate. "Still—pretty interesting."

"It's what we've got," Castillo said more definitively. "What does your gut say, McCoy?"

McCoy looked up at his boss, surprised to be asked. He considered a moment. The information itself was certainly far from damning, and yet his inner voice was whispering to him.

"Do we have any information at all from any other sources that would suggest the secretary could be here in the Khartoum area, Junior?" he asked.

The spook shook his head. "No, and we have more density of assets, operators, agencies, and task forces here in Khartoum than anywhere else in the country."

McCoy nodded, feeling Castillo's eyes—all of their eyes—on him. Surely, the boss wasn't going to have him make the call.

"If it was me," he said, looking up at Castillo, "and I was a terrorist group holding a high-value hostage, I wouldn't hold them in Khartoum. Far too dangerous." He pointed to Kuraymah Barkal on the map. "We were told that SIF had a concentration of operations in the northern areas of Sudan. This region sits halfway between Khartoum and the Egyptian border."

"So, what are you saying exactly?" Castillo pressed. "That we leave Khartoum?"

He let out a long sigh. "Yes. My gut tells me we need to expand our search outside Khartoum. For one thing, we're blown here. We're not going to be able to move about without attracting attention, and we have hit squads looking for us." He fixed his gaze on the map. "I would have Junior's boys analyzing both the Ad-Damir region and the area around Kuraymah Barkal with ongoing imagery and any assets to find known SIF affiliates in either area in real time and with historical archived feeds. At the same time, I say we head north. We load up with as much ISR gear and weapons as we can cram into a truck and head to Kuraymah Barkal."

"Okay, you have me convinced," Castillo said, taking McCoy by surprise. "Junior, shake your asset tree and find us some place to safe up in the area. See what your office has for organic assets we can tap if we need to turn a rescue op on short notice." He rose from his seat. "In the meantime, I'll trade our Land Cruiser for a new vehicle with the CIA lead here."

"Good luck with that," Ani snorted. "The guy in charge here is a lifer from analysis, not CS."

"Well, there's task force guys here as well," Castillo said with a smile. "And don't forget, I have that magic letter from the President that got us into your apartment."

Ani laughed. "You ordering Junior to wait in the hall got you into my apartment. That damn letter ruined my life."

"I'll make sure to requisition a new, better life for you when this is over," Castillo said with a chuckle. "Deal?"

"No, thanks, Charley," Ani said, her expression suddenly going sour. "My old life will do just fine."

McCoy pressed to his feet, feeling the pull of duty. "I'll get with the GRS guys and get us some fresh ammo and see what else they can scrounge for us."

"I'll work on the ISR gear we might be able to borrow from the CIA element here," Ani said. "Cool?"

"Perfect," McCoy said.

"I have my marching orders," Junior said to Castillo, "but I also want to make sure we get Wardi and Shaker's families secured somewhere. And, Charley . . ."

Castillo turned to him, eyebrow up.

"Yeah?"

"I need you to promise you'll use that letter of yours to relocate these families to the States," he said. "They've sacrificed enough."

"Done," Castillo said, and McCoy said a quiet prayer that the old-timer meant it.

He watched Ani and Junior leave, Ani whispering something to the spook, who put an arm around her and gave her a hug while whispering something back.

Castillo followed McCoy as he went over to freshen his coffee before finding the GRS man to scrounge ammo and supplies.

"Nice call back there," Castillo said, standing beside him with his arms crossed.

McCoy laughed. "Just doing my job."

"Look, McCoy," Castillo said, and his voice sounded different—enough that it made McCoy turn to look at the man. "I may have underestimated you. When I saw the file on you, I'll be honest, I wasn't sure you were the right call. You're a Marine through and through, and Marines are notoriously rigid . . ."

"I'm a Marine Raider," McCoy corrected him with a smile. "We're a different breed of Special Operator, Colonel. We're fluid, adaptable, and creative."

Castillo smiled and nodded. "Even so, very few people, even elite operators, can adapt to this environment. But you are doing exceptionally well. You're the right man for this job, and I thought I should say so."

"Thanks, Charley," McCoy said, feeling a swelling of real admiration and gratitude for Castillo. He'd underestimated the old spook, too, but saw nothing to be gained in the admission. "I just want to get the secretary of state home safely and then return to my team in Iraq."

"We'll see," Castillo said, clapping his shoulder and heading for the door. "I've got a call to make that won't be fun and then we'll get our shit together for what's next."

"White House?" McCoy asked.

Castillo sighed and smiled.

"Afraid so," he said. "Though I'm tempted to call Director Fleiss directly and let *him* deal with President Cohen."

And, with that, Castillo was gone.

McCoy chuckled. The call would suck either way . . .

Thank God I'm not the one who has to make it.

PART III

CHAPTER THIRTY-FOUR

President Natalie Cohen paced back and forth, aware that it made her look indecisive, but frankly not giving a shit.

"I will tell you, Marty, that I'm not sure this was the right call," she said, shooting her DNI a look. The fact that Fleiss had green-lighted the Presidential Agent team to head north out of Khartoum seemed reckless in light of all that had happened in the last forty-eight hours. "Castillo and his new boy are on a rampage—first in Cairo and now in Khartoum. It's bad enough that we may have to smooth this out with our foreign partners, but now it looks like we have to placate our own intelligence community, who are loudly complaining that they don't know what's going on in their own sandbox."

She watched Fleiss, hands clasped behind his back, give her a nod. His face was a mask, but his eyes were smiling.

"You can leave the IC to me, Madam President," he said. "And I think we can dispel any concern about our interests in Sudan and Egypt. Nothing in the footprints in Cairo or Khartoum suggests involvement of U.S. operatives, at least not publicly. The body count is higher than we would like, obviously, but we have cover and deniability—which I feel is the biggest advantage of using this program, quite frankly. Charley tells me they are on the trail and that they believe they may have located the region where Secretary Malone is being held."

Cohen let out a long, frustrated sigh, then walked around the *Resolute* desk and dropped into the chair that now, like those before her, provided more frustration and tension than comfort. She looked up at the DNI, who had barely moved.

"Marty, no bullshit—do you really believe Frank is still alive?"

Now Fleiss took a moment, clearly considering the question carefully and formulating his answer.

"I believe he is, Madam President," he said finally and firmly. "If he were dead, there would be an announcement and claiming of responsibility—likely to include some graphic photos or videos along with bragging about bringing America to her knees. We also now believe that there may be elements within the Sudanese transitional government involved." She watched Fleiss hesitate, and he shifted his weight slightly.

There was something he wasn't telling her.

"Are you telling me the Sudanese government is involved in the kidnapping of the secretary of state?" she demanded, the very thought making her blood boil.

"No, ma'am," Fleiss answered quickly. "Not at all. In fact, we're working with representatives at many levels who are involved to assist us—directly and with information otherwise difficult to obtain. It's possible that a rogue asset may be embedded in the Sudanese government, however. We don't know whether his involvement is to capitalize on information streams for money—common practice in most North African countries—or if this is someone actually personally and ideologically involved."

Cohen leaned back in her chair, exhausted now for some reason. She'd not slept well since the secretary had been taken, but the reports of bodies left in Castillo's wake had kept her from sleeping at all the last two days.

"So," she said, folding her hands on her desk and leaning forward. "You've given Charley permission to move into some vague area north in Sudan to prosecute a lead on Frank Malone's location. And then what? What assets would need to be involved in the extraction, or does Charley just imagine his Merry Outlaws riding in on white horses and rescuing the secretary single-handedly?"

"No, ma'am," Fleiss replied, unable to contain a subtle smile. "Charley has high confidence that we'll have an exact location very soon. I recommend that we spool up a Special Operations element on a short fuse to respond and augment his team for the rescue, should Charley prove right—as he seems to almost always do."

"What element?"

"We have SEALs operating as part of a Joint Special Operations Task Force out of Djibouti. I'd like to reposition a fire team from that JSOTF to stage aboard the USS *America*, an LHA-class amphibious assault ship currently in the Red Sea. From there, we could insert them via HALO or air assault using the twelve MV-22 Ospreys the Marines have aboard as part of their MEU. We also have F-35Bs aboard, should it come to that."

"F-35s?" Cohen said. He couldn't possibly be serious. "We're not looking to start a war with Sudan, Marty. Just kill the terrorists holding our secretary of state and get him the hell home."

"Yes, ma'am," Fleiss agreed. "But I've never regretted having more assets than I needed, ma'am. If Charley confirms the location of the secretary, we'll use the SEALs for a covert rescue mission, thanking the Sudanese government for the help it didn't know it provided so they save face. But you just never know. We certainly don't want to lose the secretary to these assholes for lack of firepower."

She saw a fire in Fleiss's eyes, the army general inside always stepping up in a crisis.

"I agree," she said, but her gut churned. "Just don't let Charley put us into some land war in Africa, Marty. Get the secretary back and everyone else home without casualties."

"Yes, ma'am, Madam President." He turned to leave, spinning on a heel, military style.

"Marty," she called. He turned back from the door.

"Yes, Madam President?"

"Keep me in the damn loop. And tell Charley he can't call Dad because he's afraid Mom will say no. Mom . . ." she said, leaning in and holding his eyes, "is the President of the United States. Mom is in charge. Is that understood?"

"Yes, ma'am," Fleiss said. "And I'll make sure Charley gets the message as well."

"See that you do."

Then he was gone, closing the door gently behind him.

Cohen leaned back in the chair and pursed her lips. With a long sigh, she couldn't help but wonder if bringing Castillo back might be the mistake that would bring down her presidency.

CHAPTER THIRTY-FIVE

Castillo paced while Ani and Junior argued.

You could tell a lot about two people by how they argued—how intimate they were, how much trust they shared, how much emotional baggage they carried, and how much respect they had for each other. When it came to Ani and Junior, the cup runneth over in every category. You could see it in every interaction, including the last several hours sitting side by side poring over data pieced together from their combined connections at CIA and NSA and wherever the hell else Junior got his data dumps. They had scoured through satellite feeds and HUMINT summaries, and now focused on a complex along the river in Kuraymah Barkal—the compound where the intel said Minister Khalil had spent considerable time yesterday.

". . . yeah, but this was a *National* Islamic Front compound,"

Junior said. He stood beside her, hunched over with both palms resting on the table, looking at her computer. "When the NIF dissolved, that compound was abandoned. NIF and SIF are completely different animals. The latter is not an extension or rebirth of the former. Different leadership, different objectives, different funding channels."

"I'm not debating that," she said, tapping her index figure on the table like a metronome. "My point is simply that this compound was not occupied for years and then three months ago satellite archive data starts showing traffic. I've gone through all of it. First visit, you have three guys scoping it out. They stay twenty minutes. Five days later, they come back, but this time there's a second car. My read is that they're showing it off to their boss. Then nothing for days. Then they come back. Then more traffic. They start bringing in building materials and a generator. Now we have our number one suspect dropping by again, staying at this one location—which is definitely not a polling station, by the way—for five times longer than any other stop."

"Okay, Ani, but first of all we don't even know for sure Khalil was in that vehicle. He could as easily have been in the vehicle in Ad-Damir. And we don't have a single image of a single dude with a weapon. Not one lousy AK-47. That's just not how Islamic terrorists roll. This could be a legit operation—a real estate purchase and renovation."

"Oh, please, be serious."

"I am being serious."

"Then your point is?"

"My point is that even if we *were* watching dudes patrolling the grounds right now with weapons, it would hardly be conclusive evidence that the Sudanese Islamic Front is occupying the compound, that they were the group responsible for the attack and kidnapping in Cairo, and that this compound is where they took the secretary. If I was sitting on the seventh floor in Langley and you brought this to me, I'd tell you it's thin and to find me more."

Castillo watched her turn to look up at Junior.

"I understand you're playing devil's advocate but hear me out. What if they assume we're watching their every move? What if they understand OPSEC—understand that pickups with machine guns mounted in the back and roving watches with assault rifles patrolling the perimeter is a giant red flag that screams, 'Hey, CIA, we're terrorists—shoot Hellfire missiles here.' Add that to the fact that there was a noticeable uptick in vehicular traffic coming and going from this site in the two days immediately preceding the secretary's kidnapping and the days since. Terrorists evolve more quickly than a fucking virus."

"Yes, but if they brought Malone here, we would have seen a convoy arrive. You don't kidnap the U.S. secretary of state and drop him off in an Uber. But that's not what happened here. The day after the secretary was kidnapped, imagery shows a flatbed truck delivering a sofa, some bookcases, and a freezer. I don't know, Ani, it's just—"

"Enough," Castillo said, cutting them off. "I've made my decision. I'm with Ani on this one. I've said it before and I'll say it again—there are no coincidences in our business. Imagery and SIGINT confirms that Irshad Khalil paid this place a visit five times during their spool-up phase and then again yesterday, so whatever this site may be, it's not clean. And we now have reason to believe that Khalil is involved in the kidnapping of Malone, so that's enough for me. We hit it tonight. The secretary is out of time and so are we. End of discussion."

McCoy, who'd been sitting quietly at the table listening but not talking, nodded, scooted back in his chair, and got up.

"What do you think?" Junior said, turning to the Marine.

"What he said," McCoy replied with a nod at Castillo, and turned to leave.

"Where are you going?" the spook pressed.

"If you must know, Junior, I'm going to take a crap, which I have not had an opportunity to do for two days, thank you very much. So, if you yahoos need me in the next ten minutes, then too fucking bad."

Castillo just shook his head and laughed as the Marine officer wandered off to the toilet, which at this dilapidated compound was a closet-sized room with a hole in the floor.

At least it has a door, he thought.

Once the Marine was out of earshot, Ani turned to Castillo. "His face is looking a little better. He took quite a beating the other day."

"Yeah, he can open both his eyes all the way now," Castillo said, walking over to the oversized, already warm Igloo cooler they'd brought with them. He opened the lid. "Either of you want a bottled water?"

"Please," Ani answered.

He tossed her one, which she deftly caught in midair.

"Junior?" he asked.

"Hit me," the spook said, and Castillo tossed him one, too.

"So, um, what's McCoy's story?" Ani asked as she twisted off the cap from the half-liter bottle of lukewarm water. "Did he volunteer for this operation or did you know him from before?"

"Volunteer? McCoy?" Castillo said through a chuckle, glancing at Junior. "Hell, no."

"We practically had to drag him kicking and screaming out of Iraq. He didn't want to leave his unit," Junior said.

"Then why him?" she asked.

Castillo blew air through his teeth for theatrical effect. "The DNI gave me a short list—a very short list, I might add—and I picked him," he lied.

The fact that McNab had picked McCoy as his successor purposely without Castillo's input or consent still chafed, and being reminded of it was like picking at a scab that had not quite healed.

"Why? I mean, why not pick an experienced and decorated CIA field officer? Maybe someone from Ground Branch with Special Operations experience and field intelligence work."

"Look, it wasn't really my call," he said, softening the lie. "That said, it was a good one because, out of all the candidates, I know McCoy wanted this assignment the least."

Ani narrowed her eyes, confused. "I don't get it."

"Look, McCoy doesn't need to be here. Just like he doesn't need to be a MARSOC officer in Iraq, wandering around the countryside risking getting sniped or blown up every time he steps outside. Most kids with his resources and connections would be rubbing elbows with the Silicon Valley elite, summering in the Hamptons, or partying on some billionaire's yacht in Majorca. Not McCoy. That's not what motivates him. For McCoy, getting his face pummeled and crapping in hand-dug latrines in the desert is just the price of admission."

"The price of admission?" she echoed.

"For the show—to serve his country at the pointy end of the spear. McCoy is here and serving in MARSOC because he chooses to." When he saw that it still hadn't clicked for her, he said, "You ever heard of American Personal Pharmaceutical?"

"Sure," she said. "Multibillion-dollar publicly traded company that competes with Johnson & Johnson. How's that relevant?"

Castillo nodded. "McCoy's great-grandfather founded the company, which makes him the youngest living heir of the Sage family fortune."

"For real?" she said, her eyes going wide.

"For real."

"I never, in a million years, would have imagined," she said, and Castillo could see the gears turning in her head.

"So, he joined the Marines to distance himself from that life."

Castillo shrugged. "It's more complicated than that. Pharmaceuticals is the Sage family business. Being a Marine is the McCoy family business. Our boy Killer is third generation—both his dad and granddad were jarheads, his father a Marine Corps fighter ace. He chose a different path and became a Raider."

"Why?"

"You'd have to ask him, but if you want my opinion, I think it's because he wanted to get his hands dirty. Fighter pilots were last generation's knights. Special Operators win the wars now. Given a choice between the sky and the suck, he chose *the suck* . . . something that both of you have in common, Ani. You passed on a desk job at HQ knowing that wasn't you. You chose the suck—living under a NOC, running assets in Cairo, walking in the shadows and putting your life on the line every day because somebody has to do the dirty work, and by God, you don't trust anybody else to do it, because they'll just fuck it up. Am I right?"

She nodded. "Sounds to me like you might be speaking from a place of personal experience."

He didn't reply, his gaze going to the middle distance.

Story of my life, he thought.

Nobody said anything for a long moment, each of them lost in thought. Eventually, Junior broke the silence. "If we're going to hit the compound tonight, then we have lots of work to do and phone calls to make. I assume, Charley, that you're going to get the President's authorization for this?"

Castillo shrugged, showboating just to amuse himself.

"All righty, then," Junior said.

"Please tell me you both realize we can't do this by ourselves," Ani said, eyeing Castillo.

"Do what by ourselves?" McCoy asked, walking back into the room.

"Hit the compound."

"Impossible. As much as I hate to admit it, we're going to need the SOCOM element from Djibouti," McCoy said, walking over to the cooler to fetch a water of his own. "We asked the DNI to position them closer for a short-fuse spin-up. I haven't heard back yet. Damn Navy SEALs . . . always nearby and ready to crash every party."

"And when we rescue the secretary and kick the Sudanese Islamic Front's ass to kingdom come," Castillo chimed in, "two years from now one of them is going to write a book about it—something Delta and MARSOC would never do."

"But that's only because in the army and Marine Corps they don't teach you guys how to spell, right?" Junior came back with a crooked grin.

McCoy flicked the mouth of his bottle at the spook, hitting him with a perfectly targeted dollop on the chin.

"Don't tell me you were navy before you became a spook?"

McCoy said. "Because then I'll be forced to have an even lower opinion of you than I already do."

This got them all laughing, even Castillo, and for the first time since McNab had dragged him off his front porch in Texas and out of retirement, he felt like he did in the good old days. McCoy glanced at his watch, his face set and determined. He was beginning to understand this kid—right now his mind was spinning through various assault scenarios and contingencies. He was putting together a plan.

"While the boss gets us the green light," McCoy said, giving Castillo a confident nod, "we have work to do before we try to sleep ahead of a very busy night. Rest is an important weapon here, so let's divide and conquer. I suggest we look over the most current data on the compound and formulate an assault plan." He turned to the spook. "Junior, we need you here to coordinate logistics for the infil and the exfil. We can't drop our assaulters into this compound by air without raising suspicion, so we need to get them to HALO in and set up a staging area and FARP out in the desert—at least five klicks out. We're going to need desert-worthy off-road vehicles to shuttle them from the FARP to our compound with a low footprint that raises no eyebrows. Then we'll assault the compound from here using the SUVs."

"Okie dokie," Junior said, with a button-pushing grin. "Go on . . ."

McCoy rolled his eyes and continued. "Now, assuming we get the secretary and we make it out of the compound, the safest option is probably to exfil to the FARP in the desert, but where do we go from there? Helo south to Khartoum and fly out, or helo north into Egypt? Either way, we need to put the secretary on a secure aircraft.

Ideally, we all hop on a long-haul asset that can get us all the way to the States."

Castillo watched the next Presidential Agent take control and bring his team into focus. From the looks of it, McCoy was going to do just fine in this job.

Castillo picked up the satellite phone and crossed the room, heading to the roof where it would be quiet. He hoped Fleiss had convinced the President to reposition a team of SEALs out of Djibouti and into the Red Sea with the MEU aboard the *America*. Permission for the op was less important than getting the assaulters he needed from the JSOTF, but he didn't see an easy way to get one without the other. He could get forgiveness more easily than permission for this sort of thing, but without the SEALs to augment his force, the rescue op was a failure before it started.

McCoy had proven himself to be a one-man annihilation machine more than once in the last few days.

But not even he was that good.

CHAPTER THIRTY-SIX

The White House Situation Room

Washington, D.C.

March 23, 2:10 a.m.

President Cohen nodded curtly to the Marine standing watch over the entrance to the WHSR, where her carefully chosen director of national intelligence waited for her. The Marine snapped to an even more rigid stance, staring at the wall beyond her as she pressed her hand onto the glass panel and entered her PIN into the keypad.

He gave her no less courtesy and respect at two A.M. dressed in jeans and a GW sweatshirt than he would have afforded her at ten A.M. in the Oval Office dressed in a pantsuit. Never relaxed, never casual, and always on point, you just have to love a Marine—dedicated, passionate, committed to duty, and, most important, loyal. It was why the short list she had come up with, in consultation with McNab, included the only real choice in her mind, and that man had been a Marine Raider they knew would be fully committed to duty, honor, and country. A Marine would not slip into Castillo's rogue asset mentality. A Marine could be trusted.

The magnetic lock released and the Marine, who reached over

without shifting his eyes away from the nowhere at which they stared from his chiseled, impassive face, opened the door for her.

"Thank you, Gunnery Sergeant," she said.

"Ma'am, yes, ma'am," the Marine nearly barked.

Cohen smiled and entered the Situation Room where Fleiss waited for her. Unlike her, Marty Fleiss had found time to pull on dress slacks and a black polo. Unlike her, his hair was perfectly in place. Perhaps he'd never left at all.

He looked up and took his reading glasses off, setting them on the conference table beside him.

"Good evening, Madam President," he said, his eyes as bright and focused as if it had been noon. She reminded herself that the former SOCOM commander was used to working mostly at night. Special Operators were like vampires.

"Good evening, Marty," she said, standing beside him at the table, arms across her chest. "That was certainly quick. I assume Castillo's team has something concrete and that's why we're here."

"Yes, ma'am," Fleiss said, but his tone suggested he didn't think she would like what she was about to hear. He gestured with a hand and tapped on the laptop, the image then mirroring onto the large screen on the wall at the head of the table.

Cohen stared carefully at the screen, which showed what appeared to be some sort of industrial compound, with several corrugated metal buildings that could be anything at all, a large central warehouse, and a trailer up on cement blocks, like one might find at any construction site in America.

"What am I looking at, Marty?" she asked, her tone softening though she was still refusing to sit. It wasn't personal, she just had far too much nervous energy to sit without fidgeting. And a President should never fidget.

"This is a compound along the Nile River in the northern Sudanese city of Kuraymah Barkal, just under two hundred miles north of Khartoum," he said. "The complex was once a known operations center for the National Islamic Front. It changed hands several times since, then stood empty for nearly a year when a commercial company . . ."

She held her hand up, stopping him. If he didn't cut to the chase, she was going to explode.

"It's just you and me here, Marty. We can get into the weeds another time. Is this where Castillo believes Secretary of State Malone is being held?"

"Yes, ma'am," he said, but didn't elaborate further.

She sighed and, finally, took a seat. Less than a year in office and she was already exasperated from constantly having to read between the lines.

"And what do *you* think, Marty?"

Fleiss took a long, slow breath. He wasn't covering his ass—she knew him far better than that and it wasn't in his nature. He'd turned her down twice before finally accepting the job as DNI. And that was what she wanted. She needed someone serving the country and her administration, not themselves. He was the reluctant public servant with decades of service and a comfortable retirement waiting for him, maybe a book about a life devoted to military and public service. He didn't have to be here and maybe didn't even want to be here. He'd answered the call, period.

"I think the odds are better than fifty-fifty, Madam President," he said, watching her carefully for her reaction. "But I would be lying if I told you there's definitive evidence that Malone is here now—or ever has been."

"That's not very reassuring, Marty." She leaned back in her chair as she studied the compound along the river. "Make the case," she said at last.

She listened as he presented Castillo's arguments for how and why he believed the secretary of state had come to be in this compound. Links to Sudanese Islamic Front that had been suggested by McCoy and Castillo, but supported strongly by NSA and CIA. Links between the SIF and the compound, including a new piece of evidence from NSA—a facial recognition hit on a man frequently seen in the compound and presumed to be the head of SIF in the region. The link between Khalil and SIF and stealthy visits to the compound in the run-up to the kidnapping. The team's concerns about Awadiya Khalil, a remarkable woman who, if Cohen could find a way to help make it happen, could be leading a democratic Sudan by this time next year.

Signals intelligence.

Satellite images.

And gut instinct.

She heard enough evidence to begin a surveillance operation and to dig into the life of Irshad Khalil. But a Special Forces hit inside a country with whom they had poor diplomatic relations? Without permission?

"This is part of the job I hate," she said, tilting her head back to look at the ceiling. After a slow, whistling breath, she lowered her gaze and looked Fleiss in the eyes. "You really think I can justify a combat operation in Sudan on this circumstantial evidence? Flimsy circumstantial evidence, I might add."

"Extraction operation, and yes, ma'am," Fleiss replied without hesitation. "When combined with the instincts of a man who has yet to be wrong, I think it's the right call, yes. These types of things are never open and shut. We make the best call with what we have when the fuse is this short. Honestly, Madam President, assuming he's there, if we wait much longer, he'll be dead. Khalil knows that Castillo's team is on to him. He'll need to pull the trigger on his long game quickly or else lose the opportunity. That, or kill Malone and bury him in the desert. If they're wrong and he's not there, well, then we've failed in any case."

"Perhaps," Cohen said, "but we're talking about an unauthorized military incursion into a sovereign country, for God's sake. If we're wrong, we're the devil in the Middle East yet again, violating sovereign territory and killing foreigners on their own soil on a hunch. There is a huge downside risk here, Marty."

"Not necessarily, ma'am," Fleiss said. "If we hit this compound and it's a dry hole, we've still hit a major terrorist compound in Sudan, assisting a fledgling democracy to rid itself of terrorist influence ahead of their election. Hell, we give the Sudanese Ministry of Interior credit and say we were there only as advisers, providing assistance. We just fire up the spin machine and let your press secretary do what he does best."

"The provisional government will know we're lying . . ."

"And they'll say nothing, Madam President. They need the win. If we offer them the public relations coup—both within their own country and on the international stage—of conducting a successful counterterror intelligence operation followed by a successful military operation on a terrorist compound to ensure their fair elections, they'll take it and feel they owe *us* a favor."

Cohen smiled. Marty was persuasive. They could move now and rescue the secretary if he was there, and still be winners if they were wrong.

"What does Charley need?"

"I repositioned a Navy SEAL element from Djibouti to the USS *America*, as we discussed previously, in preparation for this scenario. We can insert that team with almost zero footprint into the desert north of Charley's team and they can link up for the hit—a staging area with a fuel bladder, medical support, and helos. After the hit, the SEALs and support team will go back to the *America* while Castillo and his gang escort the secretary to Joint Base Andrews."

"That's it?"

Fleiss smiled broadly now. "That's probably all you really want to know, ma'am."

She nodded. This was the job. If she'd learned nothing else during her time as secretary of state before running for President, it was that making no decision was usually the worst decision of all. It took guts to make the call—yet, in her experience, indecisiveness coupled with inaction invariably led to a worse outcome than making the wrong call.

"Do it," she said, rising from her seat.

"Yes, ma'am," he replied.

"When will it happen?"

"It's midmorning there," her DNI answered. "My guess is they kick off in about fourteen hours. But it's my intention to assign operational autonomy to Castillo and his team."

"Very well."

Of course, Castillo was going to take operational autonomy whether they gave it to him or not. Him making the call made sense, since he was on the ground with eyes on. It also gave her political cover if things went to shit.

"Keep me in the loop," she said, heading for the door.

"Yes, Madam President."

Castillo would be the scapegoat if this went to hell, but that didn't change the reality of the situation. The buck stopped with her, and she'd have to deal with the consequences.

Four years might be long enough in this shitty job anyway.

CHAPTER THIRTY-SEVEN

McCoy scanned the horizon through the split armored windshield of the Joint Light Tactical Vehicle he was driving. Having spent more hours than he could count having his brains bounced around in Humvees over the years, he simply could not stop smiling as he piloted the smooth-riding JLTV with its Rocky Balboa heavyweight suspension over the harsh, uneven terrain. The landscape reminded McCoy of the deserts of western Iraq—nothing like the trite imagery of rolling sand and dunes most people thought of when they imagined the desert. *That* Sahara was farther west.

How in the holy hell Junior had secured two of the latest, most bad-ass military transports in the Marine and Special Operations inventory for them was a mystery. When he and Castillo had arrived at the turnoff point from Route A1 in their SUV and crested the hill, the JLTVs had simply been there, unattended and waiting. When asked over the radio how he'd pulled off such a coup, Junior had simply said, "They fell from heaven." With their feline-like headlights, muscular flanks, and snout-shaped hood and grille assemblies, the JLTVs looked like two crouching desert lions waiting to spring into action. He and Castillo had actually given each other a high five as they walked up to climb behind the wheel of the machines.

McCoy glanced down at his GPS watch and checked his coordinates.

Almost there . . . so far so good.

"Mako, I show you in position," Junior said in McCoy's ear a moment later, watching their two JLTVs from above and the inbound SEAL team element. "Javelin is three mikes out."

"Check," McCoy replied as he parked the JLTV and pushed open the heavy-as-shit driver's-side armored door.

"Your six is still clear all the way to the highway," Junior added.

"Roger that," Castillo said.

Knowing that they had a stealthy Sentinel in orbit watching their six is even better than the powerful, up-armored tactical vehicles, in McCoy's book. His MARSOC ass had been saved on more than one occasion by Hellfires from above, and he operated better just knowing a drone was up there. Castillo walked up and stood beside him at the front of his idling JLTV, where they scanned the rocky desert stretching out to the east through their NVGs. The SEALs would emerge any minute.

"Talk about a bad-ass truck," Castillo said, leaning against a fender.

"Oh, hell, yeah," McCoy came back. "Makes the Humvee look like a World War II jeep."

"These bad boys drive better than my F-150. I hit a ditch at fifty and barely felt it."

"Yeah, me, too . . . gonna hate to have to give them up."

"Are you sure you don't want to hit the compound in these?" Castillo said. "Just sayin', we could smash through the perimeter and take heavy fire all the way to the target without a scratch."

"I know it's tempting," McCoy said, "but the SEALs would never go for it. If SIF has spotters in the neighborhood, which I guarantee they do, they'll see us coming from a mile away. We'd lose our stealth and our element of surprise and give the bad guys time to dig in, defend from cover, and execute Malone before we can get to him. We're going to need to approach on foot and capitalize on the chaos."

"I know," Castillo said with a heavy sigh. "But wouldn't it be nice for once to get to bring a tank to a gunfight?"

"Amen, brother . . . sure would."

"Mako, this is Javelin," a new voice said, whisper-quiet in McCoy's earbud. "We are on approach. Confirm your position."

McCoy smiled. The SEALs were watching them right now, out there somewhere, and neither he nor Castillo had seen them on their approach. This call in was to check their frequency before making contact.

"Javelin, Mako—we're the two dudes standing in front of the JLTVs over the rise." He pulled out an IR strobe from his pocket and rotated it a half turn. "That's me strobing in the green."

A heartbeat later, eight SEALs materialized from nowhere, appearing on the rise, spread out in two separate arrowhead formations of four operators each. Moments later, the newcomers were gathered around the desert tan vehicles, holding a tactical perimeter and scanning as the guy in charge walked up to McCoy.

"You Mako?" the SEAL asked, tipping his NVGs up on his helmet.

"Pick McCoy," he replied, extending his hand. "Thanks for coming."

"Thanks for inviting us," the SEAL replied with a grin, shaking his hand and instantly reconnecting with the assault rifle on his chest. "I'm Terrence Cameron."

"We're clear to the road, Cam," one of the SEALs to McCoy's right announced.

"Roger that, Bubba," Cameron replied.

"We've got dedicated drone coverage, so we're checked clear," Junior told the SEAL.

"We're streaming from satellite—coverage from back home," Cameron told him. "If you got dedicated eyes, we can break from ours now. We're all yours."

McCoy nodded. "Let's load up and get the hell out of here, then. Four in each vehicle if you like. Ride with me and I can get you up to speed."

Moments later they were speeding over the moonlike landscape, the JLTVs taking the irregular, rocky ground as if they were floating on air.

"Nice ride," Cameron said, pulling off his helmet and running a gloved hand over the tight curls of his dark hair. "Haven't had the pleasure of riding in this beast yet. Should work with you guys more often . . . whoever you are," he added with a grin.

"Yeah, well, working with this group has its pros and cons."

"No doubt," the Hollywood-handsome African American operator said with a chuckle, the unspoken message that he could relate. "So, what can the United States Navy do to help you guys out tonight, Mr. McCoy? I hope it's taking some terrorists out of the game ahead of the Sudanese elections."

"You following the geopolitics in Sudan, Senior Chief?"

The man shrugged. "I'm just an operator, Mr. McCoy, but being mentally stronger than my enemies means I need to know and understand them."

"I couldn't agree more," McCoy said. He liked this SEAL NCO. A lot. "I think what I have for you might be even more exciting, Senior." He shot the SEAL a big, shit-eating grin. "Speaking as an operator myself, this is a dream op."

Cameron looked him over, perhaps trying to see if he knew him from somewhere, now that he knew McCoy had a Special Operations pedigree.

"You got my attention," the SEAL said.

"I'm sure you're getting daily, maybe even hourly, updates on the kidnapping of the secretary of state since you deployed to the region . . ."

"You gotta be shitting me," Cameron said. "You guys found him?"

"We found him," McCoy said, and uttered a silent prayer that they were right about Malone being in the compound in Kuraymah Barkal. "Was hoping you and your boys might enjoy helping us get him out."

Cameron had a smile on his face now rarely seen outside of children on Christmas morning.

"Oh, hell, yeah."

A bearded face poked through the center console from the rear of the armored vehicle.

"Did I hear you right? We're doing a hostage rescue on the secretary of state?"

"You heard me right," McCoy said, his own enthusiasm at being on a for-real, no bullshit Spec Ops hostage rescue growing inside him. The Presidential Agent spooky shit of the last few days was fine, maybe, but he was an operator above all else. This phase of the operation was in his world now. "We have all the details to share once we get back to our compound, which is only seven miles from the target. We have eyes, heavy air support, as well as your dust-off and exfil birds, and we are going tonight."

"Fuckin' A!" the SEAL replied, and then returned to the back to spread the word and collect high fives.

McCoy looked over at Cameron, whose smile was just beginning to fade as the X's and O's of the operation were clearly starting to populate in his mind's eye.

"How many shooters have you got on your team?" the SEAL asked.

McCoy wished he could tell the senior chief they were falling in on a full team of Ground Branch or even FBI HRT operators.

"Just two of us," he admitted. "With your eight, that makes ten."

The SEAL shook his head. "A bit light in my book for an op like this."

"But we have surprise on our side," McCoy came back, hoping that was true, "and good ISR that shows the compound to have fewer shooters than you might suspect. I think they never imagined we could find them."

"What is *few* in your world, McCoy?" Cameron asked.

McCoy got it. He'd been burned before, too. Shitty intel leading to poorly planned raids, where he and his boys were out on the tip of a poorly tossed spear.

"We'll go over the ISR together, Senior," McCoy said, "and I promise you and I will plan the hit together with equal say on tactics and strategy. I know you're putting your brothers on the line . . . I've been where you are now."

"How many tangos?" the SEAL repeated, unassuaged.

"Less than thirty," McCoy said.

Cameron nodded. "Depending on the layout that might not be too bad—if your bad guys really are in the dark that we're coming. I have two snipers with me and the rest are all my best breachers. If you guys are worth a shit, we might be okay."

"Look, Senior, I can't tell you what group we're with, but I do think you deserve to know our operational pedigree. I'm a Marine Raider, my boss is former Delta. I wish we had more shooters, but it is what it is. We have two incredible spooks who will be running our TOC with eyes in the sky; they saved my ass more than once in the last few days. We can make this op work and get the secretary back, so long as we all work together."

Cameron laughed. "Well, that makes me feel a little better. At least you and your boss Charley have skin in the game. But I've never had a spook read me all the way in before, so please, just keep the surprises to a minimum."

"Senior, other than exactly who we are, you will know everything that I know. Fair?" He stuck his hand out.

"Fair enough," the SEAL said, shaking McCoy's hand with his powerful gloved hand. "Let's go get some."

McCoy maneuvered behind Junior's vehicle as they pulled into a semi-arc beside the SUVs sitting right where they'd left them.

"You're all clear," Castillo said in his ear. "No visitors to the trucks while you were gone, and nothing between you and the highway."

"Roger that," McCoy said, turning to Cameron. "Switching vehicles," he informed the SEAL.

He got out, and walked over to his black SUV, as SEALs poured out of both JLTVs.

"We just supposed to leave a half million dollars' worth of equipment in the desert?" Cameron asked, with a wary look at the abandoned JLTVs.

"Don't worry, fella," Castillo said with a grin. "They'll make it home—we have a guy who knows a guy."

McCoy chuckled as the SEALs tossed gear into the rear of the two SUVs and then mounted up. Then he slipped into the driver's seat, smiled at Senior Chief Cameron, and started the vehicle with the key he'd tucked up into the visor.

"We present a smaller footprint if we swap wheels heading into our compound on the main roads," McCoy added.

"Gotcha," the senior chief said.

McCoy pressed the accelerator, spraying sand as he fishtailed in behind Castillo. Once on the road, he glanced in the rearview mirror at the SEALs, talking softly among themselves with an intimacy and familiarity that was the hallmark of Special Operations teams.

A wave of nostalgic *something* washed over him.

He shook off the feeling.

With any luck, this nightmare would be over and he'd be back with his Raider family by the end of the week.

CHAPTER THIRTY-EIGHT

McCoy moved swiftly and quietly in a combat crouch as his five-man team advanced in an arrowhead formation through the night. He had elected to let Cameron lead the element, not just because the SEAL senior chief knew his men and their movements so perfectly that he could lead them in his sleep, but because it was just the right thing to do. While McCoy might be a blooded, experienced, and competent Special Operations officer, to these guys he was just another spook. The SEALs needed their NCO on point and he wasn't about to get in the way.

"Mako One, I show you one block from the target," Junior reported from the TOC seven miles away where he and Ani were watching the team's movements in real time via streaming thermal imagery from the stealthy Sentinel drone—call sign Atlas—cruising twenty thousand feet above.

McCoy resisted the urge to answer. He was Mako Three for this op and on Cameron's stick. Cameron was One. The SEAL everyone called Bubba—a tan, tattooed Southerner—was Two. Bubba was leading the second fire team, which included Castillo, who was Four, converging on the target from the north.

"One, copy. Two, One—sitrep?" Cameron said.

"In position in two mikes," came Bubba's relaxed reply.

"They'll have spotters in all of these neighborhoods, boys," Castillo chimed in. "Be the night . . ."

Cameron double-clicked his mike in affirmation.

"Mako, we have Greyhound in orbit, just three mikes out. Channel three," Junior reported.

"Roger, Mother," Cameron said, his voice smooth and calm, acknowledging Junior's report that helicopter air support was orbiting nearby. They had two Blackhawks—call sign Greyhound One and Two—for a quick pickup after mission success, as well as two MH-6M attack helicopters—call sign Greyhound Three and Four—to rain down death should the op go to hell.

At the end of the alley, Cameron took a knee at the corner of the stucco building and held up a closed fist. McCoy crossed to the other corner and stopped. Two SEALs moved in behind him, one giving a squeeze on his shoulder to confirm they were in position behind him.

"Stand by for last update from Atlas," Junior said, as he readied his final report on the number and position of thermal signatures inside the target compound.

"One, roger," Cameron said, waiting on this last critical update before he called the breach.

McCoy stared across the dark, empty street at the eight-foot-high chain-link fence topped with concertina wire. The most dangerous part of their assault was crossing the large, empty expanse on the other side of that fence. The compound had no roving patrols, but that didn't mean there wasn't hidden security. The main gate was manned by two guards in a trailer, about seventy-five yards farther north, but those guys weren't McCoy's primary concern. His worry was shooters set up in hides inside the main warehouse and the building beside it. He and the SEALs would be easy targets as they crossed the long, seventy-yard stretch of open gravel lot, their only cover a single truck parked off to the right of the building.

He looked over at Cameron, who must have been thinking the same thing.

"You wanna move Greyhound Three and Four closer in?" Cameron whispered. "If we lose surprise, then those are gonna be long minutes waiting for the Little Birds."

McCoy wrestled with the question. That long stretch of well-lit no-man's-land sure looked ominous now in person. On the other hand, bringing the attack helicopters in close would tip off the enemy and announce their presence.

"Let's see what Mother has for us first," he whispered back, and Cameron nodded agreement.

McCoy flipped his NVGs up on his helmet, watching as a pickup truck inside the compound cruised toward the trailer at the front gate.

"Mother, Three—you got eyes on that pickup that just pulled up?" McCoy asked.

"They just came from Building Two," Junior came back. "I'm thinking it's shift change at the gate, cuz that truck's been inside the fence the whole time."

"Check," he said.

Two more shooters we can take out from a distance . . .

"Eight, One—you in position yet?" Cameron said, querying the SEAL sniper in Bubba's element who should have already split off to set up on the roof of a three-story building just two blocks away— the tallest building in the area.

"Eight is in position," came the breathless whisper of their sniper overwatch. "Eight is now God."

"Roger, God. You got a line on the trailer at the gate?" Cameron came back.

"Yeah, I got 'em. I see three guys through the window. I can probably take them inside but will drop them fast if they come out."

Cameron looked at McCoy.

McCoy held up one finger. He wanted that final thermal report from Junior before they kicked things off. "Sitrep, Mother?"

"Mako, you have four thermals inside the trailer by the gate— two who just arrived in the pickup plus the two originals. There are two stationary concealed sentries north and another two south, just to your right, Mako One, toward the east side of the compound. Inside, we hold a total of seventeen thermals. Inside the main ware- house, we have five milling about in a large room, perhaps a break room of some sort, which will be the first room encountered by Mako Two if they enter from the north side, on their left. The main floor of the warehouse complex has another three signatures on the west side of the room. There are then two thermals stationary by a third on the east side of that open area. Best guess is that this is where they're holding the secretary. That thermal is supine, and a bit plumper than the others. The other two are seated outside the room, probably door guards . . ."

As Junior talked, McCoy populated the mental map warehouse

complex with figures. He'd watched thermal imagery from the drone for more than an hour before kitting up, and he had burned the layout into his brain.

". . . That's it for Building One. We then have four more in Building Two north and west of the target building. This might be sleeping quarters, as three are supine and appear to be sleeping and the other is sitting in a chair in front of a thermal signature appearing to be a TV. Building Three due north has two signatures, one asleep, it appears, and the other looks to be pacing back and forth as if standing night watch."

That was it—and completed the tactical picture for McCoy, with very little unexpected. The northmost building might be the site for the ringleader of the terrorist operation here. Alone with a single bodyguard . . . McCoy pegged him for a high-value target. But tonight, they only had one mission objective and that was to recover the secretary of state.

Assuming Malone is even here at all . . .

"Mako Two is set," came Bubba's soft voice in his earpiece.

McCoy looked at Cameron and gave the SEAL a nod.

"Two, One—on my call breach from the north. God, simultaneous fire to take out the tangos at the gate. My element breaches in the chaos."

The plan was for Mako Two's element to secure Buildings Two and Three first and then supplement Mako One as they breached the target, Building One. After recovering Secretary of State Malone, they'd exit together out the main gate to the west under sniper overwatch and exfil with Greyhound two blocks west of the sniper's position.

Maybe fighting through whatever kind of QRF the bad buys have in place . . .

The acknowledgments came a heartbeat later from Bubba and the team sniper respectively:

"Two."

"God."

McCoy watched Cameron take a deep breath. He could feel the tension in the air as the team leader prepared to make the call and kick off the op. A heartbeat later, Cameron gave the order:

"Mako Two—go!"

McCoy watched the front gate. He never heard the shot, but he did hear the tinkle of breaking glass and shouts from inside the trailer. The trailer door burst open and two men charged out, AK-47s up and ready, turning west to engage the unseen threat.

Bad move.

The first man dropped dead to the ground before he took his first step. The second, realizing his mistake, spun on a heel to head for the pickup truck and took a round from the SEAL sniper to the back of the head.

"Four tangos down," came the sniper's cool voice.

"Two is inside the wire," Bubba said.

On this report, Cameron was up, surging across the street to the fence in a combat crouch with a second SEAL in tight behind him, scanning to the west. McCoy mirrored the motion, moving offset to Cameron's right and scanning east. He crossed the gravel perimeter road with long quick strides sighting over his Sig 716. At the fence, he took a knee and scanned for targets inside the fence line. A SEAL behind him confirmed his position with a squeeze on his shoulder while a second SEAL cut an opening in the fence with rapid snips using a wire cutter.

Two figures running inside the fence line crossing his peripheral vision caught his attention. They apparently hadn't seen McCoy's element, because they were crossing the open expanse at a diagonal, heading toward the front gate. Simultaneously, he heard the sound of suppressed rifle fire to the north—Mako Two, with Castillo embedded on the team, being engaged by shooters.

"Two tangos down north," came Two's call a second later.

Upon hearing the crack of gunfire, the two runners stopped and looked north. Frozen in place, they made great targets, and McCoy placed his floating red dot on the first man's temple and squeezed. The man fell to the ground, dead, as the second fighter took a 5.56 round to the face from the SEAL beside McCoy.

"Three—two tangos down," McCoy reported.

With only fifteen seconds elapsed, they'd already killed eight of the twenty-five bad guys.

So far so good, but they would have to move very fast now to capitalize on what, if any, element of surprise remained. All of their rifles were suppressed, so the gunfire was muted but not silent. The gate sentries and the shift replacements were dead, but if the pair inside the trailer had raised an alarm before stepping out to engage the threat then the rest of the compound would soon be swarming with activity.

"Move, Mako," Cameron growled, addressing both elements together.

A SEAL stood in the gaping hole in the fence, holding the cut flap of chain link mesh up on his back. McCoy followed Cameron through the breach, with the other SEALs in trail. They moved with practiced fluidity, spreading out, scanning every degree around them like a single, unified creature with five rifles and ten eyes, floating across the wide, open lot quickly, but without taking enemy fire.

So far so good.

Seconds later they were spread out beside the heavy door in the wall of the sprawling warehouse, and McCoy took a tactical knee, scanning his sector instinctively for movement and threats. Beside him the same SEAL who had breached the fence now pressed a small breacher charge into the seam of the door beside the lock, then inserted a single detonator the size of a pen into the malleable explosive, pulling out several loops of wire attached to the detonator.

Gunfire again broke the quiet, followed by another call from Mako Two.

"Two is in contact—Building Two."

McCoy shuffled away from the door, still scanning over his Sig 716, giving him safe distance from the breacher charge the SEAL had set in the door. On the other side of the door Cameron and his teammate did the same. Then they scanned and waited for Mako Two's call.

"Two, Six—Building Three is a dry hole."

"Where'd those guys go, Mother?" Bubba growled.

"I have them for you, Mako Six," Junior chimed in. "Two tangos exiting the west side of Building Three, moving toward a vehicle."

"Let 'em go, Six," Cameron called. "We need you on Building One."

"Check. Building Two secure," Bubba announced after another smattering of gunfire. "Moving to Building One."

At this point, the entire compound knew an assault was underway, which meant both elements had to move fast before the kidnappers decided to execute the prisoner. But before Mako One could breach, they needed Mako Two to distract the shooters on the other side of the door and draw their attention away from the primary breach. The seconds stretched out like minutes as they waited for Two to breach first. McCoy felt a burning tension in his shoulders and forced himself to take a long, slow breath. Finally, he heard a dull *whump* from the other side of the building.

"Two is in," came the report from Bubba.

Gunfire erupted inside.

Cameron nodded to the SEAL with a small trigger in his hand, linked by two wires to the detonator in the molded plastic explosive on the door. The SEAL nodded his head in a *one . . . two . . . three* cadence, and on *three* McCoy squeezed his eyes shut tightly to preserve his vision. The breacher blew the door open, and then McCoy was up, pressed against the wall beside the wrecked door, locking eyes with Cameron, who tossed a flashbang grenade through the hole into the building.

The grenade detonated with a bang and a burst of light so bright it flashed through McCoy's shut eyelids. A heartbeat later, McCoy was trailing Cameron across the threshold and into the warehouse. Cameron moved left through the door and McCoy immediately turned right, clearing the corner as he moved, before turning back to engage targets forward. Like a perfectly choreographed ballet, two other SEALs had surged forward up the center lane in perfect step and the fifth member of the team pushed forward between them as they angled left and right thirty degrees to cover the expansive space of the open warehouse floor.

McCoy saw a target in his lane, a small-framed shooter spinning his head around in confusion, no doubt still blinded by the flashbang. McCoy, moving forward in a combat crouch, dropped the insurgent with a round to the chest and one to the head as he fell. Confusion reigned in the warehouse, the terrorists shouting and running haphazardly. Not so for the SEALs, as they methodically worked the problem with controlled precision fire.

McCoy locked up another enemy shooter, but the SEAL to his left shot first and the young terrorist pitched backward, his AK-47 sliding across the concrete floor.

"Mako One, you guys have three more tangos on the west side, moving quickly south along the wall," Junior called in his ear.

That was his lane. McCoy angled right, looking through the white smoke drifting slowly upward as he heard two more gunshots to his left, then a burst of machine-gun fire and three assault rifles fired in response farther forward.

"Got him, Seven. He's down."

McCoy saw them—three figures in a single line, moving rapidly along the wall, trying to flank them. He dropped to a knee and fired, driving the middle terrorist into the wall where he slid to the ground leaving a trail of dark blood behind. McCoy felt the leg of a SEAL press against his side, letting him know he was there and to the left, and so he engaged the man to his right, placing his red dot on the man's head as he spun toward them, raising his rifle. He and the SEAL fired almost simultaneously and the two remaining jihadists both fell to the ground.

"Clearing left, Three," Cameron said. "You and Five surge forward and right. Engage the door guards."

"Mission objective is located fifty feet beyond those dudes you just shot," Junior reported, updating them on the thermal signature believed to be Secretary Malone. "I hold one figure pacing in a room, two thermals beside the door."

On that news, McCoy took off in a sprint, aware of the SEAL keeping pace with him to his left on a matching vector to rescue Malone.

"Two tangos down north, one moving south in the open, One,"

Bubba said. "Clear north, but I lost that one guy. Might be headed your way."

"Copy, Two," Cameron said. "One will engage."

As he closed the distance, McCoy saw two young jihadis flanking a door. Their rifles were up and at the ready but wavering back and forth on uncertain legs. He fired as he moved, dropping the right-side guard. The other young jihadist saw his friend collapse to the ground, and threw his rifle and hands over his head, but too late. The bullet from the SEAL on McCoy's left tore through the insurgent's forehead and he, too, collapsed, dead.

On reaching the door, the SEAL beside him tugged his arm.

"Just a second, sir," the SEAL said. McCoy watched the SEAL pull a glove off and drag his fingers along the seams of the door, then pull out a light and shine it along the seam as well. "Had a couple of these scenarios in Libya where the door was wired to blow. Lost one guy."

"Three! Shooter coming toward you fast . . ." Junior warned in McCoy's ear.

McCoy spun and registered the threat—a jihadi with a black vest over his long, gray tunic, eyes wide and glazed with religious zeal, drugs, or both. In his right hand he held a pistol and in his left he clutched a button detonator with wires stretching back to the vest . . .

McCoy dropped to a knee, spun his selector to three-round burst. As he squeezed the trigger, he yelled, "Explosive!"

The jihadist pitched backward as McCoy's heavy 7.62 rounds found their target, dropping whatever was in his hand, and McCoy's worst suspicions were confirmed when the suicide vest exploded. McCoy reflexively put his body between the explosion and the SEAL beside him, wrapping up the SEAL and driving him to the ground. Seconds later body parts, hot and wet, rained down on them and he heard shrapnel from the vest's payload—washers, probably—pinging off the warehouse's sheet metal walls.

And then it was quiet.

He was back on his feet, scanning over his rifle for the next threat, but found none—just a smoking hole and a greasy stain of flesh on the concrete floor where a human being had just been.

He felt a squeeze on his arm.

"Holy shit, dude. Thanks, bro," the SEAL said, his face full of gratitude and astonishment. "That was like Medal of Honor–type shit right there."

"You good?" McCoy asked.

The man patted his hands over his body and across his face and neck. "Yeah, bro, you?"

McCoy gave himself a quick once-over. "Yeah, let's get what we came for."

"Hell yes," the SEAL said.

Adrenaline flowing like liquid lightning in his veins, McCoy kicked his boot into the door at the level of the lock. The door burst free of the frame under the blow and swung open. "Hold my six, bro," he said to the SEAL beside him as he entered the room.

"One thermal inside," Junior said. "Back left corner of the room."

McCoy reflexively cleared the room, before fixing his gaze on a figure in an orange jumpsuit, huddled into the corner. He lowered his rifle and pushed his helmet up on his forehead to show more of his face.

"Mr. Secretary?" he said, extending his open left hand to the trembling man. He noticed a large, growing stain on the crotch of the jumpsuit. "Secretary Malone? Frank Malone?"

"You . . . you're American?" the man stammered, and his shoulders drooped. For a moment McCoy worried the man might pass out.

"Yes," he said, moving forward now. "We're here to take you home, sir. Are you injured? Can you walk?"

The man shook his head as if clearing cobwebs from his face, then straightened up.

"My . . . my knees and hips are a little fucked up. But, son, if you're here to take me home, I'll do cartwheels outta here. Screw the pain."

McCoy smiled. He had done only a handful of these type of missions, but rescue ops were the best.

"Good, sir," he said. "Because we're going to have to move fast."

McCoy wrapped an arm around the big man's waist, and let the man wrap a thick arm around his neck, resting some weight on his left shoulder.

"Mother, Three—jackpot. I say again, jackpot. Move Greyhound into position for pickup in five mikes."

"Hot damn, Three!" Junior shouted. "Jackpot it is."

He listened to Cameron rallying the boys to the west exit of the warehouse as he maneuvered the limping secretary of state through the door, hanging halfway off its hinges. Immediately, the SEAL at the door moved into the secretary's left side and wrapped a second arm around the man's waist.

"We gotcha, Mr. Secretary," the SEAL said, his voice scarcely containing his joy. McCoy got it—these were the missions that made all the months and years toiling in the suck worth it.

"Are you SEALs?" the secretary asked, looking at McCoy.

McCoy grinned.

"These guys are, but you got really lucky today," he said, winking at the SEAL on the big man's other side. "Today, you got me, and I'm a Marine."

"My God," the secretary mumbled as they crossed the smoke-filled space, weaving around body parts from the suicide bomber. "He really did it. Man, we owe that guy . . ."

"What guy?" McCoy asked, confused.

"Khalil," the secretary said, giving a little maniacal laugh now. "Irshad Khalil. He came to see me. He said he was negotiating my release. Somehow he got word to you guys, right?"

"Uh," McCoy said, his mind reeling. Negotiating his release? Khalil? What the hell was the secretary talking about? He had an ass-load of questions, but instead said, "We don't always know the source of the intel used for our ops, sir. We're just glad we got to you in time. If this Khalil guy was a part of the intel, then we're glad he got it to the right people. We're just relieved that you're safe."

A cocoon of operators formed around them as they exited the warehouse's west door, shuffling like a single large organism, the secretary of state in the center, toward the gate. McCoy and his teammate assisted the secretary, while six other SEALs and Castillo protected them, scanning all directions.

McCoy looked over at Castillo, whose face had the same confused look that he felt. "You caught all that on the hot mike?" he asked.

Castillo nodded. "We'll sort it out once we're on our way home with the secretary," he said, ending any discussion as they headed for pickup.

As they approached the gate, the team spread out a bit, two operators in the lead and offset left and right. McCoy had trouble suppressing the big, shit-eating grin at what had gone down as a flawless hostage rescue operation. The objective was secure and not a single operator had been injured.

Amazing.

"Mako, we've got a problem," Junior said in his ear, and McCoy cursed his premature mental celebration. "Three pickups headed your way, each with a technical in the back. They're hauling ass to the main gate."

"Shit—I got 'em," the sniper called out. "Tangos on the gate in five seconds. Pull back, pull back!"

"This way," Cameron called, and vectored the entire team north, toward the edge of the warehouse where a car and a pickup sat under a makeshift carport formed by two beams and corrugated metal for a roof. "Fan out into defensive positions and get the secretary covered."

McCoy watched as three sets of headlights fanned out along the perimeter fence, only one set at the gate and the other two pairs diverging from the vehicle for greater coverage. In the pickup beds, he saw what looked like tripod-mounted FN MAG machine guns.

"Son of a bitch," he mumbled. "Get ready for the rain."

Armed fighters began pouring from the pickups like clowns from a clown car at a circus and took covered positions while the gunners turned the heavy machine guns, setting up to unleash a thousand rounds per minute of 7.62 on their position.

"I have air inbound, but it's gonna be more than five mikes," Junior announced in his ear.

"Two, push left and prepare to engage," Cameron said. "This may be over in less than five."

And on that cue, the world lit up like the night sky on the Fourth of July.

CHAPTER THIRTY-NINE

McCoy quickstepped around the corner of the warehouse toward where two of Cameron's SEALs had the secretary of state pressed behind a large, brown metal dumpster, just as the tongues of tracer fire from two heavy machine guns strafed the warehouse's corrugated metal roof and cinder-block façade. Immediately after the first barrage, small arms fire rang out and muzzle flashes lit up the night, followed by the sound of the SEALs returning fire.

"They'll try and retake the secretary for a few minutes, but eventually they'll cut us to shreds," he called, joining the SEALs behind the dumpster, crouching low.

"We need to pull back to the east side of the compound and change our exfil," Cameron said.

"Mother, did you copy?" McCoy said, when no response came from Junior.

"Yes, but you've got a new problem," came Junior's tense voice in his ear. "You have more tangos arriving to the north edge of the compound, where Mako Two breached, and several circling to the south. And believe it or not, there's a fucking fishing boat pulling up beyond the east perimeter fence line on the river, with not one but *two* mounted machine guns and . . . holy shit . . . they have rocket launchers on the boat."

"We're fucking surrounded," Bubba called in his ear.

"Air is seven mikes out," Junior called, referencing the inbound attack helos.

It would be too late.

They needed out, and that meant west, picking up Mako Eight on their way to a dust-off in the MH-60s. McCoy scanned right, tracing up north along the fence. It was a full hundred and fifty yards to the north perimeter where the new trucks were arriving. Clearly the SIF had a robust QRF in place—damn near the entire community around the compound from the look of things. The gap between the left truck and shooters there and the approaching force from the north was nowhere near enough to move their entire team of ten guys and the secretary.

But one quiet and competent Marine Raider . . .

McCoy turned to the SEAL beside him.

"Keep the secretary here until I clear a path," he said.

The SEAL looked at him, eyebrows raised.

"Clear a path where?"

McCoy didn't answer, just squeezed the SEAL's shoulder and headed northeast along the wall of the warehouse in a low crouch, sticking to the shadows.

"Mako Three is moving north and then cutting west. I need two minutes, and then I'll have us a path out of here to the west."

"Three, Four," came an irritated grunt from Castillo. "Wait up. I'm with you."

"Negative, Four," McCoy replied, his voice a soft whisper picked up in the ultrasensitive mic of his comms gear. "Stay with the secretary, boss. I'll see you outside the fence."

"Damn it," Castillo barked in protest, but another burst of sustained machine-gun fire drove him behind cover.

McCoy seized the opportunity and sprinted for the fence line sixty yards north to flank the terrorists in cover behind the northernmost pickup, while its bed-mounted machine gun spit flames and tracers like special effects from a Star Wars movie. Rifle up, he reached the fence and took a knee, watching the seven fighters huddled behind the truck as the machine gun rattled out its tongues of death. He retrieved a pair of wire cutters from his kit and quickly snipped a hole in the fence big enough to crawl through. As he slipped through the opening, the machine guns quieted, and after a beat a loudspeaker started broadcasting from one of the pickup trucks.

"American Special Forces," the voice said in perfect, albeit heavily accented, English. "There is no reason for you to die here tonight."

Ducking low, McCoy sprinted across the dirt street that ran along the perimeter of the compound and dropped into a drainage culvert. He belly-crawled south, his arms burning as the lactic acid built up from the exertion as his elbows relentlessly pounded the gravel.

"We have you completely surrounded. We have overwhelming force with more than a hundred fighters and machine guns on all sides of you. Negotiations were near completion for the release of your secretary of state when you attacked us. Either you surrender now or I kill you and parade your bodies on CNN as proof of American military operations inside Sudan without authority or government permission. Let us be reasonable."

While the terrorist talked, McCoy peered over the edge of the drainage ditch at the closest pickup. Seven fighters armed with AK-47s were sighting on the compound with their backs to him. The heavy machine gunner in the truck bed stood with his arm draped over the butt, waiting for the barrel to cool after his last prolonged engagement. McCoy worried that the next barrage would be meant to kill, rather than to demonstrate their overwhelming fire advantage. While the leader undoubtedly would prefer to take the SEALs and secretary alive, he was also smart enough to know that his own death—dealt from above—was inevitable if he waited too long.

It's now or never.

McCoy slowly pressed to his feet—letting his rifle hang from the sling on his chest—and grabbed two grenades from his kit. With one in each hand, he pulled the pins with gloved thumbs and stepped up out of the ditch.

"Three, this is God," came Mako Eight, the sniper holding overwatch a few blocks away, in his ear. "I see your play, bro. Let me get you a few steps closer."

He didn't hear the shot, but heard the screams from the next truck over, the one directly at the main gate, as the SEAL sniper behind him unleashed deadly covering fire.

The terrorist fighters sprang to life, some turning south in confusion, others ducking for cover.

McCoy threw both grenades—the one in his left hand he tossed underhand, rolling it into the cluster of jihadis behind the truck closest to him, and the other he lobbed overhand into the bed of the next truck over.

The simultaneous explosions cued him like a bark from a starter's pistol, and he sprinted *toward* the carnage. Sighting over his

Sig 716, he fired at the heavy gunner in the bed of the truck. His round hit the man in the right side of the face, spinning the fighter completely around and dropping him like a pile of garbage in the bed next to the tripod. In his peripheral vision, he saw movement at his ten o'clock. He swiveled left to find a wounded fighter stagger- ing toward him—one hand clutching his bloody hip, his other bringing up an AK-47. McCoy squeezed off two 7.62 rounds, the first tearing open the terrorist's throat and the second raising a puff of blood and gore as it took off the right side of his head.

McCoy leaped into the bed of the truck, quickly strafed the row of grenade-felled bodies on the ground behind him—just in case— before stepping up to man the heavy machine gun.

"Return fire, Mako!" he hollered, grabbing the stock of the heavy machine gun and spinning the weapon to his right on the tripod. "Three is manning the gun in the truck to the north, so don't fuck- ing shoot me."

He squeezed the trigger as he turned the weapon on the tripod toward a cluster of fighters to the south. A tongue of flame and tracers lashed out across the confused fighters, tearing them to rib- bons in seconds. He swept his line of death away from the com- pound back toward the fence line, cutting down three terrorists who'd charged into no-man's-land, then he unloaded on the second truck he'd fragged with a grenade, shredding the cab, the machine- gun nest, and several fighters trying to take cover behind the tailgate. The machine gun cycled dry a heartbeat later, and McCoy— fueled by battle and adrenaline—leaped over the siderail and landed in the dirt. His rifle was up a split second later, scanning for targets when his gaze found the third pickup—where the megaphone talker had been.

McCoy sprinted toward the target, scanning fallen bodies as he ran—most mutilated from either his grenade or his strafing with the 7.62 machine gun. Not wanting to get shot in the back, he delivered only a final kill shot to a squirming shooter, en route to his objective. Covering fire from the SEAL sniper, Mako Eight, cleared the path for him and he almost didn't see the well-dressed man crouched beside the rear fender of the truck he closed on. He spun left, dropping his red dot onto the man's forehead as he talked into his hot mike.

"Clear through the front gate now, but move fast and watch for shooters who might have squirted."

"Mako, Greyhound en route dust-off at the primary LZ in under three," Junior said in his ear. The primary landing zone was four blocks west in a large open lot behind another, much smaller industrial compound—this one free of a fence. "Plan for hot LZ, get moving, Mako."

The bearded terrorist in suit clothes stood, defiantly, an AK-47 still clutched in his right hand and his eyes glowing with malice. "Who are you?" the man asked, in clipped, clean English.

"I'm the Presidential Agent," McCoy growled, "and the last face on this earth you're ever going to see."

He squeezed the trigger and the terrorist leader pitched backward into the dirt, dead.

McCoy took a knee beside the truck, aiming now at one of the two fighters struggling to decide whether he would be safer in front of the truck, where the rest of Mako's team now poured fire onto his position, or behind the truck, where Mako Eight was thinning the herd with his sniper rifle. McCoy settled the terrorist's indecision with a 7.62 round to his head. A single remaining terrorist now made his own decision, dropping his rifle and sprinting south, but Mako Eight ended his sprint three strides later.

"Holy shit, dude," a voice said behind him. McCoy turned to see the tall SEAL who'd breached Secretary Malone's cell by his side now standing over him, scanning the carnage everywhere around them. "How did you?"

"Well done, Three," Cameron said as he jogged by and gave McCoy's shoulder a squeeze as he passed. "Haul ass to the LZ, Mako."

McCoy waved the quickstepping formation of SEALs protecting Secretary Malone toward the gate. "Two minutes. I'll hold here for a second in case any stragglers try to engage."

"You didn't leave stragglers alive, from the looks of it," Cameron said, chopping a hand forward to move everyone out. "Eight, fall in on us as we pass."

"I'll hold with you," the SEAL called Bubba said, scanning the massacre site and then shaking his head and shooting him a wry smile. "Probably safer here with you," he added with a chuckle. "Apparently you're *that* guy."

"I thought we agreed no more Captain America bullshit," Castillo said, jogging up to McCoy, but he was grinning. Then the former Green Beret stuck a finger through the bullet hole in McCoy's shirt, just below his armpit on the left and outside his body armor. "Talk about one charmed son of a bitch."

"You're welcome," McCoy came back, but held his gaze over his rifle.

Castillo slapped his back and took off running west with the rest of the team.

"Your boss is a strange dude," Bubba said, still scanning over his rifle. "And he ain't no leader if he doesn't put you in for the Medal of Honor for this one."

McCoy laughed. "No medals on this op for me. I just did what any operator would do, bro, you included."

The SEAL shook his head. "Yeah, right."

"Well, it doesn't matter anyway. My team's not eligible for medals."

"Why's that?"

"Because we don't exist," he said, flashing the SEAL a crooked grin.

Fifteen seconds later, they were up, moving swiftly to the west, scanning over their rifles to the thrum of the MH-60s on approach and the beautiful sound of the MH-6 Little Birds going to work with their miniguns—clearing the enemy QRF boat and fighters on the river.

Better late than never.

McCoy could scarcely keep his grin contained.

Somehow they had done it. Rescued the secretary without a single casualty.

As he ran to the hovering helo, he suddenly found himself thinking, *Maybe this Presidential Agent gig isn't so bad after all.*

CHAPTER FORTY

It took all President Cohen's willpower to sit quietly and listen to what General Kerry Rydman had to say, despite the vital importance of the information. Rydman, she realized, would love McCoy . . . if only she was able to read him in on the operation they had going on in Sudan. Rydman was a Marine, too, after all—he and McCoy were cut from the same cloth. Unlike McCoy, however, the Marine General had come up the ranks the long, hard way. He had no family pedigree to help him secure admission to a service academy, and instead had joined the Marines at seventeen, with parental permission. Nearly forty-five years later, he served at the highest level with a lifetime of experience both leading and following Marines.

The teen Marine from Grundy, West Virginia, now had a wall of degrees, including a master's in foreign policy, and life lessons worth a thousand times more.

She would most certainly need to order a military response to the kidnapping—and possible execution—of a sitting secretary of state. The various options that Marine General Rydman and his aide, Colonel Brandon Land, laid out seemed sound and measured and, perhaps most important, appropriate, but all Cohen could think about was how she *really* should have heard something by now. Even if Castillo's mission succeeded, a response would still be required, though the outcome of the deeply secret mission carried out by her Presidential Agent with a contingent of U.S. Navy SEALs would no doubt heavily impact the option she chose.

Make no mistake, there will have to be blood.

The message she sent in the next day or two would not only define her Presidency and her personal strength of character; it would, she knew, prevent violence against her nation and people. *Peace through strength* was no longer just a bumper sticker, a lesson America had learned the hard way.

If I could just pay attention . . .

"Madam President?"

She looked up, about to respond to what she thought the general had said, when the double-chirp saved her. She picked up the phone beside her on the desk.

"Yes?"

"Madam President, the director of national intelligence is here to see you. He says it's urgent. I told him you were in a briefing . . ."

"Send him," she said, with more patience than she felt, and set the phone in its receiver. "Gentlemen, I apologize, but I need the room. So stay close by. I may need you in a moment."

"Yes, Madam President," Rydman said.

The door opened and Marty Fleiss stepped aside for the two soldiers to leave.

"Marty," Rydman said, with a genuine but curious smile.

"Kerry," Fleiss replied, then came into the office, crossing the room quickly to meet her by the desk. "Mike Charlie—mission complete—we've got him, Madam President," he said, unable to conceal his huge grin. "Mission success, ma'am."

"Oh, thank God," she said, pumping a fist in the air. "Marty, that's fantastic. How is he?"

"From the sound of it, he's well. A little banged up, but otherwise well."

"Did we take any casualties in the assault force—the SEALs or any of Castillo's team?"

"No, ma'am," Fleiss reported. "As you know, they lost an asset in Khartoum, but the organic team is all squared away and no serious injuries to our SEALs. It was a flawless op."

Cohen felt suddenly exhausted, as if perhaps the only thing keeping her going was the fear and anxiety about the outcome of Castillo's operation. With that removed, she found herself too tired to stand. She crossed to the couch and collapsed onto it.

"Well, thank God for Charley Castillo and his Merry Outlaws," she said, unable to contain a laugh.

"And for a President with the stones to put them in play . . . if you don't mind me saying so."

Fleiss dropped down with a long sigh onto the couch across from her.

She smiled and nodded at him. Fleiss was incapable of false platitudes, so she took the compliment at face value.

"I know you're aware I couldn't have done it without having someone I can trust completely in the ODNI, Marty."

He nodded back.

"I'm glad you feel that way, ma'am. It's an honor to serve."

"So," she said, her mind reeling, "this was Sudanese Islamic Front?"

Fleiss pursed his lips, something she hated because it was never followed by good news in her experience.

"It's looking a bit more complicated than that, Madam President," he said. "We'll get the full download once Charley and the gang have a secure channel—likely aboard the jet standing by for them in Khartoum."

"Where are they now?"

"Airborne," Fleiss said. "En route from the exfil to the airport at Khartoum via helicopter. The SEALs are on their way back to the USS *America* and are nearly clear of the border and over international waters. Once we have the secretary's jet in the air and headed home, we'll get with Charley for a detailed debrief. But I thought you would want to know once they were clear of the target."

"Excellent," she replied, her heart rate settling. "I was just briefing potential military responses with General Rydman, so I'll need Charley's take ASAP."

"Of course," Fleiss said, rising now. "I can tell you that the bad guys on the X are all dead except two squirters—two got away. I'll get back at it, so our analysts can give you the best assessment on what we get from Charley, as well as target package assessments from the usual sources."

"Thank you, Marty," she said, rising and shaking his hand firmly. "For all of it. Let's focus on getting everyone safely back on American soil, and the rest we'll sort out over the next twenty-four hours. And we should plan a press briefing. Silence from this office is deafening, so announcing the secretary's rescue to the world explains our silence nicely."

"That press brief should come from you, Madam President."

"I agree," she said, her political gears now turning. She hated that the optics mattered, but they did. "I'll address the nation from the Oval Office in the morning. We'll notify the press by six and make the announcement three hours later, just ahead of the stock market opening."

"Sounds right," Fleiss said, but his voice suggested these political issues were not his area of interest.

Nor his problem, she supposed. She missed those days.

Fleiss headed for the door and she returned to her desk, picking up the phone.

"Send General Rydman and Colonel Land back in, please. And get my chief of staff in here right away."

She hung up without waiting for an answer. The door opened immediately and Rydman and Land returned to the room, anticipation on their faces, no doubt from the jubilation evident in Fleiss when he'd passed them.

"Positive developments, Madam President?" Rydman asked, unable to conceal his eagerness to be in the know.

"Oh, yes," she replied, aware she was beaming. "The secretary of state has been recovered and will be in the air on his way home within the hour. The rescue was a success and no Americans were lost or wounded."

"Fuck, yeah," Land replied, pumping his fist by his side. Then he looked at her sheepishly. "My apologies, Madam President."

"Don't be," she said, smiling broadly. "Fuck, yeah, indeed."

"Who rescued him?" Rydman asked, the fact that he'd not been involved in what had to have been a military, or at least military-*style* operation dawning on him.

"Assets answering directly to this office and the ODNI," she replied. "Now, let's get back to the discussion of my options so the terrorist world understands what happens when you mess with the United States of America."

CHAPTER FORTY-ONE

Castillo shook the hand of the army aviator in the right seat of the MH-60M Special Operations helicopter, the door open and his right leg hanging out as he laughed with his copilot in the other seat, waiting for the refueling truck to arrive and top them off with JP-8.

"Major, can't thank you enough for the ride," Castillo said.

"Our pleasure, sir," the aviator said, gripping his hand firmly and smiling. "Honor to be part of this operation—not that it ever really happened, of course," he added with a wink.

Castillo headed for the Gulfstream 550, partially concealed within the open hangar doors. He had already decided that if President Cohen decided to keep this program going, he was going to need to have Junior with them full time. The man was a maestro of logistics, as evidenced by this remote hangar—across the runway from the commercial operations on the west side of the field, and remote even from the government hangars several hundred yards north of them. The hangar contained their ride home and, more impressive, swarmed with Secret Service agents and CIA Ground Branch operators, including four snipers positioned on the roof.

As he entered the hangar he got a nod from the black, Nomex-clad operator clutching a compact Sig MCX Rattler on his chest for close-quarters combat if needed. A man in a sport coat and open-collar white shirt approached him, hand extended.

"Mr. Castillo?"

"Yep," he said, shaking the man's hand.

"I'm Gary Morrison, the station chief for North Africa. Would've loved to have had more of a heads-up on your operation, sir."

"What operation?"

Morrison made a sour face but went on: "We definitely could have provided Agency assets to get the job done. We have a large contingent of Ground Branch and CS guys here, you know."

"I'm aware of that, Gary," Castillo said. "But we got it done. We appreciate all the security you guys have for us here now. This was a real short-fuse thing we grew into as our operation evolved. You get it."

"Yeah, sure," the man said, hands by his side now. "Who'd you say you're with exactly, Mr. Castillo?"

"I didn't."

"Gotcha," Morrison said, visibly unhappy with the answer.

"But I'll be sure to let the President and the DNI know that you guys did great work supporting us, Mr. Morrison." With that he slapped the guy on the shoulder and headed to the jet.

"Pilots tell us we can have you airborne in less than forty-five minutes," Morrison called after him.

"Great, thanks," Castillo called back over his shoulder without stopping. "Keep us secure until then, okay?"

Not surprisingly, Morrison didn't answer.

Castillo took the ten steps up the airstair in five, feeling young and, he realized, alive again. This was where he was meant to be. This was the life he was born for. He ducked his head through the doorway and turned toward the cockpit.

"Hey, man," he said with a nod to the pilot, sitting half in and half out of the seat in a desert tan flight suit and boots. "Thanks for being ready to go, Colonel."

"Mr. Castillo," the pilot said, smiling. "Good to see you again. Seems you had a very productive couple of days."

"We did indeed, my friend. We appreciate the lift. What's our ETA into Andrews?"

"Well, with the current winds and altitudes we're planning, I can get you there in just over twelve hours. Hope to shave a little off that for you."

"Awesome," Castillo said. "Where is the package?"

"The secretary is in the VIP suite in the rear. He's getting a once-over by the navy surgeon who's traveling back with us, I understand. We're fueled up, and I've got people deconflicting our route and checking provisions so we can get you guys fed and hydrated en route. Hope to be taxiing out in about thirty."

"Sooner the better," Castillo answered.

"Understood," the pilot said. "Oh, and we have fighter escort all the way to the Atlantic and partway across the pond."

"Great," he replied. That sounded more like Pentagon and White House than Junior. He didn't think that the SIF was operating an air force, at least not yet.

He exited the cockpit and found Ani and Junior bent over a laptop and talking in hushed whispers. At the rear of the main cabin, beside the door to the VIP suite, McCoy reclined in the wide leather seat, head against the bulkhead and eyes closed, though he still wore his kit and his Sig 716 still rested against his thigh, his right hand gripping the weapon.

"Nice job thinking to have a medical team aboard, Junior," Castillo said, clapping the man on the shoulder.

Junior nodded and turned to Ani, raising his eyebrows as if indicating for her to get to it.

Ani looked up, her eyes concerned.

"Charley, we have a problem," she said, gesturing to him to take the leather seat across the table from her.

"Okay," he said, not sure what *problem* possibly mattered now.

The package was on board. Their mission was not only complete, but a rousing success—Malone recovered intact, their presence relatively anonymous, and no organic injuries or losses. The loss of Shaker was of course tragic . . .

"They're going to kill her, Charley," Ani said, squeezing his forearm.

"What? Who's going to kill who?"

"Awadiya Khalil," she said, her voice strained, leaning into him across the small table between them in the superbly comfortable leather seats. "The Sudanese Islamic Front plans to assassinate her. Today, I think . . ."

"What are you talking about?"

"Charley," Junior said, "the computers the SEALs snatched off the X from Building Two were heavily encrypted. I sent everything on them via a secure satellite link to a team I'm tight with at NSA. They just started returning data to me. I'll go over whatever you want, but SIF has been tracking her movements, evaluating her security—in this case, lack of security—and even probing with practice runs. The firebombing at her campaign headquarters was a test of what security she might have covertly in place. I'm sure they liked the answer."

"What makes you think it happens today?"

"There are communications between the SIF leader at the compound and assets affiliated with them in Khartoum," Ani said. "He ordered the hit on the campaign headquarters as a probe, as Junior said. They had tons of images evaluating her lack of security. They've been sharing information back and forth on her movements and vulnerabilities. Look, Charley, we don't have time to make the case. You just need to trust us. Junior's pals are sure the data suggests an attack today."

"Well, we just annihilated their command and control," Charley countered. "What makes you think they can even pull it off now?"

"Because SIF appears to be taking a page out of the AQ and Taliban playbooks," Junior said. "They've fragmented their communications and are working under a multiple autonomous cell model, according to my buddy. They do that just in case of an attack like we did today. If the head of the serpent is cut off, it doesn't matter—plans already set in motion unfold anyway. The cells are completely compartmentalized."

Castillo raised a hand to his face, his thumb and ring finger massaging his temples as his mind ran through options.

"We're mission complete here," he said, looking up. "We can pass this on to that dude Morrison outside. He and his Ground Branch assets can handle it. Our job is to get Secretary Malone all the way home, safe and sound."

"Come on, Charley," Ani said, throwing her hands up. "The secretary's on board a military VIP transport with his own damn doctor and a fighter escort. What the hell do we have to contribute at this point other than handshakes and smiles at Andrews? You don't strike me as the kind of guy who gives a damn about any of that, Charley. Did you meet Gary Morrison? All this took place right under his nose. That guy is so by the book he wouldn't take a shit without orders in writing. You know that. Awadiya Khalil helped us. She also represents our best interest in Sudan—something you know from meeting her. If we had time to brief her, President Cohen would agree, I'm sure, but there's simply no time."

Castillo let out a long sigh, but he already knew what he was going to do. And it was the kind of call that the Presidential Agent program was invented for. This wasn't his team being a rogue asset, it was them doing the noble thing. Them doing what they were re-cruited and empowered to do.

"We could notify Sudan's government security forces," he said, his last pitch, but he already knew they were going either way.

"Can't," Junior said. "An insane number of the communications catalogued by the NSA team are between the SIF commander and servers and phone lines located within the government complex. We could tip off the ringleaders, if they're inside the government, and she'd be dead in minutes. Only we can stop this."

Charley rose, looking to the rear of the aircraft where McCoy had yet to stir.

"Shit," he said, blowing air through pursed lips. Then looked at Ani and met her pleading eyes. "You convinced me. Let's go."

Castillo headed aft and kicked McCoy's boot. The Marine Raider bolted upright, his rifle coming up as he snapped from sleep to combat-ready in a millisecond.

"Easy, Killer. We have work to do. Get with Ani and Junior and stay kitted up."

"Bad guys coming?" McCoy asked, and Castillo saw the Marine's hands begin to fly instinctively across his kit, checking his load.

"No," Castillo said, knocking on the wooden door in the bulkhead. "We're taking the fight to them. Apparently, SIF is planning on assassinating Awadiya Khalil. Today."

"What?" McCoy said. "Shit. I'm on it."

"Come in," came a voice from behind the door, and Castillo opened it and entered as McCoy headed forward. The aft third of the jet contained the VIP suite, with a double bed, a full desk with computer and sat phone and a comfortable couch and flat-screen TV. Another door at the rear led to a full bathroom and shower.

"Mr. Secretary," Castillo said, addressing the man who now lay on the large bed wearing a blue and white sweatsuit. Beside him sat a man he assumed to be the navy surgeon, though he wasn't in uniform, but instead dressed in khakis and a blue polo shirt. "How is he, doc?"

"Remarkably well, I would say," the doctor replied. "We're getting him hydrated up and fed, and with some rest he'll be in great shape when we land."

"The White House will want a conference call with you shortly after takeoff, Mr. Secretary, and then you should rest for the remainder of the flight," Castillo said, shifting his gaze to Malone. "I'll leave instructions with the cabin crew to assist you in setting that up."

"Leave instructions? Where are you going? I thought you were escorting me all the way home."

Castillo heard real fear and anxiety in the man's voice. He imagined Malone had been at his breaking point, and that fear would not disappear soon.

"I know, Mr. Secretary. I'm afraid something came up. My team has something else we need to attend to."

"To hell with that. Pass it on to someone else. After the ordeal I've been through, Mr. Castillo, I want *you* to take me home. I'm not taking no for an answer."

"You're safe now, Mr. Secretary. You're aboard an air force jet that will be airborne in just a few minutes. I'm told they have arranged for a fighter escort for you until you are home. The crew here is more than capable, I assure you, and there is an army of CIA Ground Branch operators outside right now, keeping you safe until you're wheels-up. I wish I could take you all the way to the finish line, believe me. But this has to be done. I'm sorry."

Before the secretary could argue, Castillo turned to the surgeon. "Keep him healthy, doc."

"Be safe," Malone called after him. "And thank you for getting me out."

Castillo nodded and closed the door behind him.

Shouting on the tarmac outside the jet got his attention and he hustled forward, stopping only a moment at the cockpit.

"My team is staying back, Colonel. Get the hell out of here as quick as you can," he said.

"Happy hunting, Mr. Castillo," the air force pilot said, then returned to the checklist he was running with his copilot.

Castillo hustled down the airstair to where Ani was standing chest to chest with Gary Morrison, CIA station chief, having words.

"And I'm telling you, I have no intention of committing Ground Branch operators to an operation in Sudan just on your request," Morrison said, shouting down at Ani. "I don't even know who the hell you people are."

"Well, you know we're someone, bro," Junior said. "We just

delivered the secretary of state to this plane—a kidnapped American official you guys couldn't find. Clearly, we're operating here on authority. Do you really want to be the guy to explain to your DCI why you let Awadiya Khalil, the woman likely to become the first democratically elected President of Sudan, be assassinated while you waited for paperwork? I thought you were in charge here."

"I am in charge here, and I'm not committing my assets to a bunch of cowboys without proper authorization."

"Stop it, guys. This solves nothing," Castillo barked.

"So we're just gonna let Awadiya die because this guy is a CYA, paper-shuffling pussy?" Junior snapped back at him.

"Of course not," he said. "Have you learned nothing about me? We'll go get Awadiya Khalil ourselves. Forget this guy."

"Now see here," Morrison protested.

Castillo shouldered Ani out of the way and leaned into the man so close their foreheads almost touched.

"Listen up, asshole, we're not letting Awadiya Khalil die on our watch—especially after she helped us locate the secretary of state. Truth is, we don't need your help, or your blessing. Besides, you'll only slow us down."

He knocked Morrison with his shoulder as he walked past.

"I don't know who the hell you think you are!" the bureaucrat shouted.

Castillo spun on a heel, his eyes full of rage and violence. "I'm the guy who will let the President know that you and your team were a great help in protecting Secretary of State Malone today. Or, if you don't give me a fully fueled, up-armored SUV right fucking now, I tell her how you obstructed our attempts to save one of our few true allies in the region. And make no mistake—I'll be having dinner with President Cohen thirty-six hours from now and I fucking promise your name is coming up one way or the other."

All eyes in the hangar were on them as Castillo stood, hands on hips, glaring at the man.

Morrison flinched first.

"Give them a truck," Morrison said, turning to one of his guys nearby. "And get them extra ammo if they need it."

"Thank you, Mr. Morrison," Castillo then said, evenly. "You've been a great help. I'll be sure to let President Cohen know."

Two Ground Branch operators drove a black Chevy Suburban beside them only a moment later. The driver exited and held open the door, giving Castillo a nod of approval.

Castillo looked at McCoy. "You drive," he said, moving toward the front passenger door.

With Ani and Junior in back and McCoy behind the wheel, the SUV squealed out of the hangar and headed to the gate.

CHAPTER FORTY-TWO

Africa Road, southbound out of Khartoum International Airport

Khartoum, Sudan

March 24, 6:25 a.m.

McCoy tapped the steering wheel with his thumbs, dissipating the nervous energy as he drove the team to Awadiya Khalil's private residence. They had a killing to stop and so far, nobody was feeling particularly good about their probability of success.

"Still not answering her phone?" Castillo said, turning to look at Junior and Ani in the back.

"She must have turned it off," Junior said. "Every call goes straight to voicemail and her mailbox is full."

"Keep trying," Castillo said.

"I am, and I'm sending her text messages, too."

"I hear you tapping away on that laptop, Ani. Have you got visuals?" Castillo asked.

McCoy glanced in the rearview mirror and saw her gaze was laser focused on her computer screen. She answered without looking up.

"The drone is in orbit with good viz, but I've got nothing suspicious at all in a several block radius around Awadiya's house. I don't know, guys. A hit at her private residence doesn't feel right to me, even though the data points Junior's guys pulled off that computer suggest it."

"Agreed," McCoy said, returning his attention back to the road. "We need to think about motivation here. Why is SIF going after Awadiya Khalil in the first place?"

Junior grunted. "Because she represents a very real threat to all the fundamentalist values that the Islamic Front and other proponents of Islamic rule of law embrace. If she wins the presidency, she'll usher in a new era of change and turn the established hierarchy on its head. A democratic, secular Sudan is a world where the Sudanese Islamic Front has no future."

"Exactly," Ani said. "So, is this just an assassination or a public statement they're trying to make?"

"Both," McCoy said.

"Agreed, so by killing her, what message is the Islamic Front trying to send?" she asked.

"It's a message to her supporters, a message to the reformers, hell, a message to every Sudanese—this is what happens to you when you try to upset the Islamic order," Junior said.

McCoy nodded. Oppressive regimes in the Middle East all had one thing in common: a fundamentalist, hard-line interpretation of Islam where Sharia law formed the foundation of governance.

"I'm not convinced SIF is acting unilaterally on this," Castillo said.

"What do you mean?" McCoy said with a sideways glance.

"I think Irshad Khalil is behind this hit," Castillo said.

"Hold on. You're saying you think he's helping the Islamic Front to assassinate his own sister?" Junior said.

"No," Castillo said. "Take it one step further. Not just helping them, I'm suggesting assassinating her was his idea."

"Murder his own sister? That doesn't make any sense."

"Honor killings are a dark and long-rooted practice that still exists in the Islamic world," Ani said, her voice taking on a dark and hard edge, "especially in societies governed by Sharia law. A daughter, sister, or wife who engages in disgraceful behavior or commits an act that is perceived to bring public shame to the family will be punished—and in extreme cases murdered for it. Last year, five thousand women around the world were murdered by a family member in the name of honor. Is it so difficult to imagine a man like Irshad Khalil, an ambitious man in a position of governmental power, becoming jealous of his sister who could become the *President* of Sudan?"

"He doesn't strike me as a fundamentalist," Junior said, stepping into the devil's advocate role. "When you interviewed Awadiya, I was under the impression that her brother was supportive of her campaign."

"What if that's just the mask he wears in public? What if privately he's not only diminished by her success, but offended by it?" McCoy said, jumping in.

He'd spent enough time dealing with village elders and tribal hard-liners to understand how important honor was in devout Muslim families. What Ani suggested resonated with him. It just felt right.

"Bingo," Castillo said, cocking and firing a pistol finger at McCoy from the passenger seat.

McCoy eased off the accelerator.

"We're heading in the wrong direction," he said. "They're not going to kill Awadiya at her private residence. There's no bang for the buck. To drive fear and control the narrative, he'll want the murder to happen at a time and place the world will notice."

"Ani," Castillo said, "you still have the contact at her campaign HQ? Can you call her and see what big-crowd events Awadiya has coming up?"

"Wait," Ani said, clicking her laptop keys again. "Okay, according to her campaign website, she's giving a speech this morning at the march for democracy event in downtown Khartoum. They're having a mass morning prayer—the Salat al-Fajr—to show they are not abandoning their faith by pursuing a secular government. That prayer will be wrapping up about now, with a short speech by a cleric supporting her campaign. She takes the stage right after."

"What time?" Castillo asked.

"In twenty-two minutes."

"Get an address into the GPS," McCoy said, a wave of adrenaline washing over him at the news.

"Entering one now," Junior said.

"How do you think they're going to do it?" Ani asked with heightened tension in her voice. "Suicide bomber? Rooftop sniper? Lone gunman in the crowd . . . it makes a difference how we prosecute the threat."

"It makes a huge friggin' difference," Castillo said.

A computerized female voice speaking with a British accent from Junior's GPS told McCoy to make a U-turn and then reported it would take fifteen minutes to reach the destination.

"We're not going to make it in time," Ani said.

"We're going to make it," McCoy said, his voice drowned out by the roar of the SUV's V8 engine as he pressed the accelerator to the floor. "So we still have the drone in orbit?"

"I kept it on station until the jet gets airborne, so yeah, we still got it," Junior replied. "I'll extend the tasking right now." The spook opened the laptop he had sitting on his thighs in the middle row captain's chair behind McCoy.

"Ani, get the drone refocused on downtown and the march. Scan the rooftops for possible snipers, but my money is on a suicide bomber rushing the stage. These guys are going to want to go big— shock and awe—to intimidate and scare all her supporters."

"I'm on it," Ani said, her fingers tapping with renewed purpose on the keyboard.

McCoy felt Castillo's eyes on him. When the old man didn't say anything after thirty seconds, he couldn't take it anymore. "What?" he said with an annoyed sideways glance. "I can tell you've got something to say, Charley, so just spit it out."

"I want you to promise me that this time, you're not going to go all Captain America on me and charge off into the crowd to take these guys on single-handedly, leaving me in the dust like you did in Cairo," Castillo said.

His expression deadpan, McCoy replied, "Look, I'm not gonna walk across the finish line just because your old-man legs can't keep up."

"I'm serious, Killer," Castillo said, using the one and only nickname that McCoy despised. "Don't do it."

"I'm just messing with you, Charley. We absolutely need to keep this tight and coordinated. This march is going to be teeming with God only knows how many civilians. Their safety needs to be our number one priority."

"Good," Castillo said, but there was plenty packed in that single-word answer that McCoy picked up on, not the least of which was Castillo's own recognition that at fifty-seven years old he'd lost a step. Also, he noticed that the old man never passed on an opportunity to reinforce the fact that he was the ringmaster of this pop-up circus of theirs. They weren't partners, and the same held true for Junior and Ani—in Charley's mind they all worked for him.

It's all good, McCoy thought, tightening his grip on the steering wheel. *I never wanted this gig in the first place. When this is over, Charley gets to go back to his ranch a hero and I finally get to go back to being a Marine.*

CHAPTER FORTY-THREE

"Concentration is like a camera aperture," his father, P.K. McCoy Sr., had once told him. "It takes practice, but with a little effort you'll figure out how to dial in the amount of light you can handle without washing out your mind."

At the time, McCoy had been attending Annapolis, home on leave for Christmas. His grades were not meeting his father's expectations—or his own, for that matter—and he'd confessed that he felt pulled in too many directions and was having trouble focusing. When giving advice, his Marine fighter pilot father had a habit of drowning his son in aviation analogies. Not this time. The metaphor, co-opted from the world of physics, had taken McCoy by surprise. And, strangely, it had worked for him, both as a midshipman and later as a Marine Raider.

Here and now, in the crush of chaos, his mind automatically did what had once required great effort—he closed the aperture until his concentration was hyper-focused on a young Sudanese man in a white tunic moving through the crowd toward the stage. All the shouting and noise, all the bumping and jostling, all the shifting colors and distracting movements trying to usurp his attention fell into a sensory abyss. The target was the only thing that mattered, and his brain crunched the data: The terrorist's white tunic bulged in all the wrong places, indicating the presence of a suicide vest beneath. The way the young man moved was discordant with the rest of the crowd. A vector manifested in McCoy's mind that pointed straight at the dais where Awadiya Khalil would be stepping up to speak at any moment.

McCoy picked up his pace, closing on his target like a heat-seeking missile.

"Move!" he barked, using his arms to swim through the ocean of bodies. "Move. Out of my way . . ."

In his earpiece, he could hear Castillo arguing with the Sudanese policeman who'd stopped him. As if having Castillo out of the fight wasn't bad enough, the next report was even worse.

"Possible shooter, north side!" Ani announced.

"Where?" Junior asked.

"There's a group of counterprotesters," Ani said. "West corner of the roundabout to the left of the stage. He's standing two persons to the west of the imam in the white turban and jalabiya. I'm pretty sure I saw him reposition a long gun slung under his tunic."

"Check, I have eyes on him," Junior came back.

McCoy successfully resisted the urge to take his eyes off his target and look left. The crowd suddenly erupted in a cheer as a male voice spoke in Sudanese Arabic over a speaker system.

"Awadiya just took the steps on the east side of the stage," Ani reported. "Looks like she's about to be introduced."

A surge of adrenaline flooded McCoy's bloodstream as that old familiar *now-or-never* urgency gripped him. He'd closed within ten feet of the suicide bomber, but the crowd density was too great to take a shot at any distance but point-blank range. He shoved forward, aggressively closing the remaining gap as the bomber made his way toward the stage.

"Please welcome your next President of Sudan—Awadiya Khalil!" a man said in Sudanese Arabic and the crowd roared with enthusiasm to greet her.

I'm not going to make it . . .

"Move, move!" he growled, surging forward to close on his target.

Awadiya Khalil's voice echoed triumphantly over the speakers in Arabic: "Thank you, thank you. I come before you today with a message of peace and hope . . ."

He scanned the martyr's hands looking for a trigger or deadman's switch—and there it was, a wired device clutched in his right palm. In that moment, McCoy understood that he would probably die trying to stop the bomber. But unlike falling on a grenade, in this case his sacrifice would not save Awadiya or the lives of all the innocents around him.

If I don't try, we're all guaranteed to die.

He pulled his Sig P356XL from the concealed holster, switched it to his nondominant left hand, and shoved the final civilian blocking him from his target out of the way. Feeling McCoy's presence, the terrorist tried to turn, but it was too late. McCoy clutched the bomber's right hand inside his own, clamping his thumb on top of the bomber's, which was keeping a deadman's switch depressed. At the same time, he pressed the muzzle of his pistol behind the terrorist's left ear and squeezed the trigger. The bullet punched a hole out the top of the bomber's skull and he collapsed like a puppet whose strings had just been cut.

McCoy immediately dropped his Sig and eased the dead jihadi to the ground, using his left arm to cradle the dead man's torso to his own—his entire focus on maintaining positive control of the deadman's switch.

A woman screamed.

Awadiya abruptly stopped speaking and the crowd woke up to the realization of what was going on. Around him, pandemonium ensued.

"Stay back," he shouted, knowing if the crowd trampled him he'd lose his grip and the bomb would detonate. "I said stay back, damn it!" he repeated, this time in Arabic.

Behind him, gunfire erupted, followed by more screaming.

"Tango Two is down," Junior reported. "But now I've got law enforcement coming for me."

"Roger, Three, surrender if you have to," McCoy said.

"Not going to happen," Junior came back.

"Mother, report threats," McCoy said, knowing that SIF probably assigned a shooter to watch the bomber and take him out to ensure detonation in the event the young martyr changed his mind.

"Scanning," was all Ani came back with.

Fresh gunfire echoed and a civilian running past McCoy took a round and fell to the ground. McCoy immediately ducked, making himself small while clutching the dead bomber's right hand inside both his own.

"One is back in the fight with backup. Khartoum's SPF is on our side," Castillo barked, referring to the national police. "I've got eyes on the new shooter."

A moment later, McCoy heard the double crack of Castillo squeezing off two rounds from his Sig accompanied by rifle fire.

"Tango Three is down," Castillo said.

"Confirmed," Ani chimed in. "No new threats."

"Two, One—I'm coming to you," Castillo said. McCoy could hear him breathing heavy over the comms.

"Negative," McCoy said, "Maintain maximum standoff range. The bomber was using a deadman's switch and, well, he's a dead man now, which means that I'm the one keeping the button pressed."

"I don't know how in the hell you pulled that off, but I think we're going to have to change your nickname from Killer McCoy to Miracle Man."

"Yeah, well, if somebody doesn't get me some duct tape soon, my name is going to be KIA McCoy."

"Why's that?"

"Because I have a feeling I'm gonna have to hold this thing a long-ass time before EOD shows up," McCoy said, wondering how long he had before his fingers started to cramp from the strain, "and my hands are already getting sweaty."

"Hang in there, brother," Junior said. "I might know a guy who can help."

"Of course you do," Ani chimed in.

Around him, McCoy noticed that the crowd had formed a wide perimeter, with the Khartoum SPF pushing everyone back fifty meters in all directions. Aware that his grip was suboptimal for the long haul, McCoy carefully shifted his fingers to make it easier to hold the dead man's thumb depressed on the button. Repositioning complete, he exhaled with relief at not blowing himself up.

You can do this, he told himself, closed his eyes, and mentally prepared himself for the long wait for a bomb tech to arrive at the scene to disarm the suicide vest. A moment later, he heard footsteps, and when he opened his eyes, two booted feet were standing in front of him.

"What the hell are you doing?" he said, looking up to find Castillo standing over him. "I told you to stay back."

Castillo flashed him a crooked grin. "Thought I'd provide a little incentive not to let go when you start to get tired."

"You're such a stubborn asshole, you know that, Castillo?"

"I know," the old man said, tapping his left breast pocket. "But I got a letter here from the President that says there's not a damn thing that you or anyone else can do about it."

CHAPTER FORTY-FOUR

Irshad Khalil took both his sister's trembling hands in his.

"I'm so glad you are safe," he said with a tender, comforting squeeze. "If those American agents hadn't been there to stop the terrorists this morning, who knows what would have happened."

"What would have happened is that I would have been killed—along with dozens, if not hundreds, of other innocent people," Awadiya said, making no attempt to hide her emotions. The attack this morning had clearly shaken her, yet she had put on a brave face and been strong all day in the aftermath. Now, alone with him in the kitchen of her modest home in southern Khartoum, she was finally letting her guard down. "Why does the world have to be this way—so angry, violent, and cruel?"

He met her tear-rimmed gaze. "Maybe now is not the right time, Awadiya . . ."

"Not the right time for what?"

"For you to run for President. It's too dangerous. Your life is more important than some political crusade," he said with empathetic decisiveness.

She jerked her hands from his grip, as if his touch was scalding her. "Irshad! How can you, of all people, say such an awful thing to me? This is not just some *political crusade*—we're talking about the fate of this nation. We're talking about democracy and liberty and whether Sudan is going to be a country where women have a voice in government or a place where women are silenced, oppressed, and discriminated against. Yes, running for President is dangerous, but do you want to know what is even more dangerous?"

"What?"

"*Not* running for President."

"Now you're just being hyperbolic."

"No," she said, with a defiant stomp of her foot. "I refuse to turn the clock back out of fear. I refuse to go back to living in Sudan before the coup d'état. Don't you see, brother, what you are suggesting is exactly what they want. But I will not be intimidated into dropping out of the race. I will not let their threat of violence silence my voice."

This was the response he'd expected from her, which is why he'd enlisted the Islamic Front to kill her in the first place. His sister would not be deterred. She was determined and relentless, just like he was. She would see this through to the end, and if the size of today's crowd was any indication, that end would most likely be her ascension to the presidency.

"Okay, okay," he said with a chuckle. "I take it back."

"Why do you always do that?" she said, plenty of ire left in her voice.

"Do what?"

"Say something serious and inflammatory and when you get a serious and inflamed response you make it out to be a joke and run away from the conversation."

"Is that really what I do?"

"Yes."

"Then I apologize, sister. It's been a long day. I'm tired and only want what's best for you."

She stared at him for a moment, then her expression softened.

"I know, Irshad. Thank you for supporting me today. And thank you for arranging the security detail for me. I will sleep better knowing they are there."

"You're welcome," he said with a nod. "Try to get some rest and we can talk more tomorrow."

"Okay, I will," she said, leaning in for him to give her a kiss on the cheek, which he did before seeing himself out.

"Call at the first sign of trouble. Wake me up if you must," he said to the lead member of the three-man team he'd assigned as her personal protection detail for the next forty-eight hours.

"Yes, Minister," the man said, popping him a salute, despite the fact neither of them were active-duty military.

Irshad suppressed a grin, walked to his government-issued sedan, and left without a backward glance.

The uneventful drive home was just long enough to give him time to assess the truly disastrous last twenty-four hours. He'd spent the last six months meticulously and methodically positioning all the chess pieces on the board to ensure his rise to power. First, facilitating the tragic death of his predecessor at the Ministry of Interior—another unfortunate traffic accident in a city where such accidents were commonplace—had been the first step. Making himself the hero who nearly secured the release of the American secretary of state from brutal terrorists—just moments too late to prevent his execution, and then using Ministry of Interior forces to kill any SIF left behind—had been the second.

But his sister's murder was the final, brilliant step that all but assured his rise to power.

The idea of painting Awadiya as a martyr had first come to him nearly a year ago, while watching her work the crowd at one of her earliest campaign events. She was a truly gifted and inspirational orator, and he marveled at how quickly the masses had embraced both her and her message. In that moment, he'd known she would win the election, and, like a fever dream, he saw his own path to the presidency take shape.

In death, her campaign could become his own. In death, he would amplify her message. By simply announcing his candidacy, her millions of supporters would instantly rally around him. And when, as minister of interior, he launched an investigation into her assassination, all evidence would point to the Sudanese Islamic Front.

The pursuit and prosecution of SIF would then lead him to Secretary of State Malone—whose rescue and safe return to the United States he would publicly and loudly take credit for. With the backing of the Sudanese people and the support and goodwill of the United States, his ascension to the presidency would all but be guaranteed . . .

But instead of letting the game play out, a hotshot team of American agents had showed up and flipped the board upside down.

"Fucking Americans," he said through gritted teeth as he pulled up to his driveway. "Forty-eight hours . . . that's all I needed to pull it off."

He pressed a button on the remote control clipped to the driver's-side sun visor to open the iron gate of the security fence surrounding his property. When the gap was sufficient, he pulled through, and parked in the courtyard in front of the house. His two-story stucco residence was opulent by Sudanese standards. He lived alone, so the extra bedrooms were wasted space, but that wasn't the point, was it?

The point was the message that living in such a grand place sent to his countrymen.

I am important. I matter. I possess money, power, and influence.

The house was completely dark; not a single light shone inside. He'd been meaning to install smart lights so he could turn them on with his phone, but never seemed to have the time. Khalil unlocked the front door with his house key, stepped inside the foyer, and reached for the light.

Rough hands grabbed his wrists before his fingers found the switch. He tried to scream, but the sound was stifled by a hand clamped over his mouth, a viselike arm around his throat. Then someone dropped a canvas bag over his head and cinched it tight around his neck. Panic gripped him as he flailed and thrashed ineffectively against the many powerful hands clutching him. He kicked his legs as they dragged him, but then felt himself lifted in the air, transported against his will like a toddler throwing a tantrum. He writhed desperately, trying to free himself, but the effort proved futile.

He was dropped unceremoniously and painfully into a wooden chair and his arms were quickly and expertly bound behind the chairback with a nylon strap. They left him alone for what felt like an eternity, letting fear and uncertainty soften him up. Not being able to see who had captured him, how many men were present, and what fate awaited him quickly frayed his nerves.

"Take this bag off my head and talk to me," he said, trying to take some modicum of control over the situation. "Whatever prompted this, I promise we can work it out."

Several long moments passed, then he heard footsteps and the hood was torn roughly from his head, scraping across his face and tearing painfully at his nose. He instantly recognized the trio of intruders standing in front of him in the dark—the American *diplomats* who had called on him at his office. With the tools and resources available to him at the Ministry, he'd been unable to pierce their NOCs, but he'd never had any illusions about who and what these men really were. His mind kicked into high gear, playing out a half dozen possible tacks he could take to potentially weasel his way out of the incredibly weak negotiating position he suddenly found himself in. While his first reflex was to clap back with indignation and outrage, he settled on composed supplication.

"It is very nice to see you gentlemen again, but I don't understand why you are doing this. You could have just knocked on my door and I would have let you in. If you untie me, I can open a nice bottle of wine and we can talk like civilized men around the table."

The American team leader pursed his lips in disapproval.

"I assure you guns and ropes are not necessary. I am willing to—"

"Once upon a time," the leader said, cutting him off, "there was a little boy named Irshad, who thought he knew everything and liked to prove it by hurting people. He found that the easiest way to hurt people was to justify his actions with Islamic scripture and align himself with other like-minded men who used terror and murder instead of diplomacy and hard work to get what they want. When this little boy's sister became more powerful and important than he was, it made him very jealous and angry. Her success became his own private outrage and so he decided to have her murdered in the name of honor and Islam."

Irshad laughed. He simply couldn't help himself. They had it wrong, of course, pegging him as a jihadist rather than a tactician. But that was to be expected. In the modern American strategic vernacular there were only two types of people: partners and terrorists. Now, it seemed, his life depended on convincing them that he was the former and not the latter.

"What's so funny?" the tallest of the three Americans said.

"I think there has been a terrible misunderstanding here. I do not support the Islamic Front nor do I condone their actions today. To the contrary, I've been leading a Ministry investigation into their activities," he said, trying his damnedest to flip the script. "And let me add that I owe you my sincere and deepest gratitude for your intervention at this morning's march for freedom and equality. Without your swift and courageous action, my sister would be dead. You say I am jealous of her. You say I am dishonored by her rise, but nothing could be further from the truth."

The tall one, who from his pronounced military bearing most certainly was a soldier, turned to look at the leader. Even in the dark, Irshad could see a flicker of doubt in his eyes. Unfortunately, the man with the pistol was unmoved by his words and wagged a disapproving gloved finger at him.

"We're not here to play games and trade lies. We already did that in your office, remember? We gave you an opportunity for candor and cooperation, but instead of working with us, you tried to have us murdered. The time for diplomacy has passed," the American said, cocking the pistol's hammer.

A lump formed in Irshad's throat, and for the first time in as long as he could remember, he felt real fear.

"You can't kill me, I'm the minister of interior," Irshad said, with as much conviction as he could muster. "You don't have the authority to execute a foreign official."

"You're the *acting* minister of interior," the man with the gun said, correcting him. "As the Presidential Agent, I have the authority to prosecute terrorists and enemies of state who commit crimes and acts of violence and treachery against America and her citizens. You kidnapped the United States secretary of state and murdered members of his staff and security detail in Cairo. You sent hit squads after us and nearly succeeded in killing us, too. And even though I don't have ironclad proof, my gut tells me you were the mastermind behind this morning's failed attack. You are a terrorist, Khalil. Whether you are motivated by religion or thirst for power changes nothing about who you are. If you have any last words, speak them now."

The leader raised the pistol to Khalil's forehead.

"Hold up," the tall, square-jawed American said. "I thought the plan was to get his confession and turn him over to the Sudanese authorities."

"Yeah, well, men like Irshad Khalil don't confess. They don't cooperate. And, most important, they can't be reformed. Sudan's homeland security apparatus works for him. So, I ask you, which authorities can we turn him over to? He has allies and co-conspirators inside the government right now. If we turn him in and walk away, then the second we're airborne and out of Sudanese airspace he'll be set free. And if that happens, then we both know that Awadiya will not survive to run in the next election . . . a tragedy that would short-circuit Sudan's chance of becoming a legitimate democracy in Africa."

"It's the classic scorpion and the frog parable," the third man said, the spy who had been silent up until this point. "Whatever negotiated agreement we reach with him tonight will not change his calculus. The second we turn our backs on him, he will sting us dead. It's simply in his nature."

Irshad suddenly felt his remaining time on this earth slipping like sand through his fingers. Desperate, he looked back and forth between the three Americans—the soldier, the spy, and the boss—his gaze finally settling on the soldier. "You know this is wrong. You're a military officer, not an executioner—I can see that. Turn me in. I will confess to whatever crimes you want. Justice will be served."

The soldier met his gaze. After a painfully long pause, he said, "He has no remorse. It's your call, Charley."

The boss frowned.

The pistol's muzzle flashed white.

Thunder roared.

And Irshad Khalil was struck by hollow-point lightning.

CHAPTER FORTY-FIVE

Aboard United States Air Force C-17 Globemaster III

3rd Airlift Squadron, 436th Airlift Wing

42,000 Feet over the Atlantic Ocean

March 25, 1:15 a.m.

McCoy stretched out on a sleeping bag beside a cargo pallet in the rear of the massive transport jet, hands behind his head and a ball cap pulled over his closed eyes, enjoying Junior's grumbling more than he could express.

"I mean," Junior said, "I'm glad we were able to save Awadiya Khalil—like, no joke, I'm proud as shit to have been part of this— but what the hell kind of hero's welcome is this? We're crammed into a flying garage full of military cargo?"

"The Special Operations kind, bro," McCoy shouted forward to where Junior sat on one of the nylon web bench seats. "You shared your world with me, now enjoy mine. Stretch out and get some sleep."

"I'm just sayin', Pick," Junior continued, "on the C-37B I had set up for us, we'd be stretched out on plush leather, eating filet and lobster, and sipping cocktails, or champagne, or whatever the hell you Marine cavemen drink."

"Sounds nice, you're right," McCoy said, tipping up his hat to see Ani grinning back at him and Junior pouting, arms folded, tapping a foot up and down. "But this is the comfort of the familiar. You need to embrace the advantages of the whole thing. Grab a sleeping bag, stretch out in your own little campsite and take a nap, or watch a movie on your computer or something. It's not the Ritz like you set up, but it sure as shit beats sitting up in the middle seat in coach on some damn Delta flight."

"At least Delta has cocktails," Junior grumbled again, but the man smiled now, and rose as if to head aft to where McCoy lay in his own little campsite. Instead he turned forward at the sound of Castillo's voice.

"All right, people," Castillo called out, and now McCoy saw he carried a small cooler. "It may not be champagne or Glenlivet, but I got us something to toast our success."

"How did you know what I was bitching about?" Junior laughed.

"I'm the boss," Castillo said with a wink. "I see everything, hear everything, know everything. Why haven't you yet figured that out?"

"Yeah, then what am I thinking now, boss?" Ani said with a chuckle.

Castillo narrowed his eyes as if probing into her mind.

"Disgusting language for such a pristine young girl, Ani."

She laughed. "Fuck you, Charley."

Ani and Junior followed Castillo aft, Junior taking a seat beside the older spook on the nylon bench and Ani sitting cross-legged on the corner of McCoy's sleeping bag. Castillo pulled out four long-neck bottles of beer, passing them around. McCoy accepted his, small chunks of ice slithering down the wet sides of the bottle, with a big grin as he sat himself up against the bulkhead. He twisted off the cap in unison with his teammates and raised his bottle in a toast.

"Mike Charlie," he said, clinking his bottle against Ani's.

"The first of many," Castillo said, and McCoy felt his eyes on him, studying his reaction.

"Ha," he said, and took a long pull on the icy beer, savoring the cold brew. "I believe I'll be headed back to my team in Iraq," he said, now meeting Castillo's blue eyes. "I have some unfinished business out in western Anbar to attend to."

"Maybe," Castillo said, taking his own long swig. "You should consider this, though, Killer. There are a lot of Marine Raiders who can do what you were doing in Iraq, my friend. But no more than a handful of men or women in the world are suited for what we just accomplished."

"Maybe," McCoy replied. He refused to admit to Castillo—and maybe himself—that he'd had that very same thought. "And why the hell do you keep calling me that?"

"Killer?" Castillo asked, grinning. "I would think you would appreciate honoring your father and grandfather. They both carried that name as their call sign, I understand."

"How does that honor them, exactly?" McCoy asked, frustrated. "By graciously accepting without question the nickname my dad hated and, I'm told, my grandfather loathed even more? I think I honor them better by just kicking your ass if you call me that again. I'm not a killer."

Castillo smiled and Ani laughed out loud.

"There's a stack of bodies in Cairo, another in Kuraymah Barkal, and several piles of corpses in Khartoum that I think would disagree," she said. "If they could."

"Being good at killing isn't what makes you a killer," McCoy said, feeling himself getting uncomfortably serious. "I love my country and will defend her with my life if called to do so. And, yes, I'll even kill for her, as you've seen. But I take no joy in it. Killing is a tool I employ as judiciously as possible, and with serious forethought when time permits, to carry out my mission of defending America and her interests."

A wave of nostalgia swept over him at the memory of his dad sharing the same sentiment a decade and a half ago when McCoy had asked him about the call sign. He'd not understood at the time.

He understood now.

"Fair enough, Pick," Castillo said, nodding to him.

"Well," Junior said, "good for you, Pick—and you, too, Charley. But I'm looking very much forward to returning to a life of luxurious covert adventure, as far from you jackasses as possible."

"We'll see about that," Castillo said, exchanging glances with McCoy and Ani.

"Don't even joke, Charley," Junior said. "You guys work too hard. Happy to help anytime, but I don't want a job with you."

"I can't imagine there will be a job to offer," McCoy said, studying Castillo again. "Didn't we just go rogue and execute an operation on foreign soil, resulting in the deaths of numerous foreign nationals in their own country, without even trying to get authorization? I mean that Morrison dude was an asshole, but he wasn't wrong." He cooled the thought with more cold beer. "Can't imagine the President will be thrilled by that."

"Maybe," Castillo said. "But it's big boy rules here, Pick. You make independent decisions—unilateral decisions—in this job all the time. But then you own the outcome, and the consequences if there are any. We saved the life of the best hope for a stable Sudan—

something of great benefit to the United States. The United States will likely give credit to the Sudanese, saying we provided 'minimal advising and technical assistance' or some bullshit. It turned out okay, and we get to own that, too. You remember that moving forward. Do what you think is right, and I'll have your back."

"To big boy rules," Junior said, raising his beer.

"Big boy rules," McCoy agreed, and they all drank.

McCoy watched Castillo lean back and begin a paternal back and forth with Ani and Junior. He realized, watching the former Delta operator turned super-secret Presidential spy, that he was in the presence of greatness. Castillo was not the dinosaur he'd imagined when they'd met. There was more to learn from this man than he might be capable of digesting.

Still, the idea of sponging up as much as the original Presidential Agent could share was tempting. He leaned back against the bulkhead, let his ball cap slip lower on his brow, and smiled as he listened to the all too familiar banter of a well-oiled special missions team.

He had plenty of time to worry about the future . . .

Tomorrow.

CHAPTER FORTY-SIX

Feeling more than a little déjà vu, Charley Castillo took the same seat on the sofa opposite the President that he'd sat in the last time he'd been summoned to the most powerful office in the world. General McNab was absent this time around, but DNI Fleiss was present for what Castillo assumed was going to be his "atta boy" debrief for the successful rescue and recovery of Secretary of State Malone.

And perhaps an ass chewing for what followed.

"I've got to hand it to you, Charley," President Cohen said, knitting her fingers together in her lap. "You never fail to disappoint."

"Thank you, ma'am," he said. Then, seeing her tight-lipped smile, he added, "Assuming that was meant to be a compliment?"

"It's a compliment," she said. "Frank is back home on American soil with his family because of you. From what Marty tells me, it appears you also managed to save the life of Sudan's rising champion of democracy. If she wins the election, she's almost certain to become an invaluable regional partner for this administration."

He nodded. "I sense a 'but' coming my way . . ."

"Oh, there's a *but*, all right," she said. "In the future, when you pull off these miracle covert operations for your country, can you please try to work a little harder on the *covert* element? Plausible deniability is part of the Presidential Agent program charter, but I would prefer not to have to exercise that option. You left a trail of bodies in your wake everywhere you went."

"Well, technically, it was all self-defense. In most cases, they shot first."

"Oh, really?" she said, dipping an eyebrow at him. "Is that how you're going to spin it?"

He flashed her a crooked grin. "I promise I'll try harder next time . . . assuming there is a next time."

Cohen glanced knowingly at Fleiss, apparently handing off the matter.

"Well, I think that all depends on you, Charley," the DNI said, and Castillo could already predict what was coming next. "We dragged you out of retirement against your will. If you want to consider this a one-off and head back home to Texas, the President and I will completely understand. You answered the call of duty and served your country, yet again, without complaint or condition. So, if you're ready to get back to your ranch and kick up your boots, you have your nation's permission and blessing to do so."

"That does sound pretty good," he said, playing along. "What's option two?"

"Option two is we let you keep that letter in your pocket and you and your Merry Outlaws continue doing what you do best— making the world a safer place for the rest of us."

Castillo rubbed his chin. "Can I have twenty-four hours to think about it?"

Cohen chuckled, but instead of calling his bluff, said, "Sure, Charley. Take as long as you need."

She stood and extended her hand to him.

He got to his feet and shook it. "Thank you, Madame President."

"For what?"

"For having the guts to be a President who serves the nation's needs, rather than the other way around."

"I think that might be the greatest compliment anyone has given me since I've taken office," she said, visibly taken aback. "Thank you, Charley."

So as not to spoil the moment, he simply nodded, bid her good-bye, and left the Oval Office with Director Fleiss. The two men walked through the West Wing, each waiting for the other to make the first move.

Fleiss broke first.

"You wanna grab dinner in the Navy Mess?" the DNI said. "The food's really quite good."

"Ah, the Navy Mess. I haven't been since before the remodel of the Executive Dining Room."

"Well, in that case, you're in for a real treat. They did a great job."

"You buying?" Castillo said.

"Do I have a choice?"

"Nope."

"Then looks like I'm buying," Fleiss said with a chuckle. He turned serious, adding, "You gonna stay on with us?"

"Do I have a choice?"

"Nope."

"Then looks like I'm staying on."

"Good," the DNI said, clapping him on the back. "We can talk turkey over dinner."

"I'll make it easy for you. I want to keep my team: McCoy, Junior, and Ani."

The DNI nodded, then stopped midstride and screwed up his face. "Hold on, who's Junior?"

"Smith, Jones, Rogers . . ." Castillo said through a laugh. "The dude's got so many names we couldn't take it anymore, so we started calling him Junior."

"Huh?"

"Long story."

"Fair enough," Fleiss said, "but to answer your question, who you want on your team going forward is your business. It's big boy rules, Charley. I'm going to give you and McCoy enough rope to hang yourselves and then some."

"Understood and appreciated, sir," he said.

"You can dispense with the honorifics, too," the DNI said. "Call me Marty."

"Roger that."

"What's your opinion of McCoy, by the way? Do you think the kid has what it takes to take the reins someday . . . whenever that day comes?"

Castillo bristled inside at the question but made sure not to show it. Both Cohen and Fleiss had deftly avoided that elephant in the room up to this point. The assignment had forced him to take a look in the mirror and come to grips with the fact that—at least when benchmarked against McCoy—he had lost a step. Was he still a damn good operator? Yes, no doubt about it. Was he as good as his MARSOC prodigy? If he was being honest with himself, tactically speaking, the answer was clearly no. Strategically speaking,

McCoy still had lots to learn; the kid simply wasn't ready to be the Presidential Agent—yet. If Fleiss asked McCoy the same question, Castillo felt pretty confident the Marine would give the same answer. To do the job the DNI and the President asked, they needed each other. Yes, he would be mentoring McCoy, but they would also be partners.

"If you had asked me that on day one," Castillo said, finally answering the question after a dreadfully long pause, "my answer would have been no. But over the course of the op, I saw him quickly evolve and step up to the challenge. Not everybody is cut out to be a lone wolf, and the Corps certainly has no tolerance for cowboys and rogue assets. I suppose that's just a long-winded way of saying yes, Marty, I think he definitely has what it takes."

Fleiss nodded. "Good. That's what I was hoping to hear."

The DNI led the way to the West Wing's iconic gourmet restaurant located directly across the hall from the Situation Room. Once seated at a round table in the stately, wood-paneled dining room, Fleiss retrieved a brown envelope from his inside coat pocket and handed it to Castillo.

Stenciled on the outside were the words TOP SECRET—SENSITIVE COMPARTMENTED INFORMATION.

"What's this?"

"Your next assignment," the DNI said, not bothering to look up from the menu he was now perusing. "But don't open it now."

"Because of the security level?"

Fleiss flashed him an impish grin. "There's that, but mainly because I'd hate to ruin your dinner."